WHISPERED ECHOES

STORIES BY PAUL F. OLSON

Let the world know:
#IGotMyCLPBook!

Crystal Lake Publishing
www.CrystalLakePub.com

ISBN: 978-1-64007-474-3
This book was originally published in 2016 as a limited
edition hardcover by Cemetery Dance Publications

Cover Art:
Ben Baldwin—www.benbaldwin.co.uk

Interior artwork:
Luke Spooner—www.carrionhouse.com

Layout:
Lori Michelle—www.theauthorsalley.com

Proofread by:
Hasse Chacon
Tere Fredericks

OTHER TITLES BY PAUL F. OLSON

Novels

Night Prophets

Alexander's Song

Anthologies

Post Mortem: New Tales of Ghostly Horror
(co-edited with David B. Silva)

Dead End: City Limits
(co-edited with David B. Silva)

Better Weird
(co-edited with Richard Chizmar and Brian James Freeman)

OTHER COLLECTIONS BY CRYSTAL LAKE PUBLISHING

Embers: A Collection of Dark Fiction by Kenneth W. Cain

Visions of the Mutant Rain Forest by Robert Frazier and Bruce Boston

Tales from The Lake Vol.3, edited by Monique Snyman

Gutted: Beautiful Horror Stories, edited by Doug Murano and D. Alexander Ward

Tribulations by Richard Thomas

Devourer of Souls by Kevin Lucia

Wind Chill by Patrick Rutigliano

Eidolon Avenue: The First Feast by Jonathan Winn

Flowers in a Dumpster by Mark Allan Gunnells

The Dark at the End of the Tunnel by Taylor Grant

Or check out other Crystal Lake Publishing books for more Tales from the Darkest Depths

CONTENTS

THE COUNTRY OF THE STRANGE:
PAUL F. OLSON'S UPPER PENINSULA

ROCKS AND WATER, trees and sky haunt Paul F. Olson's work, along with other, less comfortable elements. Olson is above all a regionalist. His work's bone, sinew, muscle, and spirit all spring organically from the Upper Peninsula (the U.P.), that part of Michigan surrounded by three of the Great Lakes. While it has twenty-nine percent of the state's land mass, it claims only three percent of its population, so it is, in Olson's own description of his home, "rugged, remote, lonely, beautiful, and quite weird." Those very words might be used to describe Olson's fiction as well.

If the works of M. R. James, master of the malevolent ghost story, and those of early Ray Bradbury were to wed in unholy union, their offspring might be something like the works of Paul F. Olson. Strange things abound in the U.P.'s lakes and woods, and Olson slowly reveals them to us, stripping away the shadows one by one until we see them—or at least *think* we do. These stories are rich in suggestion, in glimpses and echoes and whispers. But don't worry,

I

there are enough true horrors here to make the hair crawl on the neck of even the most seasoned aficionado of the horror tale. When Olson chooses to let us fully see his arcane creations, you'll be hard pressed not to give a little gasp, to make an actual sound to remind yourself that you are here in the real world, safe, and that this vision exists only in your imagination, lodged there by the even *darker* imagination of Paul F. Olson.

It's uncanny how Olson's nightmares are so close to our own, but not unexpected, since one quality that we all share is guilt, and that uneasy theme weaves itself through a number of stories in this volume. There is guilt at what we've done to others, at how we've shirked our familial responsibilities and disrupted our families, our loves, our lives. There's the horror of seeing that guilt made manifest by the return of those we betrayed, of those we loved and who loved us, but are not as they were, not as we remembered them, but as something *other*, lonely and quite weird indeed.

And we all dream, literally sometimes, of not just our own lives turned upside-down but of the whole world turned that way as well. You'll find those moments too, with the U.P. as the planet's microcosm. You may never have been to northern Michigan, but it doesn't matter, since Olson will take you there by the power of the written word and make you see, *see* in the Conradian sense: "That—and no more, and it is everything."

Olson does this the simple way, or rather the way that *looks* simplest, but is actually the most difficult to achieve, with plain, unadorned prose, the kind the best storytellers and poets use. It creates a quiet and altogether *haunting* voice that has no need to grab the reader by the shirtfront and order him to *look at this writing, look at how clever I am, doesn't my prose sparkle and scintillate?* No. Instead, Paul F. Olson says *I want to tell you a story. Sit with me, and listen.* And if you like a good story, good writing, and good fiction, you'll do as he asks and be the better for it.

You're also fortunate enough in this book to see how a good writer grows and develops. The stories are offered in the order in which they were written, and you'll start with those early tales, solid and well-crafted and nothing to be ashamed of in the least, but a young man's stories, with plots not as complex nor a style as polished as it would become with the years. And as those years go by, the stories become longer, more involving. Even in the span of eight years or so during which most of these earlier stories were written, there is a vast improvement in quality in such a short time.

"The Visitor," the earliest of these tales, is a quirky, open-ended story that would have been at home in the old *Twilight Zone Magazine*, but one can already see a fertile imagination at work. There's no reliance on genre tropes here. In these pages, you won't find vampires or werewolves or zombies, at least not the mind-numbingly predictable ones. Ghosts are as close to tradition as Olson comes, but ghosts stand head and shoulders above all other supernatural figures, since we all, one way or another, will become ghosts one day, if not actually, then in the memories of those who have known us (or read us). And Olson's ghosts are spirits to be reckoned with. These stories really hit their stride with such gems as "Through the Storm," "Down the Valley Wild," "Faith and Henry Gustafson," and "Getting Back." If you must, read the first few stories at one sitting, but give these later, richer tales a day each to enjoy and appreciate.

My greatest praise, however, is for Olson's new novella, *Bloodybones*. If this is the kind of work a fine writer does after letting his literary crop lay fallow for several decades, it may behoove *all* of us who write to do the same and get honest jobs for the next ten years. *Bloodybones* is an utterly delicious work, and fans of horror (and just good writing) should find it irresistible. It begins brilliantly, almost as metafiction, but Olson is too solid a storyteller for that angle, and twists our perceptions just long enough to tease us. I don't want to offer any spoilers, but *Bloodybones* is not only a classic ghost story, it's a mystery, a serial killer tale, a love story, and an adventure yarn. And it's *scary*. I read it in broad daylight, and still felt chills. If you don't read it in darkness, don't worry—Paul Olson will supply his own.

The novella is a perfect length for horror. There's plenty of room for development, but no necessity for padding, and you won't find a superfluous sentence in *Bloodybones*. What you *will* find is a beautifully written and constructed story, simply and elegantly told, one that will fill you with unease while you're reading it, and will remain with you long into the night and nights to come. It's the finest and most haunting story in a volume *full* of them.

So welcome to Paul F. Olson's Upper Peninsula, a place of deep lakes and deeper mysteries, ghosts and memories, whispers and echoes that will follow you down the wind and into the coldest chambers of the human heart.

Chet Williamson

INTRODUCTION

ASSEMBLING THIS BOOK is the scariest thing I have ever done. And I'm not talking about the stories. Oh, don't get me wrong: the tales in this collection have their share of thrills and chills. But most of them were written a long time ago by a young man who was just starting out in the business, who was just getting his feet wet and learning as he went along, who didn't always recognize the mistakes he made, and even when he did, wasn't quite sure how to fix them.

That was pretty terrifying to me.

With the exception of the final tale in the book, my brand new novella, *Bloodybones,* these stories were all long gone and long forgotten. They were dead and properly buried and slumbering peacefully. It was Rich Chizmar of Cemetery Dance Publications who first approached me with the idea of resurrecting them, of actually republishing them between hard covers. My first instinct was to laugh. My second was to run screaming deep into the woods and never return. It was like that moment you bring your new girlfriend home to meet your parents, feeling all proud and happy and grown-up and manly, until mom drags out the old battered photo album to show her pictures of you as a two-year-old, naked in the tub with a soapsuds beard. I mean, come on. When that happens, the only rational reaction is to try your best to sink into the floor and disappear.

After I calmed down and talked to Rich a little more, after I ascertained that he was, in fact, being quite serious and not making an elaborate joke, my third instinct was to take the stories and write them all over again, updating them, cleaning them up, polishing and streamlining them—in short, *fixing* them. I finally talked myself out of it, for a couple of reasons. The first was that it felt, somehow, dishonest. If I was going to show the world my stuff, then I had to be brave enough to show them the real thing, warts and all. I had to show them the original, grainy, black-and-white print with all the flaws intact, not some spiffy 3D director's cut with every blemish removed.

The other reason I decided to leave well enough alone was that I actually sat down and read the stories again—read them for the first time in many, many years—and I discovered something. For the most part, they were much better than I remembered. They were written by a much younger man, true. But they held up well, better than passing time and my nagging writer's insecurity had led me to believe. Were there a few embarrassing bathtub moments? Oh my, yes. Were there parts I dearly wanted to rewrite? Of course. Were there youthful mistakes that made me shake my head and laugh? Definitely. Were there ideas that made me blush? Phrases that made me groan? Absolutely. But I was delighted to see that the stories largely succeeded despite all that, remaining today exactly what they were back when I first wrote them: solid efforts by a kid who loved the horror field more than anything and only wanted to do one thing with his life: write good, honest stuff.

That was a happy discovery. It was the moment after the terrifying revelation of the naked bathtub photos, when you realize your girlfriend isn't traumatized, that she's laughing with you, not at you, that she doesn't think you were some grotesque, creepy little dweeb but rather sort of adorable. It's the moment you realize your past is perhaps not as embarrassing as you had thought, and yes, damn it, Mom was right all along: you were kind of a cute kid.

Just how old are the tales in this book? The earliest were written in the very early 1980s, several years before I owned my first word processor. They were done on my old, much-mourned Olympia Report De Luxe electric typewriter, that cranky old machine that hummed and rattled, sometimes groaned and sometimes growled, my favorite writing tool ever. Several others were written in a wonderful early software program called Wordstar and only survived on 5.25-inch diskettes—those salad-plate-sized floppies that really were floppy. Others were done in my post-Wordstar years but using various programs that were just as obsolete. Only a few of these relics had been converted to a more modern digital format over the years. The rest could not easily be transferred, so I had to get copies of the original magazines and plead with my dear friend Laurie Jasmin to type everything for me, which she happily did, bless her heart. Most of the stories were written before my children were born, and those children are now in their late-twenties. Most of them were written before I became a published novelist with the release of *Night Prophets* in 1989. Many were written before I even launched my magazine, *Horrorstruck: The World of Dark Fantasy,* in 1987. In short, these stories are *old.*

Now that I've survived my initial terror, I can look back at the stories with a fond sort of nostalgia. I can walk through the table of contents and precisely retrace those early years of my career, from the days when I almost suffocated underneath the pile of rejection slips on my desk to the days when editors were actually contacting *me* to solicit tales. I can remember how long and hard I worked on most of them, how I struggled to say what I wanted to say (my highest admiration and deepest envy has always been reserved for accomplished short story writers. I am awed by them. I was always okay at the long stuff, but never talented enough to become as good or prolific a short fiction writer as I wanted to be). I can remember the explosive joy I felt on that day in March—the Ides of March, as luck would have it—when I received my first acceptance letter from Dave Silva of *The Horror Show*, and somewhere, I still have a faded photocopy of that first $10 check. A quarter of a cent per word. I had arrived. I can remember the friendship and guidance and support of everyone who helped me along the way, those who bought the stories, like Dave, Gretta Anderson, Tom Monteleone, and Rich Chizmar, and those who didn't, most notably my idol, Charlie Grant, who professed to like my work, though never quite enough to actually publish it, but who unfailingly offered kind words and invaluable advice in lieu of sales.

Since those heady days, I spent many years doing

INTRODUCTION

other things. I worked in arts marketing for a time, followed by seventeen years doing a very different kind of writing from the kind you'll find in these pages, covering a community's foibles and triumphs as the editor of a small-town newspaper. During that time, according to my records, I wrote approximately 25,000 news articles, feature stories, interviews, blurbs, editorials, cutlines, and other journalistic pieces, but precious little fiction. In fact, there were days I was convinced that I had forgotten *how* to write fiction. I unhappily fell away from almost everything that felt creative, and I almost fell away from the horror genre itself, except for a few projects here and there, like co-editing the *Hellnotes* newsletter in its early years.

Now, I feel a bit like Rip Van Winkle awakening from his twenty-year sleep, and by all rights, it should be just as disorienting. After all, I have been gone from the business long enough to make the transition from young turk to old fart overnight, with nothing in between. But here's the thing: it doesn't feel like I've been gone. When I finally left the newspaper in 2012 and began writing fiction again, it almost felt as if no time at all had elapsed. I struggled for a while with the mechanics of it all; my fiction muscles had definitely atrophied, and they needed months of hard daily workouts to regain their strength. But the rest of it was the same as always. The excitement was still there. The sense of exploration was still there. The feeling that I was making new discoveries every day was still there. So, too, were the occasional bouts of agony and despair. The story ideas that spent several decades tucked away on little scraps of note paper, or lurking even further back in the recesses of my mental filing cabinet, were still clamoring to get out. The work itself was as challenging and happy and crazy and frustrating and rewarding as ever. And my love affair with the dark was as fresh and exhilarating as it was when I was nine or ten years old and first discovering guys with names like Poe and Lovecraft, Leiber and Bloch and Matheson.

The title of this collection, *Whispered Echoes,* was meant to evoke long-lost voices from the past. But I have a confession: most of it, at least the important parts of it, don't feel past to me. Realistically, I know how long ago it was. I've seen those oversized diskettes, after all. But when I move beyond that and get down to what really counts, time no longer seems to matter. I can close my eyes and immediately conjure all of it. I can vividly recall sitting hunched over that venerable Olympia, a scratchy LP playing on the stereo, venturing tentatively into the dark worlds of "The Visitor" or "Forever Bird" or "Through the Storm" or "Guides." I can remember struggling to find my way, feeling like I was in the dark with a candle that kept flickering and blowing out. And I can remember what happened next, that indescribable, overpowering thrill that courses through your body when the initial hesitation slips away at last and you realize you might be on to something. The words begin to come a little faster, and pretty soon, they are literally spilling out of you. Your fingers are hammering away at full speed, but somehow, there is no more keyboard, no paper, no screen. There's just you and your story. I can remember that so clearly. It's the same thrill I felt not long ago, when I was working on *Bloodybones.* This

X

INTRODUCTION

time, I was hunched over a Macbook Pro, and the music came from Pandora or Spotify, not a vinyl platter. Three decades had elapsed between that new story and the earliest tale in this book, and all I have to do to remind myself of that is look in the mirror and wince. But does it feel like three decades? Honestly? It scarcely feels like three days.

That's magic, I think. Good magic. The magic of fiction.

My sincere hope is that you find some of the same magic reading these tales, that they carry you away for a while as they did and still do for me, that it won't matter when they were written—last week or last month or last century—that such things won't even enter your mind. I'm fairly sure that's the way it's supposed to work. My world and yours are supposed to gradually fade away, until only the world of the story is left.

We can put that theory to the test right now, by turning the page and seeing what these fictional echoes do for you. If you choose to follow the echoes, if you chase them into the dark until you're suddenly lost, until you can't see ahead or behind, until it's just you and the words and nothing else—if that happens, we will all have gotten what we came here for.

And if, by chance, you catch a glimpse of a soapsuds beard from time to time, please be kind. I knew the kid. His heart was in the right place, and I can assure you he meant well.

Paul F. Olson
Brimley, Michigan

THE VISITOR

THERE IS NO more beautiful season than fall in Upper Michigan, although that is strictly opinion. Certain folks love spring above the rest, and certain more love summer. There are even those few—snowmobilers, skiers, and the most avid of the tourist-haters—who champion winter. But to my mind, there is nothing greater than autumn and its crystalline mornings, its steady afternoon rains, its haunting winds that are never quite still, even in the quietest hours. Despite that, there is something about the season that is not quite right. Something that hasn't been quite right, in fact, since Kent Barclay began coming into town each October first, taking a room at Elvira Martin's boarding house, and leaving again during the first week of November.

Kent Barclay.

Precisely who he is, I don't know. Or maybe I do . . . maybe I do and am just afraid to speak it. He certainly seems harmless enough on the surface. A gentle wisp of a man, he merely strolls the narrow main street and even narrower side streets, nodding to people, kicking at pebbles, and searching the sky as if for treasure. On days that it rains you can see him at his window in the boarding house (and always the same room, always room number 3, up front, second floor) looking out passively. He smiles pleasantly, always treats our dogs and children well. He's even capable, on those occasions he's approached in the park, of holding a rather stimulating conversation.

Perhaps what troubles me about the little fellow is only the blunt and prosaic fact that here is a man who comes into a tiny burg like Patterson Falls once a year, stays a month or thereabouts, and leaves, for no apparent reason that anyone has ever been able to tell. He's never fully answered questions on that score, that much is certain. He's apt to just smile sadly and say in that fine, thin voice of his, "Vacation" or "Just sightseeing."

But more likely my fear is deeper, more complicated. In fact, I know it is. It's fear of the way accidents seem to follow Kent Barclay while he's in the Falls. Fear of the way those accidents grow slightly worse each year.

The first year, nine years ago, he tripped and fell over an admittedly wide and dangerous sidewalk crack along Appleton Street. He happened to fall in the path of little Billy Hardesty on his Schwinn. Billy swerved and plowed the Schwinn into a rather large oak. Both were relatively unhurt, although Billy had a nicely abraded elbow to show off at the grammar school in Ishpeming the next day.

It went on like that for several years, one or two incidents each October, no one really hurt or put out, no one really troubled. But then . . . was it four years ago? No, I believe it was five. Barclay, on his afternoon rounds, was going into the IGA when the wind suddenly snatched the door from his hand and slammed it outward. That in itself would not have been so bad, but it just so happened that Joey Wenderson was following immediately behind. Automatically, he thrust out an arthritic hand to keep from being hit, but his hand went straight through the glass, shattering it, leaving jagged shards hanging. According to Barb Foley, who was running the register that day, Joey let out a squawk like only a startled and wounded old man could and foolishly jerked his hand back, gashing his arm in five places, three deep enough take stitches.

After that, those of us who gathered around the card table every Saturday at Kendrick's True Value Hardware (and I must say on my own behalf that as a retired teacher from the Marquette School System and probably the most educated person in the Falls, I still fit into those gatherings rather well) took to calling little Kent Barclay "the jinx" and "the curse," jokingly speculating over coffee about what sort of trouble he was going to cause next.

We didn't have long to wait. Two weeks later, just before he left town for the year, he strolled absently across the intersection of Parsons and Appleton, directly in front of a Chevy driven by an out-of-towner salesman who had just been pitching his wares to the manager of the Knife-N-Fork Diner. The salesman hit the brakes a touch too hard and cracked the steering wheel. To say nothing of his skull. I believe he took nineteen stitches, but I don't recall the precise number.

The next year was the same. Two people hurt to bleeding by our visitor's bumbling or clumsiness or ignorance or whatever it was. The year after that, three people. The year after that, two again. One of those was our mayor, who nearly severed two fingers on his left hand trying to catch an axe that Barclay knocked off its display rack in the hardware store.

Our Saturday accusations against Barclay grew stronger, and Paul Kendricks, who had driven the mayor to the hospital in Marquette, even suggested (only half-humorously) that perhaps there was some ordinance to keep such a dangerous soul out of town.

"What's he come here for anyhow?" Joey Wenderson said, touching his scarred arm ruefully. "What's a fella like that want here ever' year?"

We only looked at each other and shrugged. It was a question all of us had asked for the last five or six years, and one to which none of us had an answer.

But as always happened, by December we had more or less forgotten about Barclay and taken up the threads of our more mundane existence. His name came up only occasionally in the winter and spring and summer, and even those hurt by his blundering seemed to harbor no ill will against him during those months. His presence in Patterson Falls each October was still a mystery, but so, in their own ways, were the coming of the birds each spring, the freezing of Conley Lake each winter, the turning of the autumn leaves. You see? We had already, in one form or another, come to accept him as an ordained and inexorable part of our simple lives. It wasn't until that last year, months ago now, that all that began to change.

Barclay came into town just before noon on October first, wheeling his little blue Pinto up to Elvira Martin's and carrying his single faded tartan suitcase inside. It was cold for that early, and raining steadily. An hour after his arrival we saw him from the hardware store, sitting in the window of room number

3, gazing out at the somnolent main street with the blandness that had become his trademark.

"Little guy's back," George Loveworth noted, tapping ash into the dregs of his coffee.

"Looks that way," I said.

There was a pause, and then Paul Kendricks asked the time-honored question: "Whaddya spose he wants here, anyway?"

We gave him the time-honored response: blank, silent expressions.

"He ain't got no family around," Kendricks said, persisting. "Not even what you'd call friends. All he does is walk around in circles . . . and set up in that window there. I don't know. I just don't get it."

That was the extent of our Kent Barclay discussions that first day. There was no mention of the accidents, although I suppose all of us were wondering just when the first one would happen, just what it would be.

For a while it appeared that we were going to be disappointed that year. There was usually one incident during Barclay's first week in the Falls, one or two more during his last. This time, however, the first three weeks of his visit passed uneventfully. Perhaps, using hindsight, I could attribute that to the fact that it rained almost continuously during those weeks. Barclay was rarely seen outside. Still, he was at his window every day, like a silent but certainly sentient guardian, or a prisoner staring out longingly at the streets of freedom. Then one day the rain stopped. The next morning the sodden pavement gleamed in the early sunlight. Barclay was up, according to our chief of police, Harv Bennedict, by seven o'clock, strolling down Main, turning almost absently at Bridgeton, and swinging past the old, abandoned school. Bennedict told us later (but not in his official capacity) that he had been out on morning rounds when he passed Barclay, that he nodded and said hello, received a similar greeting back. All perfectly ordinary. It was what followed later that morning that was not ordinary at all, that shattered routine and changed our muddled thinking about Barclay for good.

It happened around eleven-thirty, and on this, I don't need to rely on secondhand accounts. I was there. I saw it. I saw it all.

I was out on morning rounds of my own, enjoying the crispness and the just-washed freshness of the day, breathing in great lungs full of air, watching drenched, dull-brown leaves drop limply to the earth. I had stopped by the post office to say hello to Vinnie Pierce, then by the IGA to greet Barb Foley and buy a roll of Certs. My next stop was John Barlow's State Farm office. I was inside with John, chewing over the local high school football scene and the high cost of getting by, when Barclay ambled past the big picture window out front.

"There he goes," John said. It was a simple statement, and I saw no need of reply. John went on: "Strange little guy, don't you think? Nice enough, though."

I nodded and savored a Certs. "At least he's staying out of trouble this year."

We laughed over that and swiveled a few degrees to watch his progress down the street.

It was about that time that things seemed, to me, to suddenly slow down, as though we were watching film on a screen and the projectionist had pulled some lever marked slow-motion or low gear or whatever. Later, remembering with John, he said it was nearly the same for him . . . vaguely unreal . . . not at all a comfortable feeling.

We saw Barclay moving casually along, then moments later saw the front door of Bud McKennon's house swing open, saw little Sarah McKennon dart out. I remember thinking it was strange Sarah would not be in school—she was at least eight years old—and then realized it was Friday, the end of the first grading period of the year. The grammar school was out until Monday.

Sarah was clearly in a hurry, charging forth to meet some friend or to complete some errand for her mother, for she madly scrambled along the sidewalk, a large grin on her face, something clutched in one chubby fist. It did not take her long to catch up with Barclay.

That was when it happened.

As she attempted to pass Barclay on his right, the visitor quickly and agilely, without so much as glancing over his shoulder, side-stepped in that direction.

Sarah McKennon skidded on the still-damp pavement and almost fell, but like most children, she was blessed with a natural grace and regained her balance. She did not seem deterred at all and simply swung to the left.

Barclay, still walking, still not looking back, moved right with her, blocking her path.

"What the hell's he think he's doing?" John said, and it seemed as though his voice came from a great distance.

I did not answer. I had no answer. But I felt a very palpable sense of impending trouble gathering in my chest. I had no idea what the trouble would be, but I knew as surely as I knew the date and the name of my town, as surely as I knew *my* name, that it was coming. I had never experienced anything quite like it before, and I clutched the windowsill as though it were a life ring and watched.

Out on the sidewalk, I saw Sarah half running, half walking now, swing right, then left, then right again. Each time, wispy little Kent Barclay moved with her, moved ahead of her, blocking her route.

They had reached the corner of Wislow and Main, crossed into the next block. Barclay continued to amble on, as though unaware of the child behind him trying to pass. Yet he couldn't truly be unaware, could he? No, no, of course not. He was playing a game with the girl. They were old friends from the park or the playground behind the Municipal Building and this was just a game they played when they happened to meet, a tradition, a ritual.

But I did not believe it.

That sense of trouble had mounted, like a squeezing hand around my heart, and I could only watch and wonder what in the name of God that crazy little tourist thought he was doing.

Then, outside, Sarah McKennon, surely irritated now, made her move. I have no doubt she saw only two options. One, veer wide to the right across the front lawns of the houses, and two, veer left into the street. Yes, even to this day I'm quite certain the most sensible courses of action, taking another route or slowing and stopping, waiting for Barclay to disappear in the distance, never even entered her eager eight-year-old mind.

THE VISITOR

And so she did what any impatient youngster would do. She chose from the two options she saw, and she chose what she doubtless thought was the simplest, which in this case, since she was already to the far left of the sidewalk, meant darting out into the street.

I heard the car before I saw it, heard its dreadfully squealing tires as the driver floored the brakes, heard the protesting wail of its horn. Then I saw it flash into view, saw it strike the running girl. And then I heard the final sound . . . the final sound, that is, until the shouting began moments later. I heard the dull and thickening sound of the girl being hit.

"Jesus," John Barlow said. "*Jeeezus.*"

Barclay simply kept on strolling, not glancing back, as though nothing at all had happened.

I remember the next hours only dimly, as though I viewed them through a sheet of gauze, or through a thick fog bank that distorted thought as well as vision.

I remember John and I running to the scene.

I remember the shocked white face of the driver, his protests that he hadn't seen her, that she had just run in front of him, just like that, my god, just right out in front.

I remember the volunteer ambulance pulling up.

I remember Dr. McCauley coming and pronouncing her dead.

I remember her sobbing mother, her goggling three-year-old brother.

Most of all, I remember the sudden new loathing I felt for Kent Barclay.

I remember all that, but as I just stated, I remember it only vaguely, as though from a dream.

The early minutes of our gathering in the True Value the next morning were bleak and silent. Then things turned quickly and bitterly angry. John and I were the only ones who had witnessed the accident, the only ones who had seen the bizarre little duel on the sidewalk prior. The others were perfectly willing to believe us, however, as though they had been quietly waiting all these years for something tangible to pin on our annual visitor. Still, we all knew there was nothing legally to be done. There is no actual law against lurching back and forth on the sidewalk, impeding the progress of an impatient eight-year-old girl. And he hadn't forced her to run into the street. Even if he had, there was no way we could prove it, certainly no way we could prove he had known the car was coming. But if our legal channels were nil, there seemed to be a harsh consensus around the card table that morning that our moral course was open and extremely clear-cut.

"We gotta kick the bastard out," Paul Kendricks said. "I dunno what his game is, but we don't need him in the Falls."

Joey Wenderson coughed and nodded. "Shoulda done it long ago."

A brief silence ensued, and then Frank Bishop said, "Think we can keep him from coming back next year?"

Kendricks laughed jaggedly. "Damn right we can. Our town, ain't it? We'll just tell him he ain't welcome. Tell him if he shines his pussy-lickin' face round here next fall, we'll kick him right out. Kick him out, hell. We'll *kill* the bastard."

"The law," I said weakly.

"Fuck the law," Joey Wenderson said. "We gotta

duty. He can count himself lucky we ain't gonna walk over there and kill him right now."

I nodded. Despite my newfound hate for Barclay, I had no doubt he could consider himself very lucky indeed.

There was some short discussion of who would get the honor of speaking to Barclay. Harv Bennedict was suggested and rejected. We all knew the police chief had a difficult enough time mustering the courage to hand out a speeding ticket. He could not be entrusted with such a delicate matter as this, even assuming he could be convinced that Barclay had to go.

Then Frank Bishop looked at me and said, "How about you, Matthew?"

My eyes widened, but before I could protest there was round after round of agreement from the others. I was well-spoken and diplomatic, yet just tough enough from my years in the north to make my words stick. It was that old specter of superior education and experience come to haunt me at last. Besides that, it was pointed out, I believed as deeply as any of them that Barclay was dangerous, and I had been there when Sarah McKennon was killed. That gave me additional ammunition.

After one or two flimsy arguments, I agreed.

I had no doubt in my mind that Barclay should go, that Patterson Falls would be infinitely better off without him. I did doubt, however, our position if the little man should decide to press his legal right to "vacation" or "sightsee" where he wished.

Still, what choice did I have? In my new angered state of mind, it seemed to have come down to an us-or-him proposition.

The next day, Sunday, it rained again, and as I approached Elvira Martin's boarding house, I looked up and saw him standing in the window of room number 3, simply looking out, and I felt my loathing wash back over me like a wave of hot water.

The first moments of our meeting in the dingy but astringently neat little room were harmless enough. He remembered me from occasional encounters in previous years and even remembered to inquire if I missed teaching. However, when I came to the subject at hand, the tension seemed to mount almost immediately.

"Leave?" Barclay repeated, his bland little face clouding. "Leave town?"

I nodded. "As soon as possible."

"I'm afraid I don't understand."

I took a deep breath and attempted to explain to him our position, explain how the mounting accidents over the years had changed our good opinion of him, how it would be better for all involved if he were to just slip away and forget about the Falls. I withheld mention of Sarah McKennon and what John Barlow and I had seen, thinking rather obscurely that I might need that as leverage later.

Barclay heard me out politely enough, but his expression grew darker by the moment. When I was finished, he leaned toward me so quickly that I thought for one absurd moment he was going to strike. But instead, he merely coughed and then leaned back, frowning.

"You have no legal right," he said.

"I realize that, Mr. Barclay. We all realize that. But you've got the town set on edge. Some are talking about violence. Now don't you think it would be better for everyone if you ju—"

"Violence? *Violence?* Because of a few harmless accidents? You have no right . . . you . . . you have no grounds, you—"

"Mr. Barclay, there's no sense in arguing about it. The town's made up its mind, and you're not likely to change it. Now, you're going to leave today. And you're not going to come back next year. If you feel such an urgent need to sightsee in this area, why don't you try Ishpeming or Michigammee or Champion? Why don't you go north to the Copper Country? All very lovely, I can assure you. Just . . . just don't come back to Patterson Falls."

For a moment, he said nothing. He merely stared at me. I thought my cool enforcer posture had been successful. Then he smiled—a sweet, dripping, horribly sickening smile—and said, "I'm afraid that would be impossible, Mr. Jacobs, and you'd better go back and tell your friends I said so."

"There's no such thing as impossible, Barclay."

"Oh, indeed there is. I have work to do here. I must come back."

I almost laughed. "Work? What work? Walking around the streets looking at the sky? Hurting children on bikes? Making old men put their hands through glass doors? Knocking axes off the wall in the hardware store?" I felt my reserve crumbling, my anger come boiling through. But anger mixed with an odd glee. As though I had been waiting for this moment a long time. "What work?" I grinned maniacally. "Forcing little girls into the street so they get struck by cars?"

I expected some expression of surprise at that statement, but I was disappointed. He only maintained that nauseating smile and . . . there was something else, something above the smile. It was in his eyes, a dark look of gleaming hatred. Or perhaps it wasn't hatred. Perhaps it was . . . I don't know. But it was there, and it drove an ice shard of fear into my heart. I felt the pain of it and drew back as he spoke his next words.

"I think that's all, Mr. Jacobs. Be sure to tell everyone what I said. Good day, now."

I opened my mouth to speak but could find no words. The pain in my chest was now above the tight constriction of simple unease. It was shattering. I rose, backed away, and fumbled my way out the door.

I was halfway down the stairs when I lost consciousness.

***

I stayed in the hospital nearly two months. The doctor said I was extremely fortunate. It was a massive heart attack, he said, the kind that frequently refuses to give folks my age a second chance. I'm back in town now, though, spending my time much the way I spent it before, only at a much slower pace. There were some days in July and August when I had to forego the Saturday sessions at the True Value, when it was just too hot, too stunningly humid to consider the long walk downtown, the strain of the discussions. But I don't have to worry about that anymore. It's September, you see, and the weather has turned blessedly cool and most pleasant.

He's coming back.

I admit there were times throughout the bleak

winter months when I tried to delude myself into thinking Barclay was bluffing. After all, he was just a little wisp of a man; I must have intimidated him somewhat. Even in spring and summer, I clung to that hope, foolish as it was. Barclay was bluffing. The attack was just ugly coincidence.

But it's autumn now, the time of beauty, the dying time of leaves and grass and foolish dreams.

He's coming back.

He has work to do here.

There is nothing I can do, nothing any of us can do, to alter that. In some comic, horrible way, he's like an absurd little postman, refusing to be stayed from his duties.

Work to do.

I wonder why.

And oh God, I wonder what it's going to be this year.

FROM A DREAMLESS
SLEEP AWAKENED

"I COULD LOSE my job for this, you know."

The police chief and the priest stood at the base of the small rise that led into the mouth of the cave. It was several hours past sunrise, but the day was overcast, the sky a sky of twilight.

The priest smiled, a gentle smile that he might use to comfort a parishioner in a moment of need. "I doubt that," he said.

"I don't. Can't you see the headline in *The Beacon*? COP COPS OUT TO SUPERSTITION."

"Is that what you think this is? Superstition?"

The police chief, whose name was Carl Holt, grunted. It was hard to tell what he meant by it. "I don't know. I just don't know."

"But you know what you've seen here, and what you've heard."

Holt opened his mouth to reply, but he never got the chance.

The priest took two steps up the rise, moving closer to the cave. Holt's hand went reflexively to the butt of his holstered S&W, and then he followed along.

That was when the voice spoke to them out of the cave. The voice of Tommy Gallagher.

FROM A DREAMLESS SLEEP AWAKENED

***

They had been playing in the cave for over an hour. All the local kids played there, despite the fact that the rutted and rocky road that led to it had been fenced off and posted sixty ways to Sunday for years. On this particular day, three of them had climbed the fence: Perry Lincoln, Jim Bowker, and Tommy Gallagher. They had indulged in a brief and desultory game of hide-and-seek and were now engaged in an all-out-red-blooded-American-kid game of War. Perry and Jim were enemy infiltrators; Tommy was the special agent assigned to track them and "kill" them. Their whispers seemed like shouts in the echoey corridors of the cave, their shouts seemed like cannon fire. It was impossible to tell where the voices were coming from. Were they on this level, or down the narrow washout on the larger sub-level below? Were they around the corner, or a quarter-mile back through the winding maze of rock, in the deepest part of the cave? As a result, Tommy soon became overwhelmed with the fruitlessness of his assignment and decided to hunker down for a while in the little cul-de-sac off the main passage. He would eat the Baby Ruth he'd hooked from Madison's Rexall and wait for them to stumble on him.

He wolfed the candy bar and used a piece of jagged rock to dig a small grave for the wrapper. He'd gone down no more than a few inches when he discovered the bone. It was poking upward at a sharp angle, and he worked quickly to move away enough of the soft, damp earth to get a grip on it and pull it out. That was more difficult than he thought; it took him several minutes to get a firm enough hold. Even then, he had to get to his feet and really whale on the bone before it came loose, tumbling him backwards like a catapulted stone.

"Holy jeez," he muttered, and his words came back at him five-fold. He held the bone up and looked at it. It was huge, well over a foot long, the ends roughly chipped, the center section smooth, slicked with mud and a greenish slimy substance.

He'd seen enough animal bones in his career as a kid to have no doubt this particular bone belonged not to a dog or a coyote or a bobcat but to a man. It was too long, too large. It looked suspiciously like a part of the skeleton that hung in Mr. Krycraft's science classroom, the one the kids had nicknamed Otto. A little rougher, more ravaged, but clearly of the same origin.

He set it down gently, almost reverently, and attacked his small hole with the jagged rock. Within five minutes—the deceptive sounds of Perry and Jim still coming to him from all around—he had unearthed several unrecognizable bits and shards and something that could only be a finger, small and crooked, but whole.

"Hey, guys!" he called, awestruck. "C'mere a second! I found some stuff!"

There was silence for a long moment. Then he heard their giggles echoing through the cave.

"No!" he cried. "Really! Game's off a minute! I found some bones!"

"Liar!" he heard Jim say.

"You gotta find us, fartface!" Perry said.

Tommy sighed. "Assholes," he said. He allowed his hands to play lightly over the surface of the large (thigh?) bone. He became aware of a tingling sensation as he touched it, a prickling almost like an electrical current that passed through his fingers, up his arms, into the very center of his chest.

And then his breath clogged in his throat.

There was a thin, fine line of mist rising from the bone, as though it had been taken from a very warm room into a deep-freeze. It circled upward like lazy campfire smoke, swirling.

He drew his hand away and crabbed backward a few feet, watching the mist creep upward. It began to circle over his head, much more of it now. It was beginning to form itself into a dense wall and . . . beginning to take shape.

Tommy heaved himself to his feet and took a halting step away from it. Yes. The mist was beginning to take shape. It was almost like one of those hidden picture puzzles in the *Weekly Reader*, the ones that consisted of bits and pieces of a real object and lots of other shapes as well. You had to look at the picture and figure out what it was supposed to be, separate the important from the deceptive. This was like that. He was certain that something was developing before him, but it was sketchy and vague, half-real, half-there. He could not tell what it was, though he felt a desperate urge to know.

He backed up again and bumped the cave wall behind. The mist was moving forward now, the tendrils of its new shape reaching for his face.

"Perry?" he said uncertainly, his voice little more than a choked whisper. "Hey, Jim . . . you guys c'mere, would you?" But this time he could not even hear their whispers.

He turned then and tried to run from the cul-de-sac, but he moved too quickly and stumbled on the loose rock underfoot. He went down hard, his breath driven from him, his vision blurred. A great blackness began to seep into his mind, but before it took hold, he was fully and dreadfully frightened of the cold touch of the mist closing over his feet and ankles, moving hungrily upward.

***

Carl Holt's face had drained of all color. His hand tightened painfully on his service revolver and he glanced at the priest. But Father Jurgens seemed calm and composed, almost serene.

"Welcome," the voice from the cave said again. "It's such a pleasure to see you here, Father, Mr. Holt. How thoughtful of you to come."

There was something almost laughably frightening about those tight, formal words uttered in Tommy Gallagher's high nine-year-old voice. It was like a symphony played on a calliope.

Carl Holt felt numb. He had seen and heard things here since Tommy's disappearance last month. The things that had made him approach Jurgens in the first place. But those words . . . that voice . . . they seemed not unusual and mysterious but unutterable, horribly obscene.

"Tommy?" Father Jurgens said then. "Is that you, Tommy?"

The voice in the cave laughed harshly. It was still the sound of a child, but it was underplayed with other tones as well, dark tones that were not the domain of any child anywhere.

"Is that you, Tommy?" the priest repeated slowly.

"It is," the voice said. "And it isn't."

Jurgens turned then to the police chief. "You were right to come to me, Carl," he said.

"Was I?" Holt said. And then he laughed. It had absolutely no humor in it. It was the sound of ice cracking underfoot.

"You were. You're aware that this cave was an Indian burial ground, aren't you?"

Holt only stared at him, as though he had just spoken a Latin Mass that was beyond Holt's Methodist comprehension.

"I researched it once, years ago," Jurgens continued. "This cave is sacred ground, as are all tribal burial places. It was not meant to be disturbed. Likely, it was protected by charms and curses. It was not meant to be violated."

"Kids play here all the time," Holt mumbled, as though that had some significance.

"Doubtless," Jergens said. "But perhaps this time something was disturbed. You told me what happened to you in there. You were lucky to come out unharmed. Once the sacred ground is violated, there's no telling—"

"Funny words from a priest!" Holt snapped. "Sacred grounds? Charms and curses? *Curses* for gods' sakes? Do you really believe that?"

"Don't you? Come now, Carl, it was you who came to me, wasn't it? I didn't drag you out here. You asked me to come, am I right?" Holt did not answer. "Carl, speak to me! *You* approached *me*, didn't you? You asked me to help."

Carl Holt released a shuddering sigh. It seemed to come from his very center. At last, he nodded miserably.

***

The search for Tommy Gallagher was called off after two weeks. The cave, as well as miles of surrounding woodland, had been repeatedly searched by all manner of volunteers and officials. Nothing had been found—not a shoe or a shirt and certainly not a kid—and except for the near decapitation of Henry Lewis by a falling stalactite, the search had gone without incident.

On the last evening, after everything had been officially terminated and the others had gone home, Carl Holt remained behind in the cave, unwilling to let go. He had known Tommy quite well, had taken supper with his parents more than once. It was Tommy's father who had helped him secure his mortgage six years earlier. He simply did not want to admit that a kid with so damn much life in him could be dead now. He was constitutionally unable to admit it. And so, when he was alone, he unsheathed his utility flashlight, clicked it, and began a final tour of the corridors of the cave.

"Tommy!" he called. "Hey, Tom Gallagher! It's Carl Holt! You c'mon out now, you hear?"

But he heard nothing but the sound of dripping water somewhere in the vast expanse around him.

He wandered around for nearly an hour, until it was full dark outside and blacker than midnight inside. It was all ridiculous, he knew. The cave simply wasn't that big. There just weren't that many places to search. And twenty to thirty people had been searching it for nearly fourteen days. They had covered every possible inch of the place at least five times. The official chalk markings on the walls were ample proof of that, the endless Xs that meant an area had been checked and checked and checked again.

He started up the washout to the main level, ready at last to let go. Not happy about it, but ready. That was when he heard the giggling from above. He paused and held his breath, listening closely.

It had been a giggle. He was certain it had been a giggle. A child's merry little laugh. Sudden and irrational hope surged through him.

But there was nothing now. Nothing but the natural sounds of settling rock and the drip of the underground spring.

"Tommy?" he said tentatively. No answer. "Anyone?" he said then. "Hey, who's there?"

He sighed and continued upward. When he reached the main level, he turned toward the entrance, pausing to glance behind once or twice, seeing nothing.

And suddenly, he noticed the faint glowing light ahead. He halted momentarily and then hurried toward it, slipping on the rocky floor, using the walls for balance. As he approached, he could see where it was coming from. It issued from the little dead-end corridor that bent to the left off the main passage, the little cave within a cave. He knew that area had been searched—had searched it twice himself—but that did not explain why there was now that faint but very clear light coming from within that little space.

He reached it and knelt down, looked into the cul-de-sac. He just made out the faint outline of something crouched in there, something gnarled and hulking and grotesque, when the light exploded into a blinding, magnesium-bright flare. He threw up an arm to shield

23

his eyes and tumbled backwards, partly from protective instinct, partly from the brute force of his surprise.

The cave was brighter than noon. The light was seemingly coming from the walls themselves, devastatingly sharp, numbing.

Carl Holt let out a small cry of fear and began to scramble on his hands and knees back toward the entrance. He was so intent on getting out that he did not even realize the light had suddenly vanished until he was actually outside, back in the cool night air. He lay on the crest of the rise for a moment or so, gathering his breath, collecting his senses, and then at last he got to his feet and looked back into the cave.

It was dark, its gaping mouth no more than a dividing line between the shades of black. The only glow was from his flashlight, and even that was growing feeble as the batteries slowly wound down.

"Jesus," he whispered to no one. "What in good Christ was that?" It seemed to him that he was answered by the high, faint laughter of a child, carried to him from within the cave on the breath of the nighttime breeze.

***

"Yes," Holt said now. "I came to you."

"And you haven't changed your mind?" Jurgens persisted. "You still think I can help?"

"I don't know if you can help, Father. My God, I told you I thought for two weeks before coming to you. I don't know what you can do . . . but no, I haven't changed my mind."

"Cop cops out to superstition?" the priest said gently. "Yeah. Yeah, I guess so."

FROM A DREAMLESS SLEEP AWAKENED

***

Carl Holt made two trips back to the cave after that night. He never went in but only stood at the entrance, waiting to see if anything was going to happen. Nothing did, but once, he thought he heard the giggling he had heard that night, and once, he heard something within fall, like a large rock tumbling from a great height. He was not a superstitious man, nor was he particularly religious. But a drowning man does not question the fact that he is drowning. He doesn't rationalize, and he engages in precious little debate. He only does whatever is necessary to save himself. And that was why, on that Saturday afternoon one month after Tommy Gallagher's disappearance, he stole out of his town hall office and went to the rectory behind the Catholic church. That was why he had risked ridicule and disdain and even the possible ruin of his career. That was why he had seriously used the word exorcism for the first time in his life.

***

They waited several minutes for the voice to speak again. When it did not, they went the rest of the way up the rise and into the cave. Immediately inside, Jurgens reached into the folds of the vestments he had worn and retrieved a small vial. He uncapped it and sprinkled its contents of holy water to the right and left.

"In the name of the Father and of the Son and of the Holy Spirit," he said, crossing himself, and then uttered several more phrases that Holt did not catch. Latin, perhaps.

If either of them had expected anything to happen, they were disappointed. There was only deep, dead silence. Holt allowed his grip on his weapon to lessen slightly, but he kept his hand at the ready.

"The cul-de-sac," Jurgens said then. "Where is it?"

"Up ahead here, around the corner."

"Show me."

Holt nodded and started forward, the priest close behind. When they reached the small passage with its low-ceilinged dead end, Jurgens took out another vial of holy water and sprinkled it over the entire area.

The water splattered against rock, and this time something happened. The walls and floor of the cave began to glow, as though the surfaces were slightly radioactive. A faint light. A light that was almost imaginary.

"What—" Holt began, but Jurgens silenced him with a firm grip on his shoulder.

"This is it, Carl. This is the burying place."

"How do you kn—"

"Shhh." Jurgens straightened himself regally and raised his voice. "Is anyone here? Speak to us now."

Silence. And then Tommy Gallagher's voice again: "A little child shall lead them, priest. Do you understand?" It was odd the way that voice seemed to come from everywhere, from behind and above and below them. Odd the way it lingered in the air like a memory after it had finished speaking.

"Explain yourself," Jurgens said, and for the first time, Holt detected a note of uncertainty in the priest's voice.

"Explain yourself," the voice repeated, mocking. "Really now, Father. You must understand. A little child shall lead them."

A long moment ticked by. That time, with its

accompanying silence, seemed to stretch and spiral, and although Holt was sure it was only a handful of seconds, it seemed a half-hour at least.

At last, Jurgens nodded slowly. "A catalyst," he murmured. "A human catalyst."

"What are you talking about?"

"Spirits, Carl. And catalysts. Tommy awakened the spirits. And he paid the price. He was inhabited. He was used. He—"

"Wonderful, priest!" the voice boomed, and it was no longer Tommy's voice at all. Now it was something flat and dull, something coldly inhuman. "You do understand after all."

"You . . . you must rest," Jurgens said. "You once knew peace, and you must return to that. There is no need to—"

There was an enormous and blinding flash of fire, similar to the flash that had stunned Holt on that night two weeks prior. It came with a thunderclap explosion that drove them backwards, a murderous tidal wave of sound. Holt struck the rock wall behind and slumped to the floor, his head lolling from side to side. Jurgens struck the wall too, but was able to right himself. His hand went to his neck and darted forward, brandishing a crucifix.

"Rest!" he intoned. "In the name of the Holy Father, I command you to—"

The laughter swelled up, deafening and hideous, swallowing the last of his words into a chasm of malevolent humor.

"A child shall lead them," the voice said. "But a child is weak. We seek strength, priest. We prefer someone strong, someone like yourself."

"NO!" Jurgens bellowed. The light flashed again, but he stood his ground against it. "You must not! You were disturbed! But now you must rest! Our Father, through me, commands you to—"

"There is no rest, priest. Not now. That was our promise. You speak so wisely of charms and curses. Such a wise priest. But you know nothing of the tribal promise. You know nothing of what must occur after awakening."

Jurgens had gone pale, and his eyes were speckled with fear, but his voice was a stormlike shriek. "*In the name of almighty God, I command you to sleep!*" A large vein pulsed madly in the center of his forehead.

"Strength," the voice said then, almost soothingly.

And at that, something dark and formless hurtled out of the cul-de-sac and drove into Jurgens with the force of a runaway truck. The priest flew backward like a scarecrow. He cried out briefly, terribly, and then was silent. A quick and triumphant laugh filled the cave, followed by the complete quiet of the tomb.

Holt blinked and began to right himself from the cave floor. "Father?" he said softly. "Father Jurgens?"

The priest whirled around, eyes flashing with a bestial and predacious fire. Holt cried out and spared no further time for thought. He raised his revolver and fired. The shot went wild, ricocheting around the cave like a crazed pinball. He fired again and again, this time on his mark, but the shots had no influence on the body before him. Jurgens was not there anymore, and in his last moment of life, it was that thought that filled Carl Holt's brain. Jurgens was not there anymore. Only a shambling, skulking Jurgens-thing. Only a priest body with something entirely different within.

FROM A DREAMLESS SLEEP AWAKENED

***

When it was finished with Carl Holt, when its centuries-old appetite was appropriately whetted, the priest-form turned away from the remains and headed for the mouth of the cave.

There was a shabby country road out there, with a little town waiting at the far end.

There was a whole world beyond that.

And there were all manner of promises to be fulfilled.

THE FOREVER BIRD

S HIFT CHANGE WAS at four, and two hours after that, Hank and Gilbert were well on their way to fulfilling the Friday goal they had set for themselves at the beginning of the week: that is, they were almost as drunk as it was humanly possible to be in that short length of time. Since leaving the mill they had been cruising the back roads around Caldwell, chugging Pabst and listening to Seger on the tape deck slung below the dash of Hank's car. They were on the last of the beer and singing along to *Ramblin' Gamblin' Man* for the fourteenth time when Hank brought the car to a stop in a spray of gravel, jerking it over to the shoulder and almost dumping them into the drainage ditch alongside.

"Hey man, what're you doing?" Gil said. "I thought we was gonna head back into town for some more brew."

"Don't havta," Hank said. "I just remembered."

"Yeah? I remembered too. I remembered you're an asshole.

What're you talkin' about?"

"The glovebox." "Huh?"

"Open it."

Gil looked at his buddy as though he had just ordered him to put on a tux and call on the Queen.

31

"Open the glovebox, man."

"Okay, okay." He bent and snapped it open, ignoring the spill of greasy maps and broken Foster Grants that tumbled out. "Now what?"

"In the back. Behind the insurance shit."

Gil shook his head. "You're crazy, Hankus. Purely crazy." But he fumbled past the legal papers and came out with a small foil-wrapped package. He held it up and stared at it so closely that his eyes crossed for a moment before focusing. Then the significance of the find dawned on him. "Holy jeez, partner. Is this somma Carl's stuff?"

Hank nodded proudly. "You betcha. Pure Columbian. Oughta be some papers back there someplace too."

Gil plunged his hands back into the glovebox and dug out a tattered packet of Zig Zags. "Fantastic," he murmured. "How long you had this stuff, anyhow?"

Hank shrugged. "Couple months. Three maybe."

"Christ, you shoulda remembered it before! We wouldn'ta needed the brew."

They got underway again, Hank goosing the car up to seventy and cranking the volume on the tape deck up to the maximum while Gil rolled them each a bomber. The pot seemed to be just what their beer-soaked minds needed, and within a half-hour they had rewritten the words to *Ramblin' Gamblin' Man* at least seven times, each new version throwing them into giggle fits of immense proportions. They passed out of Caldwell Township and into Champion, passed out of Champion and into Republic. The day's rain ended, and a creeping, swampy fog came on with the sunset, oozing out of the woods and enveloping the road. It did not deter Hank at all; he bravely kept the speedometer pegged where it was, convinced his old driving instructor from high school would be proud of his control. "Hope you're watchin, Mr. Bankard," he said at one point.

"Yeah," Gil agreed, with no idea who Mr. Bankard was. "Hope like hell you're watchin."

They no longer knew where they were. At several points, they had actually circled back to within a few miles of Caldwell without being aware of it. Each town they passed was just a brief twinkling in the fog, every other car a phantom beast ripping by.

"I'm stoppin," Hank announced after a time.

"Aw . . . why?" They had just lit up their third joints, and Gil felt as though he could cruise along forever, felt that perhaps he already had.

"Munchies, man. I think I saw a restaurant back there. Sides, Gilly, I gotta piss something wicked."

He stomped on the brake and threw the car into reverse, swerving backwards up the road. Their taillights cut through the mist like red stage lights in a play about hell.

"There ain't no restaurant, Hankus. We ain't passed nothin for ten—"

"You're fulla shit, old buddy. Look there."

The fog suddenly gave way on one side of the road, revealing a gravel-and-dirt parking lot and a building about the size of two mobile homes placed side by side. A sign atop the building said CLYDE'S in blinking white letters.

"Told you I saw a restaurant. Told you."

"Yeah, you're a regular genius. Clyde's? What kinda place is that?

Where the hell are we, anyway?"

Hank didn't know—had never heard of the place—and so wisely kept silent.

"Pro'bly some kinda Ptomaine Palace," Gil muttered.

"Who cares? I'm so hungry right now I'd eat a whole truckload of ptomaine."

"You don't eat ptomaine, you asshole. It's food poisonin, man."

Hank frowned. "I knew that. Whaddya think I am, Gilly? Some dope or something?"

That struck them both as extremely funny, and they remained in the car for some time after coming to a stop in the empty lot, laughing and howling and exchanging good-natured insults.

At last, they got out and headed for the door. They had to pause halfway there while Hank relieved himself.

"Some fog, man," Gil observed. "Yeah."

They went in.

The place was a dump—you could see that right away. The handful of booths and tables were nicked and scarred, heavily grease-splattered. Some of them had not even been bussed since the last customers had left. The checkout counter by the door was dusty, its glass display front foggy and grime-streaked. There were overhead lights, at least, but many of them were burned out, giving the place the shadowy look of a long-empty house.

And it *was* empty.

They approached the back counter, each choosing a padded stool and plopping down.

"Hey!" Hank called. "We're hungry!"

"Yeah, c'mon! Whaddis this place, anyhow? A restaurant or what?"

The door behind the counter swung open then, revealing a kitchen even darker than the dining area. They caught a brief glimpse of things that looked like cutlery and cookware hanging from overhead racks, and then the view was obscured by the figure that came through the doorway. In the shadows, that figure looked quite large—large and lumpy—like some kind of retired strong man gone from muscle to fat.

"About time, man," Gil said. "You oughta learn how to treat your customers a little—"

He broke off sharply, the words dying on his lips. The figure had stepped fully into the light, and as it did, something had registered in Gil's brain. It was having a hard time cutting its way through the beer-and-marijuana haze that was swirling around in there. He stared at the figure dumbly, his mouth working without a sound, making connections. Then it came to him.

"Dean?" he said. "Is that Dean Hardwick?"

The figure nodded. "Yeah. Who are you?"

"Aw, c'mon, man, you gotta remember me. It's Gil ... Gil Duchamp, from high school."

"Gilly? Is that really you? Well, Jesus H, it is. How are you doing, pal? It's been a long time."

The figure, undoubtedly Dean Hardwick, stepped forward and thrust out a beefy hand. They shook, and Gil studied the face before him.

"You're lookin good, man. Cept for them scars. What happened?

Football?"

"No, I don't play anymore. Little cooking accident is all. What about you? What have you been up to?"

35

"Not much. Working at the pulp mill over to Caldwell. What about you, though? How'd you end up in a dump like this? An where are we, anyhow?"

Dean laughed. "You're at Clyde's, Gilly. In Strunk Corners."

"Strunk Corners? Where the eff is that? There ain't no Strunk Corners in Michigan."

"Well, there sure as hell is. You're sitting smack in the middle of the town limits. Only about fifteen miles from Caldwell."

"There ain't no Strunk Corners in Michigan," Gil repeated. "Is there, Hankus?"

Hank snorted, coming out of a dreamy doze. "No sir, no Strunk Corners round here."

"You guys are fucked," Dean Hardwick said. "I moved here right after my football scholarship was up. Been here almost ten years. Ought to know the name of my own town, wouldn't you think?"

"Strunk Corners," Gil repeated softly, musing over it. "Strunk Corners? Whatever you say, man. This here's m'buddy, Hank Brody. Went to high school over to Negaunee, so you wouldn't know him. How bout fixin us some burgers or something, Dean-boy? We're starved."

Dean nodded, turned to the grill. "Two special Big Clyde Burgers coming up."

He bent his huge frame over the freezer chest and brought out two frozen patties, throwing them onto the grill. There was a hiss and a sizzle, and Gil grinned broadly.

"Love that sound, Dean. Love it. So what're you doin here workin for old Clyde?"

"There isn't any Clyde, Gilly. He died ten years ago, right after I bought this place from him."

"Too bad."

"Oh, not really. That old coot was as crazy as crabs on a mad dog. You should have seen the stuff I had to clean out of here when he left."

"Yeah? What kinda stuff?" Hank said, before slipping into his doze again.

"Don't mind him," Gil said. "He's a little stoned. What kinda stuff?"

"All sorts of shit," Dean Hardwick told him. "Witchy stuff, if you know what I mean. Crystal balls and amulets and old dusty books and these little bottles or something. I kept some of the books—make good winter reading—but I dumped the rest of it right out. Don't need that kind of crap in a family restaurant."

"Boy, I guess not," Gil said wisely. "Not in no fambly restaurant.

Not in Strunk Corners."

Dean turned away from him again and moved to the shadow-struck far end of the counter. He came back a moment later with a tremendous loaf of French bread.

"So, Gilly," he said then, and his voice seemed a shade softer than it had before. "You're working in a mill, working pulp. Is that all you've been up to since you stole my girl?"

Gil drew back, so far back that he almost fell off his stool. "What?"

"You stole my girl in school. Debbie Lee Ison. Don't tell me you forgot old Debbie Lee."

"Debbie Lee. Debbie Lee Ison? I didn't know no Ison, I didn't steal . . . oh. Oh-oh. Debbie Lee? Was she yours?"

"Come on now, Gilly. Don't tell me you forgot that. You were the talk of the halls for two years. Everyone said you had guts to steal a ballplayer's meat." He bent to retrieve something from under the counter. Gil watched him warily as he came back up, saw a brief metallic glint, which materialized after a moment into a mammoth cleaver.

"Hey no, Dean-boy. I didn't know she was yours. She was hot for me, was all. An that was years ago, buddy. That was . . . it musta been twelve years back now. You ain't gonna get crazy on me for something that happened twelve years ago, are you, partner?"

Dean stepped closer. The cleaver rose. It seemed to hover in the shadows above the counter.

"C'mon, Deanie . . . twelve years. I mean, that's ancient history.

It—"

The cleaver fell.

It split the loaf of French bread neatly in two.

Dean Hardwick laughed. "Not to worry, Gilly, my boy. I'm not mad at you. You stole my girl. So what? You said it yourself—ancient history. Truth be told, I was happy to be rid of the slut."

"Hey now, that ain't nice. Debbie Lee wasn't no slut. She—"

The cleaver rose again. Gil shut up quickly. The cleaver came down and cut the halves of bread into quarters.

"Twelve years is a long time," Gil muttered then, as if to convince himself.

"Well hell, sure it is, Gilly. Not to worry. I told you I'm not mad."

"You sure?"

"Sure I'm sure. One thing Dean Hardwick was

always good at, beside football, and that was making up his mind. I made up my mind about that one right away. I wasn't mad at you then, and I'm sure not mad at you now. Hey, tell you what. Burgers are on the house for you and your friend."

"We got money."

"Sure you do. But old friends don't have to pay around here."

"Not in Strunk Corners," Hank slurred from the depths of his

doze.

"Not in Strunk Corners," Gil echoed, and grinned. "Thanks, Dean-boy. You always was good people. And about Debbie Lee—"

"Drop it," Dean said. "We're shut of that subject." Gil nodded obediently.

A few minutes later the hamburgers were ready. Gil gave Hank a poke in the ribs, and they dug in. While they ate, Hank muttered unintelligible phrases, and Gil and Dean talked over old times, old parties, old friends. When the food was gone and the conversation seemed to have run its course, Dean turned suddenly and headed for the kitchen.

"Where you goin, Dean-boy?"

"Hang on a second. I want to show you my bird."

"What?" Hank said. "What about a turd?"

"He said *bird*, Hankus," Gil told him. "You gotta bird, Dean-boy? I didn't know that."

"Oh, heck yeah. Another thing that belonged to old Clyde that I hung onto. Makes good company for an old football player."

He said something else as he disappeared into the kitchen. To Gil's frazzled mind it sounded like *magic bird*, but he knew that couldn't be it. After several moments, their host returned with a small black mynah bird perched on his wrist.

"Flicker? Want you to meet an old pal of mine. Gil Duchamp. And his friend Hank. Boys, this is Flicker."

"Hey there, Flicker," Gil said. "How ya doin? That one a them talkin birds, Dean?"

"Talking bird," Flicker said then, quite clearly. "Flicker, the talking bird."

"Whoa—fantastic!" Hank said. "What else does he say?"

"Flicker talks," Flicker said. "Flicker likes football."

They all laughed hysterically.

"Old bird," Dean told them. "Clyde had him four or five years, and I've had him ten more."

"How long'll he live?" Gil asked.

"Don't know. Clyde told me he'd live forever, but Clyde was crazy, like I said. He was right about one thing, though. Flicker's magic."

"Huh? Whaddya mean, magic?"

"Probly shits and talks at the same time," Hank said, and Gil cast him a withering gaze.

"He's magic," Dean said again. "He grants wishes. Go ahead . . . try him."

Gil shook his head slowly. "A bird that grants wishes? Tell you, Dean-boy, I think livin in this place's gone to your brain. There ain't no magic birds."

"Oh, yes, there are. I guarantee it, Gilly. Go ahead."

"I wish for a million bucks," Hank said. "I wish for five million bucks. I wish for five billion-trillion bucks."

"Shut up, Hankus. Dean was talkin to me."

"That's right, Gil. I was talking to you. Go ahead, old pal, make a wish."

Gil stared at Dean for a long time, then turned and stared at Flicker. He suddenly felt as though every trace of beer and pot had left him. His mind felt open and sharp and clear, almost too clear.

"Make a wish," Dean repeated. "Anything for my old friend."

"Aw, I don't want nothin. Go on an give Hank his money. I don't need nothin."

"I insist, Gilly. Make a wish."

"Shit, magic birds—birds that live forever. Ain't no such thing."

"Gilly . . . *make a wish!*"

"I, uh, okay, okay, here goes . . . but just to make you happy, Dean-boy, just to make up for takin Debbie Lee from you. I wanna live forever. How's that? I wanna be like Flicker there. I wanna live forever."

"Done," Dean said.

"Done," Flicker repeated in an uncanny imitation of his master's voice.

And then they were all laughing—Gil, Hank, Dean, even Flicker—laughing as though they all wanted to burst.

"Magic birds," Gil said, tears rolling down his cheeks. "That's a good one, Dean-boy. You always were a funny guy. Birds grantin wishes. Jesus, that's rich."

"I thought you'd like it," Dean said, and carried Flicker back into the kitchen.

"Let's go, Gil," Hank said while he was gone. "I don't like it here so much. I wanna smoke another joint."

Gil looked at him and nodded. That unnatural sensation of sobriety had not left him, and another joint, or for that matter just another beer, sounded like

41

exactly what he was after. When Dean came back empty-handed, Gil told his friend they had to leave.

"Oh really? We were just getting close again. Just getting the memories going. You can stay awhile, can't you?"

"Fraid not, Dean-boy. We gotta get back home. Both of us workin Saturday shifts tomorrow."

Dean nodded with clear regret. "I get you. Work comes first. But hey! Now that you know where I am, don't be a stranger. Come on back anytime."

"Sure will," Gil said. "Back to Clyde's. Back to Strunk Corners." They started for the door, thanking Dean for the food.

"No problem. We'll do it again next time. Maybe I'll have Flicker grant you another wish."

"Yeah, that'd be nice."

Then they were outside in the parking lot, out in the heavy fog, and the door to Clyde's was closed behind them. An instant later the lights in the front window went out, and then the blinking sign overhead, leaving them in utter, dripping darkness.

"Let's roll," Hank said. "I wanna get outta here."

"Sure thing," Gil said. "We'll smoke a joint an head on back to Caldwell an—"

He stopped, cocking his head slightly to one side. For a moment, he thought he had heard something, something moving overhead in the fog, something sailing by like a glider. A whisper of displaced air. But then it was gone. He shrugged and clapped Hank on the back. The two of them started for the car.

When they were back on the road again, headlights piercing the mist, Seger growling through another tune, pot smoke heavy in the air, he let out a gusty sigh.

"Sure is good to see old friends again," he said without much conviction.

"Must be," Hank agreed. "You was a crazy fucker, you know that? Stealin a girl from a mountain like that?"

"Crazy, yeah. You know, I'd clean forgot all about Debbie Lee. I remember her now, though. Whooo, what a sweetmeat."

"Hope she was worth it."

"Every inch, Hankus, every inch. Nothin to worry about, though. Old Dean's gone soft. Playin with birds now. Jesus."

Something thumped against the back window then, and Gil whirled around just in time to see a glimpse of some shape fluttering back there in the fog. A suggestion of movement.

"What the—?" he said.

"What the—?" Hank responded, and sped up a bit.

Then the thumping came again, more powerfully, and the car swerved a little. Gil looked back again, and at first he thought he was seeing the headlights of some distant car. Then he realized they were not headlights at all but eyes. Yellow eyes. Peering into the car. Peering at him.

"Hit it, Hankus," he said, struggling to keep his voice level. His stomach had become a cluster of icy lumps, and those lumps seemed to be alive, knocking and rolling against each other.

The car swerved again and then leapt forward, eating up the road, chewing up the fog.

Thump . . . thump . . . thump . . .

"Jesus, Gil, I can't keep er straight!" Hank's voice was now as clear and sober as it had ever been.

43

But Gil wasn't paying attention. He was staring, transfixed, out the back window. The shape had materialized into a solid form. He saw it moving back there, black wings twitching, black claws groping.

"Goddammit, Hank, would you get this car *ROLLING!*"

"I'm tryin, man, I'm tr—"

The car was struck again, and this time it bucked a little too far. The tires caught the gravel on the right shoulder, pitching them around. Gil saw flashes of roadside weeds, and then he saw one final glimpse of the thing that was behind them: the mammoth, hulking bird with the shimmering yellow eyes and the piercing beak. The bird had grown suddenly larger than any creature from a dream, much larger than any bird was meant to be.

Wings beating at the car as it spun around and left the road, wings enveloping them.

"Wish granted, Gilly," the voice of his old friend's mynah bird said then, filling the air, filling his brain. "Wish granted," Flicker told him. "Live forever, old pal."

And the world went upside down, while white fire lit the night.

HOMECOMING

IT WAS FRIDAY NIGHT, yet there were only two other people in the place. Beckett, who the Lord knew had been in enough crappy roadside dives the last twenty years to learn they usually did their best business at the end of the week, considered asking the bartender what was wrong but decided against it. A short time later—after his third beer and second cigarette, as the baseball chatter they'd been exchanging wore a bit thin—he asked anyway.

"Stiffed," the bartender explained. "I beg your pardon?"

"We been stiffed . . . stood up. See, usually we got this band outta Green Bay. Good group, name of Moonrider. Tonight they found a better job over to Iron Mountain. First weekend in more'n two years we ain't hadda band." He grinned and gestured at the empty tables, the darkened dance floor. "I guess word gets around pretty quick."

Beckett ordered another pitcher, and the bartender set it up before taking off to adjust the picture on the TV. He filled his glass, counted bubbles for a moment or two, then turned and looked around the place for the fifth or sixth time that evening.

Now that was strange, he thought. He hadn't noticed the boy before.

Earlier, the only other patrons had been an older couple in the back, drinking something with Canadian Club in it and studying an Arctic Cat snowmobile catalog with the avidity of academicians. Now the boy was here as well.

He couldn't have been more than fifteen (fourteen was probably closer to it), wearing a ratty pair of jeans and a T-shirt that promoted the local high school pep club. His hair was greasy and unkempt, swept back from his forehead at comical angles. A bottle of Pabst sat in front of him, hardly touched, and a cigarette dangled from the corner of his mouth.

Beckett watched him for a while, discomfort creeping into his bones. He thought of his son, just about that age. Absolutely no way in this sweet world that Andy would be allowed in a place like this. But of course, that meant nothing at all; Andy was in St. Louis with his mother, and there was no telling *what* she was letting him get away with. He grimaced, felt the discomfort changing rapidly to bitterness, and took several swallows of beer, hoping to wash it away before it took hold.

The bartender returned, eager to pick up with the National League where they'd left off with the American, but Beckett confounded him by jerking a thumb over his shoulder.

"Who's the kid?"

The bartender shrugged. "Who knows? Never seen him around before."

"You check an I.D. on him?"

"Huh?"

"I mean, do you make a habit of serving alcohol to fifteen-year-olds?"

"Hey, bud, take a look around. On a night like this I'd serve my five-year-old nephew. What's the gripe? You work for the state or something?"

Beckett shook his head. "I told you before, I'm a manufacturer's rep."

"Then it's no big deal, right? Shit, I was drinking when I was his age."

Beckett turned again. The boy hadn't taken any more beer but had the cigarette down to the filter. As he watched, the kid crushed it out and slowly lit another.

"So you think the Cubs are gonna take the Mets? I say you're crazy. That Gooden can outpitch everyone in—"

Beckett waved him off distractedly and got to his feet, not precisely sure what he was up to but feeling driven by some quiet inner imperative. He stretched, waited a moment for the muscles in his back to loosen, then started across the room.

"Hey, bud, you can't throw him outta here, you know. It ain't your place. You can't give him the toss."

"Shut up," Beckett said, and the bartender drew back sullenly, turning to polish a few glasses, suddenly and pointedly detached.

The boy glanced up as he approached. "Hi'ya, son."

The boy said nothing . . . didn't so much as nod.

"You mind if I have a seat?"

Still nothing.

Beckett hauled up a chair and lowered himself into it, resting his elbows on the table. "How're you doing tonight?"

The boy's mouth opened slowly, as though it operated on stiff, rusty hinges. It stayed that way—open and speechless—for a long time. Beckett felt his stomach tighten painfully. He swallowed.

"She had no right," the boy said at last, softly.

"I'm sorry?"

"She thought she was the goddamned Queen or something. But she had no right. No fucking right."

His voice was low and hushing, the sound of cedars in a summer breeze.

"Do you mind if I ask who you're talking about?"

"I wanted to show her she was wrong, that's all. I just wanted to show her."

Beckett's belly clenched again. The lady (she of the older couple and the snowmobile catalog) dropped a quarter in the juke. Hoyt Axton began to sing about Spain and a place called Needles. The bartender dropped a glass. Its shattering death sounded distant, unreal. Beckett fumbled in his shirt pocket for his cigarettes, got one, lit it, and drew in a huge amount of smoke.

"I just wanted to show her," the boy said again.

"Son, I really—"

The boy turned, looking at him directly for the first time. The effect was startling enough to chop his words off. Dark eyes—wounded, nervously tense. Mouth set firmly. Nostrils flared. Beckett frowned, wanting nothing so much as to return to his beer and the desultory baseball talk.

"D'you ever think about oil rigs?"

Beckett blinked. "Oil rigs?" he repeated, staring at the boy and trying to figure out what was going on, hoping to home in on whatever track this kid was traveling. Those dark, hurting eyes shifted back and forth, and he wondered what was behind them, ticking steadily away. Or if there was anything at all.

Uncomfortably, he was reminded of a sales call he'd paid almost two years before to a small but profitable company that dealt in several ways with Michigan's boom-and-bust lumber industry. He'd had no difficulty getting in to meet the CEO, a pleasant, fortyish man with a full head of hair and a charming smile. Once in the man's office, settled in a padded chair and about to launch his spiel, he'd experienced the not-very-happy sensation of being watched, became convinced there was someone else in the room with them.

Irritated, whirling around, he had found himself looking into a pair of cold, black eyes that were peering at him from the depths of the closet in the corner.

The CEO had laughed (a little pathetically, it seemed in retrospect) and said, "I see you've noticed Max."

"Max?"

"My boy. I'm afraid his counselor—caretaker, really—had to check into the hospital this week for tests, and my wife, well, she never could relate to Max very well, never could control him. So I brought him to work with me. I enjoy his company, and he just loves to explore."

Max, it turned out, was the CEO's sixteen-year-old son, severely retarded and capable of only the most rudimentary conversation, able to care for himself to only the slightest degree.

The sales call seemed to last forever, and although Max remained in the closet throughout, staring noiselessly, it was one of Beckett's least successful days ever. He just couldn't shake the sensation of being watched by those black and piercing eyes.

Eyes.

With nothing behind them but a skull full of dark and abstract impulse.

Eyes.

Masking mystery and god only knew what kind of intent.

It was Max's vapid but sentient gaze that he thought of now, looking at the boy.

"Oil rigs," the boy said again after a moment. "They're pretty dangerous, you know. But some things are more dangerous."

He tossed his head back and threw off a light, musical laugh. The sound of it was utterly unexpected, unreal, chilling.

"She really had no right."

Beckett leaned forward. "Are we talking about your girlfriend?" "No goddamned right."

"Or your mother? Is it your mother?"

The dark eyes flickered, and for a third time Beckett felt his stomach clench. The hairs on the back of his neck prickled.

"Someone had to show her. That's all I wanted to do, cause somebody had to do it. She had to be shown. Jesus, she had no right!"

"Did she leave you?"

"Leave?" Another laugh. "Yeah, she left me." He took a swallow of beer and gave a very boylike grimace. "Will you come home with me?"

"*What?*"

"I wanna show you."

HOMECOMING

"Uh . . . no, I don't think so, son. I'm sorry, but . . . I mean I—"

"You afraid?"

Beckett stiffened. "Should I be?"

The boy shrugged. "I just wanted to show her."

***

It was a lovely night but a long drive—ten miles back up the highway Beckett had traveled earlier in the day, then nearly four more down a dusty, godforsaken stretch of trail marked County Road 420. Deeper and deeper into moon-speared woodland, underbrush crowding the car, swaying branches reaching for them like animated creatures in a dream. The boy leaned against the side window and stared out at the wilderness, now and then muttering something Beckett couldn't make out. He wondered how the kid had gotten into town in the first place, wanted to ask but didn't and could not say why.

Then suddenly the boy was bouncing up and down, gesturing wildly, telling him this was it and he'd better pull off, pull off now, pull off quick! He pumped the brakes and swung hard right, pulling into a gravel drive less than ten feet long, coming to a stop just scant feet from a house trailer sitting there on cinderblocks in the middle of the clearing.

"Is this your house?" he asked, but the boy was already out, yanking open the trailer door. He followed, stumbling on something in the yard but not looking to see what it was. There were no front steps; he had to hoist himself up by the jamb to get inside.

It was dark in there. Beckett wondered where the boy had gone and caught a whiff of copper and smoke, like hot metal on a forge. Or perhaps it was something else, but he didn't even want to speculate on what that something else might be.

He simply stood there like an idiot, trying to see, cursing himself for coming. He should have stayed in the bar and continued working on his buzz, should have tried harder to convince the drink-jockey that the Cubs were a cinch to win the National East.

And then the room was dazzled with light. Beckett blinked . . . gaped . . . gasped.

The place was a wreck.

The faded tartan couch in the middle of the tiny living room was overturned, the end table that had once sided it lying with its legs in the air like a murdered animal. There were broken bottles everywhere, glass shards winking dangerously in the harsh glare. Papers were scattered, chairs upended, clothing strewn about.

"She threw Dad out," the boy said, startling him by coming from the light switch in the corner and standing a few feet away with his hands on his hips, apparently eager to spill everything at last. "He wanted to work it out. He told her they could do it. You know, he even offered to go to one of them pussy marriage counselors they have in the city. He said he'd do that if they could only pull it all together. That's what he said . . . he said, 'Marge, we gotta try and pull this all together.'

"But she wouldn't listen. She *never* listened. She was a bitch, and she had no right, but she threw him out, right the fuck out the door, like he was some kind of bum or something.

"He went down south, thought he had some people there that would take him in. I don't know if they ever did, cause all he ever wrote me was that he was going to give the bitch her divorce. Said he was gonna get a lawyer, the best one he could buy, and fight like hell to get custody of me. He thought we had a good chance cause he'd gotten this big job on an oil rig and he was making all this money. He thought he could find a high-class lawyer in maybe a month or so."

He paused, his face a neatly-divided mask: part youthful helplessness, part adult defiance.

"Did she hurt you?" Beckett asked, thinking, *Why? Why'd you have to get involved, you old fool? Why didn't you let the kid drink in peace?*

"She hurt me," the boy said. "She hit me . . . she threw me around. Like she hurt Dad. She threw *him* out and he went to work on that goddamned oil rig and he fell and broke his neck. It was her fault, and she would have done the same to me. She would have killed me too, if I'd let her."

Something was trying to break through the confusion in Beckett's mind, but he couldn't tell what it was. He felt as though he were scuttering around in the dark, trying to scoop up a bundle of spilled straws and build something out of them. He struggled to see clearly, but that look in the boy's eyes—*Max's eyes . . . Max's eyes peering out of the closet*—kept getting in the way.

"She left you," he said, a simple statement designed to force something definitive from the boy. "She ran away. Do you have any other family? Any friends? Someone you can stay with until she—"

"C'mon!" the boy said, grasping his hand and tugging. "C'mere!"

He started across that battle zone of a living room,

heading for the narrow hallway that led to the back. Beckett went along helplessly, his throat hot and tight, his free hand bunched into an impotent fist at his side.

Another light came on, and the boy shoved open a door, revealing his bedroom. There was a small, unmade bed, a tiny dresser and desk. Tigers posters and music magazine tear-outs of Van Halen decorated the walls. All completely normal, perfect, and right.

Except for the mess in the middle of the floor. A circle of candle stubs with a small pile of sticks and stones in the center. A jumble of books to one side. A litter of notebook paper with scrawled calculations.

"What—" he began, but the boy was already pulling him away, forcing him along the hallway again, pushing open yet another door and revealing an area of destruction as bad as the living room. The master bedroom, larger than the boy's but still claustrophobic, was torn apart and filled with awful relics of the struggle—broken pictures, shattered pottery, furniture dismembered and disemboweled.

"Oh my god," Beckett murmured. His mind was sodden and heavy, incapable of lightning thought or great deduction, but still, he was beginning to see the full scope of what had gone on inside this trailer earlier in the day. Details capered just beyond the edge of coherence, and for no reason, he thought again of coal-black eyes gleaming from a dark closet.

The boy was still pulling, not allowing him time to think. This time he propelled him across the hall, into a miniscule bathroom and the absolute worst of it.

Warm bile flooded his mouth. He staggered backward, clutching vainly for support. He fell against the wall and struck his head, almost collapsed before he was able to pull himself up by sheer strength of will. He swallowed . . . breathed . . . swallowed again . . . grimaced . . . and took a step forward . . . into the bathroom.

It was like some crazed, surrealist painting or a photograph of a nightmare. There was blood everywhere—across the floor and the ceiling, the tiles and the mirrors. That cloying, coppery smell was strongest here, and there was no doubt anymore about what it was.

The boy's mother was in the corner, between the tub and toilet, her days as a bitch finished for all time. She was not going to throw any more children around or give any more husbands the one-way bum's rush. Her flesh was torn and tattered; her limbs lying at bizarre, impossible angles; her face a sliced and shimmering mask of agony.

Beckett vomited, stumbled forward, and vomited again.

"Eyes," he groaned, for no particular reason. "Oh my Christ, those staring eyes—"

He wobbled and spun. He felt the boy's hand on his arm but shook it off violently, starting for the living room, staggering like the Lord's most pitiful drunk, banging back and forth off the walls but keeping his feet through some innate sense of balance that was beyond understanding.

"Wait!" the boy cried, pleading.

"You killed her," Beckett said thickly. "You killed your mother." The words were alien to him, foreign and awkward, yet he couldn't stop saying them. "You killed her, you killed—"

"Not me! It was *Dad!* It wasn't *me!*"

Beckett stopped at the verge of the living room, turning back. "You said your father was dead."

The boy nodded, and for the first time, his eyes showed something other than fear and loathing. Now, they were wide and innocent, wet with tears and full of confusion deeper than Beckett's.

"He died last week, and I wanted to go down south to the funeral, but she wouldn't let me. I showed her the money I saved, and she wouldn't let me go. She called him a scum and a bastard and said we were better off with him dead. I tried to leave, but she hit me." He paused, and a great, shuddering sigh escaped him. "She beat me up."

"But you said—"

"She wouldn't let me go, but I had to see him one more time, so I brought him back. I brought him here."

"You brought . . . ? What the hell are you talking about?"

"I brought him here," the boy said again. "It wasn't easy. It took three days, working all the time, all day and night. Not easy at all, no way, but I got him here. Dad always said hard work pays off, and I worked hard, you know? I busted my ass for a long time to get him here, and we got paid all right . . . we all got paid sure enough . . . when he got here."

The boy was babbling, hysterical, and Beckett knew he had to get away. The realization that he had actually been in a car with this lunatic for almost half an hour was terrifying. The fact that he was alone with him now, in a small trailer in the middle of miles of wilderness, was even worse. He had to run. This was a little town, but there were still police, authorities to keep him safe and take care of this crazed kid, this murderous little sonuvabitch.

"*I didn't think this would happen!*" the boy screamed, and the trailer shook with the force of his cry. "You think I planned it? I just wanted to *see* him! I just wanted to touch him and say goodbye! I didn't know . . . I *didn't!*"

He was sobbing, his small body wracked with wave after trembling wave. His face was a contorted, working machine; his mouth moved, but no words came out.

And there was something else.

Another sound that came from the last room in the trailer, the one with the closed door at the end of the hallway.

A bump.

A soft and slithering thump. Something wet. Something slippery.

Beckett's muscles locked. He tried to take a backward step and couldn't. The lights in the room seemed to flicker momentarily and things began to swirl, as though he were seeing everything from an out-of-control carnival ride. Once again he groped for the wall, but this time he missed, went to his knees, and was unable to rise.

"I didn't plan it," the boy repeated through his tears. "But she deserved it . . . She deserved everything he gave her when he got here, when he came home."

The door at the end of the hallway crept open, just a crack at first, then slowly and steadily.

" . . . when he came home . . . "

THEY CAME FROM THE SUBURBS

YOU SAW THEM the first few hours of every weekday morning. They wandered in and out of the stores but never bought, rarely spoke. They sat on the benches in the center court but never chatted with those nearby. They filled the tables of Woolworth's Cafeteria, cups of decaf in front of them, untouched. At noon, when the lunching businessmen appeared, when the kids from the nearby high school flooded in, they were gone, and it was easy—oh, so easy—to forget all about them.

They were the elderly, mostly, but there were young mothers with infant children and a few wayward teens as well. There was no one constant about them but this: they were always there. From ten until twelve, they were as much a part of the mall as the gaily rushing water fountain and the dusty plastic plants that never died.

David Finley was one of the few employees in the mall to notice the quiet ones. He always thought of them that way, as *the quiet ones,* and the only reason he saw them—really saw them—when others didn't was because he was new. Small-town bred, he'd moved toward the city, to the suburbs, for a better job. Not seeking his future, precisely, just trying to get ahead. He hated the mall with its dry air and windowless walls, hated the national chain of record and video stores that he worked for. Still, he had to admit that it was better in terms of salary and the possibility of advancement than anything back home.

He noticed the quiet ones toward the end of his first week, when the nervousness had subsided and the routine had begun. The store manager, a dour company brownnoser by the name of Fred Schultz, had just shown him how to open the registers for the morning and then had left him alone on the sales floor while he went back to call the national office about a planned Bruce Springsteen promotion. The mall was quiet, as it always was in the morning; the store was completely empty. David was standing by the counter, aimlessly straightening the current Top 40, when he heard someone come in behind him.

"Good morning," he said, turning around with a bright smile that was already forced after four days on the job.

It was an old lady. She stopped and looked at him suspiciously. "Help you find something?" he asked, suspecting the answer; there was nothing in here for her unless she was seeking a gift for her favorite grandson. More likely, she wanted to know where the restrooms were.

The old lady continued to stare, her eyes filmy gray, unblinking. He tried again: "You looking for anything in particular?"

She walked away, heading cross-store, toward the video racks that lined the better part of one wall. David shrugged and went back to work, didn't look up again until he heard the crash five minutes later. He hurried over.

The lady was standing, bewildered, amid a jumble of VHS cassettes—the cheap ones, the public domain B-flicks from the forties. Apparently, she'd tried to pull one from the back without removing those in front, bringing down fifteen or twenty tapes from all sides.

"Don't worry about it," he was saying before he even got to her. "Happens all the time . . . it's these silly racks. I'll pick them up."

The old lady turned toward him and mumbled a single word that might have been, "Mess." Then she was gone, drifting toward the entrance and vanishing into the mall.

David looked after her for a moment before kneeling to pick up the tapes.

***

Coincidentally, he saw her again later that morning as he headed toward the Cookie Palace for a cup of coffee during his first break. She was sitting on one of the benches between Sears and Sportsworld, staring straight ahead. She had a cigarette between her fingers, but it was unsmoked; the ash was over an inch long, just seconds from dropping to the floor.

His steps faltered; he gave her a quick nod.

She looked at him with those filmy, unblinking eyes. "Mess," she said then, softly. "Tapes."

He hurried past before he had to think of something to say.

***

You saw them the first few hours of every weekday morning. They wandered in and out of the stores but never bought, rarely spoke, and eventually he asked somebody about them. It was the beginning of the Christmas season, and although their business had not yet picked up, their allowable hours had; there were now three people scheduled in the mornings. Fred Schultz was holed up in the back, doing the weekly figures. David was up front with Karen Bach, a part-timer. The third quiet one of the day had just drifted in and out without touching a thing or saying a word.

"Who are these people, anyway?"

Karen, who was always flashing a vapid idiot's grin, looked at her watch and said, "Huh?"

"Who are these people?"

"What people, David? Who're you talking about?"

"The people in the mall every morning. They're in here all the time, but they never buy. Christ, they hardly even look. And always the same ones, the same forty-fifty wanderers. Who are they?"

Her grin almost made him feel like an idiot. "They're shoppers, David," she said, explaining the facts of life to a child.

"No, they're not. Shoppers are the afternoon crowd, the night time people, the ones who come on weekends. Shoppers *buy*."

"What's the difference?"

"There's a big difference. I mean, Jesus, don't they have anything better to do?"

Karen was growing tired of him. "You wouldn't understand.

You're from Hicktown. Around here, shopping's important."

"There has to be something better, *more* important."

61

"There's nothing more important. There's nothing else, period. Downtown, maybe, where the parks and museums are. Out where you were, on the farm or whatever the hell it was. But in the suburbs, all we've got is shopping. Even if we don't have any money."

"You—"

"It's all there is."

"And these people—"

"It's their whole life. Their world."

"Sad," David murmured. But what he was really thinking was,

scary.

***

By the end of his first month the quiet ones had become his hobby, a sort of low-grade obsession. He'd asked about them several more times—how could anyone go to a goddamned shopping mall five days a week?—but had given up hope of getting satisfactory answers. Instead, he waited. He kept an eye on the way they floated in and out of the stores, the way they reached out to touch a certain record, the way they stared for long minutes at a particular display, or worse, the way they stared at him when he bid them good morning.

It was a matter of mechanics, he decided.

For the quiet ones, coming to the mall was a habit. There was no human reasoning in it, and even less of the human heart. They were like someone's collection of wind-up toys, click-clicking around their silent, mysterious business until they ran out of power for the day.

That image clarified frighteningly just a week before the holiday. He was dusting the registers and swiveled to watch a young, pasty-faced mother push a stroller past the store. Stunned, he watched her continue blindly on her way until she ran the carriage into one of the benches near the elevator a few hundred feet away. The stroller bucked and stopped, but the baby did not cry. For almost ten seconds, the young mother's legs continued to move, taking wooden steps that led her nowhere, until at last she came to a halt. Then she backed up a few paces, swung the stroller to the right, and went on.

David blinked and looked around, but none of the other employees had seen it. He wondered what they would have thought if they'd noticed. Probably nothing. She was only shopping.

He swallowed, leaning against the registers for support, and felt a slow, chilly sensation move up and down his spine.

Shopping, he thought dimly. *It's all there is. It's their whole life. Their whole crazy friggin life. Shopping.*

He had to bite down on his tongue to keep from crying out.

***

It unraveled three weeks later.

With Christmas finished and their allowable work hours cut back again, he was pulling a lot of night shifts. Coming in at one and working until nine-thirty was hard—it kept you from doing anything worthwhile in the morning, and it shot the afternoon and evening as effectively as if the day had never existed. Still, he had reached a position of some authority in a very short time, and being trusted to close the store by himself, to shut down the registers and do the day's bank deposit, was at least partial compensation.

He was in the back, classic Deep Purple on the stereo, finishing the figures and getting ready to leave, when he heard the crash out front.

"Dammit," he muttered. It was that NEW RELEASES rack; it had to be. He'd warned Fred the thing was too shaky to last long. But before he could get up, the crash came again. And again. A fourth time and a fifth. Frowning, he realized what it was. Someone was pounding on the front gate, banging a fist against the cheap metal grillwork so that it shook and rattled against the lock.

Probably Karen. Somehow, almost every time he was scheduled, she was scheduled too, her and that damned idiot's grin and that almost total unwillingness to work more than five minutes without taking a break. He'd let her out ten minutes before, but she must have forgotten something. He pushed away from the desk and went out to see what she wanted.

The overheads were off, only two wall-mounted spots left on as nightlights; the store was dark, shadowy, utterly still but for Karen's persistent banging away up front. He hurried toward the gate, anxious to stop that crazy noise, and he was just a few feet shy of his goal when he saw it wasn't Karen Bach at all. It was an old lady, and it took less than a moment, less than a foot's further progress toward the grill, to recognize her. It was the lady he'd seen almost two months earlier, the one who'd upset the cassettes, the one who'd been sitting on the bench near Sportsworld, holding an unsmoked cigarette in her small, gnarled hard.

He stopped.

"We're closed," he said through the gate, the words spoken through a grin much like Karen's.

The old lady didn't stop banging. She looked at him with wide, milky eyes and brought her fist down on the grillwork again and again.

Jesus, he thought, *what is this? What's she doing here now? The quiet ones don't come out at night!*

"What do you want?"

Bang . . . bang . . . bang.

The grillwork trembled all along its twenty-foot length, and it occurred to him that the strength she was generating was improbable. Incredible.

"Ma'am, we're closed. You'll have to come back tomorrow. The registers are all shut down. I couldn't sell you anything if I wanted to."

Bang . . . bang . . . bang.

Drowning out his words.

He stared at her, perplexed, thinking about insanity (hers or his, it didn't matter, just plain, old-fashioned, you-flipped-your-lid insanity), as another person approached the gate from the side. This one was an elderly man he'd not seen before. Gray hair, gray stubble on his cheeks, a brown-checked shirt and baggy, green work pants. The old man fell into place beside the woman and began pounding right along with her.

David backed up a step, a thin trickle of sweat meandering down the side of his face. His collar and tie felt suddenly tight, noose-like.

"What do you want?"

The old lady opened her mouth and spoke—a single word, perhaps two, he couldn't tell—but it was swallowed by the ratcheting cacophony of their assault on the grill.

David Finley was trembling. "Go away," he said, not nearly loud enough. "Both of you . . . go away. We're closed now."

They continued to pound.

A solution came to him, an answer to this nightmare of senior citizen nonsense. He turned from the gate and hurried toward the registers, where the number for mall security was taped alongside the numbers of the IBM service people and the credit card authorization service. He grabbed the telephone and punched in the digits. There was nothing but silence for an impossibly long time . . . silence . . . and then at last, it began to ring. Once. Twice. Almost a third time before the line went dead and the receiver became a sleek but lifeless lump of high-tech plastic in his hand.

Bang . . . bang . . . bang.

"Oh Jesus," he whispered. "What the hell is this?" He looked up.

For a moment, it was as though he'd been struck with a sledgehammer. His knees buckled, and he had to grip the counter to keep from falling. He screamed. Or perhaps he only imagined the sound of his voice raised in terror. The skin on the back of his neck tightened. Cool water shot through his veins.

The quiet ones were everywhere. The mall was full of them. There were five at the grill now, some pounding, others reaching out with crooked, sculptured hands and scrabbling against the metal. A dwarfish old lady, her filthy scarf lopsided on her head, was pulling at the lock as though she wanted to rip it out.

And behind this bizarre quintet were hundreds more, old and young, wandering, sitting, banging on the gates of every store in sight. Across the way, at B. Dalton, a group of punkish teens had the entire grillwork damaged. As he watched, they threw their weight against it for what might have been the fifth or sixth time. It sagged inward but somehow held. Slowly, they backed off and prepared to attack again.

He saw many of the quiet ones he'd seen before, even more he didn't recognize. To the right, the young mother who'd run her stroller into the bench by the elevator was there again, with her silent child. Just as before, the carriage was wedged against the seat, and just as before, her legs moved regardless, faster and faster, taking her nowhere but trying . . . oh, good Lord, trying.

He dropped the receiver and fled, hoping to escape out the rear delivery door. But when he got to the back room, he realized it was hopeless. They were in the service hall too. He could hear them pounding on the door, banging against the cinderblock walls, attacking the back doors of every other shop in the wing.

Breathing hard, he stood there, his mind spinning helplessly. It came to rest for a moment on a movie he'd seen once, some ridiculous horror thing called . . . what? *The Dead at Dawn?* He couldn't remember, but the images of the film stayed with him. A suburban shopping mall filled with murderous zombies.

But what were these? Not zombies, of course, but what? Who were the quiet ones?

There was a tremendous, shattering roar as the front gate collapsed at last under the pressure of their attack. The sound of it snatched him cruelly from the popcorn-scented darkness of memory and thrust him back into the present. He heard footsteps—ten of them now? twenty? even more?—and he cowered against the employee break table.

They were in the store.

Sounds of destruction reached him. He heard racks being overturned, albums being stepped on, merchandise tumbling from his carefully-crafted displays. He waited, kneeling there, trembling and whimpering, praying for it all to stop, for the quiet ones to go away, for his mind to wake him up and show him that he wasn't at the mall but was only dreaming, creating a sleeping hash of absurd images out of the mental snapshots he took each weekday morning.

He waited until he could wait no more, until he was forced to admit this was nothing as simple as a dream, until he had to see what was happening out there.

He moved toward the door and peeked out. His mouth dropped open.

The quiet ones were shopping, moving through the store in their damned mechanical way and looking at everything, browsing, filling shopping bags from up front with records and tapes, posters and videos. They were cramming the bags so full the merchandise was spilling out. Paper seams split, and 45s slipped to the floor, unnoticed, trampled. They were everywhere, blundering into racks and knocking them over, moving on to another and doing the same, all the while filling bags and purses and pockets with things they never could have wanted.

Obscene. Darkly hilarious.

Shopping is their life, Karen had said. *It's their world. It's the only thing.*

"Their life," he murmured, and for the first time he

wondered if it was their death as well, if perhaps these weren't zombies after all.

The quiet ones. The shopping dead.

Thinking these jumbled, insane thoughts, he stood there and watched the surreal, almost violent shopping spree. He didn't even move when he was spotted by one of them. It was an old man in a grimy Red Sox cap, his white hair poking crazily from underneath, who passed by inches away and stopped to look at him. His face was utterly blank for a full ten seconds, and then delight seized his features. He grunted, exhaling a foul smell, and reached out with a knotted, bone claw hand. His touch on David's shoulder was hard, chillingly cold.

"No," David whispered. "Please."

But it was too late. The old man looked back at the others—over fifty of them now—and grunted louder, again and again, making crude, bestial noises until they were all looking up, staring at David with eyes that glowed in the half light.

"We're . . . not . . . open," he said. "*Please.*"

Two or three of them started toward him, dropping their bags, spilling things everywhere. They crunched the records underfoot, kicked them aside as though they'd never really been interested in the first place.

David backed up a step and tried to speak, but the words were gone. His throat was a clogged channel.

The shopping dead, his mind whispered. *They're here and they're real, oh boy are they ever. It used to be some kind of crazed obsession that brought them out every morning, but now, good Lord, now something's gone wrong in a big way. Maybe it's something in the air or the water. Maybe it's the goddamn moon. But whatever it is, it's got them triggered, and I'm in the middle of it. The middle of* them. *The shopping dead.*

The quiet ones took hold of him then with the same bloodless touch of the man in the Red Sox cap. He struggled—at least he thought he did—yet they seemed to have no difficulty pinning his arms to his sides and shoving him forward.

Silently, they propelled him up the center aisle, and he realized that the rest of them had stopped what they were doing and were watching. He could see them staring and sensed something very much like glee emanating from them like waves of heat.

On and on they pushed him, past the classical and the country, past the jazz, past the backlist and the current hits. On and on until he was behind the counter, where at last they released him.

He tried to read their expressions, but it was hard to tell what they were thinking. Or if *thinking* was even the word.

One of them, a scarecrow of a man in wool trousers and a dingy white shirt, grunted and made a few vague motions with his bony hands. David blinked, took a moment, and at last understood what was wanted. He shook his head slowly, but the scarecrow would not accept that. Again he grunted and waved his hands in the air, wanting David to turn the registers on. He rapped his knuckles against the keyboard.

"I can't," David said. "It's all shut down for the night."

The scarecrow pointed to the key that dangled from the register lock.

"No . . . I can't. I won't—"

THEY CAME FROM THE SUBURBS

One of them grasped his shoulder from behind and squeezed, very hard. The scarecrow rapped his ancient knuckles near the cash button again.

David groaned. "I won't do it," he said, even as he turned the key and ran through the series of strokes that would open the machine and get it ready for business.

And out on the sales floor the quiet ones were queuing up. Shuffling, staggering, limping forward like a pathetic army, they made their way toward the register, forming a line and thrusting albums and tapes in his face.

David looked at them, knowing what he was about to do, realizing that he was about to start ringing sales for people who had no money, understanding that he was about to start punching in figures and giving totals to creatures that would only grunt at him and walk away because, money or not, waiting in line to pay was part of their dim cultural memory. He was going to be a sales clerk for an endless line of the shopping dead.

Obsession.

Yes indeed. That said some of it. And boredom. And rampant consumerism and the daily grinding existence of life and death in suburbia. And magic. Bad magic. There had to be some of that in it too.

Life without meaning . . . towns without life . . . the inescapable draw of the mall, a draw that reached even beyond—

The grip on his shoulder tightened, causing real pain. But still he didn't move. He was picturing an endless succession of malls, each one becoming a victim of what they themselves had helped to create. He saw lines of the shopping dead in Chicago and

Miami and Los Angeles and Denver and Tulsa. He saw weary clerks ringing sale after unconsummated sale. He saw the terrible results of what happens when obsession reaches into the grave.

But there are so many of them! his mind screamed.

It was his last thought before, mechanically, he began to ring.

THROUGH THE STORM

ANDY FROST SAT on the back porch of his great aunt's summer house, staring at the lake, absently pushing checkers around the board in front of him. Several of the black checkers had been lost years before and had been replaced by large buttons from someone's sewing kit. It didn't matter. It wouldn't have mattered if they'd never been replaced at all. There was nobody to play with anyway.

In the past hour, the afternoon sky had begun to darken, and a breeze hurried across the lake, riffling his hair. There was that potent, unmistakable smell; a thunderstorm was coming, a big one.

"Andy?" his great aunt called from the house. "I want you inside now. Radio says it's going to rain."

Andy glanced toward the screen door momentarily then returned to pushing the checkers around the board. *Gonna rain?* he thought. *You needed the radio to tell you that? What kinda witch are you, anyhow?*

"Andy?"

He began to hum softly to himself. Across the lake, the first great streaks of moisture appeared in the air. It was probably already pouring in town. That meant he had another five or ten minutes.

Behind him, the screen door banged open. He

caught a brief whiff of lilac bath powder before the breeze snatched it away.

"Andy! Did you hear me, boy? I said I want you inside right now. There's going to be a storm."

"I'll be in soon, 'delle. Hang tight."

He could feel her staring at him, those rheumy but devil-sharp eyes trying to penetrate the back of his skull. He longed to remain still but squirmed a bit, helplessly.

"I will not hang tight, Andrew Joseph. I will not hang tight at all. I told you to come inside. Now gather up your things, and get in here."

"Witch," he muttered under his breath, and thought, *Oh, you're Mr. Cool, all right, a regular ice man. But if you were looking right at her, you wouldn't be so cool, would you? You'd be dyeing your Jockey shorts brown.*

"What did you say?"

"Nothing, 'delle. I'll be right in."

He could still feel the eyes. They were like blazing drill bits applied to the back of his neck. Then at last they left him. The screen door banged again, and she was gone.

Andy looked up from the checkerboard, trying to gauge the storm's progress. The streaks of moisture were a little darker, a little closer. The wind had picked up too. For the first time in practically two weeks, there were whitecaps on the water. He heard the mutter of distant thunder although he'd seen no lightning yet.

It was going to be a bad one, maybe the worst yet. Might be hail.

Might lose a couple of trees.

So what're you sitting here for? Why don't you motivate your buns and get inside where it's safe?

That brought a small bubble of laughter to his lips. He picked up a red checker and placed it two squares to the left. The first trace of moisture touched his cheeks. Not rain yet, exactly, but closer. The wind was now a constant, driving force. The screen door opened again, not with a bang this time but with an almost imperceptible whisper of wood. The sound made him shiver.

"Andy?" Apologetic now. Dripping with kindness, with sweet buddy-buddiness. "I'm sorry I was short with you."

"It's okay, 'delle."

"I *am* sorry, though. I didn't mean to yell."

"It's okay. Really. No sweat."

"If you come in now, I could bake some cookies. Tollhouse, maybe?"

"It's not storming yet, 'delle. I just wanna stay out till it starts.

I'll be all right."

She went on as though she hadn't heard. "I know Tollhouses are your favorite. I'll bake a double batch, and after . . . well, maybe I'll show you how to do a reading."

Andy stopped, his hand frozen an inch above the checkerboard, poised to grab one of the pieces. Something twisted violently inside his belly, like a great restless beast trying to claw its way to freedom. Appropriately—oh god yes, so appropriately—there was a jagged slash of lightning over the lake, followed by a whipcrack of thunder. He didn't jump, didn't move.

"Would you like that, Andy? Would you like me to teach you how to do a reading?"

No way, 'delle, he wanted to say. *I don't want nothing to do with your readings. I don't want nothing to do with you! I just wanna sit here till the storm carries me off, if you wanna know the truth. Or until I get fried by lightning. That's all I want.*

He wanted to say all those things to his great aunt, but when he opened his mouth, the only noise that came out was a reedy little squeak, as though that creature in his belly had just snapped the head off a mouse.

"Andy? What's wrong, honeybunch?"

Again the open mouth. Again the strange little squeak. The beast was sure a hungry sucker. How many mice was it gonna eat, anyway?

"Andrew . . . please . . . I can't imagine what's the matter, but if you'll just come inside, we can talk about it. You can let me know what the problem is. We can make it all better. We . . . there! Look! It's starting to rain."

It wasn't raining really, not until she mentioned it. Then the wind rose at least ten miles an hour, surging over them like invisible surf. There was another burst of light and sound, and the rain began to fall. It splattered on the back steps and began to soak the edge of the porch planks, just inches from Andy and his checkerboard.

"The storm's here, child. Time to come in." She came a step closer, and without looking, he felt her reaching for the back of his neck. He ducked away.

"Andy! What's gotten into you? Don't you want to learn how I do my readings?"

Andy felt sick. The beast had quieted down, but in its place was sour nausea. He swallowed hard.

THROUGH THE STORM

"You're ten years old, honeybunch. Your mind is ready. You're ripe. It's time I showed you how to read."

Oh man, he thought, oh Jesus. I don't wanna know that stuff. No sir. Running gnarled old hands over the bumps and ridges on your skull. Phrenology, she called it. Or peering at twisted roadmap lines on the hand. Palmistry. Casting small pebbles into a chalk circle on the kitchen linoleum. Pessomancy. You name it, she had a thousand of them.

And what power do you use on the things in the cellar, 'delle? What do you call that, huh? Zombie-ism? Is that what it is?

He turned to face her at last. There was moisture on the back of his sweatshirt—part rain, part perspiration. She was standing just two feet away, wearing the same yellow and green flowered dress she'd had on at breakfast. Gray hair pulled back in a huge, uneven bun. Too much makeup. Too much lilac bath powder. And those eyes. Always the eyes. Deep and red, watery but always sharp. Always incredibly sharp and somehow terrifyingly alert.

"Time to come in now, Andrew. The storm's here."

The words finally came out, spilling in a frantic jumble. "I'll go in, 'delle, but I don't want you to show me anything. Okay? I don't wanna see any readings. I don't wanna learn that crap. I'll go in, but only if you leave me alone. Okay? Will you just leave me alone? Please? Will you?"

His great aunt stared at him, offended. "Of course, Andrew," she said after a moment. "You don't have to learn a thing, if you don't want to."

"Promise?"

"Of course. Have I ever lied to you, Andrew?"

He almost laughed, caught himself just in time. "No, you never lied, 'delle. Just let me pick up the checkers, and I'll be right in."

She nodded, a proprietary little gesture, then disappeared into the house. Andy looked after her before bending to gather up the board and its pieces. The rain came driving across the lake, across the yard, onto the porch. It stung his face, but he didn't spare it a thought. He was too busy hating his parents for going to Europe again. For sending him back here a second summer, against his objections. For returning him to this place after everything he'd told them.

He had been excited when they had first told him he was going to spend the summer with his great aunt Adelle at her lake cottage. He'd been to Europe before, and it bored him. The museums and shops, the long drives through the countryside searching out obscure little vineyards, the endless gibbering babble of the locals, the disdainful looks they received as Americans. Europe was horseshit. Dead horseshit at that. On the other hand, he'd never met his great aunt, so *that* would be an adventure.

It hadn't taken him long to change his mind that first summer. Adelle Stuart, his maternal grandmother's sister, was old and fat. She smelled of woodsmoke and lilac bath powder. She lived alone on the lake, her husband having died before Andy was even born. The nearest neighbors were seven miles down County 271, the nearest kids his age three miles beyond that. The yard was surprisingly small, the lake passable for swimming but cold, always cold, even on the hottest July day.

Worse than all that, however, was the fact that

THROUGH THE STORM

Adelle Stuart was a fruitcake. He'd decided that in five minutes flat. She talked to herself. She watched him far too closely. And she was into fruitcake kinds of things. Phrenology and pessomancy, tarot and ovomancy. Astrology. Alomancy. The things she called her "magic friends." She kept all sorts of strange, smelly herbs around the house, along with a real crystal ball and a shelf of dusty books and an endless array of tiny bottles filled with red and green and amber fluids. Sometimes, she would pour the contents of one of those bottles into his morning orange juice, changing the taste from sweet to rancid, sharp to dank.

Fruitcake. You got it, Charlie. A real fruitcake witch.

Within ten days, he'd been as bored as he ever would have been in Europe. He'd exhausted all the possibilities the place had to offer. He missed his friends, his chance to play Little League. He even missed *school*. Wasn't that a rip? Nine freaking years old, and he missed school! He knew the house inside out. He knew every inch of the yard. He knew the small utility shed backwards and forwards, spent so much time in there that the smell of gasoline, grease, old grass clippings, and the twice-a-month caretaker's pipe tobacco made him want to throw up.

He needed something new, something else to discover, to keep him occupied. He needed a way to escape from crazy old 'delle, who was always tracking him down, wanting him to read some Latin gibberish from one of her books or try out a new divination technique on him.

That was when he discovered the cellar. And after that, nothing was ever quite the same at the summer place.

"I could still make the Tollhouses if you'd like," she said to him when he came through the door with the checkerboard under his arm, hair and clothes dripping.

"No thanks. Gotta go change."

"Hurry back. We'll sit here at the table and watch the storm."

"Sure thing."

He left the kitchen and headed for his room, pausing briefly in the living room and glancing toward his left, at the low door in the wall. A ghost-chill wandered up his spine. He remembered seeing that door for the first time, thinking it led to a storage space, like the cedar closet back home where his mother kept her good wool dresses and his father stored the Pendleton hunting jacket he never wore. He remembered opening that door. He remembered seeing darkness, the beginning of a steep stairway. He remembered finding the light switch and turning it on, starting down into forty-watt gloom.

He hurried away.

Inside his bedroom, he stood at the window for a very long time, watching the rain pound down and the wind sweep the trees back and forth like strange dancers. It was all lit by the almost constant flickering of lightning, punctuated with rhythmic waves of thunder. He ran a hand through his wet hair and wiped that hand against the denim of his jeans.

He used to think the storms were great. Being a city kid, used to gray, smoky drizzle, the first few wilderness storms had been exciting. They'd gotten his blood and adrenaline pumping, often made the small hairs on the back of his neck tingle and rise. But now, the storms scared him. It had been storming the day he'd gone into the cellar, when—

He wheeled around sharply. For a moment, between thunder bursts, he thought he'd heard footsteps outside the door. He held his breath and listened. Yes. There it was. Soft breathing just beyond the knotty pine. She . . . but it was gone, and he knew it had never been there. He knew it was something else he'd heard. Not his great aunt spying on him (although she did that on occasion) but another sound from elsewhere, from much deeper in the house. It was the storm. The storms got them going somehow. The storms always juiced them up.

Thunder again, and the spell was broken. He let out his breath with a mighty, shuddering sigh and stripped off his wet clothes, draping them over the back of the desk chair. He laid down on the bed and closed his eyes. Wind rattled the glass. Thunder made the bed quiver with secret energy. The rain sounded like skeletal fingers playing across the panes, searching for entry. He opened his eyes momentarily, then closed them again.

Why had they sent him back here? Why, when he'd tried to tell them about 'delle's craziness? How could they do it when he'd struggled so hard to explain about the cellar?

"Nobody's denying that your great aunt's a bit on the eccentric side," his father had said to him in his maddeningly rational way. "Why, I remember a family reunion about ten years ago, around the time you were born. Sixty or seventy relatives at least, from your mom's side. And there was Adelle practically running a fortune telling concession in the middle of it. She had an hour-long backup of cousins and uncles and aunts waiting for one of her readings."

Eccentric, Andy had thought, wondering how he could make them understand.

"I won't have you saying things about Aunt 'delle," his mother had told him later, when he'd gone to her. "She might be a bit silly, but that's all. And it's either stay with her again this summer or come to Europe with us. You know how much you'd hate that."

Andy had opened his mouth, ready to beg to be taken to Europe, but it was no good. The case was closed with them. He was going to spend another summer with dear old, eccentric old, silly old 'delle. He had no choice. They didn't understand.

And what would he have really told them if he could have found the words? Could he have told them straight out about the dusty, cobwebby, low-ceilinged cellar beyond that three-foot door? About the workbench with its understandable jumble of tools and scrap wood and its not-so-understandable jumble of burned candle stubs and dried herbs and bottled spices? About the empty fruit cellar and the door *inside* the fruit cellar? The door that was padlocked shut and sealed with draped strings of the same herbs that were on the workbench, like a castle entrance sealed with garlic against a vampire in some stupid old movie on Dr. Dementia's Theater of Blood? About the sounds inside that place? The slow, dragging footsteps? The scrabbling of frantic hands against the wood? The furtive, fruitless tugging on the latch? Could he have told them what he really thought about silly, eccentric Adelle Stuart? That her passion for "magic things" went beyond divining the future from piles of salt and candlelit eggs, oh so very far beyond?

His eyes snapped open, and he sat up straight, gooseflesh crawling across his arms and back. Footsteps again. But this time, it *was* 'delle, and she was coming toward his room quickly, obviously not intending to spy. She rapped on the door.

"Andy? Are you all right in there, honeybunch?"

He swallowed back the last of the memories and a good deal of the fear. "Yeah. I'm fine."

"Well, I want you to come out now. You said you'd sit at the table with me and watch the storm."

He sighed. "I'm coming. Just putting on some clean clothes."

Silence for a moment. Then: "I'm waiting for you, Andrew."

There was something in the way she said it that made him shiver again. The smell of lilac bath powder came through the door.

"I'm coming," he said again, but he didn't get out of bed and begin to dress until he heard the retreat of her steps, until the cloying scent had faded.

She was waiting for him at the kitchen table. Her flabby, twisted hands were resting on the oak surface, enveloping a steaming mug of one of her herbal teas. He flashed her a small, forced smile and pulled up a chair.

"What were you doing in there?" she asked.

"Nothing," he said softly, avoiding direct contact with those piercing eyes. "Had to hang up my wet clothes and find some dry ones, is all."

She nodded, said nothing else for several minutes. The storm had already abated a bit. Andy made a show of watching the patterns formed by the rain as it ran down the window above the sink.

"I want to ask you something," 'delle said then, just moments after he'd begun to relax. "Will you give me an answer?"

Ask me something? Jesus, 'delle, what're you gonna ask? Why can't you just leave me alone? Why can't you just let me stay in my room, for Pete's sake?

"Will you give me an answer, Andrew?"

"I suppose. I can try."

She smiled. "Good boy. I want to know why you won't let me teach you things. Why you seem so afraid of my readings. You know, when your dear mother called me in April and said you'd be coming back for another summer, I was delighted. I thought this would be the year I could begin passing some of my knowledge on. I'm not as young as I used to be, you know. So why, Andrew . . . why are you so afraid of my readings?"

It's not the readings, 'delle, believe me. It's not the readings at all.

"They're only entertainments, little party games. I should think you'd like to learn the secrets. Think of your friends at school, Andrew. Think of the way they'd laugh and applaud if you could tell them their futures by feeling the ridges of their skull! Think what an absolute smash you would be!"

Smash . . . skull . . .

"There's no harm to any of it, boy. No harm at all. You don't think I'd try to hurt you, do you?"

Andy didn't answer. He just stared at her blandly.

"You can't be serious!" she said, her voice rising several notches. "You don't honestly think I would harm you, do you? Answer me! Do you think I would try to hurt you?"

Andy shook his head.

"Well, I should hope not! Now I'm afraid I'm going to have to insist. I'm an old lady. I have to pass these things on to someone, for heaven's sake."

Andy swallowed hard again. The beast in his belly had come awake for real this time. She'd promised him, dammit! She'd told him he didn't have to learn those—

"Andy . . . what's wrong, dear boy?"

"Nothing," he said, studiously avoiding her gaze.

"Andrew Joseph, look at me."

He did, and thought the beast was going to literally explode from inside, breaking free into the outer world in a shower of blood and flesh and his own poor guts.

There was something in her eyes he'd never seen before. Always rheumy but always sharp, yes. Now, however, there was a light in there. A burning, fiery glimmer that, impossibly, seemed to dance and move sinuously while at the same time penetrate the center of his skull.

"I'm going to teach you everything, child. All I know. I'm going to teach you marvelous things."

Andy pushed his chair back and got up. "I wanna lie down, 'delle. I'm tired. That walk I took this morning and all. I—"

"Sit down."

He summoned the courage to look directly at her. He shook his head. "No way. I'm gonna take a nap."

He started past her, was almost free, almost clear, when her beefy arm shot out and grabbed him by the wrist. He felt pain go spiraling up his arm, peaking in a fireburst at the shoulder blades. He cried out, almost wrenched his way loose, and then was dragged to her side.

"Listen to me, Andrew Joseph Frost! Listen good! You're living under my roof and will do what I say. I want you to sit down now. It's time for your first lesson."

That was when he crossed the line. Perhaps he could have obeyed and encountered nothing more terrible than a sleepy kind of boredom as she rambled on about palmistry or such. Perhaps. But it was a chance he didn't want to take, so he stepped across the line in a big way.

As she was twisting his arm, trying to maneuver him back toward his chair on the other side of the table, he simultaneously pulled with all his strength and reached out, striking his great aunt a glancing blow on the side of the head.

'delle cried out in squawking, birdlike protest. Andy seized the moment and pulled again, breaking free and darting out of the room.

"Come back here!" she shrieked.

He heard the sound of her chair tumbling over as she rose from the table, heard the pounding of her footsteps. She was faster than he'd imagined, unnaturally quick for her size and age. She caught him again before he'd even reached the stairs, her gnarly hand snagging his shoulder and jerking him back. A huge arm encircled his neck and shoulders, drawing him close to her heaving bosom. He felt her hot breath on his cheek, thought he might pass out from the stench of that lilac bath powder.

"Let me go!"

She chuckled, a sludgy, thick sound that seemed to coil its way around him and hold him even tighter.

"Please, 'delle. I just wanna go lie down, okay? Will you please just let me go? Will you—"

"It's lesson time, boy."

"I don't wanna learn nothing! You promised!"

She began to drag him backwards, back toward the kitchen, and in that half-moment when she was in between steps, slightly off balance and a tiny bit unprepared, Andy pulled his arm forward and brought it back with all his strength, driving his elbow into the soft folds of her stomach. The wind rushed out of her at gale force. He didn't wait to see if it was enough but instead repeated the blow, this time aiming the elbow higher, at the notch just below her ribcage.

His great aunt's grip loosened. He broke it, charging headlong at the steps. He'd reached the first one when she caught him yet again, her thick fingers nipping the cuffs of his jeans. He fell, tried to get up, and stared in wonder as she moved past him, catlike, and blocked his access to the stairs.

"You'll learn, boy," she said, laughing again with what appeared to be genuine good humor.

He pulled himself to his feet and began to back away, moving blindly across the room. He refused to take his eyes off her, even when she broke into a wide, mostly toothless grin.

"You don't want to go down there, Andrew. No . . . I don't think you'd like that at all."

He struck the wall and with dawning horror felt something digging into the small of his back. He knew there would be no getting to the stairs now. There would be no getting back into the kitchen or even outside, where the storm's second wave had descended in whooping, walloping splendor. He realized, with sick dread, that he'd backed himself directly into the cellar door.

"I suppose you'll come and take your lessons now," 'delle was saying. "See, I know you've been down there, child. Surprised? You thought I was busy in the kitchen, but I knew. I knew the moment you opened that door and went down. I knew when you went into the fruit cellar and found my locked room. I knew right away when you heard what was in there. I'd hazard a guess and say you don't want to go down there again, do you, dear boy?"

He didn't want to speak—loathed giving her the satisfaction—but the words slipped out before he was aware they were coming.

"W-what's in there?" he asked.

His great aunt smiled again. "Oh, that's hard to say. Might be any number of things. Could be spooks. Think it's spooks, Andrew? Or maybe it's a cellar full of bad little boys, children who wouldn't take their lessons. Could be they disobeyed me and were locked away down there forever. Do you think that might be it?"

Andy shook his head. Behind him, the cellar latch seemed to be moving, twisting and turning slowly, probing his spine and kidneys like a living hand.

"Or," 'delle went on, "it might be something else altogether. Could be the living dead. Could be my witch's familiars. Could be strange, blind animals I summoned out of the bowels of the Earth." She laughed richly. "With my powers, you can't be sure what it is. So why don't we forget about it and get on with the lesson?"

88

THROUGH THE STORM

In a strobe-flash of lightning, she took a step toward him, then a second, and a third. Andy's eyes darted left and right, desperately judging the chances of escape. They were slim, and he knew that wasn't being honest. They were nonexistent. Break toward the kitchen and she would be there. Break for the steps and she'd be there too. With her crazy agility and speed, there was only one place for him to go.

"Ready, child?" Thunder roared. She was another step closer, and still another. "I think we'll start with the palms. Those are the simplest. Excellent training ground for a boy your age."

Andy reached behind him and opened the latch, spinning around and ducking through the three-foot entrance. He yanked the door shut behind him, snapped the light on, and went down.

The walls were sweating down there. The workbench loomed ahead of him like a mass of shadows. He imagined the flickering of angry lightning all around, although there were no windows giving on the outside. The door above opened again and Adelle came forward, wedging herself through the narrow space, ducking under the beams, thumping down the steps.

"Come back, boy! You shouldn't be down here! It's a dangerous place for a child, it's—"

"Quit chasing me!"

He reached the workbench and began frantically shoving the herbs and candle stubs aside, searching for some kind of weapon. Nails and picture hooks, a screwdriver, a wrench, little bits of plywood and two-by-fours.

"Leave me alone, you bitch!"

She appeared at the bottom of the steps, wide and

impenetrable, her hands resting on her fleshy hips, her face quivering with joy. Or was it something else? Was it something new?

Behind him, he heard the noises in the fruit cellar— or rather in the room *inside* the fruit cellar. The shuffling, scuffling footsteps, the first hands beginning to tug at the latch. He heard the padlock rattle up and down, the sound of fingers scraping against wood, the sound of long, slow breath . . . or perhaps *that* was just the constant murmur of the wind overhead.

"I'll be happy to quit chasing you, child, if you'll listen to reason. Don't shun the opportunity I'm giving you. Come away from this filthy place. Come upstairs and learn."

Andy found it, the weapon he'd been looking for. He whirled around, the hammer raised before him like a shield. He waved it back and forth in what he thought was a properly threatening manner.

"If you don't leave me alone, I'll kill you. Do you understand that, 'delle? I'll kill you."

Yeah! he thought, insanely proud of himself for having the courage to say it. *Dig on that awhile, you old witch! Think of this hammer smashing your fat head! Chew that awhile!*

But Adelle only smiled sadly. A heartbeat later, she advanced on him again.

"I'll kill you," he repeated. "I'm serious, 'delle. Really." He sidled along the side of the workbench, retreating and hoping it didn't look as though he was. Then a new inspiration struck him. "If you don't go away, I'll use this hammer. I'll break that padlock and let out those . . . those things . . . whatever you've got locked up in there."

She stopped.

Her face changed.

That new look he thought he'd seen in her eyes was there for sure now.

My god, she's afraid, Andy thought wildly. *She believes me, and she's afraid of whatever's in there . . . as afraid as I am.*

"I don't want you anywhere near that fruit cellar, child," she said at last. "You listen to your great aunt. Don't you dare go in there."

"I will if I have to, 'delle." He waved the hammer in the air, almost dropped it when a particularly loud thundercrack burst overhead a second later.

"Andrew—"

He moved toward the fruit cellar.

"Andy . . . child . . . ."

The latch of that inner door was moving violently up and down, making the padlock that hung there look pitifully small, horribly cheap.

"My sweet boy—"

"Stop!" he commanded, surprised to find that he actually *was* inside the fruit cellar. In fact, he was only a few feet from the inner door. The noises that came from beyond that opening were now loud enough to drown out the last sounds of the storm. "Stop, or I'll break the door open."

In a final show of bravery, he allowed his free hand to reach out. His fingers danced lightly across the latch.

"Come away from there, Andrew. Now."

Whatever was inside began to bang on the door. The latch rattled. The hinges creaked. The wood trembled, bulging with each blow.

"What's wrong, 'delle? Are you afraid I'm serious? You starting to believe me, witch? Are you?"

He stared into her eyes and thought, *My god, she's practically shitting bricks. Look at her. Listen to her. What's in there, anyway?*

He thought about what she'd said. The living dead, spooks, bad little boys. He thought about blind animals from the pits of hell. Was it one of those, or was it something even worse? Was it maybe—just maybe—the failed outcome of one of her experiments, the awful result of some of her unnatural tampering?

Do you really wanna find out? he asked himself. *You think you honestly wanna know?*

He pondered that, staring into his great aunt's wild eyes, feeling the cool metal of the padlock beneath his fingertips.

"Andrew, please . . . "

"Go away, 'delle."

Whether or not she truly meant to do what she did next was unclear. It could have been a simple, instinctual reaction to her fear, a panic attack, for he suspected that deep down, she wanted nothing more than to get away from the fruit cellar and whatever was in that room. Yet intended or not, she came for him, blundering forward, her arms stretched out, questing. He leapt aside and shocked himself by simultaneously bringing the hammer down against the lock.

Adelle shrieked. It was a single, pained cry. She reached for his free hand, but he twisted away. Her momentum carried her into the fruit cellar wall; the whole room shook as she struck it.

"Child, please," she said. Her breath was coming in great, rasping bursts. Her eyes jittered back and forth, from him to the door to the stairs, which led to safety, like BBs in the eyes of a child's toy clown. "I'll leave you alone. I promise it, Andy. I swear it. But you'll have to put the hammer down now."

Andy stared back at her. The moment seemed to hang there, waiting for resolution. The cellar had become strangely quiet. There were no more storm sounds from over their heads. And whatever was in the locked room had fallen silent too. He thought in shorthand fashion that the entire world was waiting to see what would happen next.

"Andy . . . "

He allowed his arm to relax, let the hammer hang at his side. She had beaten him, and she knew it. She knew that he didn't—couldn't—let those things out of their prison. She knew that he had nowhere left to run. He was backed into a corner, a small, young, hopelessly trapped boy without the guts to do the only thing that could save him.

He stared at his great aunt for a full minute. Then he shrugged. "I guess you win, 'delle. Palmistry, huh?"

The look of terror faded from her face, melting away like a cheap wax mask. Her grin of triumph returned.

"Palmistry, indeed. Just the first of my many secrets." She held out her hand to him, but he refused to take it. *I'm not gonna bend that far, witch. No, ma'am.*

She shrugged. "Come along then, child. It's time."

She turned and left the fruit cellar, heading for the stairs. Andy watched her go, overwhelmed with shame at his cowardice and loathing for that fleshy mound of bad things that had such control over him. She'd beaten him. He was whipped. She—

He snapped those thoughts off before they could go any further. He spun about and raised the hammer high, bringing it down against the lock. It snapped like a bad toy, flying a foot or two through the air, dropping, and skidding across the floor.

Adelle turned in time to see the latch go up, the door begin to creep open.

And Andy ducked aside, thinking that there were worse things—worse things by far—than having his last sight be the look on that fat face as her prisoners came out to meet her.

THE MORE THINGS CHANGE

I.
THE CIRCUMSTANCES

FIRST THE SUN didn't set.

Then there was the day that all the deer showed up in town.

Then all the books in the local library became juvenile coloring books.

Then the river reversed itself and began flowing northward.

Then—perhaps the cruelest cut of all—that horrible week when our TVs would only play for five minutes every hour, reverting for the other fifty-five to blank snow.

Today the sky is green.

Yesterday it was pink.

I'm betting on yellow tomorrow.

We used to think it was the end of the world, but now, I guess we know better. An author we had to read in high school, in the days long before the prudes got him banned from the required reading lists, said it best, I think. He said, "Hi Ho." Now, that could mean a lot of things, but I always took it to mean that life just goes on, no matter what. That author's name was Kurt Vonnegut. I've been rereading his stuff lately, in the wee hours of the night. He's become my personal prophet in this new age.

There was a town meeting this morning, the first since those wild early days when Mrs. McCardle was stirring folks up with her talk of End Times and the Revelation to John. This meeting was different.

The mayor, whose beard had begun to grow on the inside of his cheeks, making him look like a late-autumn chipmunk and sound like the Godfather after a hit of really good acid, stood before the town council and the electorate with a chubby, paternal frown.

"My friends," he said. "I'm sorely troubled by the amount of wagering that's going on these days, this betting on all the changes in our world."

We said something. I'm not sure what, but it was appropriately noncommittal.

"Why, I understand that the line at Jerry Winkler's Rexall this morning was twenty-seven people long. What's more, I understand that none of those fine people were there to buy film or pick up a prescription. They were there because Jerry was giving good odds on maroon as a sky color tomorrow.

"Now, friends, the world has altered. But need I remind any of you that we're still a society of law and order? Must you be told to hang onto your rationality and reject any hints of barbarism? Do you need to be reminded that gambling of any sort is still illegal? If we allow ourselves to be drawn into this web of cynicism and greed, we—"

His voice had become more intense, nearly impossible to understand: "Mmmmm mooormm odds

... mrrom grrrummum mro grumm maroon ... mmm frumm umgruummm still illegal ... "

His eyes were flashing with preacher's fire, but a few of us didn't much feel like being saved and slipped out the back door of the council chambers.

"Whaddya think?" George Hoover said as we started walking uptown. "You think Winkler's right? Gonna be maroon tomorrow?"

I shrugged. "I've got ten bucks on yellow myself, at seven-to-one. But I can afford it. I won big on the falling-trees pool last week."

Ken Tatum grunted. "You were damn lucky. Who would've believed all of Fisher's Woods would go at once like that?"

A bear rode by on a big Harley. We waved. The bear gave us the finger.

"Jesus Christ, I'm tired of this crap," Ken said. "Bears flipping us off. I gotta tell you boys, I'm sick of all this bushwah."

I left them at the corner and went on home, past what used to be respectable houses full of respectable people. Now, there was something wrong with every one of them. Or maybe I shouldn't say *wrong*. You see, my values have been changing lately. While I used to have a rigid set of moral ideas, I'm finding it harder to believe there's any such thing as right or wrong left anymore.

Different, then.

I think that says it best.

Brian Forrester's place has portholes now instead of windows. His siding, which used to be a normal if not very flashy white, is now a vivid, shocking green. Roger Chalmers' place has a flurry of shrubbery growing out of the roof. Mrs. Davis' place no longer has a front door. Where the door used to be is an amateurish painting of a flamingo smoking a cigar and wearing a Budweiser cap. The painting is done on a swatch of green silk, and every time Mrs. Davis rips it down in anger, it appears again within a few hours.

But the worst . . . sorry. The *most different* of all is poor Roy Hooper's house. No doors *or* windows. Just bright red siding. A steel roof of bright and glaring blue. None of us have seen Roy in the last two months. Our repeated attempts to get into his place have proved fruitless. That house of his is impregnable.

Different. Yessiree. If that's not different, I don't know what is.

II.
THE CONJECTURE

My doorbell rang at two o' clock, but I didn't recognize it right away. It went ding-dong, the way it always used to go. But that was a bit of a surprise; for the last three weeks or so, it had been chiming the Georgia Tech Fight Song.

I opened the door and saw Ken Tatum out there with Buddy Mills and Carl Brinkley. I hadn't seen Carl lately and noticed right away that he had a nasty bruise underneath his left eye, no doubt from that violent, drunken bitch he's married to. The bruise wasn't really what I noticed, though. I mean, I saw it, but it was no big deal. Carl always has a shiner or a lump or a cut. What I noticed was that this particular bruise was a bright banana-yellow color, like gaudy clown makeup.

THE MORE THINGS CHANGE

I nodded at everyone. "How do, gentlemen?"

"Not good, Elvin," Buddy said. "Can we come in?"

"'Course you can." I stepped back from the door and ushered them through. "Let me get you all a beer."

I passed out cold Stroh's all around—but when we opened the cans, we found them full of fruit punch. Except for Ken, that is. He had some kind of cola.

"We gotta talk," Buddy said. "We've been hashin' this over all day, and I . . . that is, we think we got this thing knocked."

I figured he was talking about the changes, but the rest of it, I didn't understand. "Just what do you mean by 'knocked?'" I asked.

"Well, y'know, Elvin. We got it knocked. Licked. Figgered out."

"Is that so?" I smiled. If I had a nickel for every time I'd heard that lately, I'd be wealthy. Especially since those nickels probably would have turned into gold pieces by now. "Tell me what you figured out."

Carl leaned forward, his shiner gleaming. "Jock Bartholomew," he said softly.

The name threw me. "Jock? What about him?"

Ken flashed a sad frown. "I'm disappointed in you, Elvin; truly, I am. You're just about the smartest fella in town. Don't you see the connection?"

I shook my head. "Afraid not." "When did Bartholomew move here?"

"I don't know. Three, four months ago. April, I'd say."

"And when did all these changes start?"

"I remember that exactly," I said. "The middle of May. It was Mother's Day, the day the sun didn't go down."

Ken leaned back with a smug look. "Y'see?"

I was afraid I did, but something inside me wanted to play it ignorant a little longer. "What are you getting at?"

"Jesus!" Carl said. "It's Bartholomew! He's behind everything!"

"Look at the evidence," Buddy told me. He pronounced it *ev-ee-dence.* "You ever known a stranger man than old Jock? He lives out there on the Blackwater Road, all by his lonesome. Hardly ever comes to town. When he does, he buys a lot of them natural foods and shit like that. And he even buys a lot of . . . " He paused, and when he spoke again, his voice was low and whispery. " . . . a lot of *books,* y'know, them paperbacks from over to the Rexall. And whenever anyone sees him out in the woods, he's joggin'. *Joggin',* for Chrissakes!"

"Not only that," Ken added, "but what did he move here for, anyhow? That's what I wanna know. He don't know nobody in town."

"Well, that part's easy," I said. "That cabin belonged to his uncle. You fellas remember him. Pete Bracken. He used to go fishing with us. He used the place every summer for thirty years, and when he died last winter, he left it to Jock."

"And how would you know that?" Carl said. "How would you know when none of us ever heard it?"

I shrugged. The fact that Jock and I had become good friends over the last few months wasn't such a big deal, but suddenly, it didn't seem like the time to mention it. "Heard it around, I guess."

"Well," Ken said, "I don't care if he's related to the Goddamn Queen of England. It's too much to be coincidence. It—"

THE MORE THINGS CHANGE

He broke off suddenly, after taking a healthy swallow of his beer/cola. He coughed and grimaced and swallowed with great effort. "This crap just turned into vodka!"

Buddy grunted. "Y'see, Elvin? That bastard Bartholomew, he's got witchy powers. Why, I'll betcha he's listenin' in on us right now. He knows we're onto him, so he's gonna make it tough. Shit, everyone knows Ken can't hold his vodka."

I got up and paced across the room. This didn't make sense. For months, we'd been living with the changes in our town. For months, we'd accepted everything that came our way with good grace and a fair measure of humor. Well, sure, there were the bad apples like old Mrs. McCardle, but they were the exceptions. The rest of us had learned to roll with the punches. Hi Ho, and all of that. Occasionally, some fool would try to escape, but when the roads changed on him, circled around, and returned him to the town limits, that person would learn to go with the flow, just like the rest of us.

Then why the sudden reversal? I wondered. Why this new effort to pin blame?

I sighed, remembering the hints of growing anger I'd seen lately. A fist fight over last week's falling-trees pool. Some bullet holes discovered in the WELCOME sign on the edge of town, which had just lately been reading $E = MC^2$. People claiming in soft voices to be fed up, like Ken this morning, saying, *I'm tired of this crap . . . I'm sick of all this bushwah.*

I suppose everyone reaches a breaking point after a while. In the final accounting, the best excuse for any of our actions is that we're only human. When we reach the point past which we can't or don't care to venture, well, then we want to strike back.

"What do you plan to do with this information?" I asked.

"Simple," Carl said. "We're gonna pay a visit to the bastard, make him 'fess up. Soon as he does that, we'll have Mike Weathers lock him in jail. Or mebbe we'll go one better and just string him up ourselves."

I frowned. "And if he tells you he's innocent?"

"That's easy," Buddy said with a laugh. "He does that, we'll string the lyin' witch up for sure. Just for spite, y'know." He hesitated, smiled, and laughed again. "Just for spite."

III.
THE CONVERSATION

I had been to Jock Bartholomew's cabin perhaps five times in all. Mostly, we did our socializing when we'd meet out in the woods. I'd be cruising along on one of the walks Doctor Barker told me to take or maybe heading off to one of my favorite fishing holes, and I'd run into him jogging. Except Jock didn't call it jogging. To him, it was always *running,* and mister man, did he take it seriously? I hope to tell you.

He was a former high school track star who had also done quite well in the mile during his college years at one of the Ivy League schools. Although those days were long since past (he had spent the years in between bouncing around as a ranger for the National Park Service, a sometime high school teacher, a freelance journalist, a photographer, a potter, and now a newborn wilderness dweller and oil painter), he still lived for his long daily runs.

Even though I knew the Blackwater Road well, it still took me a fair amount of time to get to his cabin that day. I hadn't been there in at least a month, and there had been plenty of changes. No matter where I looked, I kept seeing things that made me stop and take a second glance.

There was the trailer that belonged to Joe and Ellen Friedrich. It used to be a regular old silver Airstream, but now, its silvery hue was dull and reddish. After a moment, I realized I was looking at what might be the world's only house trailer made out of brick.

Or then there was the grove of trees growing upside down, leafy crowns buried in the earth, roots waving in the air.

Or the little waterfall on the side of the road—Drake Falls, we locals called it—that was running backwards, the steady flow rising like a charmed snake out of the water pool, slithering ten feet straight up the rocks, and vanishing back into the woods.

Or the sign marking Buck Haven Road that now said BERLIN 140 km.

Or the squirrel that came up to me and asked—in a fine French accent too, I might add—for directions to town. That made my mouth drop open in astonishment. And *that* made the little critter laugh. When I hurried off, I could swear I heard the beast singing "Do You Know the Way to San Jose?" in a pleasant high tenor—like Wayne Newton during his glory days, if you know what I mean.

I got to Jock's place an hour after leaving home. It's

a trip that normally wouldn't take more than thirty, maybe thirty-five minutes.

"Elvin! It's good to see you! What brings you all the way out here?"

He had his easel set up near the cabin, and there he was, perched on his stool, trying to capture the big oak that stood at the northwest corner of his property.

"Howdy, Jock. It's nice to see you too."

"You want a beer? I picked up a fresh case yesterday." He started to rise, but I waved him back down.

"We've got to talk," I said. "It's . . . it's about the changes."

He grinned. "Ah, you've returned for some more of my crackpot Dartmouth philosophy." He put his brushes aside and made himself comfortable.

I ambled over and looked at his painting. It was fine, although that weird greenish sky that had been hanging over us all day had played hell with the tones. "Very nice," I said absently. "And no, I'm afraid it's not philosophy I'm after today."

His eyebrows went up. "Oh?"

"No, it's . . . something else. You know we've talked about the changes a lot. You mentioned the way it might be the last punishment of an angry God or maybe just the—what did you call it? The vivid manifestation of a universe gone mad? I'll tell you straight, Jock, that stuff's over my head, but in a crazy kind of way, it made sense to me. I've got no trouble believing it could be either of those things, or any of a hundred others. And I liked the other thing you said, about how maybe it was all part of a test, a cosmic exam. Do you remember that? We were sitting at Pike

Lake when you came up with that one. You said our humanity was being tested, and to pass, we had to hold up under the pressure."

"Yes," Jock said, smiling. "I remember."

"I think I liked that answer best of all. I mean, I don't know how to fight against an angry God, and I sure don't know anything about universes going crazy. But a test I can handle. I can take the pressure. I can fight the strain. That's a snap. I know how to keep on keeping on."

Jock looked troubled. Maybe he had picked up on the worried note in my voice. He might have seen something in my face. I'm not sure.

"Elvin," he said. "What's wrong?"

"It's some of the other fellas in town," I told him. "They don't care about God and tests and all that. All of a sudden, they have their own ideas. They came to my place a little while ago to tell me they've got the changes all figured out."

"Yes?"

"Yes," I said. And I told him.

As I talked about what Buddy and the others had said, Jock grew noticeably pale. At one point, he picked up a paint brush and held it lightly between his thumb and index finger; I could see it trembling.

When I was finished, he turned a sad-eyed gaze on me. He didn't say anything for a full minute. Then, softly, he said, "You don't believe them, do you?"

"Hell, no! Whatever else happens, we're still friends. And even if we weren't . . . well, good lord, I know nonsense when I hear it."

He sighed. "Thank you for that."

"You've got to understand something," I said,

rushing on in a lame attempt to explain. "The way it is with outsiders and newcomers in a small town, they're just naturally under suspicion. And you don't act like most of the folks around here. Your reading and all that running you do, it's—"

"For godssakes, Elvin, I know all about that! I was prepared for it when I moved here. But if you ask me, there's a pretty big difference between second glances in the hardware store and accusing someone of witchcraft. What next? Assuming they don't string me up, as they so quaintly put it, what's their next move? I sold some paintings at that little craft shop on Winthrop Street last week. Are they going to storm the place and rip those paintings off the wall? Burn them in the street?"

Truth to tell, I thought they very well might. I had seen those paintings. They were wonderful representations of the way the town looked with all the changes: the strange skies, the funny houses, even some of the people, like the mayor with his inside-out beard. It wasn't unrealistic to suppose that Buddy Mills and the others would interpret those pictures as admissions of guilt, Jock's way of boasting about the things he had done. But I didn't see any point in saying that—not then.

"That doesn't matter," I said. "What's important is to get you out of here before they come rushing in all half-cocked and do something that can't be taken back."

He was trembling again. "What do you propose?"

"There's a road," I said. "I drove down it a few weeks ago, just for a lookaround. Things are pretty strange out there. I saw a house made out of something that looked like cotton candy and a car that I'm pretty sure had feet instead of wheels. But I kept driving, and I got almost all the way to Dollarton before everything went topsy-turvy and I found myself back here. Dollarton, Jock. That's almost thirty miles away, and more than twice as far as you can get on any of the other roads. I think we ought to try going down there again."

"I don't like the idea of running," he said. "Perhaps if I met with your friends and explained—"

"Believe me, they're not in the mood for explanations. And if you tried any of your philosophy on them, they'd string you up for sure. Think for a minute. They want to hang you because things have gone wacky around here. But that's not the real reason. When you boil it down, they're after you because you're different. Because you go running in the woods and because you like to paint. Men who take those things as lynching offenses can't be reasoned with. We've got to run. Later, if things ever calm down, we can come back and try talking sense to them."

He didn't say anything for a time but finally nodded and allowed me to lead him into the cabin. He pulled a suitcase from under the cot on which he slept, and together, we began packing whatever clothes we could find.

We had really only gotten started when we heard the mob coming down the Blackwater Road.

IV.
THE CONFRONTATION

"Yo! Witch! C'mon out! We wanna talk to you!"

They were out there, ringing the cabin. Twenty or thirty strong, their babbling voices blended into a shrewish chorus, but I could hear Buddy Mills' voice cutting clearly above all the rest: *Yo! C'mon out!*

When I peeked through a chink in the cabin wall, I could see pale and angry faces. I could see hands clenched into fists. I could see sunlight glinting off gleaming rifle barrels.

I was amazed at how rapidly things had happened. One minute, you have a couple of friends batting around a crazy idea; the next, you're on the edge of something irrevocable. This morning, things had been normal, or at least as normal as they had been for the last few months. We had been talking and laughing as buddies, watching armies of deer trot down the main street, ducking out of the way of motorcycle-riding bears, lining up at the Rexall to bet on the sky color. There had been some baffled amusement in our voices, a touch of weariness, perhaps even a trace of fear. But there hadn't been anger. Not anger like this.

I suppose I had been deluding myself. I had been pretending that if I just kept moving straight ahead, if I waited for the mad universe to find its sanity once again, if I read enough Vonnegut and kept the faith . . . well, I guess I had figured that if I did all of those things, I'd wake up some day and find everything back to normal. The bottom line? I had supposed that if I just kept laughing long enough and hard enough, that invisible cosmic comedian would tire and move on to find a new audience somewhere else.

What I hadn't noticed was that while I was busy laughing, a subtle line had been crossed. My friends, it seemed, had been nurturing something much darker than laughter.

"We're trapped," Jock whispered.

I shook my head. "No. I'm going out there. I'll talk to them. With any luck, that'll bring the ones out back around to the front. I'll keep them busy. You slip out that back way and head into the woods. Wait for me at Pike Lake. I'll meet you there later and show you that road to Dollarton."

"Elvin, they'll kill you."

"No, they won't. They won't much like that I'm here, and they'll hate me when I tell them I'm your friend. But they know me, they trust me . . . or they used to, at any rate. I'll be able to stall them long enough for you to escape."

Jock sighed. He still looked pale, but who could blame him? Like all of us, his life had been turned upside down lately. But for him, it was worse than that. Today, his life had just been flipped over *again*—and in a hell of a big way.

"All right," he said. "We'll try it."

Outside, Buddy Mills raised his voice above the crowd again: "Goddammit, witch! Get out here right now! You got five minutes before we blow our way in there!"

Jock hurried to finish packing. While he gathered his things together, I wandered around the cabin, looking at his books and canvases. I walked over to the fireplace and studied the collection of aging track trophies on the mantle. I picked one up and read the inscription:

OSBORNE HIGH SCHOOL TRACK TEAM ALL AROUND CHAMPION 1963 JOCK THOMAS BARTHOLOMEW

It wasn't fair. The man liked to run. He liked to paint. He liked the solitude of the woods. He liked to read. As I did. All he wanted was the chance to start a new, quiet life in a new, quiet place.

A cosmic test. A cosmic joke. And in the grand tradition of mankind, we had turned the joke back on ourselves.

Two minutes later, Jock signaled that he was ready. I put the trophy down and pulled in a deep breath. I nodded. A moment later, I went out to face the crowd.

I suppose you're thinking that they tore me apart out there. But they didn't. Once they got over being stunned by my presence at the cabin, they seemed surprisingly ready to listen. At least in the beginning.

I told them honestly that Jock and I were friends. I also said that I thought what they were doing was small-minded and cruel and insane, and I told them that I'd come to warn Jock of their asinine intentions. After that, I ventured off into the Land of Lies, stating that I'd found the cabin empty when I got there, that Jock had obviously run away some time earlier.

"I knew it," Carl Brinkley said. "That proves he's a witch. The bastard knew we was comin'. He got away before we could punish him."

I shook my head sadly. "He isn't a witch, Carl. He's a man, just like you and me."

"The hell he is," Buddy said. "Men like you and me don't make shrubs grow outa Roger Chalmers' roof. They don't make the fish in the river turn red and blue. They don't make the sky look like a Vegas neon sign. Or at least men like *me* don't." He gave me a long, steady stare. "I don't know about you anymore, Elvin."

The crowd gave a low, rumbling murmur.

"What's the matter with you?" I asked. "What made you turn all of a sudden? This morning, we were getting along fine. We sat together and laughed while Mayor Chipmunk scolded us for gambling. Nobody was talking about witches then."

"We're tired," somebody said. "We're decent people. We'll take the crap someone throws at us for a while. We'll stand for being pushed around a little. But eventually—"

"Eventually, you push back," I said, remembering my very thoughts on that subject earlier. "I can understand that; believe me I can. Do you think I like what's been happening here? Watching my dog stand up on two legs and run away from me? Listening to my doorbell play that damn Ramblin' Wreck song? Trying to rescue poor Roy Hooper from that fortress he's trapped in? Do you think I've *enjoyed* that?"

"You've been laughin' a lot through all of it," Ken Tatum observed.

"So have you! Jesus, so have all of you! We had to laugh or go insane! That's what the betting was for, wasn't it? That's why we had the sky pools and the falling-trees pool and—"

"Just how *did* you win that tree pool, Elvin?" Buddy said softly, and the crowd murmured again. Somewhere, two or three rows back in the throng, I heard the click of someone snapping off the safety on his gun. That was all it took. I bolted and ran. I scrambled around the side of the cabin and darted into the woods before they had even absorbed the fact that I was gone.

But once they absorbed it, they took to the chase with fierce enthusiasm.

V.
THE CONSEQUENCES

I found Jock waiting at Pike Lake, just as we'd planned. We took to the woods together, running as fast as we could, while the angry townspeople—my old friends, I kept thinking—followed. We ran up hills that hadn't been there before and past thick stands of pine that were coated with glistening sleeves of shining silver. We jumped over creeks of bright yellow water and scurried past animals that waved at us or swore in perfect English at being disturbed. On and on, farther and farther we ran, until the green sky darkened and the pinpricks of red and purple stars had appeared overhead.

The world had changed, I thought. Not right or wrong, not better or worse, just different. Perhaps we would get to Dollarton and find normality in control, or maybe we'd get there and find that it, too, had changed, that the whole world had been affected. Or maybe, just maybe, we'd never get there at all. We had to face that possibility, I knew, but we also had to keep going, keep trying.

After several long and painful hours, even Jock, the

expert runner, was fading. We tried to cheer each other on, but it was difficult. Our bodies ached and our lungs burned. No matter how fast we went or which direction we ran, the hunters stayed close behind.

The world had changed. Yes. And we all cope with change in our own ways. Some of us laugh. Some of us paint. Some of us run. Maybe somewhere there was someone writing new songs about all the differences. We read. We talk. And some gather in angry clusters to look for the solution.

Changes.

No matter how drastic the movement of the world, there are always a few things that resist it, some elements that cannot be altered. The spirit of man. The fate of the different.

On and on, into the night.

Hi Ho.

The mob howled in the darkness like wolves.

GUIDES

ART MADIGAN HAD been living in Kelly's Corners his entire life. From his childhood on Truman Street in the town proper, he had succeeded to a cabin on Raymer Road, then to a trailer on County 630 (known locally as That Long and Dusty Stretch), and finally to his current living accommodations, a cabin on a large lot at Conley Lake. Since the quality and overall *worthwhileness* of your life in Kelly's Corners was based on how far out of town you lived, Art considered his own life to have been one of spectacular upward mobility.

He made a living the same way most of his friends did—working at odd jobs, hauling trash, raking leaves, splitting wood, watching cabins for the summer people during the off-season. But he considered his true calling to be the same as his father's, and his father's before him. He considered himself a guide, and a damn good one. Nobody knew Conley Lake as well as he, or the other lakes in the area, either, for that matter. No one could find the walleye with such unerring accuracy. While the two fish and hunt shops in town offered "professional" guides with fancy bass boats and fish-finders and hourly rates, for a relatively humble forty dollars a day, Art could take even the greenest horn out and come back with the limit every time.

Or so he had always thought. So he had staked his reputation—and even more importantly, his ego—on for the last thirty-nine years. But on the second Saturday in May, something went wrong. On that day, he went out with Mr. and Mrs. Bert Evans of Valley Forge, Pennsylvania, and what did they catch? Nothing. Not a walleye, not a perch, not even a goddamned sunfish.

"Perhaps we should try over there," Bert Evans said after more than three hours, pointing across the lake at the crooked finger of Big Walker Point.

Art laughed. "Only if you wanna catch rocks and stumps. Water's too shallow over there. With this bright sun, there ain't gonna be any walleye within a half-mile of the place."

Evans shrugged. "With all due respect, Mr. Madigan, there don't seem to be any here either."

Art ignored the comment and kept on trolling, working the southern shore of the lake with everything he had. After another hour he puttered over to Merriam Bay and tried there, and then tried the unnamed inlet near Kramer's Rest-Ezy Resort. No luck. By three-thirty, the Evanses were growing noticeably cranky.

Art couldn't understand it. Six hours and not a catch? Not a strike? Not even a nibble? If nothing else, the little guys should have been pecking their leeches and worms away, and yet he'd only had to rebait twice, and then only because the bait had grown too pale and waterlogged to be attractive to any sensible fish.

At the end of the day, as he was bidding goodbye

to his customers (putting on a brave front that even he didn't believe), Bert Evans stopped him and said, "I suppose you don't offer a money-back guarantee."

Art was startled. He had never thought of that; he'd never needed to think of it. "Sorry," he said, recovering his composure. "I can't do that. But I'll make you a deal. Come back any time, and I'll take you out again for . . . oh, let's say half-price."

The Evanses looked at each other and laughed. The sound of it was like the tail of a whip laid against Art's face, and it echoed in his head for a painfully long time afterward.

***

He had a sign taped over his bathroom mirror. On it were three words, which he had taken from a late night movie—a black-and-white war film—he'd first seen as a teenager. In the movie, some towheaded, freckled-faced private had just gotten shot in the chest. As he lay dying, his sergeant ran up to him and said something along the lines of, "Davis! Davis! Are you all right?" To which towheaded Davis had replied, "Don't worry about me, Sarge. I'm gonna be fine. I'm a gamer." Those were the three words Art had scrawled on a piece of scrap paper and placed over his mirror. I'M A GAMER. They helped get him going every morning and pushed him on when times were hard. They formed his credo, his entire system of belief. Because he was a gamer, Art told himself repeatedly that his experience with Mr. and Mrs. Evans had been a fluke, a bizarre one-shot, an aberration. But as the chilly mornings and pleasant afternoons of May faded into the heat and humidity of June, his confidence was shaken.

With the coming of Memorial Day, the tourist season started for real. He was busy every day with clients—lone businessmen on vacation, groups of men on getaway weekends, couples, entire families—taking them to Twin Lake, White Lake, Bartlette Lake, Pine Stump Lake, but mostly to Conley Lake, for what he continually promised was the finest fishing in the north.

While reports from his friends and competitors told Art that the fishing was better than usual that year (on June 11th, a state-record walleye was taken in Merriam Bay), he and his customers were continually shut out. Day after day, he started with high hopes, and day after day, he came home empty-handed. He tried everything from his usual leeches and crawlers to minnows and hoppers and even a few dreaded artificial lures, but he couldn't buy a strike.

By the end of the month, as the word leaked out and gradually spread throughout the area, he noticed a marked decrease in the number of people calling for his services. On the Fourth of July, he actually had no customers at all. For the first time in years, he was able to go into town and watch the annual VFW festivities, although he did so moodily and found no pleasure in the parade, the afternoon barbecue, or that evening's fireworks display.

"I'm a gamer," he muttered to himself a week or so later, when he found himself without clients for the second time. "But this is ridiculous."

That day, he went to the IGA and bought a bottle. That night, he took his first drink in almost ten years. It tasted surprisingly, refreshingly good; not even his guilt and shame could ruin the smoky flavor of the whiskey or silence the words the liquor whispered to him: *It's gonna be all right, Art ol' man. Just wait'll next time, wait'll tomorrow. You'll take your limit by noon.*

That night, he fell asleep early in front of the TV (watching Babe Winkelman, of all people, who could catch a half-dozen fish in the time it took Art to get his outboard started). For a long time, he dozed in and out, tossing feverishly, muttering drunkenly, but sometime past midnight slipped into a deep dream. In the dream, he was chased along the shores of the lake by a pale, shambling creature with no face. The creature reached for him with gnarled, algae-encrusted hands but providentially was too slow to catch him.

When he awoke in the morning, the couch was soaked with his own sweat. He couldn't help noticing it. What he didn't see was the series of puddles on the floor—six or seven in all. They started at the cabin door, led across to the couch, and stopped there. They had begun to dry, and while most of them were just indistinct patches of wetness, one or two still held the perfect shape of a footprint.

***

The next night, he didn't drink, but he did go to the Bear's Lair, the better of the two bars in Kelly's Corners. There, just as he knew he would, he found his old friend, Bill Raven. Bill was sitting at his usual table in the back, nursing his usual pitcher of beer. He seemed inordinately glad to see Art and tried to encourage him along several paths of conversation. Art, however, wanted to keep it short. In the Bear's Lair, a friendly talk between two friends could grow helter-skelter into a conversation with three men, and four, and five. Eventually, what you ended up with was an all-out bullshit session involving anywhere from ten to thirty of the town's loudest mouths.

"Look," Art said after a few minutes, "I gotta ask you somethin'."

Bill nodded. "Fire away."

"You 'member my dad, doncha?"

"Of course I do. I was a couple-three years behind him in school. We were pals. Say, you sure you don't want some of this beer?"

Art waved it away. "You 'member how he died, right?"

Bill's expression darkened. He lit one of his foul-smelling cigars and leaned back, shaking his head. "I'm getting old, Artie, I'll grant you. But I couldn't forget that. Helluva note. Helluva thing for your family. Helluva mess for the town."

"That it was," Art said. He had only been six at the time, but his mother had passed the story along like an heirloom. "I was wonderin' . . . well, hell, Bill, I was wonderin' about what happened before he died."

"I don't know what you mean," Bill said, but his expression said otherwise. Not only did he know what Art was getting at but he had already made the connection. It would have been hard not to. The jokes had been going around town for almost a month: *Yeah, old Artie's lost his touch. Artie used to have the fish jumpin' into his boat; now he couldn't catch 'em with a stick of dynamite and a net.*

"I think you do," Art said now. "I'm talkin' about his bad luck."

"Hell, boy, that wasn't just bad luck. That was a curse. You think you're a good guide? You couldn't hold a candle to your daddy. When he started coming back dry every day, that wasn't just a funny stretch. Something happened to him. Something had changed. It was like he was . . . I don't know . . . almost like he was *doomed*. Doomed to live out what happened to your grandpap."

Art stopped breathing for a moment. He felt his heart stop beating then lurch into action again. "What're you sayin'?" he asked in a choked, husky whisper.

"You know what I'm saying, Artie."

"Uh-uh. No sir. I don't getcha. Grandpa ran off with that Stuart woman, didn't he?" He laughed harshly. "Jesus, what am I askin' you for? I know he ran off."

Bill Raven didn't say anything for a very long time. He stared at Art with narrow, winter-chilled eyes. The gaze made Art shift and squirm uncomfortably; he felt as though Bill were trying to see into his brain, or worse, into his soul.

"You're not kidding, are you?" Bill said at last, after nearly a minute.

"'Course I ain't. Why would I be kiddin'? Grandpa ran off with

Hedda Stuart."

Bill shook his head and murmured, "I can't believe you don't know. It's your own family, for godssakes. I can't believe no one ever told you."

"Told me *what?*"

Bill sighed. "Things were different in those days. People didn't want the truth. When your grandpap went out, his buddies took it on themselves to pull what you might call a cover-up. There were six or seven of them in on it—my pop, Gunnar Seppala, Dave Atkinson, a couple of others. Hedda Stuart, well, she really *did* run off, just the day before. Except she ran off with a brush salesman, not your grandpap."

Art felt dizzy. The world seemed to be spinning much too fast, whirling away from him. He felt a powerful urge to grip his chair with both hands, as though to do otherwise was to risk being flung out into the vastness of space.

"What happened?" he said.

"He died." Bill sighed again. "Just like your daddy about twenty-some years later. He ran into a dry spell, couldn't catch a fish for all the tea in Shanghai. His business shriveled up and blew away. He lost his hope. He lost his faith. He lost everything."

Art groaned inwardly. "And?"

"And what? I told you, it was just like your daddy. He couldn't stand it anymore. Took his boat out one day and went overboard. They found the boat floating off Big Walker Point. Only thing in it was your grandpap's old hat. Back home, they found a note. Like I said, in 1931 that was news you didn't spread. Lucky for my pop and the others, Hedda took her powder and made it easy on them." He hesitated, puffing his cigar thoughtfully and eyeing Art with a look of infinite sadness. "I still can't believe no one ever told you the truth."

Art pushed away from the table and got to his feet. Everything was still spinning, even faster than before. Although Bill called out to him, he never looked back. He simply stumbled out of the bar and hurried home.

This time, he noticed the wet footprints immediately. They formed a wide circle just inside the cabin door.

GUIDES

His first reaction to Bill Raven's story was to ignore it completely. His second reaction, several hours later, was to prove that it had been a lie. He spent the rest of the night and most of the next two days going through old family papers, searching for the truth. He had to cancel several customers to do so, but the irony in that act never occurred to him.

The papers were in several boxes marked variously FISHING and GUIDING and IMPORTANT RECORDS. There were old tax forms, customer receipts, maps of the area lakes, pamphlets and flyers, faded letters, and even an old fishing journal his father had kept for several years. He sifted through them repeatedly, but there was almost no evidence that his grandfather had even existed, let alone committed suicide. And as far as his father's journals were concerned, they stopped in 1953, a full two years before his dry spell and death. He drank on and off during his search, but did so almost absently. He didn't feel the obsession, the compulsion that had driven him during that time some years ago when drinking had become a problem for him. In fact, it was drinking that finally showed him the truth. It happened toward the end of that second day, after he'd been through the boxes at least nine times.

He had just finished his third whiskey and water in the last few hours, and as he tried to put the glass aside, the moisture beaded on its sides caused him to drop it. It landed with a thump in the open box at his feet. When he reached in to retrieve it, several papers were stuck to the bottom, and when he pulled the papers free, he discovered two of them plastered together. The top form was an old receipt for gasoline that he'd already looked at a dozen times. But glued to the bottom of the receipt was a handwritten note he hadn't seen before. He unfolded it with trembling hands and read his father's spiky writing:

Nothing for weeks. Friends laughing. Good customers going to Pete Brady. No good. Just like dad. It's going to end the same way and I

The note ended there, but its few words (and the palsied uncertainty he could see in his father's hand) told him everything he needed to know.

He put the boxes away after that, back up in the crawlspace attic where he didn't have to see them or, with any luck, think about them either. As he came back down the ladder and mixed himself a fresh drink, Bill Raven's words were going around and around in his head like the waking memory of a vivid dream: *Something happened to him. Something had changed . . . almost like he was* doomed. *Doomed to live out what happened to your grandpap.*

Even with the alcohol buzzing in his brain and the feel of the cryptic note still fresh upon his fingertips, Art found it hard to credit the concept of being doomed to do something. It reminded him a little too much of movie curses, voodoo dolls, or at the least a fatalism he could not accept. But the choice of that word—doomed—didn't lessen the impact of what Bill had said. It didn't take away the obvious connection between the deaths of both his grandfather and his father. And it didn't lessen the unhealthy dread he carried with him to bed later that night.

***

He dreamed again. In the dream, he was fishing a

quarter-mile off Big Walker Point with one of his regular customers, a man named Johnny Hammond who went out with him two or three times every summer. He didn't like fishing near the point. As he had told Mr. and Mrs. Evans, the water there was simply too shallow for walleye. But they'd already been out for nine hours and hadn't caught a thing. Big Walker Point was the last place to try.

Suddenly, Johnny Hammond was on his feet in the boat, staggering from side to side, calling at the top of his voice, "I got one, Artie! Sweet Jesus, *I got one!*"

Art felt a burst of joy that was almost nuclear in its intensity. The dry spell was over, he thought wildly, watching Johnny's rod bend almost double. The curse was broken, the doom had been shed. Thank God, thank God.

Johnny battled his monster fish for ages. Every time he thought he had weakened it enough to haul it in, the fish would run deep again, and all the instructions Art could offer did no good.

"Can't . . . can't hang on anymore," Johnny gasped after more than half an hour. "You gotta help me, Art . . . gotta . . . gotta take the pole."

Art did, and for the first time felt the sheer power of the catch take hold of him. He, too, fought until his arms were on fire and his chest hurt, until his back throbbed with pain, until the sweat stood out on his forehead and ran down his face in stinging rivulets. After an eternity, the struggle broke. It was so sudden that he almost fell overboard. One second he was fighting with everything he had left, and the next he was reeling quickly, effortlessly.

The fish was heavy. Even with no fight, he could

tell that. He couldn't imagine what it was. No walleye could be so big or battle so long and hard. But what else could it be? There were no muskies in Conley Lake, and the thought that it might be a prehistoric sturgeon was laughable.

Then he saw it coming up.

Not a fish, but a person.

A white, bloated corpse.

Its head was lolling, its face framed by weeds and twigs and long, floating strands of hair.

And its pale hands floated beside it, reaching upwards.

He looked around for Johnny, but Johnny was gone. He was alone in the boat. Just before the corpse broke the surface, he dropped the pole and screamed. Even with no tension on the line, the corpse kept rising slowly, inexorably. It crested out of the water and hooked one hand over the gunwale.

Art sat up in bed, sobbing and wild-eyed, just in time to hear the whispering click of the cabin door being quietly closed.

***

It was raining that day, a light but steady drizzle. He had customers scheduled, the Donahues, a family of three from Cleveland, Ohio. He reached them at their motel in town and cancelled, mumbling a variety of excuses all having to do with the weather. After a quick breakfast of oatmeal with a whiskey chaser, he bundled into his slicker and rainpants and took his boat out on the lake.

It took fifteen minutes to reach Big Walker Point. Once there, he dropped both the bow and stern anchors and pulled his bottle out of the tackle box. He took a quick slug and gazed at the rain-dimpled surface of the lake. He didn't know what he expected to happen, but he was coolly determined to wait there until it did.

It didn't take long. Less than an hour after dropping anchor, he heard something behind him, a noise that sounded like a bucket of fish being dumped onto the floor of the boat. He whirled around, heart hammering, and saw his father sitting in the stern.

The man was dead. Drowned. Like the corpses in his dreams, there was no color left to him at all. His flesh was so white that it was almost transparent. His hair, seemingly bleached, hung limply around his face. His clothes—a strapless white undershirt and faded dungarees—were rotted. They hung in wet, loose strips. His arms and chest bulged in strange places. The bulges seemed to be moving, undulating gently, as though something alive was moving sluggishly just under the skin.

Art cried out and hefted one of the paddles from its oarlock. His father's pale lips drew back into a quivering smile, revealing a toothless oral cavity that was filled with water and clogged with mud and algae. The water ran out lazily and pooled at the corpse's shoeless feet.

"We was doomed," his father said thickly, spraying Art with flecks of mud. "Both me and your grandpa. We was doomed."

Art swung the paddle frantically. He felt a slight resistance as it struck his father's body, but otherwise it was like hitting a cloud. The paddle's arc went right through the corpse and came out the other side, dripping wet.

"You're dead," Art intoned. "Jesus, Dad, what're you doin' here? *You're dead!*"

The corpse nodded, spilling more water. "Dead," it croaked. "And doomed."

And at that, his father simply leaned backwards and slithered out of the boat like a snake. The body struck the water without a splash. Art scrambled to the stern and looked over. He caught—or *thought* he did—a glimpse of pure, shimmery whiteness going down and down, but it was gone almost before he could register it.

Dead. And doomed.

Shaking badly, he hoisted the anchors and started for home.

***

I'm a gamer, Art told himself, and after that day made a strict effort to put the early summer behind him. To dwell on what had happened was to lose his mind, he decided, and so he serviced his customers when he had them and kept his thoughts on other things when he didn't. He was convinced that his urge to drink and his troubled dreams would vanish if he could just have one good day—just one—and so he fished with his clients and he fished alone. The waters of Conley Lake that had always been his favorite spot became even more than that. They became his home, day and night, as he desperately sought that first catch, the one that would break the jinx and make everything better.

But the catch never came.

Hour after hour, day after day, nothing.

In early August, another state record was pulled from the lake (a walleye unlike any that had ever been seen), and yet Art was luckless despite all his skill, the years of knowledge he brought into play, and the battalion of nightcrawlers and army of leeches he deployed in the effort.

Toward the middle of the month, he went into town to buy gas for the outboard. As he was leaving the Shell station, he ran into Stumpy Mitchell.

"Hey, Art," Stumpy said, waving him over. "Glad I ran into you, bud. I . . . say, you feelin' all right? You look like hell."

"I'm fine," Art said, a little too quickly. "What's up?"

"They're gonna be hirin' over to the mill next week. You interested?"

Art frowned. "Why would I be interested in that?"

"Well, I figgered . . . you know . . . "

"No, I don't know. What the hell're you talkin' about?"

Stumpy shrugged uneasily. "Jesus, Art, *you know.*"

Art shook his head. "You're crazy, Stump. You know I don't take no outside work in the summer. In the off-season, sure, I'll take whatever I can get. But not in August. I'm a guide, not a damn millworker."

"Hey, sorry," Stumpy said. He looked *very* uncomfortable now, as though he wanted to sink into the sidewalk and vanish from Art's sight. "I just thought, well shit, with your bad luck an' all . . . you can't be a guide if you ain't catchin' nothin'."

"I'm a guide," Art repeated woodenly, and after his friend had walked away, he said it yet again, soft, barely audible. "Goddammit, I'm a guide."

And yet Stumpy's words haunted him for a week afterward. *You can't be a guide if you ain't catchin' nothin'.* Sometimes they came alone, and sometimes they swirled in his head alongside and mixed up with Bill Raven's words about doom.

"I'm a gamer," Art reminded himself whenever those voices popped into his brain. "A guide and a gamer."

But when Labor Day came, effectively bringing the major portion of the tourist season to a close, he still hadn't caught a fish, and he was feeling far less than game. At thirty-nine, he thought perhaps his life was over. Everything he had built his reputation on was gone. The things he had staked his very being on had left him. The axis around which he revolved had been broken or stolen or both. Conley Lake had been his home, and that home had somehow, in some way, been poisoned against him.

He stopped drinking again, but no longer felt like getting out of bed in the morning. What was the point? he wondered every day. Why get out of bed when you had no life to lead?

If he had subscribed to the fatalism he had earlier rejected so strenuously, he would have plainly seen how all the pieces had fallen into place. He would have realized how neatly and unavoidably he had been prepared for the final day.

***

Late September.

Cold.

Raining again.

He awoke in the darkness of the hour just before dawn, aware of a presence in the room with him. He could feel it as well as hear it, low voices conversing in a soft, unreadable tone.

He fumbled on the nightstand and closed his

fingers around the lamp. Groping his way upward, he found the switch and turned it. The room was flooded with light, the force of which drove him back against the pillow like a punch.

"Son," a voice said, and he opened his eyes again, blinking.

They were standing above him, his father and grandfather.

Cold water dripped from their drowned corpses, and when his father spoke, his voice was the sound of waves washing across a rocky beach.

"Don't you understand yet?" his father said. "Don't you understand?" his grandfather echoed.

Art shrank away, but his pillow and headboard would only allow him to go so far. He gazed into the bloated faces and realized that neither of them had any eyes. Instead, they had small pools of dark, deep water that glimmered where their eyes should have been.

"It's a cycle," his grandfather said in his heavy, waterlogged voice. "It didn't start with me, and it ain't gonna end with you. It's a cycle—and you gotta play your part."

His father reached out to touch him. Art scrambled out of bed and ducked past the corpses, but his father came after him anyway. With squishing, relentless steps, he crossed the room and cornered Art by the dresser on the far wall.

"Play your part," his father said, those wishing-well eyes brimming as though with tears.

"Play your part," his grandfather said.

"No," Art told them. He might as well have wished them a happy day for all the reaction he got. "God, no."

Their arms floated toward him through the air. Their white fingers worked and writhed like maggots.

"Play your part," they said in thick, dripping unison.

"But I don't understand!"

"Play your part," they said again.

The pale fingers stopped inches from his face. He could smell the rot and moisture-spurred decay. It was a rich, foul odor that swept over him, covered him like a blanket.

"I don't understand," he said again, pleading.

But if he had hoped for a response, he got none. The two figures turned away without touching him. Side by side, they padded out of the room, leaving pools of fetid water behind.

When the door closed behind them, Art Madigan was sobbing much too loudly to hear.

***

An hour later he crossed the yard and headed toward his boat. When he got there and climbed in, he was amused to see that the pen he'd used to write the note was still gripped in his tight, bloodless fingers. He let it slip and watched it drop into the lake. It sank from sight, barely a ripple left behind.

He started the motor and headed for Big Walker Point. This time, he didn't anchor but merely sat and waited. The morning crept by slowly. The rain stopped and the sun came out, but it was sunlight screened by high clouds, weak and cold and ineffective.

"I'm a guide," he muttered to himself from time to time as the boat drifted free across Conley Lake. *I'm a guide,* he thought, *but it's more than that. I'm a gamer, a fighter. I don't give up easy. I don't give up* at all.

GUIDES

But he thought he could hear the grinding of a tremendous wheel turning somewhere beyond his sight.

And he waited.

Waited for day to turn to evening.

Waited for the water around the boat to darken and swell.

Waited for the ripple, for the shimmering glimpse of transparent whiteness rising toward him.

He waited.

Eventually, he knew, his father and grandfather would come to him like guides. Then he would know what he was supposed to do next.

GETTING BACK

I

THE TORNADO THAT cut a wandering path across southeastern Wisconsin on the night of my homecoming never came very near my parents' farm, yet in a way it was the start of everything. A symbolic beginning, if nothing else. A harbinger.

My father was the best weather forecaster I knew. He didn't need meteorologists' reports; he didn't rely on homilies about red skies in the morning; he didn't feel anything in his bones. He just knew what signs to look for and how to read them. So that night, while the radio issued warnings about seeking immediate shelter, my father laughed.

"That storm's not gonna hit here," he said. "Look at the sky. Might veer just to the south, maybe, but she's not coming here."

The four of us—my mother, father, grandmother, and I—sat on the screened front porch in the muggy twilight, drinking beer. Bursts of thunderstorm static cut through the damage reports from neighboring counties on Dad's transistor. Lightning slashed the sky at long intervals while it rained gently, relentlessly. My grandmother, at one time the best storyteller I'd ever met, talked about past storms. She talked about the North Atlantic hurricane that almost sank the ship bringing her parents from Germany to New York and about the Great Lakes gale that had threatened the schooner carrying them to Milwaukee. My father nodded at various parts of the tales, interjecting a comment or two and laughing at the appropriate points.

My mother was strangely quiet. She'd inherited a great many things from her mother, among them a healthy dose of the tale-spinner's art. But that night, she had nothing to offer. She sat in her wicker chair, a few feet apart from the rest of us, nursing her beer but not finishing it, her eyes focused on a point somewhere beyond the porch. I watched her for a long time while Grandma rambled on and finally leaned over to whisper at my father.

"Is Mom all right? She's so quiet."

He turned a long, slow gaze on me and said, "You had yourself a long drive today, didn't you?"

"I . . . yeah, I guess so. Yeah, it *was* a long drive."

He nodded and took a swallow from his bottle. "I could tell. You showed it when you pulled up. A long, hard drive."

I sighed. "It was a long, hard *year.*"

"Oh? I thought you wanted to be a teacher."

"I do. I just think my choice of . . . Look. Can we talk about this later? Tomorrow, maybe?"

"Sure, son, whatever you want."

"Now what about Mom?"

Again he gave me that long, languid gaze. Then he turned away, and by that time my grandmother had launched another story and my opportunity was gone.

The wind picked up as the night went by, and the sky above the barn was lit more and more often by vivid electrical streaks. Still, Dad's prediction seemed to be on the mark, for while we continued to hear about downed power lines, fallen trees, and damaged homes in an area that stretched from Madison to Milwaukee and south to the Illinois border, we were never directly threatened.

It was some time after ten when my grandmother fell asleep in her chair. Mom had gone in without a word almost half an hour earlier, and the night was now silent but for the sounds of rain, thunder, and wind. I faced my father again.

"You didn't tell me about—"

"I think we'll be lucky with the corn this year. The spring was just right and the summer looks good."

I slammed my open palm on the arm of the chair. "Dammit, Dad, I—"

"She started her chemotherapy again, Pete." His voice was small and tight, strangled.

I stared at him. His face was crisscrossed and distorted by shadows. A fifty-three-year-old man who looked aged and ageless at the same time.

I didn't know what to say, and when I found something at last, it was juvenile, utterly useless, stupidly shallow.

"You're kidding."

"No, I ain't."

"But—"

"She took sick in the Red Owl two weeks ago. Fell down, took a whole display of canned peas down with her. Finally admitted she'd had the pain again since March."

"Oh, Jesus. I thought the doctor said she was in remission."

He shook his head slowly. "That was three years ago, Pete."

The voice on the radio was saying something about a new funnel cloud sighting in an area not far distant from the farm. Perhaps that cyclone, churning along several miles away, was responsible for the distant roaring in my ears, but I didn't think so.

"I . . . I really thought . . . Oh, shit."

"Now, Pete—"

But I'd stopped listening. I rose like a stiff, mechanical doll and went outside. The jungle humidity swept over me, and the rain came with it. The wind, ripping across the yard, tore at my hair and clothes.

"Pete, the storm—" my father called from the porch, but his voice already sounded distant, unreal.

I hurried toward the barn but didn't stop when I got there. I turned right, cut between the twin hulks of the equipment sheds, and entered the field we'd always called the north pasture. It was planted in timothy that year, as it almost always was, and already it was going on shin-high, ready for the season's first cutting in a week or two.

The sky was still charged with electricity, but I went on anyway, not caring that being out there in the middle of that field was one of the more foolhardy things I'd ever done. My mother was dying. The cancer was back. Three years of relief and the blackness had returned to the horizon. The past year—my first of full-time teaching—had been one mighty kick in the gut. And now, coming home for the summer to recoup and recover, I had just been kicked again.

It took me forever to cross the field. Several times, lightning stroked toward the ground less than a half-mile away. My shirt and pants were drenched, my hair dripping, hanging across my forehead like a lunatic's wig. Still I went on until I'd reached the property line at the back of the north pasture.

Here was a gap-toothed row of box elders and Norway maples my father had planted twenty or twenty-five years earlier. They were swaying wildly in the wind, and the rush of air through their branches made a sighing, whistling chorus of eerie pain. Running just behind the trees was a barbed-wire fence, then a stretch of overgrown no-man's-land that separated the property from the north-south highway.

Standing there, looking through one of the gaps in the treeline, gazing down the highway toward the south, I heard another rumbling sound in my ears, this one much louder than before. It was a sound very much like a long, powerful freight train. A sound like a million running feet. It shook me to the roots of my teeth and the center of my bones.

And then I saw it, perhaps seven miles off, distinguishable in the night only as a darker patch of blackness. A roiling, churning, whirling swatch of midnight. A funnel cloud.

It was moving away from our land, away from the highway on a northwest-southeast line. I thought about running but didn't. It was moving away, and I was fascinated. Watching it vanish across flat farm land, hearing that roar in my ears and feeling the steady vibration beneath my feet, I felt chilled. The power of that swarming darkness made me shiver; I felt a slow gnawing of primitive fear in my belly.

"God is angry today," my mother would say when we were little and tornado warnings would force us to take shelter in the farmhouse cellar.

Now, seeing an honest-to-god funnel for the first time in my life, that didn't seem far off the mark at all.

I watched until the cloud had blended with the night and the roar had faded, until the ground had stopped shaking. Then, I realized just how wet I was.

Soaked for life, I thought crazily. And on the heels of that: God is angry today.

I shook my head and turned back toward home. The wind had become a knife against my skin.

"Mister?"

I stopped in mid-step. Literally. One foot was halfway to the ground. Then I whirled around to face the trees and the place where the little boy had spoken.

I wiped the rainwater from my eyes but still saw nothing beyond swaying branches, blowing leaves snapping back and forth like tiny pennants.

"Mister, please . . . "

I took a step forward. The voice was small, plaintive, very real.

But I couldn't see the boy anywhere.

"Who is it?" I called, the words torn from my lips by a vicious gust of wind.

"Mister?"

"Where are you?"

"Mister?"

It was then that I had what I'm sure was a premonition, the first and last time I've ever experienced such a thing. I'm not positive that premonition is the right word, but in that instant, I *knew* that I had to get out of there. I *knew* something terrible was sweeping down on me. Then it felt as though a great hand was turning me around again, pushing me away.

"Mister?" Soft and small, lost and pleading. "Mister?"

I ran, heading for home, fleeing on the strength of the wind and the raw, horrible power of that black sensation . . . that fear . . . that premonition.

"Mist—"

The little boy's voice was swallowed by a shattering, splintering crash as one of the largest box elders in the row toppled to earth, sending branches and wood shards flying.

I only looked back for an instant, never breaking stride.

The wind howled at my heels.

II

The next morning was bright and sunwashed, a bit cooler. My mother's mood was considerably better; she sat at the breakfast table chatting twice as much as the rest of us, Grandma included. Her son was home, she must have said three times, and nothing could make her happier. When Debbie got back from college at the end of the week, we'd be a real family again. That phrase—*real family*—troubled me, but it was worth it to see Mom feeling fine.

My father said nothing about the night before, for which I was grateful. I'd been a fool, running on gut emotion into the teeth of a wild storm and then— alone, frightened by the funnel—suffering aural hallucinations. I saw no need to have any of that brought up.

"When's Debbie getting here?" I asked, keeping the conversation on safe ground.

Mom smiled. "Friday afternoon. She called last week, said her last exam's Thursday night and she'll drive up the next morning. You two . . . let's see . . . sweet Jesus, you haven't seen each other in almost two years!"

I nodded. "The last time was just after I entered the master's program. But we write every week and talk on the phone a couple times a month."

"Still, it shows that you don't come home enough, not nearly enough. Not at Christmas or Thanksgiving, not at Easter. You'd think you were ashamed of us or something. You'd think—"

"Faye," my father said, "the boy just got up. Don't start on him now."

I cringed at the use of what I'd always considered a pejorative but was thankful for his defense nonetheless. Mom, though, wasn't quite ready to give up.

"I know he just got up, Reuben. But he's a member of this family, and he ought to act like it. It couldn't hurt. The Manse Family sticks together. They celebrate their holidays together." She looked at me, and now, I saw with relief that the lecture was a gentle one. Her words were harsh, but her eyes betrayed a soft, good humor.

"Don't get me wrong, Peter. I'm so glad to have you home this summer, you wouldn't believe. I just think we ought to see you more often."

I shrugged, looking into my Rice Krispies. "I've been busy."

Grandma snorted. "Education," she said sagely, "is a dangerous thing."

And at that we all laughed; the tense atmosphere shattered and blew away.

***

After breakfast my father pulled on his gloves and headed for the equipment shed. I went after him, wanting to ask more about Mom. We paused just outside while he lit a cigarette and adjusted his Trojan Seed cap. He studied me with an unreadable gaze.

"Wind took down a tree last night."

I swallowed. Had he already been out to the property line? Or had he followed me last night, staying a few yards behind, to make sure I'd be okay? I said nothing but offered a tiny nod.

"I was sorry to see her go," he continued, "remembering the way you used to play in her and all. You and Stevie had a treehouse there for a couple-three years, remember?"

"Treehouse?"

"Sure. In the big oak down at the foot of the drive. You remember that treehouse, don't you? You fellas used all them old Burma Shave signs we had piled in the barn."

I relaxed. He didn't know about the box elder at the back of the north pasture.

"I remember," I said with a smile. "Burma Shave signs and rusty, bent nails from the old chicken coop."

Dad laughed. "You fellas were a couple of regular carpenters, all right." He started toward the shed again. "Gotta move along, Pete. Stop by later and meet the new hired men. We're rebuilding the engine on the Deere, be there most of the day."

GETTING BACK

I still wanted to ask about Mom but decided it could wait. I told him I'd pop in later and watched him walk away, his head lowered and the small stoop in his shoulders—a stoop he'd had as long as I could remember—just a little more pronounced than it had been when I was last home.

I stood in the yard for a long time, looking around at the house, the freshly-painted barn (white with green trim, green aluminum roof, the words MANSE FARM 1923 in black above the long, sliding doors), the adjacent stone silo, the equipment sheds, the dog kennel, the poultry pen and coop. A million scents assailed me, each one bringing a rush of memories. I smelled manure and damp earth, cut grass, gasoline, paint, and old wood. I thought of an entirely different set of aromas—pencil shavings, paper and books, chalk dust—and wondered for the first time in a long time if I'd made the right decision.

Not knowing what else to do, I headed for the barn, cutting across the lawn and climbing the driveway's slight incline to the upper floor.

Inside it was cool and dim. I could hear the cows downstairs stirring restlessly, lowing, anxious to be let out to pasture. Up here was the old hayloft, seldom used in my lifetime, and a series of large grain rooms to the right and left that had been full constantly when I was little but had been replaced by concrete cribs outside when I was in high school. The place was now used mainly for storage. The loft and grain rooms were loaded with unwanted household items, old battered beds, sea trunks with broken locks and missing hinges, backless chairs, couches minus their stuffing. The center section of the barn was used for parking. My

Escort sat next to the family pickup. In the corner were two Lawn Boy push mowers, a Wheel Horse garden tractor, and a rack of grass shears and hedge clippers, all of which would only be in the way in the equipment sheds.

I stood next to my car and looked up the length of the rotting ladder that led to the loft. I remembered Debbie, Stephen, and me playing up there, endless summer afternoons. Games of pirates and cowboys and secret agents, the kinds of games kids never seem to play anymore. Games of big city hospital and ocean-going cruise ship and hidden underground laboratory.

I remembered Stephen, two years younger than me, so much quicker, more agile, going up the ladder like a little monkey, taking the rungs two at a time and laughing at his brother and sister for being so slow. I remembered Stephen always creating new games, keeping things interesting. I remembered Stephen . . .

. . . Stephen screaming . . .

. . . Stephen crushed beneath the old Allis Chalmers . . .

. . . Stephen's life ebbing, spilling out onto the bare earth of the east acreage . . .

. . . Stephen . . .

I stood there in the barn and cried, hard and long. I'd cried at the time, of course, but not often enough in the seven years since.

. . . Stephen . . . Steve . . . Stevie . . .

It felt damn good to stand there crying like that. Frankly, I don't care what that sounds like. I'll say it again. It felt damn good to be in the barn where we'd played so often, crying for my dead brother.

***

GETTING BACK

As Mom had been quick to point out, it had been a long time since I'd been home. Three years, to be precise, ever since my graduation from the University of Wisconsin and my entrance into the graduate program there to earn a master's in education. My room, therefore, hadn't changed since my school days. A rabid sports fan then, my walls showed it. They were covered with pennants—Badgers, Packers, Brewers, even the old Milwaukee Braves—and with wonderful clippings and posters from the Green Bay glory years. My high school diploma was mounted above my desk, where I'd hung it before going off to Madison. My senior year required reading still lined the bookshelves at the foot of the bed, Salinger cheek to cheek with Dickens.

After a hamburger and potato salad lunch with the family and the two hired men (a short, stocky grouch named David Falkner and a peachfuzzed kid named Tommy Scheinholt), I said I was going to my room for a nap. My grandmother and mother flashed concerned looks as I left the table. My father mumbled something about Milquetoast teachers, but grinned as I passed his chair.

In my room, I gazed out the window at the fields beyond. The north pasture and its timothy could only be seen from the other side of the house, but from here I could see the southern acreage. It was divided into three neat sections: green wheat, very young corn, and a crop that looked like sweet peas, although they might have been beets; it was a little early to tell. It was a beautiful sight, all that fertile land, and since it seemed to be the day for it, I gave in to the rush of old memories and new fears.

I'd loved the farm life as a child but had chilled to it in high school when the playtime decreased and the workload went up. In that period, when normal adolescent rebellion runs rampant anyway, I determined to go to college and see if there was a better way before committing myself to keeping the Manse Farm going. The death of my younger brother in a tractor accident two weeks before my eighteenth birthday had wiped out that wait-and-see policy. The farm was not—absolutely, certainly, without a doubt in the world—for me. It was a stinking place. A horrible, boring, backbreaking, viciously dangerous and cruel place. It was the lifestyle of the past. It was outdated, fit only for dullwitted rednecks and their ugly, graying wives.

So I was a teacher in a small northern Michigan town. My first year on the job had been an eye-opening journey through smalltime hell, and my first day back on the farm brought with it so many incredible sights and smells that I was utterly bewildered for the first time since the tenth grade.

What in the hell *did* I want, anyway? And was the rush of hatred for this life that had spilled out of me as Stephen's blood had spilled onto the ground still relevant seven years later? Somehow, I didn't think so. If anything, crying for him in the barn today had been a release from that sort of thinking.

"Shit," I said, leaving the window and throwing myself on the bed.

My mother was dying.

Did that fit into the equation somehow? And if so, where?

Debbie was going to the University of Illinois,

thinking about art school after graduation. When Mom was gone, my father would be alone. And he was no spring chicken, although by no means old. With Debbie and me gone, there were no more Manses to carry on the farm that my father's father had begun. I'd never looked at that as a duty before, but perhaps it was . . . perhaps it was.

Thinking all those crazy thoughts, I fell asleep face down in the pillow and dreamed. Stephen was not in the dream, nor was Debbie. My parents weren't in the dream. I was all alone there, wandering through a dark house filled with closed doors, and each door was a vital decision I was unable and unwilling to make.

III

I awoke in darkness to the touch of a cool hand on my forehead and the strong smell of fried chicken in the air. I'd overslept, missed dinner, and my mother had brought a plate for me, was now trying to wake me up.

But as I blinked rapidly and struggled toward alertness, the cool, small hand moved down my cheek to the side of my neck. That was a strange way to wake—

My vision cleared and I looked up into the face of a child. A small boy with fine, delicate features, china-white skin, blonde hair in a rough bowl cut. His lips looked extremely red against his pale skin; they were drawn back in a wide, trembling bow of agony or fear.

I sat up like a shot, slapping the hand away, trying to get out of bed.

The child stumbled backward, and I noticed for the

first time that he was crying. Several teardrops were frozen on his face, as if in a painting.

"Fanny," he said in a high, quavering voice. "W-where's Fanny?"

The air in the room grew suddenly, terribly cold, and then the child was gone.

Terrified, I fumbled for the light on the nightstand and clicked it on.

I was alone.

There was indeed a plate of food—fried chicken, mashed potatoes, string beans—sitting on my desk, a glass of reddish fruit punch beside it, but my door was shut, my window closed.

There wasn't another soul in sight.

IV

Debbie was even more beautiful than I remembered, more beautiful than the picture of her I kept on my bedroom dresser in Michigan, more beautiful than the every-boy's-cheerleader-fantasy-come-to-life of her high school days. The last three years had matured her, softened her, added a certain measure of peace to her smooth, lovely face.

Good Lord, how I had adored this girl as we'd grown up. And how I'd missed her since we'd been apart.

She wheeled her car into the driveway on Friday afternoon, leaped out, and ran toward me seconds after putting it in park.

"Peter! It's true! You did come home! Jesus Christ, it's good to see you!"

We met halfway between her car and the house, embracing while Dad waited on the porch and smiled.

"Put her in the barn, Deb," he told her, "next to Pete's little Ford.

I don't want you blocking the drive."

She rolled her eyes in mock disgust and tugged my arm. I clambered into the passenger's seat while she got in, gunned the engine, and headed into the barn.

"Like the wheels?" she said, grinning.

"Yeah, not too shabby. You didn't tell me you'd bought—"

"Actually, it belongs to my roommate, but she's taking classes this summer and working on campus, so she said I could use it. Pretty damn neat, huh?"

I laughed, thinking that look of peace had been a thin illusion. She was still the same—the frantic enthusiasm was still there, undampened.

She pulled in beside my Escort and shut it off. Then she turned to me and shook her head sadly. I knew what she was saying. It had been far too long.

"So," she said after a moment. "How are you, big brother?"

I shrugged. "I've been better. You, on the other hand, look fabulous. Looks like Champaign agrees with you."

"Yeah, I've always had a taste for the bubbly stuff."

"I meant the town, pea brain, and you know it."

They were silly jokes, but we dissolved in laughter.

That night, we sat next to each other at dinner and relived enough old times to bore even Grandma. After that, we sat on the porch as we had on the night of my own homecoming. This time, with the whole family there (the *real* family, as Mom had called it), I felt secure enough to bring up the subject that had been bothering me for two full days.

When the talk and laughter had dwindled, I took a deep breath and said, "Hey, Dad, who bought the old Purliss place, anyway?"

He gave me a strange look. "The Purliss Farm? Whaddya mean?"

I was referring to our nearest neighbors, almost a mile down the road, and I said so.

"I don't know what you mean, Pete. The Purlisses ain't even had it up for sale."

"You mean old man Purliss still—"

"And old *Missus* Purliss," my grandmother said. "The bitch."

"You mean they still live there?" I found it hard to believe. The Purlisses had seemed old when I was a kid, ancient by the time I'd left home.

"Sure do," Dad said. "He still raises his smelly chickens, and she still chucks rocks at any kid who rides by on a bike. Why?"

"Oh . . . no reason." I grinned sheepishly. "I . . . I was just wondering if there were any new kids in the neighborhood. I've seen a few around the farm the last couple of days."

My father's eyes narrowed. He leaned over the arm of his chair so that his face was just inches away from mine. "Kids? Around the farm?"

Very sorry now that I'd brought it up, I tried to wave it away. "Probably just kids from across the highway, playing around in the north pasture."

"There haven't been any children here since you and Debbie went off to school. And since the Berrand boy joined the Air Force." This came from my mother. "Are you sure?"

"I thought so," I said with a laugh that I hoped sounded casual. "Guess I was seeing things, huh?"

Nobody else was laughing. "Seeing things," Dad repeated thoughtfully. "Maybe. But I'll keep my eyes open. Maybe the Arlettes have their grandkids for the summer. Helen always says she wants them to visit."

I shifted uneasily. Part of it was because of the way I'd just made myself look foolish, but a much larger part of my unease came from remembering the voice in the storm, the cool touch on my forehead and neck, the tortured face with the frozen teardrops highlighted on bone-china cheeks. Luckily, Debbie noticed my discomfort and came to the rescue, asking in the snidest possible tone if I'd seen the way the Illini had clobbered the Badgers in football the year before.

When the rest of the family had gone to bed, I lingered on the porch, staring through the screens at the yard. The house was dark and quiet. I almost screamed when Debbie came up behind me and touched my shoulder.

"You okay, kid?"

I tried to smile. "Who're you calling kid, kid?"

"Seriously. Are you all right?"

"I'm fine. Sure."

She came around and perched on the arm of my chair. We were silent for a long time; the only sounds were the chirr of crickets outside, the muted tock of the antique wall clock in the entryway behind us.

"What's this about kids on the farm?" she said at last.

I sighed. "Nothing. Like Dad said, it's probably just

Helen Arlette's grandchildren. They can probably use the help with their farm, don't you think?"

She stared at me. Her lovely blue eyes seemed suddenly dark, almost frightening.

"It's something else, isn't it? You didn't tell us everything."

I opened my mouth to protest, but she cut me off.

"Dammit, Peter, tell me! What's wrong? What'd you see?"

A cool hand on my forehead . . . a child's tortured face, there and then gone . . .

"Peter . . . "

I smiled. "Me no see nothink, *señora*. Me just a poor peasant who—"

"Peter, please . . . what's wrong?"

Once more I sighed. "Look, Debbie, believe me. I didn't see anything. And if I did, I couldn't tell you right now. If you want to know the truth, I'm not convinced that what I saw wasn't just a bad dream."

She frowned. "I don't understand."

"I didn't have a very good rookie year. Of course, you know that already."

She nodded. "You wrote about some of it. And while we were making dinner, Mom mentioned that you were in a rotten mood when you got home the other day."

"Yeah. Well. I think the things I was talking about tonight might be the result of that. You know, I had every single illusion shattered. I'd always thought the city schools were the bad ones, the inner ghettos were the hot spots. I knew all about crime and threatened teachers. I knew about the dropouts and unteachables. I knew about lousy board politics. I just didn't expect to find that in a small town. I mean, my god, I wasn't there a week before some shop class degenerate pulled a hunting knife on me in lit class! He was actually going to stab me, I think. And this is in a school of four hundred and fifty in a town of twenty-five hundred! I saw almost as many unteachables there as in my student teaching in Chicago. And I couldn't seem to stay on the right side of that nepotistic joke they call a board of education. Let's just say that I had a lot of false hopes stolen and a lot of expectations ruined."

"And your dream?"

I shook my head. "Whatever it was, I think it was an after-effect of the last nine months. I . . . I really don't know. It was frightening, but it was also two days ago. If it was a dream, I think I finally got it out of my system."

She patted my hand. It was a contrived, motherly gesture that nevertheless comforted me a bit. "Whatever you say. But don't forget that pact we made when we were kids, you, me, and Steve. You want to talk, you talk. You got a problem, I'm there to listen. Got it?"

I smiled and kissed her on the cheek. "Thanks, Deb. Really. But I think I'm okay now. I really do."

V

I woke up the next morning when a dog began barking outside my window. For a moment, lying there groggy and heavy-lidded, my mind not yet functioning, I had the uncanny sensation of being transported back in time. When I was ten, we'd owned four dogs: two collies, a springer spaniel, and a mutt. The last of them, the mutt, had died in my junior year of high school. My parents hadn't owned a dog since, and the kennel by the equipment sheds, like the grain rooms in the barn, was now used for storage.

The barking went on and on, and when I finally came to enough to realize that I wasn't ten anymore, it began to fade.

I scrambled out of bed and went to the window, yanking on the cord and sending the shade rattling up on its roller. The sun was very bright; it almost knocked me back, like a physical blow to the face. When I was able to focus, I saw it. Saw them.

A large dog was running across the yard, heading for the fifty acres of young corn. It was a huge beast, a Great Dane by the look of it, and the way it was frisking and frolicking, tossing its head and barking at the sky, seemed almost ridiculous for its size.

A dog, running away.

And at its heels, charging along pell-mell after it, trying mightily to keep up, was a small boy in coarse woolen overalls, white shirt, and old-fashioned, honest-to-god suspenders.

A dog, running away.

And at its heels, the little boy who'd awakened me from my nap on my second day home, touching me with an icy hand, crying as though he'd just lost the best friend he'd ever had.

A boy and his dog, a dog and his boy, running away.

I turned from the window, burying my face in my hands and telling myself it was another stupid dream, another nightmare brought on somehow—

inexplicably—by the experiences I'd had in my first year teaching.

It was getting harder all the time to believe that.

***

"I can't figure it, Reuben," David Falkner was saying to my father as I entered the kitchen. "I checked everything."

"Did you—"

"Every frigging thing, Reuben. The carb's fine, the filters're clean, the fuel line's wide open, the pump's dandy-great."

My father shook his head. "And she's still not getting gas?"

"Not enough. She starts up, runs a second or two, and chokes out. I mean, shit, we ground the heads and changed the rings. She's got brand new plugs. What's wrong?"

"I don't know, Dave. Tell you what. I'll be out in a minute to look at her. If we still can't get it running, I'll call Mike Hoff over to the dealership. Maybe he could take a look."

Falkner, cheery as always, growled something profane and stomped out of the house.

I crossed the kitchen and poured a cup of coffee. "Problems, Dad?"

"Your father needs a new tractor," Grandma said from her place at the table.

"Can it, Eva. I *don't* need a new tractor."

"Is something wrong with the Deere?" I asked.

He nodded. "We just finished a two-week rebuild on her, and she won't run. Even before the rebuild, we could keep the engine going." He sighed, fingering the buttons on his denim shirt. "Dave Falkner's one of the best damn mechanics in Washington County. I just don't understand it."

"Your father needs—"

"Eva!"

My grandmother only laughed at the edge in his voice.

"I don't need a new tractor. What I need is this one running before we cut the north pasture next week."

He paused and looked at me closely, as though really realizing for the first time I was there.

"You slept in," he said. "Breakfast's been over for an hour. Your mom and sister drove into Milwaukee for the day."

"I was up. I was just . . . just sitting in my room. Thinking."

He mumbled something, already distracted again by the problem of the John Deere. A moment later he'd left the house, and I was left to scrounge my meal in the company of my mother's mother.

I thought briefly of asking her about local children but decided against it. She'd been there the night before when I'd brought it up and hadn't volunteered anything then. I ate my toast and cold cereal as quickly as I could and went outside.

Heading for the north pasture, I decided that I had to get some kind of fix on this thing. Whatever you wanted to call it—waking dream, hallucination, mental effects of a bad year, *whatever*—it was just crazy enough to be frightening.

After that first night, it had been a vague kind of fright, disjointed, detached. The kind of fright you feel watching the nightly news and seeing a disturbing thirty-second film clip from a distant country.

Bothersome. Soon forgotten. The chill I'd gotten watching the funnel cloud had been much worse than the chill of the sad little voice, the falling tree.

The next day had been worse. Being awakened by the hand on my forehead and seeing that face, hearing that voice—*Fanny. W-where's Fanny?*—had brought an emotional kind of fear, as though I had, for just a quick moment, been cursed with the ability to look into my own grave. I'd seen something impossible, been touched by someone who couldn't be there. Was that, then, a fear of the unknown? A fear of *ghosts?* I wasn't sure, but it had pressed on my heart in a way I'd never experienced before.

Now this morning—the dog and the boy. What kind of fear had I felt then?

I thought I knew.

It was the fear of the unknown again, yes. Fear of something that really couldn't be. But more significantly, it was fear for my own mind.

I was seeing things. Somehow, in some way. Creating pictures, inventing scenes.

The fear I felt realizing that was the fear of a slipping grip. It was the fear of a crumbling foothold.

Say it! I had to tell myself.

It was, simply, fear of insanity.

***

Ten minutes later, kneeling at the base of the fallen tree, I temporarily forgot about fear and hallucinations and shaky footholds on reality. I was struck by something I think few twenty-five-year olds ever are: pure, childlike wonder.

The box elder that had gone over in the storm had literally been ripped from the earth. Its root system stretched toward the sky like the arms of thirty or forty religious supplicants. Large, gnarled, trunklike roots went off in every direction, narrowing to spidery, dirt-clotted capillaries that stirred gently in the morning breeze.

The ground around the tree was littered with wood chips and pieces of bark ranging from tiny to huge. Broken branches were laying as far as ten feet away, their leaves still green.

Most amazing of all was the crater.

Where the tree had been rooted was a gaping hole in the landscape, three feet deep at least, more than three feet across. The inside was littered with more wood chips and shreds of root that had been left behind. The earth was gravelly—no fine topsoil here—and only a few slugs and earthworms moved through it.

It was the crater that put me in awe. Like the unleashed power of the funnel cloud, it left me a bit weak-kneed. To think of a wind powerful enough to not only crack a tree this size, or to split and topple it, but to actually seize it and *rip* it whole from the earth . . .

God was angry, a part of my mind whispered.

And you were there to see it, another part whispered back.

Once again, I felt the tremor I'd felt that night, the tremor that'd been caused only in part by the passing tornado, the vibration of the ground beneath my feet.

And then the sun caught something small and bright inside the crater, sending a finger of light right at me. I squinted and bent over, scrabbling in the stony soil until my fingers closed on a tiny, metal object. I tugged, coming away with a small, scarred medallion.

Its tarnished fine-link chain came after it, slithering out of the ground like a snake.

I held the medallion up, brushing away a few loose particles, tilting it this way and that, looking at it.

It was the size of a half-dollar. Etched on its surface was the profile of an animal—a lamb, most likely—and below it were the words THE LORD IS MY SHEPHERD. Actually, a good-sized nick had taken away the last half of the word SHEPHERD, but the meaning was clear enough. I turned it over.

The back was rough and had but one word engraved on it: the name JASON.

A religious medallion, given as a gift, perhaps, for Christmas or baptism or confirmation. I had no way of knowing how old it was, nor did I want to hazard a guess. It was in awfully good shape, considering where it had been. There were the few small nicks, the larger flaw that blotted the word shepherd, and now I noticed that the chain that had once held it around Jason's neck was broken. Still, considering the fact that it had been buried here for God knew how long, it was close to mint.

I stood and slipped it into the back pocket of my jeans, then knelt and rummaged in the dirt again. Perhaps I would find something else buried here, something lost by someone long ago that would give a clue to the medallion's age or Jason's identity. I didn't find anything yet still found the work absorbing—an indication, I suppose, that something Stephen had always said to me was true: small things amuse small minds.

Over the next twenty or thirty minutes, I worked my way around the edge of the crater, manually turning the earth in search of history. I'd already decided to make a complete circuit of the rim before stepping down inside the hole, and was close to finishing with the perimeter when the scream shattered the air like a rifle shot.

"*Siegfried! No!*"

I spun around, almost losing my balance and toppling into the pit.

"*SIEGFRIEEEEEEEEEED!*"

In that instant I felt a panic I'd felt only once before, when that student in my lovable small-town school had pulled his deer-gutting knife on me, had pushed me to the wall next to the chalkboard and held the blade to my chest.

The dog I'd seen that morning frolicking in the yard was no more than thirty feet away across the north pasture, and he wasn't frolicking anymore. Not by any stretch of the imagination. That massive beast was charging straight at me, hackles raised, teeth bared in a terrifyingly vivid snarl. The boy was at its heels, trying to call the dog back, trying to stop it before it could kill me, but right then, there seemed to be little doubt about who would reach me first. That dog was so much quicker, more powerful than the boy.

"Siegfried! Stop now! *Noooooo!*"

There was nowhere I could run, trapped as I was at the edge of the pit alongside the treeline and the barbed wire fence, so I did the only thing I could. I raised my hands to ward the animal off, a foolishly weak gesture that, to an outsider, might have seemed comical if the situation hadn't been so deadly. I think I cried the word "no" myself, but I'm not sure if I said it or only wanted to say it. The dog was less than fifteen feet away now, and its pace had not slowed.

And then the impossible happened. The young boy leaped forward and snagged his dog around the neck, catching fur and flesh and hanging on, screaming at the beast to stop, to leave me alone. The animal's momentum carried it forward a few more feet before it came to a reluctant stop five feet from where I stood. With its owner still clinging to its neck, it planted its forefeet in a combative stance and growled at me, a low, eerie sound that came from deep in the back of its throat.

"Bad Siegfried!" the boy scolded. "Bad, bad dog. Bad boy."

The dog didn't seem chastened in the least, but it did stop growling and relaxed its position a little. After a long, silent moment, the boy released his grip. The threat appeared to be over.

The boy hurried to my side, looking up at me with wide, frightened eyes. And yes, it was the boy who couldn't exist, the boy who'd awakened me with a cool touch, the boy who'd frolicked across the yard that very morning. It was the phantom boy, the ghost boy.

"You all right, mister? You all right?"

I spoke without thinking. "Yes. I'm okay, Jason. Thank you."

At the sound of his master's name, Siegfried uttered a short growl but made no menacing moves.

"You know my name," Jason said. "How do ya know my name, mister?"

I reached into my pocket and pulled out the medallion. I held it out to him, and he opened his small, pale hand to take it from me. He turned it over

161

and over, staring at it without saying a word. Over and over, like a magician practicing a trick.

"That is yours, isn't it, son?"

"Yes, mister. Yessir, it is. You found my medal. Lord-golly, you really found my medal! Where?"

I made a vague gesture at the pit behind me, and then, aware that this was a kind of magical moment, an impossible conversation that could end abruptly at any instant, I said, "Son . . . who are you?"

The boy frowned, gripping his medallion tightly and holding it to his chest.

"I'm not going to hurt you, boy. Who are you?"

"Jason Widder," he said in a small, weak voice.

"And who's Fanny? Is Fanny your sister?"

Clearly, I'd said the wrong thing. The boy's expression changed in a flash from one of shy interest to one of hot panic. He leaped forward, letting the medallion fall to the ground, grabbing onto the front of my shirt.

"Where's Fanny? You've seen her? Where is she? Where is—"

"Whoa, Jason, hang on." I extricated myself from his grip, stepping aside. Siegfried growled again but remained where he was. "I haven't seen Fanny. I just want to know who she is. Is she your sister?"

He stared at me for a long moment, and I could almost see the wheels rapidly turning inside that small blond head. He was debating whether or not to believe me, whether or not to trust me with any information beyond his name. I stared back at him, trying to make my expression both firm and kind. I tried not to let the fact that I was standing in the north pasture holding a conversation with a ghost—for surely that's what was

162

happening—enter my thinking at all. I was very afraid of what I'd do if I thought about that too much. I was scared that if I allowed myself to admit that I was speaking to a phantom, I might run screaming into the field.

"She's my sister," Jason said at last. "But I haven't seen her in . . . in a long time. I'm scared, mister. I think my papa might've gotten her."

Puzzled, I said, "Your father? Is he around?"

"Course he is! And he wants to hurt Fanny and me." He stepped closer again and dropped his voice to a husky whisper. "He tried to kill us, both of us."

"But, son . . . Jason . . . aren't you . . . oh, Jesus . . . aren't you already dead? Aren't you already—"

I stopped in mid-sentence because the boy's expression had changed yet again. I knew right away that by asking him that question I had ruined the magical moment myself. It was going to end very soon, and something about my words had ended it. The boy and the dog began to flicker in front of me like an image on a piece of extremely bad film. Frightened, not ready to let go, I reached out and tried to hang onto him, but he was fading, fading oh so fast, and my hand closed on an insubstantial form, closed on nothing but air.

"Jason, no! Stay here, son, I'm sorry! I'm sorry, Jason, but don't—"

Again I stopped. It was too late. I was alone in the field, hard against the edge of the gaping crater, with nothing to show for the incredible thing that'd just taken place. I had no boy and no dog, no answers to my hundreds—thousands—of questions. Nothing. Even the medallion was gone.

"Jason, please come back," I said without much hope. My only answer was the rumble of traffic on the highway a half-mile away.

"Jason?" I said again, loudly. "Please?"

A gentle breeze stirred my hair, and I could feel my heart breaking when after five minutes no one had come to join me in the field.

VI

Mom and Debbie didn't get back from the city until just before suppertime, and by the time they did I'd had plenty of opportunity to think about what had happened to me at the back of the north pasture that morning.

I believed it all by then. Quite frankly, it didn't seem like I had any choice. First of all, I didn't know a lot about psychology—one of my worst courses in college—or the various manifestations of unstable, failing minds, so I had nothing to do but resort to that old line—I know what I saw, therefore it had to be true.

With that simple realization came a sort of peace. At least I no longer felt the fear I'd felt before. Whether or not I should be scared that there were ghosts haunting my parents' property—haunting *me*—I didn't know, but they seemed harmless enough, almost powerless in a way. Good lord, Jason didn't even seem to know what he was. It was as if he didn't understand that he was dead, that the world was different now than when he'd been alive. He was still looking for a sister who'd been dead for maybe one hundred years, running from a father gone nearly as long.

GETTING BACK

So I was no longer worried for my sanity or safety, at least at that moment. But I was still troubled, this time by the horrendous sense of loss I'd felt when the boy and his dog had vanished. I thought at the time that my heart had broken when they'd left me alone, and even later, that didn't seem far from the mark. And I couldn't say why. It might have been losing a chance to complete my "interview," which was, I had to admit, the opportunity of a lifetime. Yes, it might have been that, but I thought there was something else working at me too. Without understanding, I felt an even greater opportunity had vanished along with Jason and Siegfried. Without knowing what or why or how, I sensed that some mighty chance had been just millimeters away from my fingertips, a chance that had evaporated like the morning mist that lay over the farm before sunrise each day.

After dinner, Debbie and I left the family on the porch and took a walk around the property, skirting the barn and going out to the head of the driveway, along the road. We sat on the remains of the fallen tree where Steve and I had once had our treehouse and talked a lot about a lot of things. I wanted desperately to tell her what had happened that morning but couldn't. Maybe it was because I didn't have the vocabulary to describe what was happening to me. Or maybe it was because I was just too damn confused to risk embarrassing myself in front of my younger sister, the girl I'd spent my entire life idolizing.

"You still seem kinda tired," she said at one point, "worn out.

Did you have those . . . *dreams* . . . again last night?"

I forced a phony smile, at the same time feeling awful about lying to her. "No dreams," I said. "I slept like a baby."

That wasn't precisely a lie, but I knew that sleep wasn't the issue and that my answer was only artful sidestepping.

She reminded me again that she was a good listener, invoking the childhood pact between us and our dead brother, and so she wouldn't feel mistrusted or neglected, I talked to her. But not about Jason. Instead, I dredged out all the tales of my rookie year as a teacher, giving her the chance she craved to feel motherly, to provide aid and comfort.

It was much later on, when I went to bed, that I came to understand what was still bothering me about that morning. Like something biblical, the answers showed up in a dream.

***

"Hey, Peter, you c'mon outta there right now!" Stephen said to me. "You c'mon out, and we'll talk, man to man! Just me and my big brother!"

I was hiding in a familiar place, behind the mountain of bales in the lower barn, wedged between scratchy hay and baling wire and cold stone walls. Stephen knew I was there because I'd always been there as a kid. It was that lack of originality that made me "it" a lot in our three-way games of hide-and-seek.

"C'mon, Peter, I know where you are, so just show yourself. Let's have a little talk, just the two of us, whaddya say?"

Slowly, I stood up and came around the edge of the hay, flashing a sheepish grin.

"You always knew where I hid, dammit. Always."
Stephen grinned.

He looked the way I wanted him to look, the way
I've always chosen to remember him. Younger than
me, he'd nevertheless been taller, with a more
muscular, athletic build. More handsome too. Not a
sixteen-year-old Adonis, exactly; that would be an
exaggeration. But it wouldn't be untruthful to say that
he'd had more success with girls before his death than
I've had at my age.

"Yeah, I always knew," he said now. "Just like I
always knew what was on your mind. I could tell you
right now what you're thinking."

"Oh? What am I thinking?"

"You're thinking how good I look for someone
who's been dead so long." He laughed. "You were
worried that when you came out from your spot there,
I'd be all bloody and banged up, like if the Allis had
just rolled over on me. You thought it'd be closed-
casket time all over again."

Wincing, I said, "You're right. You always could tell
what I was thinking."

His lips stretched back in a long, sly grin. "I know
what else you're thinking, Peter. You're thinking about
that little kid, Jason, the one with the dog." Another
laugh. "Siegfried . . . a Nazi dog or something. I'm
right, aren't I? You're thinking about the kid with the
Nazi dog."

I nodded, aware for the first time that this had to
be a dream. Usually, discovering a dream in its middle
is a fun experience—it means you're okay, safe, free to
do anything you damn well want. Somehow, it wasn't
like that this time. I knew I was in my bed, that

Stephen and I weren't standing in the lower barn. I knew that everything was a product of my sleeping subconscious, and yet it was still a humbling, awesome experience. I was so glad to see my dead brother that I wanted to throw my arms around him and hug him close, but I couldn't. God help me, but I was afraid. Of him, of myself, of the discovery I felt barreling at me from just around some mental corner.

"Yeah," Stephen said then. "Jason. He died a long time ago, you know."

"I know. But he doesn't know he's dead. At least . . . at least I don't think so. Talking to him was strange. It—"

"Hey, Peter, I was there," Stephen told me. "I saw the whole thing. You had a million questions to ask him."

I wanted to deny it, absurdly embarrassed that my brother, the ghost, had seen me talking to another ghost. But of course, I couldn't deny a thing.

"You wanted to ask him how he died. And about that sister of his, Fanny, or whatever her name is. You wanted to ask about his father. You wanted to know what it's like over here on this side, and you wanted to know about me. You were older than me, yeah, but not a helluva lot smarter. I could always figure out what was really on your mind. You wanted to know if the kid'd seen me. You thought if *he* could come back, maybe I could too."

And that was really the end of the dream, for although I know it went on some time longer, that surreal conversation stretching out for several more minutes through Stephen's questions, Stephen's observations, and my meek acknowledgements, the important part of it passed right then.

GETTING BACK

He was right. That was why the conversation in the north pasture had seemed so important and why I'd been heartbroken when it had ended. Jason was my key to the mystery of Stephen's death. My brother had died young, and so had Jason. Jason came and went from the other side, and so might my brother.

I awoke in the dark, sharp and alert from the moment my eyes opened. A thin ribbon of sweat was trickling past my right eye. I swept it away and climbed out of bed, getting dressed without turning on the light. It was several moments before I realized I was talking to myself in a husky whisper as I zipped my jeans and tied my sneakers.

"That's it," I was saying over and over. "Go find Jason. Drag him over to this side. That's it. Get the answers. Yeah. That's it. Get the answers."

I shut my mouth as soon as I heard what I was saying.

The house was lit by moonlight coming through the windows as I made my way down the steps, through the kitchen, and outside. My mind was spinning out of control. The dream had made me think about a lot of things—Stephen for one, my mother's cancer for another, and there were more—each of which was rushing at me now, all in a jumble, demanding to be considered and debated, pushing to have their say.

I stopped at the edge of the gravel, where the front lawn of the farmhouse met the driveway. The moon was even brighter out here, lighting the barn like a floodlight; the shadow cast by the huge building looked distorted, monstrous. I swallowed and took a long, slow breath, exhaled, took another, and sighed. I wasn't completely in control, but obviously, the edgy, caffeine-like high I was on now was as relaxed as I was going to get.

Answers.

That seemed like the single most important word in the universe as I crossed the lawn heading for the north pasture.

VII

Standing at the bottom of the box elder crater for the first time, I realized it was even bigger than I'd thought. When I tried to look over the rim, I had to crane my head back and up before I could see the bases of the other trees, the barbed-wire fence they masked. I couldn't see the passing headlights on the highway at all.

My walk through the timothy had done a little bit to sober me up, and now, twenty minutes after getting out of bed, I was reaching a point of some rationality. That is, I was beginning to wonder what I was doing there.

It was two o' clock in the morning, and I was alone at the edge of my father's property, ready to conjure up the ghost of a little boy who'd been killed by his father a long, long time ago. Why? So that the little boy—who didn't even realize what he was, mind you— could point the way to the other side, could tell me, perhaps, how to bring my dead brother back, how to stop my mother's cancer before it killed her, or maybe how to turn back the clock to a time when a swelling tumor and a tractor rollover were unheard of, could possibly be averted.

Magic, I thought. That's what I'm after. Simple magic. Impossible magic.

I sighed again and thought of something a teacher had said to me just before Christmas of the last year. He was a twelve-year veteran of the school that was killing me, and he'd taken me aside in the faculty lounge, smiling and saying, "I know what your problem is, Manse. You had your head in the clouds. Small town, north woods, rural consolidated school. You were thinking heaven and roses. Shit, Peter, nothing's heaven and roses. But put your feet on the ground and you'll see it's not that bad. Look at it a little realistically and you might get to like it. But for God's sake, stop dreaming."

Hearing those words in my mind, I wondered if that's what I was doing now—looking for roses again, heaven and roses. I wondered if my head was back in the clouds.

"Jason?"

The name escaped my lips before I even knew I was preparing to say it. It startled me, and I broke out in gooseflesh.

"Jason? Jason Widder?"

A truck rumbled by on the highway. When that intrusion passed, I heard footsteps coming toward me in the dark. No longer afraid of ghosts, as I had been when that cool touch had awakened me in the dark, I was nonetheless afraid of deeper things. The soft approaching footsteps made my breath catch in my throat. I felt a band of cold pressure seal itself around my heart and begin to tighten.

"Jason? I'm here, Jason, where I found your medallion."

171

The footsteps came closer, moving like a whisper through the timothy. Soft . . . like a stealthy animal . . . soft . . . like a spirit moving before a gentle breeze.

"I'm here, Jason," I said. My voice had dropped to a rough whisper.

The footsteps paused, moved forward again, then stopped entirely. I was opening my mouth to speak the boy's name once more, but what came out instead was a scream—the sound of shock and pent-up frustration—when Debbie spoke to me.

"Who the hell're you talking to, Peter? Who's Jason? And what're you doing out here in the middle of the night?"

VIII

She had followed me easily, hearing me on the stairs and dogging my path like a spy as I crossed the yard and the pasture. Embarrassed, I allowed myself to be led back to the house but refused to go in. We sat instead on the porch steps, our backs to the screen door, our knees touching, the only sounds for a very long time the constant chirr of crickets and the distant barking of the Arlettes' dog more than a mile down the road.

Finally: "Another bad dream, big brother?"

I laughed. It was so like her, going for even a small laugh in the face of what, to her, must have seemed an insanity.

"Actually, it wasn't all that bad. I dreamed about Steve this time."

Even in the dark, I could feel her gaze sharpen. "What about Steve?"

"I dreamed . . . no, I *found* a way to change everything. To bring Stephen back. To maybe get rid of Mom's cancer. I don't know . . . but I think I found a way to make everything better again. To give me another chance at the decision. You know. To let me take over the farm, work with Dad, anyway, until he'd be ready to turn it over to Steve and me."

I stopped the rush of words as abruptly as I'd started them, felt my skin go hot and crimson. None of that was true—it was nothing but fantasy—and it was certainly nothing to be telling Debbie, whom I'd always loved and admired, whose admiration I'd craved in return.

Savagely, I wondered what was happening to me. Talking to spirits, running into pastures in the middle of the night, fantasizing things that could never be. And worse, talking about all of it.

Debbie was still giving me that hard stare. I didn't respond, pretending to be interested in the worn spots on the knees of my jeans.

"Peter?"

I still didn't answer. Jesus, I'd said enough already.

"Peter, what's wrong? Good lord, was the teaching really *that*

bad? What did they do to you in that hick town?"

This time, I responded, but it was just a mumbled word: "Nothing."

"Are you serious about staying here, on the farm? My god, don't you remember how we worked? Don't you remember how important school became to us after the accident? How it was the only way out? And we got out! Both of us! This is supposed to be our last summer here . . . I didn't tell them yet, but it is. Next summer, I'm going east with a friend, going to take classes at an art school near Cape Cod, a workshop thing. And by next year, you should be really settled . . . somewhere.

"Peter . . . look at me . . . tell me you're not seriously thinking about staying on the farm."

I turned to face her for the first time since my outburst. I felt another one coming on but managed to keep it simple.

"Debbie, this farm is haunted. There are ghosts here."

Her mouth opened, working soundlessly for a moment. Then, she began to cry. "Oh, Peter, dammit!"

She got up and fled into the house, the screen door slamming behind her, loud enough to wake the dead.

I stayed on the steps for a while, looking out across the moonstruck yard, seeing Stephen, Jason, and Siegfried in every shadow. There was my brother, leaning against the open barn doors, grinning at me, his teeth dazzling, his posture casual. There was the dead boy, with his dog, near the base of the silo, crouched and watching, as though wanting to approach but not wanting me to ruin everything again by telling him he was dead.

Close to dawn, I went inside and back to my room, pausing long enough outside my parents' bedroom to look in and see them in their twin beds. I felt a tear roll down my cheek as I stared at my mother's curled and sleeping form.

Dammit.

I'd ruined it for Jason. I'd ruined it for Debbie. My own mind was a tempest. Yet I hadn't meant any harm. I just wanted to make it all better. A simple thing. I just wanted everything to be fine, the way it had been a long time ago.

IX

I heard them talking about me as I came down for breakfast later that morning. I heard my mother protesting something Debbie had just said, heard my father grunt in surprise, heard Debbie rush on, mentioning something about professional help, a doctor. I paused only long enough to hear that before making my entrance.

I knew I looked a wreck—fifteen minutes in the shower and ten in front of the bathroom mirror had done nothing to erase the effects of the night. My eyes were narrowed and bloodshot, my cheeks surprisingly sunken. Combing my hair had been a worthless endeavor since it was as dry as straw, flying away in several directions at once.

"G'morning."

My father grunted again as I came around the corner. Debbie let out a small cry. My grandmother muttered, "Shit." Only my mother remained calm and tried to act normal, although I could tell by the way she was looking at me that Debbie had told them everything I'd said and done in the middle of the night.

"I hear we lost a tree out at the property line," Dad said then, confirming what I'd suspected. "I guess it went down in that storm."

"I guess so," I said. And then: "Deb? I really need to talk to you. Will you take a walk with me?"

What came next frightened me more than anything

else that had happened—more than the storm or the voice in the night, more than the cool touch on my cheek or the vicious charge of the phantom dog. What happened was that Debbie didn't answer me right away. Instead, she looked at Mom and Dad, at my grandmother, with a pleading expression in her eyes, a look that said plainly: "Get me out of this. I don't want to be near Peter because he's crazy."

My sister. My own little sister.

Nothing, even the dim and oh-so-distant possibility of recapturing the past, was worth that.

"Please, Deb? Give me a half hour, will you? I don't think that's asking much."

She flashed me a very forced smile and said, "All right, but only a half hour. Mom and I are going shopping again this morning."

"Debbie—" my mother said, but was cut off as my sister repeated, "Mom and I are going shopping again this morning."

The firmness in her voice as she restated the lie made me want to weep.

***

The talk didn't do any good. I tried, but in the end it was worthless.

I took her out to the box elder crater, where she'd found me in the night, and told the entire story. At one point, I had to reach out, grasp her wrist to keep her from hurrying away. She listened to the rest, shaking her head sadly throughout, and when I tried to get Jason to appear to us, she backed away several steps, watching with horrified fascination, certain, I'm sure, that the last of her brother's sanity had fled.

Jason didn't appear. Wouldn't appear. Not even

the damned dog would show up. At last, Debbie said she'd seen enough and returned to the house, leaving me sitting on the edge of the hole with my head in my hands.

He was my own personal spirit, I supposed. I didn't know why, but for some reason he had appeared to me and me alone, and now he would be with me for the rest of my life.

I looked up, knowing what I'd see.

Jason and Siegfried were standing just a few feet away, looking at me with concern.

"What's wrong, mister? You hurt?"

I nodded.

"You need help? I'd get my ma, but I can't find her. Still, you gave my medal back and all, so if I can help you, you just say the word."

I tried to tell him to leave. That's what I very badly wanted to say to him—*Go away, dammit, just go away, you're dead*—but the words that came out when I spoke were much different.

"Who are you, Jason? Tell me about yourself."

He looked surprised. I had to prompt him again for the story, which was finally told. He started speaking slowly, cautiously, but gradually gained confidence and speed. I don't believe it took more than ten minutes to hear about his life.

He was eight years old, he told me, and lived nearby (here he motioned with a small hand to the subdivision across the highway, which had been privately-owned farmland when I was a child). His mama and papa worked nearly twenty acres, grew a great deal of corn and oats, raised chickens and pigs. They had one cow and one horse. The pride of the farm was a new four-row plow that had been purchased recently.

His papa, it seemed, was a man taken with the holy word of God. It was he who'd given Jason the medallion, had given a smaller but similar one to Jason's sister Fanny. He was a strong man, a good man, but unfortunately was taken with drink almost as much as he was with the power of the Scriptures. With his drinking bouts came episodes of surliness, which served only to warn the family that an outbreak of horrible violence was soon to follow. Jason's papa had, in the past, broken some of his mother's fine china; he had smashed a kitchen chair against a doorframe; he had beaten the cow and kicked the chickens and attacked the pigs with a pitchfork. On several occasions, he had physically beaten Jason and Fanny, once so badly that Jason had needed a rushed trip to Dr. Grumbacher, who lived more than five miles away.

His mama—"the best person in the world"—tried to control these episodes and more often than not received a few licks of her own as compensation. In the end, the only good she could ever do was to help the children *after* their beatings by holding and hugging them, by crooning lullabies while they fell asleep in the single bed they shared in the loft.

One day—Jason couldn't remember how long ago now—his papa had been even more taken with the drink than usual. It had been a very, very long time between bouts, and the children had allowed themselves to believe the drinking might be over for good, that their papa's promises to cure himself had finally come true. But now, he realized that the time between episodes hadn't meant anything at all, in fact had only served to make the next attack worse.

On that final day, Jason's papa actually killed the horse and several of the chickens. Then he came after Jason with anything and everything he could find: a shovel, a hand rake, the awful pitchfork, his own belt and boots. Jason remembered being battered very badly, remembered Siegfried trying to come to his defense but being beaten back, and after that he became confused. He recalled fainting and then waking up in a world where everything was different—"It smells different, sounds different . . . it *feels* different"—and where he couldn't find his way home.

He had been wandering the area for an indeterminate time, often through a fog that he described as "a dreadful mist" and often in total darkness "even in the heat of noon," trying to find his way back across the wide road to home, trying to locate his mama so that she could help soothe him as always, and trying to find his beloved sister Fanny, who, he feared, might have been hurt very badly in their papa's last fiery burst of drinking violence.

"But it's different," he repeated in conclusion. His voice was beginning to quaver. Siegfried hovered over him protectively. "I know where I am, mister, really. I know I live just over there. But I can't get there, try as I might! I can't find the house or the barn. I call for my mama and she doesn't come. And I can't find F-Fanny anywhere!"

Now the tears exploded from inside him, and I got up and moved to his side, cradling the little ghost boy in my arms, hugging his phantom but nevertheless very real body, stroking his dead but oh-so-tangible hair. I crooned words to him that I imagined his mama might croon, if they could somehow find each other in the darkness one hundred years after their deaths.

"I just wanna go home," he murmured against my shoulder.

"I know," I whispered in his ear as my own tears started to come. "Believe me, Jason, I know, I know."

X

They found me about twenty minutes later. My father. My mother. My grandmother. Debbie. I must have been a helluva sight to them, sitting there alone on the edge of the crater, crying, shivering, speaking to the dead.

They got me back to the house, where I promptly succumbed to what my doctor later called a batch illness. "Exhaustion," he told my parents, "and influenza and a bronchial infection that's damned near pneumonia." I was treated there in the farmhouse, had to stay on my back in my childhood room for almost two weeks. During that time, I was visited often, both by my doctor and by another doctor, who was introduced as a colleague doing a paper for a prestigious medical journal on the treatment of upper respiratory ailments. I didn't find out until much later that this second man was a psychiatrist.

When I recovered, Debbie and I went to Madison for a weekend together. I looked up old college buddies, showed Deb the places of what I referred to as my flaming youth, ate a lot of pizza, drank a fair amount of beer. We saw three movies, a bad rock concert by two local groups, and a summer stock version of *Charley's Aunt* featuring a fading soap opera star whose name I've forgotten. In short, we crammed more into two and a half days than I ever had before or have since.

When we went back to the farm, I began the letters and phone calls, the newspaper scouring and cashing-in of old debts that make up the search for a new teaching job.

* * *

All of that was nearly five years ago. In the time between then and now, my grandmother passed away quietly in her sleep. My mother went into remission a second time, finally relapsed, and died just before Christmas last year. My father, burdened like all farmers by rising costs and diminishing prices, sold the property after my mother's death and is living in a Florida condominium where he dabbles in rock collecting, photography, and god knows what else. He wrote to me recently and said that he is happy, though I wonder how a man born and raised on a farm, who made his living from the land for so long, can really be happy in the land of grapefruit and polyester. Debbie graduated from U of I and has a fine job teaching art at a private New England college. She has never given up her own painting and recently had a show at a Boston gallery. Unknown to her, I have clippings from the Boston papers, good reviews of her work. I keep those clippings on my desk, where I can look at them whenever I feel the need and think of her.

Myself, I'm living in northern California, teaching high school in a largish consolidated district and loving it most of the time. I have learned, as that veteran

Michigan teacher once counseled, not to set my sights so high. I no longer search for heaven and roses. Bad students exist, obviously, but so do many good ones, even a few great ones. For every industrial arts animal who sulks in the back of the room, there is a literature lover in the front row with his or her hand eagerly raised. No one has pulled a deer-gutting knife on me recently. I am active in board politics and currently am helping design a new curriculum package for the next school year.

***

In the last five years, I've dreamed of Steve only once. In the dream, I was sitting at my desk, grading essays on—what else?—*The Catcher in the Rye* and listening to Prokofiev on the stereo. I glanced up and saw him standing in the doorway, leaning against the frame, young and healthy as always, casually relaxed. He didn't speak. But he smiled at me. It wasn't his hell-raising rogue's smile but rather something more calm. A little more sedate. Wise. Almost beatific.

As though he approved.

***

I have a good life now. There really isn't a better way to describe it than that. It's not perfect, surely, but it's comfortable. On bad days I am able to look ahead, and on good days it's difficult to imagine that there was a time when I wanted something more, something so very much different.

But there are times when I awake in the middle of the night and imagine I hear a tractor chugging away in the distance or hear a screen door slamming and Steve's footsteps racing down the front walk or hear my mother whistling bad big band music as she bakes in the kitchen. I hear those things, and my eyes fill, and I wonder what if . . . what if I could have . . . if I could . . .

At those times, I also hear another sound, one that fills my heart and mind with a longing so intense that it's quite simply beyond words.

I hear the sound of a large dog barking as it races past the house, the sound of a lost young boy following behind, calling its German name over and over and over again.

I hear that and wonder if he, alone among all the creatures who ever walked the earth, has managed to find his way back.

FAITH AND HENRY GUSTAFSON

THE RAIN HAD stopped by the time they reached the Black Pike, a fact for which Henry Gustafson was very grateful. The Pike (known locally as "The Hellbender") was tricky enough to negotiate when dry. When it was muddy, as it was now from a three-day downpour, the drive became an exercise in nail-biting adventure. Toss in the extra inconveniences of darkness and rain drumming on the windshield, and Henry supposed it would be easier to pull over to the side of the road, get out, and walk.

"Whaddya think, Artie?" he said to his partner. "Call came from the old Bible camp. That's, what, maybe two-three miles more?"

Artie nodded silently, and Henry turned his attention back to the twists and turns, rises and falls, of the road. The butterflies were still congregating in his belly. The first couple had arrived as soon as the call had come in. More were dropping by all the time. Right now, they were having a nice little caucus. He figured that by the time he and Artie actually reached the old Singing Waters Bible Camp, his gut would be in the throes of a goddamned butterfly convention.

FAITH AND HENRY GUSTAFSON

He wanted to talk over the situation but knew it was useless. Artie would listen, but he wouldn't have much in the way of input. When you got right down to it, Artie was an awful lot like an old B-movie character carried out to the extreme. The tough, rugged, silent type. That was Artie to a T.

The call had come into the Kelly's Corners Police Station at 12:37 A.M. Henry had spent the next fifteen minutes trying to raise some assistance, all to no avail. The chief was vacationing downstate. Lizzy Halprin was still on maternity leave. Bill McInnis was out east somewhere, taking a two-week course in rural law enforcement. When Henry had tried calling across the lake to Patterson Falls, the phone had rung at least thirty times without an answer. He guessed old Harv Bennedict, who had been chief of police over there longer than God had been making planets, was home sleeping off some Old Grand-Dad. Or perhaps still out somewhere drinking it. That left the volunteer ambulance, which was supposedly on the way, maybe ten minutes behind, and the county sheriff's department, which was too far away to be much help but had told Henry to call again if he found he needed a back-up on the scene.

"Shitfire," Henry muttered, because it seemed like a good, practical thing to mutter under the circumstances. He could see the entrance to the Bible camp up ahead and what he thought was someone waving them down with a weak flashlight. He realized a moment later that it wasn't a flashlight at all, just the bouncing reflection of the Blazer's headlights glinting off the mailbox at the head of the driveway.

"Ready, pard?" he asked Artie as he swung into

the drive. The trees were very close here, the darkness thick. "Somebody's gotta be around," he said, mostly to himself. "I mean, someone placed the call, didn't they? Sure they did. I heard 'em. I *talked* to 'em."

He pulled up in front of the administration building, feeling the tires sink hopelessly in the mud as he came to a stop. In the old days, when Henry had been a kid and they had come out here three or four times a summer for Sunday School picnics, they had called this place the Lodge. He had a fairly clear memory of the inside—an enormous, open room with picture windows looking out on Conley Lake, a rough stone floor, a timber beam ceiling, the biggest fireplace he'd ever seen, before or since. On the keystone of the fireplace had been engraved *Fight the good fight of faith, lay hold on eternal life 2 Timothy 6:12,* and on the wall above had been a mounted moose head, an old, bedraggled, moth-eaten thing that the kids had predictably nicknamed Bullwinkle.

But that had been a long time ago. Henry wasn't a kid anymore, he had forgotten many of his Bible verses, and the only place you saw Bullwinkle was in reruns. The syndicate of Upper Peninsula churches that had operated Singing Waters had gone bust in the early seventies, and through some sort of court fiasco, the whole shebang had been taken over by a group of Chicago idiots who had wanted to run the place as a fishing resort. That had lasted approximately an hour and a half, and the camp had sat empty, decaying, for a long, long time. Until August, as a matter of fact, just a couple of months ago, when Henry had heard that some Detroit-area businessman's association had purchased it for use as an executive's weekend retreat. That was supposed to begin next summer.

He couldn't imagine who would be there now. It was almost Halloween, for Chrissakes. But *someone* was there. Workmen, maybe, fixing the place up. Someone, somebody. Because one somebody had called the station to report that another somebody was dead.

Pulling together a dash or two of false bravado, Henry said, "Let's get going, Artie m'man," and climbed out of the Blazer. His boots immediately sank into four inches of mud, but he had larger concerns on his mind, including finding the phone caller, finding the body, and wondering how far behind the goddamned ambulance was.

There was nobody in the Lodge. That became obvious as he tried the door and found it locked, walked past the windows and shined his flashlight through the glass, picking out nothing but lots of cobwebs and ancient furniture slumbering beneath filthy dust covers. At one point, thinking he saw some stealthy movement, the butterflies flapped madly and his heart leapt almost completely out of his chest. He calmed himself, steadied his light, and chuckled weakly.

"Of course there's mice," he whispered, watching two of the little buggers scurry out of sight. "Place's been empty for years. Shit, it's prob'ly a regular Disneyland for rodents in there."

Leaving the Lodge, they tramped through the mud, past two locked storage buildings and a shack with a sign identifying it as the PX, past the collapsed roof of what had once been a picnic shelter, past the huge open-air amphitheater where long-ago campers had burned bonfires and sung hymns to the double ring of cabins on the shore of the lake.

It would have been a lie to say the butterflies were gone completely, but Henry was nevertheless beginning to feel some hope. The longer they stayed and the more they searched without finding anyone, the greater the likelihood that the whole damn thing was a prank. It surely wouldn't be the first time. Even now, he could imagine some kids, or maybe a couple of drunks using the pay phone at Worthy's Rustic Tap or the Red Rooster, laughing their asses off at the thought of cops trekking miles and miles out into the woods to search for Prince Albert in a can.

The first cabin was a ruin. Like the picnic shelter, the roof here had given way under the weight of countless old snowfalls, leaving rubble surrounded by a shell of walls. The other cabins looked all right (at least at a quick glance and in near total darkness), though most had lost their doors and windows to time and storms and vandals. Inside each one stood the stark skeletons of bunk beds—six sets to a cabin—a table, four chairs, a row of rusty lockers, and a bulletin board on which two headlines had been painted: TODAY'S CHORES on the left, TODAY'S SCRIPTURE on the right.

They went west of the cabins to the large community bathhouse. A sign above the door read KYBO. *Keep Your Bowels Open,* Henry thought. *Jesus, that's a blast from the past if I ever heard one.* He poked the beam of his light through the open doorway, studied the empty toilet stalls and the shower heads that now served as the anchoring points for great swoops of cobwebs, and shrugged.

FAITH AND HENRY GUSTAFSON

His mood was improving rapidly, his step becoming lighter, his breath coming a little easier. Even Artie seemed happier. He didn't say anything, of course, but some of that perpetual tension seemed to have gone out of his broad shoulders and strong back.

The only things left to check were the old baseball diamond (it was now just a big overgrown field dotted with sapling trees) and the lakefront dead ahead of them. They were going to come out of this okay, Henry decided. He tried but couldn't even muster any resentment toward the kids or drunks who had done this to them. What the hell, a prank once in a while was good for the soul; it kept you on your toes.

Five minutes later, when they found the body outside the boathouse, he wished he could have held onto a few of those happy thoughts just a little longer.

"Could've saved the ambulance boys some sleep," he said when he found his voice. The last of the butterflies had been suddenly replaced by a cold leaden weight sitting three inches below the bottom of his rib cage. "This fella's past hope. What we need here's the medical examiner."

He swallowed a trickle of bile that had climbed into his throat and turned around to see what Artie thought. His mouth was open to actually ask the question—*Helluva mess, eh, pard?*—but he shut it with a snap when he saw that Artie was gone.

He sighed. That had been the way of things more and more often lately. He would get a call for a domestic or a B&E or a disturbing the peace or even a grisly smash-up out at the intersection of 41 and Kelly Road . . . he would get one of those and the butterflies would start and he would try to ignore the whispering

189

voice that told him he wasn't cut out to be a cop, he had never been cut out for it, and that he didn't have the nuts to handle whatever the trouble *du jour* might be . . . that would happen, and then Artie would be there, Artie his partner, his pard, his good buddy, and everything would be okay for a while.

There had been a time when Artie had stayed with him all the way through the calls, right up through the boring paperwork at the end. But for the last year or so, Artie had gotten him going and then split when things got hairy. It was almost as though he were saying, *I'll help you get your wheels under you, boyo, but the rest is up to you. You gotta have faith in yourself, trust yourself to pull through. You gotta learn how to handle the bad shit on your own.*

Bad shit, Henry thought. It seemed safe to say that was exactly what he had on his hands right now. He turned back to the corpse and tasted bile again. *Where the hell is that ambulance?* he wondered. He felt utterly, hopelessly alone and lonely. *Goddammit, Artie, I hate it when you run out on me.*

"The problem is," he murmured, "there's never an imaginary partner around when you need one."

The victim was male, a young and healthy guy judging from the build, but it was hard to be sure because the face was missing. There was nothing there but a pulpy mass of flayed tissue clinging to the skull, and even if there had been some slight hope of pinning down an age or even identifying the man, Henry just couldn't bring himself to examine things more closely.

It seemed his original guess had been right. The fella was some kind of workman or caretaker, probably hired by those Detroit bigwigs to start a few odds and ends repairs before the snow flew, setting the stage for the real work next spring, cleaning up, getting ready. Henry made this assessment by noting the man's dirty Joe Journeyman coveralls and muddy work boots, the tool belt he wore around his waist, the big hands toughened by rings of calluses.

He wondered briefly if the guy was local, someone from either the Corners or the Falls. Probably. It would've made sense to hire someone from the area to keep an eye on things. There were plenty of men around who did work like that for the summer folks and seasonal resorts. Shutter windows, drain pipes, shovel snow off roofs, things like that. Henry knew most of them personally. Some of them were big gents, like old Joe Journeyman here, but like the ravaged face, that was something he didn't want to dwell on very much.

He paced nervously away, down to the place where the weeds and grass of the camp property dropped off into a jumble of rocks along the shoreline. The large boathouse, whose roof had sagged dramatically in old age, was a black hulk to his left, Conley Lake an even darker patch spread out before him. It was like looking at . . . nothing . . . at nothingness. Only a faint, damp, fishy smell and the gentle lapping of water on stone confirmed that the lake was even there.

He knew there was a procedure to follow in situations like this. He racked his brain but couldn't begin to imagine what it would be. In his eight years on the Kelly's Corners force, he had seen a lot of fatalities—car, motorcycle, and snow machine wrecks mostly. Only three murders, all simple domestics that had crossed that invisible line and gotten irrevocably out of hand. In each of those three cases, George Remillet, the chief, had been there to handle things. Henry's own role had been more that of chief cook and bottle washer. Or more to the point, chief dork and body bagger. Perhaps if he'd taken George's advice and gone with Bill to that two-week course out east, he'd know what to do. Of course, if he'd done that, he wouldn't be here now and this whole mess would be somebody else's problem.

He hesitated, shifting his thoughts into neutral and raising his head. From somewhere behind him, from the direction of the Lodge and the driveway and the Black Pike, he heard a noise. His initial response—*Hot damn. Them ambulance boys were slow enough, weren't they?*—changed quickly into something else: *Not the ambulance. That ain't no body buggy. Footsteps. It's the fella who called the station.* And finally from that into a thought that nearly overwhelmed him with its dark simplicity and even darker implications.

There was a murder here, you ignorant jerk-off, a goddamned murder! Who do you think them footsteps belong to? The guy who called you? Maybe. But maybe it's Joe Journeyman's killer coming back to—

Henry swallowed and felt fear as sharp as glass sticking in his throat. There were procedures again, steps he should be taking. He groped through his mind, trying to latch onto things he had read, things George Remillet had lectured him on over the years, but all he could come up with was a simple phrase, one he'd used hundreds, maybe thousands of times, the one he used when he had a speeder pulled over out on

Kelly Road or Conley Lake Drive: "Good afternoon, sir. May I see your license, registration, and proof of insurance, please?"

He didn't think a killer would be impressed with an opening line like that.

Improvising, he dropped to his knees and fumbled his service revolver from its holster. The gun had always seemed big, clunky, and inconvenient to lug around before. Now it seemed impossibly small, even dainty. *I'm trapped down here,* he thought, *trapped with my back to the water like a bug on a wall.* He tried to stay calm and trust in himself, but that was too big an order to follow, and he thought, *God damn you to hell, Artie! Why can't you be real?*

The footsteps came steadily closer, moving between the cabins now, squishing through the mud, swishing through the weeds and witch grass. He heard another sound too, a high, thin, eerie whistle, lonely-sounding notes of a familiar-sounding song. It took him a moment to pull the memory of that song out from among the yammering terror that had seized control of his brain. *A hymn, an old hymn,* he thought. *We used to sing it a lot. Jesus . . . that was it . . . Jesus Something.*

The answer came to him in a ghostly mental chorus of children's voices

Jesus Savior, pilot meeeeeee over liiiiiiiifffe's tempestuous seeeeeeaaa

and he remembered, dammit, he really remembered it.

It wasn't the camp theme song—that had been "Hail to Thee, O Singing Waters" or some hogwash like that—but every time they had come out here from town, scruffy local kids mingling with the more well-to-do (and infinitely snottier) campers who came from all over the Midwest, the camp administrator, Reverend Somebody, Reverend Douglas, Reverend Davis, Reverend Dufus, had led them in a chorus of "Jesus Savior, Pilot Me" before the barbecue or the softball game or whatever it was they were there for.

Henry remembered that now as he listened to that slow, sad whistle. It was a pretty sound in a way, almost uncannily on key, but listening to it getting closer and closer sent a scurrying chill from the back of his neck all the way down to his tailbone.

Something clicked inside him, a sticky relay switch closing at last, and he lurched into action. The way he saw it, he had two options. He could follow Artie's advice, trust in himself, and play the tough guy by turning on his flashlight, aiming it at the eyes of the approaching whistler, and barking, "Police! Hold on, or I'll blow your jewels to China!" Never having been that kind of cop, however, and finding himself constitutionally incapable of becoming one now, Henry opted for his second choice.

As quickly as he could, staying low to the ground, he moved down the shoreline to the boathouse. The door on the high side of the building was padlocked, but that didn't matter because the whole thing was off its rusted hinges, barely hanging from the hasp and lock. He slipped inside, hesitating a moment, wishing he could turn on his light and get the lay of things. Too risky, he decided. He was standing on a catwalk; he knew that much. In all likelihood, it ran all the way around the building, a safe distance above the water. That was all he needed to know right now. He could hear the sound of the lake gently caressing the pilings below, and as long as he kept that sound in mind and didn't venture too far in any direction, he would be okay.

Revolver still ready, he turned back to the door and peered out. The complete darkness inside the boathouse made it appear much brighter outside. He didn't think he'd have any trouble seeing the whistler when he broke out of the cabins and came into view.

It occurred to him that he was being awfully cowardly (though as always, he preferred to think of it as cautious) in the face of someone who might not even be Joe Journeyman's murderer. What if it was the man who had *called in* the murder rather than the killer himself? Henry considered that. It was possible. But it was also possible that the person who had called was miles away by now. There certainly didn't seem to be any working phones around here. And what if the murderer had also been the caller? Shit, things like that happened all the time on TV.

The bottom line was that he didn't think an innocent man would be strolling around an abandoned camp at one-thirty in the morning, whistling hymns. Only a candidate for the giggle mill, a genuine wacko, would do that.

His heart, which had actually been slowing itself to something approaching normal speed, took another staggering jolt. The whistler, still whistling, had appeared from behind the last cabin, a shadow of a shadow, almost formless. "Jesus Savior, Pilot Me" finished on a drawn-out note, like a perfect sigh, and began again.

Henry felt sweat break out on his forehead.

Dartmouth, he thought wildly. *The old guy's name was Reverend Dartmouth. He was from somewhere in the Eastern U.P.—Newberry, the Soo, St. Ignace— a real nut, crazy as a damned loon with some of that fundamentalist crap he spouted, strict as hell, mean to the kids, a tall guy, skinny and . . . Christ, was he really a hundred and ten years old, or did he only look that way to us kids?*

The whistler's shapeless silhouette came toward the boathouse. Henry grabbed again for that elusive inner strength, missed it, and sidestepped away from the door, moving a few feet down the catwalk. *Not far,* he thought ashamedly, *I won't go very far. I'll just slip out of sight, that's all. Maybe the guy can't see me, but God only knows what his night vision's like. He might spot me as quick as shit.*

He backed into something that wasn't the catwalk railing or the boathouse wall.

His breath snagged. His heart stuttered.

His mind registered softness, dampness, a vague sensation of radiating warmth.

He pivoted slowly, moving away from that wet embrace but simultaneously turning to face it. He had to know. Hooding the lens of his flashlight with his hand, he turned it on and stared at what was in front of him.

Four of Joe Journeyman's buddies (his mind randomly, crazily named them: Mike Mechanic, Pete Plumber, Kent Carpenter, Willie Workman) were hanging from the boathouse wall. Their shirts and jackets had been pegged over the nails upon which boater's life jackets or canoe paddles had once hung. Their faces, like Joe Journeyman's face, had been slashed and mangled beyond recognition by some object that Henry now realized must have been both heavy and wickedly sharp. Blood had flowed freely down the front of their necks to their shirts and coveralls, still wet, still warm. Henry almost choked when he understood that it was Mike Mechanic's blood he felt soaking slowly through the back of his shirt.

He was ready to turn the light off again when he noticed the legend scrawled on the wall above the victims' heads:

TODAY'S SCRIPTURE

IF THERE IS FOUND AMONG YOU A MAN WHO DOES WHAT IS EVIL IN THE SIGHT OF THE LORD AND HAS GONE AND SERVED OTHER GODS

YES EVIL BUSINESS YES EVIL $$

THEN YOU SHALL BRING FORTH TO YOUR GATES THAT MAN WHO HAS DONE THIS EVIL THING AND PUT HIM TO DEATH

DEUT 17

Deuteronomy, Henry thought wearily, finding another memory. Deuteronomy was Dartmouth's favorite book of the Bible, the book of Hebrew Laws as set forth by God and His main man, Moses. He remembered the old preacher saying once that he wished he had a book of Deuteronomy to run Singing Waters. Do this, dear little campers, do this but don't do that. You'll be blessed for one and cursed for the other.

Henry felt a wave of anger surge through him, and he thought that perhaps his years of cowardly cophood were going to boil and explode, pushing him forward, forcing him at last to find all his hidden strength and do what was right. People didn't do things like this. You didn't kill innocent people in the name of some old collection of laws that said eating pigs was a sin but it was fine to rape a captured woman if you shaved her head and waited thirty days.

He felt some mystical connection moving toward completion deep inside his body and brain, a connection almost being made, a connection that would finally banish his fear and give him the faith he needed to charge forward without worrying about what might happen to him.

But the whistling stopped suddenly, and Henry felt the two ends of that connection shrivel away in the silence. It seemed that perhaps his brain had stopped functioning and that his blood had frozen in his veins. He began to tremble, and his eyes were drawn helplessly back to that writing on the wall, the last line of which was less than an inch above the heads of the slain construction workers: *Then you shall bring forth to your gates that man who has done this evil thing and put him to death.*

"And the people shall say Amen," said a thick, slow voice behind him.

FAITH AND HENRY GUSTAFSON

Henry screamed. The flashlight fell from his hands. He caught a quick glimpse of its beam going over the railing and cartwheeling down to the water below. Then a splash and darkness. He had a moment where his mind raced free during which he wished for many things—that everything could have turned out differently; that the chief or Lizzy Halprin or Bill McInnis or even that old drunk Bennedict from the Falls had been available; that the ambulance had showed up when it was supposed to; that Artie was real; that he himself was more than just a no-brained, no-balled cop who needed an imaginary partner just to get him up out of his chair at the station. Any one of those things, and he might have had a chance.

His thoughts were chopped off by the sound of the boathouse door being pulled off the hasp. He saw a dark shape rising to fill the opening. Dartmouth? Oh God, oh no, he didn't think so. The old man couldn't be alive, he'd be a thousand years old by now, and he had always been so frail and skinny, while this thing was huge, towering, bulky, and misshapen. It held something above its lumpy head, something he could not identify in such an instant of extreme terror but that might have been a large steel cross.

Yes, he thought, a cross . . . and it was lit . . . lit by faint light, although the boathouse and the waterfront outside were utterly dark . . . lit . . . its edges glinting like sharpened blades.

His finger twitched on the trigger of his revolver, but he didn't know what would happen if he shot, if the bullet would hit its mark, if one would be enough to kill that gargantuan thing, if he would have the time or guts to shoot again. Still he hesitated, but finally broke and turned and stumbled away along the catwalk, left hand groping for the old, wobbly railing, right shoulder bumping past the dripping corpses of Mike Mechanic, Willie Workman, and the others. He heard boards creaking beneath his weight, the pattering of rotted wood falling into the water below. He heard the sound of the railing itself, as though it were crying, weakening, about to give out.

"And the people shall say Amen," the voice said again, and then came the worst sounds of all: the dragging, thudding noise of the killer coming after him, the scythe-like whisper of that weapon slicing through the air.

Henry ran faster, tripping, barely maintaining his balance. When he reached the place where the catwalk ended at the boathouse's front wall, he stumbled in surprise on the stairway that was there. He flailed his arms, felt empty space in front and below, and almost pitched over the steps before he caught himself.

His fear was replaced by a burst of understanding—perhaps Reverend Dartmouth would have called it an epiphany. He was being pursued by someone (some*thing*) that was left from the days of the old Bible camp. Someone (some*thing*) that had been here all these long years—here or quite nearby. Someone (some*thing*) that didn't cotton to the idea of a greedy businessman's association taking over. The same someone (some*thing*) that had stopped the Chicago idiots' fishing resort before it ever got off the ground. Was that it? Oh Jesus, *could* that be it? Henry didn't know, but he thought it very well might be.

As he descended one rickety step after another, listening to the ragged rasp of his own breath, the wild thunder in his chest, and the heavy sound of pursuit less than ten feet behind, he thought he might be facing something as large and fathomless as the spirit of the camp itself, the spirit of the place as established and embodied by a skinny old Bible beater who had loved to sing "Jesus Savior, Pilot Me" and preach from a ridiculous old legal code.

Madness. Lunacy.

Yes, it was that. But he had seen that inhuman shape. Accepting such madness and lunacy in the name of understanding, in the name of finding the strength to keep running . . . that had to be better than giving in to blind fear, didn't it? If he did that, if he surrendered so easily simply because he didn't know what he was facing, he might as well crumple into a ball right now and wait for that cross to part the top of his skull.

He reached the last step and the wooden pier at the bottom. It had been raining so much that fall that the water level had risen by inches, covering the boards. Cold water seeped into his boots as he went to the open barn-style doorway that communicated with Conley Lake. He grasped the edge of the door and swung himself around it. It was a good idea and a good try, but he missed dry ground by several feet, landed in water up to his knees, and had to scramble desperately up to the rocky shore.

The heavy thing was almost at the bottom of the stairs. The urge to stand and fight was growing strong within him, the urge to rest even stronger than that. But the thing was closer, was almost upon him, and that was enough to murder all those urges and set him in flight.

***

It was damned funny, Henry kept thinking, the way noises carried so well in the still night air.

He had heard the thing chasing him quite clearly, and he had not allowed himself to stop running until he had heard it stop first. That had been—what? An hour ago? Two hours? *Three?*

There had been nothing but silence after that, silence for a very long time, silence while he hunkered along the shore a quarter-mile from camp, silence while he collected his strength and what was left of his wits, wondering if he could sneak back into the camp and get the Blazer, if he'd be able to free it from the mud and escape. Silence. While he wept. While he pondered. While he tried again to make that difficult connection he had almost made several times that night already.

Eventually, as clearly as if he were standing right there, he had heard a vehicle rumbling up the camp driveway, the sound of doors slamming and the voices of Beverly Yates and Linc Wellington, the volunteer EMTs from the ambulance, calling his name.

Henry? Hey, Henry Gustafson, where the hell are you?

Other words: *We got lost, buddy* and *This place is as empty as shit, ain't it?* and *Where's this body s'posed to be?* and again, *Jesus Jumpin' Christ, Henry, where* are *you?*

Then more silence, not very long, followed by something short and high and horribly clipped that might have been a scream. Then a long, slow, perfectly clear whistle: *Jesus Savior, Pilot Me.*

Yes, it was funny how those sounds carried so well,

and how that thing that might have been and probably was a scream had gone straight to his heart like a big hand, grasping two loose ends and pulling them together.

He knew what he had to do. Artie had heard that scream, that sound of another human being suffering, and had come back to him, put a hand on his shoulder, and looked him straight in the eyes. Artie had told him.

"You can't hide anymore, boyo. This ain't playing at cops and robbers anymore, nabbing kids out breaking curfew. This is the real thing. You ran from the scene when you shouldn't have, you hid like a coward, you stayed here crying while them medics got taken out. Now you gotta get in there. Win or lose, you gotta try to clean this mess up. It don't matter that you're scared. It don't matter that you don't know how it's all gonna end. You just gotta do it. You're a cop, boyo, like it or not. That's what cops do."

Henry's mouth had dropped open in amazement. "Artie . . . I don't believe it. Artie, Jesus Christ, you're *talking!*"

But Artie had shaken his head solemnly, and after a moment Henry had understood. *It ain't Artie talking,* he thought, *it's me. Good Sweet Lord, it's actually me. It's me who felt that person's pain, me who's going to react to it. It's me who knows what's going on. It's me who knows what needs to be done.*

He thought about what he had seen back in camp and wondered how much of it had been real. Some of it? All of it? A huge creature that killed in the name of God? Was that possible? And if it was, then how could he ever hope to stop it?

He shook his head and sighed, knowing that didn't

matter anymore. What waited in that camp was a mystery light-years beyond him, but the connection, so long in the making, had been completed. The wires were hot and tingling. He had what he'd always been missing before. The ability to trust in himself and not worry about the outcome. The ability to do what was right.

He smiled. He couldn't exactly say that he'd be going into battle with God on his side. Images of scrawled scripture, misshapen beasts, and sharpened steel crosses made it impossible to think that. But something, something from within, would be there next to him, something good, something right, or at least something very simple and pure. He couldn't quite touch it, but he didn't doubt it either. When your back was to the wall and the screws were to your balls and you finally found what you'd been lacking . . . well, the power that came from that had to mean something, and you couldn't just turn away from it.

He stood up from his hiding place in the weeds and rocks, slapped his service revolver briskly from hand to hand, and drew his shoulders back. Artie was standing in front of him, tall and strong, but Henry shook his head firmly.

"Not anymore, pard. Get out of here. This is my job. I'm a cop.

It's what cops do."

He thought a smile crossed Artie's rugged features in the moment before he disappeared for good.

Henry sighed. The sound of that ageless hymn reached him across the gulf of darkness, the notes perfect and clear. *Tempestuous seas all right,* Henry thought. *Second Timothy, chapter six, verse twelve.*

FAITH AND HENRY GUSTAFSON

His lips parted, and he found the notes of his own whistling song. He took one step, and then another, and a third, his shadow huge and strong as he advanced through the black of night into the even darker heart of the eternal mystery.

DOWN THE VALLEY WILD

You ran screaming for your father because there had been a terrible accident . . .

VERY LITTLE HAD CHANGED. The terrain was more weathered, the undergrowth wilder, the cabin sadly run down—but it was still there, and nearly forty years had not altered any of it beyond recognition or repair.

Stewart arrived in the early afternoon. Of course there was no longer a family Jeep, and he had not trusted his Mazda to negotiate the roads that linked the property to Highway 41, so he had parked at the Amoco in Patterson Falls and asked the pump jockey, a man by the name of Larry Allison, to run him out in his pickup.

"Hey, I know that place," Allison said. "Used to hunt out there when I was a kid. Ain't nobody lived there long as I been alive. What, you buy it from the fambly or somethin?"

Stewart shook his head. "I am the family. Name's Don Stewart. The land and cabin belonged to my father. He died a few months ago."

"Sorry to hear that," Allison said, and Stewart nodded to show he appreciated the thought.

DOWN THE VALLEY WILD

Now he used the tarnished key that had been in the lawyer's envelope to unlock the front door. He hefted his suitcases and went inside, immediately staggering from the overpowering odors of age and decay. He gulped and blinked rapidly, but his eyes began to water and his stomach uttered a threatening groan.

There was no trace, no lingering evidence whatsoever, of his mother's fanatical housekeeping or the slightly less effective but still dedicated cleaning his father had done after her death. Everything was coated with dust and a greasy, almost jellylike slime. Cobwebs dangled from the ceiling and decorated the few remaining sticks of furniture. Newspapers, which had once been tacked over the windows to combat sun fading, now lay on the floor, yellow and faded themselves. Rodent droppings were scattered across table tops and window sills. A black and white photograph of two young boys with their arms around each other withered alongside a 1952 issue of *Life* on top of the woodstove.

Stewart swallowed hard and went in the rest of the way. It was going to take work—Jesus, was that an understatement—but it could be done. He figured that by tonight the place could be sleepable, in two or three days it would be livable, and by the end of his vacation it might actually be comfortable again.

He set the suitcases in the corner and returned to the edge of the road, where he and Allison had piled the things he'd purchased in town: cartons of food, boxes of cleaning supplies, mops and brooms and buckets. It took three trips to get everything into the cabin. After that, feeling old, Stewart forced himself to go out again for a quick tour.

The yard had been consumed by saplings and weeds. A shame, but clearing it would have to wait for his next trip north. He had neither the proper equipment nor the ambition, and he knew that the cabin would keep him busy enough, thank you.

The woodlot to the east had succumbed to chaos as well. Deadfalls and scrub growth were everywhere. Windstorms had toppled the best of the older maples and ironwoods while others were ravaged by age and disease. He would eventually need the chainsaw he had put off buying, he supposed, for someday he'd have to come in here and salvage what he could. But luckily there was still some firewood already cut, split, and stacked under the overhang on the cabin's eastern wall. Because of his father's superior craftsmanship, the overhang was still weather and waterproof. Mostly, anyway. There was at least half a cord of ironwood that was unrotted and nicely seasoned.

He saved the worst of the tour for last but finally could put it off no longer. He strolled around the back of the cabin, his hands jammed casually in his pockets, a strained but still lighthearted whistle on his lips. With his boyhood summer home squarely at his back, he ventured to the far southern edge of the property.

The ravine was still there.

Of course, that was a bit like saying that the pyramids were still standing in the desert or that Niagara Falls was still roiling and rumbling. Ravines didn't simply disappear. You didn't have to be a geologist to know that they grew with time, but still . . . still . . . seeing those sloping, canyonlike walls for the first time in so very many years, laying eyes on the tangled thickets that ran downward into seeming oblivion . . . the very sight of those things made him forget about breathing for a moment or two and kicked his heart into a crude, jittery tap dance.

An image of the faded photograph in the cabin rose in his mind.

You ran screaming for your father . . .

No.

It was too early. He would deal with it. Of course he would. Dealing with it had been one of the prime reasons (or to save a lie for a rainy day, *the* prime reason) that he had accepted the key from the lawyer in the first place. But not now, not yet.

You ran screaming—

He turned angrily and stomped back to the cabin, the gloom of the ravine and its quietly rustling trees shut off, closed off, blocked out of his thoughts.

For the first time he was grateful that such great untold quantities of work were waiting for him inside.

***

By nine that night Stewart felt that he could spend the night in the cabin without contracting a dread illness or falling prey to the March of the Marauding Mice. He had worked without a break until twilight, stopping then only long enough to fire up the woodstove, eat a quick sandwich, and down two beers. Then he had gone back to work, sticking with it until the mild complaints being offered by his body had progressed to grumbles, and from grumbles to an outright yammering bitch.

He closed the windows he had opened to air the place out and sat down by the stove with a package of Fritos and another beer. An hour ago it had begun to rain. The sound of it on the roof merged with the crackling snap of burning logs to bring back a flood of memories:

The time he and his father had driven to Conley Lake to go fishing and had somehow managed to overturn the rowboat not once but twice . . .

. . . the time he and Dale had rigged a high jump in the side yard, complete with a cross-pole made from a birch whippet and a landing area that consisted of rat-eaten mattresses from the county dump . . .

. . . the time Dale had challenged him to climb to the cabin roof and leap to the branches of the cedar tree seven feet away (little Donnie had accepted that challenge and had tumbled gracelessly to earth, fracturing his wrist and spending the remainder of the summer in an awkward, joy-spoiling cast) . . .

. . . the time when his mother had still been alive and all of them had driven into the Falls to attend a movie at the newly-opened theater. The locals had called it a "picture house." They saw a double feature with shorts, and they'd had a fine time—except, perhaps, when Dale stole all his popcorn and he had gotten in trouble for trying to snatch it back.

Memories could be a good thing, but too many memories (or the wrong kind of memories) were not. He told himself that it was for that reason more than any other he had tossed the photo of the two young boys into the woodstove first thing, before the old newspapers and magazine, before the kindling twigs, before the logs. Even still, picture or no, he seemed to have little control over the things that came to mind. They came, the good and the bad, at random, in bits and pieces, some cloudy, some clear, each demanding in its own quietly insistent way to be heard. He guessed he could have sat there by the stove for his entire vacation, listening to the fire and helplessly reflecting, letting in whatever might come (with one exception, of course), and still not touch on half the things that lurked back there in those first eight years of his life.

That night he dreamed of Dale. Not Dale on the last day, but he and Dale high jumping in the yard. He had been terrible at it. He had knocked the whippet from its supports every single time. But not Dale. Dale could fly. Dale would run and leap and sail upward, his body arched in a triumphant parabola, soaring. And then he would thud onto the pile of moldy mattresses and look up to ascertain that the pole was still in position, his grin dazzling, his eyes glistening and alive.

He awoke from that dream with the beginnings of a sob locked in his throat and the certainty that someone was tapping on the window next to the bed. He rolled over, expecting to see a gaggle of drunken teenagers, a lost camper, perhaps even a wilderness hobo.

But there was no one there. The tapping was just the sound of rain pattering on the glass.

Stewart sighed and lay down. Ten minutes later, he was asleep again, tossing, muttering.

Dreaming.

***

On the third day he took a noontime break, laid down his scrub brush, and went out. The time had come. He knew that. He *felt* it, although it had not been a conscious decision. The idea had simply come to him, unbidden, almost as casually as a man might decide at one in the morning that it is time to get out of bed and make a sandwich.

He waded through the tidal sea of grass and stopped at the edge of the ravine, trying to remember where the path had been. He shuffled slowly back and forth along the edge of the slope but finally abandoned the search and picked the clearest spot he could find to start down.

It was steeper than he remembered. He was forced to move from tree to tree, struggling to keep his balance. Brambles caught at his jeans. The gravelly soil beneath his boots gave way again and again. Several times, when there were no trees large enough to support his weight, he had to go it alone, slipping and skidding and sliding on the edge of disaster down to the next handhold.

It took nearly ten minutes to reach bottom. Once there, he paused, gazing at the junglelike lay of the land. For the first time since Allison had dropped him off at the edge of the property, he could hear the river, although it didn't sound nearly as ferocious as it once had.

He supposed it had been a dry spring.

He forged ahead, moving cautiously into the heart of the ravine. The ground was booby-trapped with the hidden corpses of trees and frost-heaved rocks. Overhead branches groped for his face and snapped viciously as he passed, cutting him off from everything behind.

"Jesus," he murmured, partially in surprise at just how wild the ravine had become, partially in response to the whole new rush of memories that cascaded over him as he moved along.

Good lord, but they had spent the time down here. He and Dale, he and his father, Dale and his father, all three of them. Sometimes he would come alone, but not often; even in those days, it had not been a good place for a child to play by himself, and little Donnie Stewart had never been a courageous sort of kid. So they had come together, inventing games of Jungle Scout, River Guide, African Explorer, and bizarre permutations of tag or hide-and-seek. Of course Dale always won. Whatever the game, Dale came out on top. But little Donnie, far from brave yet stubborn to a fault, had always gone back for more.

Their summer hideaway. Their summer playground.

The growth began to thin a little, and he broke out at the edge of the river. It was as disappointing as he had guessed from the sound. Its banks were still rocky, still wide, but the flow of water couldn't properly be called a river at all. It was, in fact, not much more than a muddy creek. He knew he hadn't been looking forward to seeing it the way it had been that final summer, but still he felt a curious pang, an unaccountable frustration, a sense of being let down. It was as if he had traveled a great distance only to find—

He whirled suddenly, staring at the wall of trees behind him. There had been a noise back there, a crisp snapping of branches and a slow dragging sound, as though someone was pulling something very heavy through the scrub.

He tried to remember if there had ever been any animals down here. There had, yes, but only squirrels, chipmunks, and the occasional jackrabbit. If there had been anything large enough to make a noise like that, they would have known about it, and they probably wouldn't have played down here as often as they had.

Bear? he wondered.

But whatever it was, it was gone now. There was nothing but the gentle sough of wind and the pitiful gurgle of the river. He listened a little longer and finally lifted his gaze to the sheer rock wall across the water. The sight chilled him. He was seized with a sense of pure, uncut sorrow more powerful than he had felt in years. Remorse he recognized. Guilt he knew well. But this . . . this was an agonizing sensation of burning loss. He felt as though someone had seared the inside of his chest with a blowtorch, making every heartbeat a weeping cry of pain, every breath a stinging jolt of misery.

He shook his head slowly.

"I'm back, Dale," he whispered. "I finally came back."

He stayed there for a long time, staring at the wall. He wasn't sure if he still wanted to keep the memory at bay or not, but it was too late for such distinctions. Choice was not a factor. Free will, if it had ever existed, was gone. The memory had arrived, and there was no stopping it as it played itself over and over in a vivid loop. The game that had soured. Little Donnie's anger rising. Dale on the edge and Dale going down. The mighty, almost mystical roaring of the river. It was very hot that summer, he remembered, but there had not been a dry spring, oh no, not that year, not by a long shot.

You ran screaming for your father . . .

Oh yes, you ran screaming, didn't you? You wailed and wept and wet your pants and kept thinking it couldn't be true. You wished it were you, wished you were the one and not Dale. You wanted to go back and do it again and have it all turn out differently, have the beginning and the ending magically alter themselves until—

Stewart left the riverbank, his steps quicker now that a path had been made. He was almost running, was running, as though the shadows and phantoms and wicked creatures thundering through his brain were actually things that could be left behind.

But they followed him.

And something else followed him too.

He stumbled along, pushing branches aside, trampling the underbrush, making enough noise to completely smother the heavy dragging sound that dogged him like a nightmare from the past.

***

He drank a great deal of beer that night, fell asleep early, but awoke sometime later in the middle of a foggy, troubling dream. He sat up in bed, gulping air, rubbing his eyes, trying to rein in his wildly galloping senses.

The tapping was at the window again, only this time, the night was dry, the sound not the whisper of black rain but something else. He looked out and saw the kind of darkness that was only possible in places like this, miles from civilization . . . except that this darkness was marred in the center by two distinct pinpoints of light.

Stewart blinked. The pinpoints didn't waver. He drew a breath and fought back the irrational fear that was stirring within him.

Those pinpoints, those dots of light—they were glowing eyes.

"Kids," he muttered drunkenly as he struggled out

of bed. He found his pants and pulled them on without bothering to zip them. He wobbled out into the main room and yanked open the back door, finally sobering a degree as the chill of the summer night struck his skin and made it tingle.

"Hey! You kids! You get outta here right now! This is private property!"

There was a brief silence, but then he heard the tapping again, still at the bedroom window around the corner from where he stood.

"I told you to get outta here! You're trespassing, and I've got a gun inside." That was a lie, but he didn't intend to give the little sneaks a chance to find out.

The tapping continued, increased, grew louder. It was fast becoming a sound of angry insistence.

"Well, goddammit."

Stewart went back inside to grab whatever weapon he could find. It took him awhile, but when he reemerged, he was brandishing the scrub mop he had purchased in the Falls. He held it in both hands, like a bat, and stepped into the yard.

"You got one more chance!" he yelled, moving gingerly through the long and dewy grass. "I want you kids outta here—right now!"

The tapping had become a banging. It seemed impossible that the intruder would not break the glass.

"You asked for it!"

He raised the mop and rounded the corner.

And then he stopped, the anger drying and dying within. In its place was an instant of stark confusion, followed by a dark, crawling sensation in the pit of his stomach.

Whoever had been at the window was running

away, into the forest, but in the dark, what he saw didn't look anything like a kid. Actually, it looked only vaguely human, rather more like a gnarled woodland animal, its body pale and twisted. It scuttled into the underbrush on skinny, bowed legs, its arms swinging spastically, apelike.

"What the hell . . . ?"

He put out a hand and steadied himself against the cabin wall. His Adam's apple bobbed up and down. His mouth opened and closed in convulsive silence. He finally managed to force something out—"You stay away from here, dammit! Next time, I'll shoot you for a thief!"—but he felt ashamed even as he uttered it, well aware of the hollow force behind the words.

Then he began to tremble violently, uncontrollably, his body wracked with great, quaking sobs. He told himself he was shivering because of the unseasonable temperature, but he knew that wasn't true. It was because of something else, oh yes, because of that moment just before the thing had scurried off into the wilderness, when it had turned toward him for one brief breath of a moment and he had seen its face. It was because of that, and it was because of the four words that had risen to his lips as he gazed at that face, the four words he had barely choked back in time.

Those words were: *Dale? Is that you?*

He wanted to laugh at that now—oh God, he wanted it so badly. But a laugh would be wrong. It would be misguided. It would be fraudulent, worse than a lie. Because even a mild laugh would not in any way change what, for that one instant, he was certain he had seen.

***

That year, a fierce, rainy spring had finally surrendered to a summer of almost unheard-of heat. Temperatures in the nineties day after blistering day had driven them to the ravine more than ever before. It was better down there in that wild valley, sheltered at least a little from the merciless, unblinking eye of the sun and the brain-busting humidity.

On that particular day the game had been a northwoods variation on the old cowboys-and-Indians theme. True to form, it had started on a free and happy note but had plummeted downhill rapidly.

The problem, of course, was Dale.

(Dale whom Donnie loved)

Dale who was tall and athletic.

(Dale whom Donnie respected)

Dale who could play baseball with the high school boys despite the fact that he was only eleven and who did better in school on his bad days than Donnie could ever hope to do.

(Dale whom Donnie idolized)

Dale who had been his mother's largest joy, who was still his father's pride.

(Dale whom Donnie envied)

Dale who could never do any wrong.

(Dale whom Donnie feared)

Dale who always seemed to find the quickest way to spoil a good game whether by obstinate bickering or by developing new rules in midstream or just by simple dictatorial domination.

Dale whom Donnie loved, and respected, and idolized, and envied, and feared.

And hated.

Dale.

DOWN THE VALLEY WILD

He could not remember now precisely what had gone wrong that day. He could, however, remember the important parts—the two of them playing well together, wading across the river like true scouts from the John Wayne school, racing through the wilderness, and then later, finally, standing on the crest of the far slope, above the sharp rock wall and the water, screaming at each other.

"Your fault!" he yelled at Dale. "You always ruin it! You always mess things up!"

Dale only smiled, that infuriating smile that was an unmistakable feature of the patented Dale Stewart up-your-ass, kid-I'm-better-than-you expression. He reached down and gave Donnie a condescending pat on the head.

"Poor, misguided, demented little brat."

"But you cheated! We had rules, pus bag! You're a creep, you know it? You're a snot-faced, nose-picking creep! I hope you die! I hope you rot! I hope you—"

Dale reached out with a lightning-stroke hand and slapped him across the face. His head rocked back and came forward sharply. His chin struck his chest. He began to cry.

"I'm gonna tell Dad! You hit me! I'm gonna tell on you!"

"Be my guest, brat. Dad won't do anything to me. Jesus, you know that. He'll blame it on you. He'll say it was your fault. So go on, I'd like to see it. Run and cry to him, blow your nose all over his shirt. We'll see what happens. Go on."

And that was when the weakening thread of Donnie's self-control snapped. It might have been the prosaic fact that yet another enjoyable game had been

219

spoiled. Perhaps the humidity was working its dark, heavy magic on him. Most likely, it was the unavoidable realization that every single word Dale had just said was true. He didn't know. He was beyond reasoning then, didn't stop to question why, and later he could never be quite sure. The thread stretched . . . and stretched . . . and snapped. That was the only thing that really mattered.

He bent down and dragged a hand across the rocky hillside, coming back up with his fingers curled around a sharp and jagged stone that was roughly the size of the grapefruits their father favored for breakfast. Dale stared at the stone as though it were a cheap toy. He began to laugh. The laugh had a taunting, frustrating ring to it, a horrible touch of mockery, an air of irrepressible snottiness.

"You cheated!" Donnie's voice was high and hoarse and bitterly triumphant as he pronounced that verdict.

And then it was time for the sentencing.

He raised the rock and with one smooth motion leapt at his older brother. Dale's eyes grew suddenly wide, comically startled. It was an expression Donnie cherished—but the moment was dreadfully short.

The rock in his hand came down. Hard. Oh Jesus, oh God, there was no denying that it came down hard.

Dale's comical eyes rolled up in his head, the lids snapping shut like shades on a roller. And then he was gone, slumping, leaning, teetering, and tumbling down the rocky hillside, body crashing through the brambles like a sack filled with dead, very heavy weight.

Donnie stared in dawning horror as his brother's body reached the bottom of the hill and the lip of the rock wall. It seemed to pause there for a heartbeat, but then it took flight, soaring up and out . . . up . . . and out.

It was that moment more than any other he would never forget—Dale in the air for an impossibly long time, completely limp, utterly out of control, sailing up and out . . . and then dropping.

He hit the river with a mighty splash.

Donnie screamed, *"DAAAAAAAAAAAAALLE!"* and took off down the side of the ravine, stumbling and sliding, scrabbling for handholds and footholds, almost out of control himself. His brother's name broke out of his throat over and over, becoming one long, uninterrupted syllable, a wailing siren of pure panic.

He reached the rock wall and peered down, but Dale was not in sight. Running parallel to the rushing water, he came to their well-worn footpath, the one that bypassed the wall and zigzagged down a shallower embankment until it reached the shore. He raced down it, falling repeatedly, skinning his hands and knees, bloodying his nose, heedless of everything but getting to the river in time. He hit bottom and charged headlong into the water.

"Dale!" he cried again. "DALE!"

He struggled against the current and waded back to shore then ran frantically up and down the bank like a frightened rabbit searching for a way across. His eyes darted left and right, searching, scanning. His older brother was nowhere. There was nothing there but an old log being churned downstream. There was just that, the log, swept along in the endless, furious flow.

The log.

The flow.

The tremendous rushing noise in Donnie's ears.

The empty river and his own bald panic.

After an unknowable time, he forded across and ran for the cabin, ran screaming for his father to tell him there had been a terrible accident. They had been playing atop the far side of the ravine, and somehow Dale had lost his balance. One slip and Dale was gone.

The underbrush flogged and flayed him as he charged homeward, but he ignored everything, kept running, kept screaming.

Oh Christ, he ran screaming . . .

***

Stewart blinked and stared at the trickling river and the rock wall behind. For a second there, he had seen it all again, that picture of his older brother's body suspended in the air, then dropping, crashing into the water and vanishing from sight forever.

He shuddered.

There had been many volunteers from the Falls and the neighboring town of Kelly's Corners. They had searched the ravine and surrounding woods for days (twenty days? It might have been that long, perhaps even longer). They had dragged the river all the way to the county line and beyond. No body had been found.

They were told to blame it on the current. The current could carry something for weeks and weeks, miles and miles. The current could trap an object against an underwater obstruction and pin it there until it decomposed. The current was a powerful, usually unbeatable force, especially when there had been such a rainy spring and the water on this branch of the Little Spruce River was so high, so wickedly swift.

No body had been found.

DOWN THE VALLEY WILD

That had been their last summer at the cabin. His father, barely recovered from the natural death of his wife two years before, could no longer cope with the summer place. The cabin had been locked, the yard left to go wild, the woodlot left to grow and die and slowly rot.

Stewart turned away, suddenly wishing he had never taken the key from the lawyer yet knowing that, all the same, it made no difference. The memory was there anyway. It always was. Unacknowledged, it waited. Patiently, it lingered. And in weak moments of drink or exhaustion or sleep or just plain boredom, it pounced—that stark mind-picture of Dale in the air.

He took a step in the direction of the cabin but hesitated almost immediately. There was something up ahead, at the verge of the trees. Somebody, staring at him.

This time there was no mistake.

"Dale," he breathed.

The trees rustled. The somebody turned away.

"Dale, Jesus, don't run! Don't go—"

But he stopped himself, because he was getting carried away again. Call it a guilt fantasy. Call it a mind ghost created by the long-buried, long-hidden, long-unadmitted, long-kept-inside. Whatever the case, it hadn't been Dale, any more than the thing outside the cabin had been. Oh, it had his brother's face, but that face was pale and broken, lumpish, freakishly grotesque. It was his brother's size, but the body was bent and twisted, cruelly deformed. And forty years had gone by . . . yes . . . his brother had been dead for almost forty years.

But there was something else that silenced him too, that kept him from giving chase. It was the sound the thing had made, that weak, whimpering noise it had uttered as it turned away, like an old dog that was very, very sick, like something ancient and weary, drowning in despair.

He stood there, hugging himself but unaware that he was doing so, listening to its hasty retreat, catching glimpses of its white and naked form scrambling away through the brush.

There were glimpses of something else as well, glimpses of the wild forest animals that scuttled along after the creature. It was a virtual parade of squirrels and rabbits, foxes and woodchucks and coyotes, waddling porcupines, wriggling badgers—fifteen or twenty wild things in all, following the leader.

Stewart groaned.

Then the thing was gone; the thing and its followers had vanished.

He stood there, catching his breath, dying inside, and finally left the ravine as quickly as he could.

He was almost running.

***

That afternoon he walked the three miles to the highway and hitched a ride into town. He returned several hours later with three purchases: more beer, a cheap plastic lawn chair from the Ben Franklin, and a shotgun with birdshot from one of the local sporting goods stores. As evening fell, he took the chair and the beer and the shotgun out into the backyard and planted himself in the middle of the grassy sea, midway between the cabin and the rim of the ravine. He drank beer, watched the sun go down, kept the weapon across his lap, and waited.

Night came, the moon rose, yet he saw and heard

nothing. He wasn't deterred. Despite the beer coursing through his system, he felt sharply and wildly alert. He knew what he had to do. For his own good, his own safety, his own protection, his own sanity, he had to get the thing that was trying to fool him, trying to con him into believing it was his brother. *You betcha,* he thought. *You've got to get that liar, that trickster, that false sibling. That's the answer.*

He waited.

It came at last, one hour past midnight.

He heard it first, grappling up the slope, coming through the brambles. He straightened, every muscle and shred of tendon in his body stiffly complaining.

It finally appeared—a moonish face peering at him over the edge. He raised the shotgun.

"C'mon out!" he called.

The face didn't move.

"Hey, now! Come out where I can see you! Your game's over!"

Something in the face seemed to twitch slightly.

Stewart's hands twitched on the shotgun.

And then the thing spoke to him, saying just a handful of indecipherable word-sounds in a voice that was thick and crusty, dirty and old, gravel-filled.

Stewart gulped and choked. The shotgun slipped from his grasp and fell to the ground, clanking against a half-full beer can and overturning it. His hands opened and closed as though trying to wrap around the weapon he no longer held. He never bent to retrieve it. His eyes never left the white and gleaming face.

The thing gargled out something else. Stewart felt

his chest constrict around a heart that was on fire with rushing blood and raging emotion.

"Dale," he whispered.

The thing was silent, staring at him.

"Dale, oh God, I don't . . . I mean I never—"

The thing's hands suddenly appeared from below the rim, ghostly claws darting forward and back so quickly that Stewart thought he must have imagined the movement. There was something lying at the edge of the grass now, something the thing had put there for him, although he could not tell what it was.

"Dale—"

The thing grunted and turned to go.

"No, wait! Dale . . . please . . . you've got to listen to me."

The thing hesitated.

"Jesus . . . aw, Jesus, Dale, it's been so long since I could talk to somebody about this. I never . . . actually, I never talked to anyone. I've never been able to talk to anyone. How could I? And you . . . oh, Dale, I didn't mean to . . . I never meant to—"

The thing cocked its head slightly to one side, listening as though it didn't understand the words, couldn't understand them.

Stewart groped for something else, some way to bridge the gulf between them. He thought he saw (hoped he saw, prayed he saw) the creature's eyes sparkling in the moonlight, a single bright drop highlighted on its misshapen cheek.

His own eyes filled with tears.

This time, when the thing turned its back to him, it vanished quickly, dropping out of sight as though it had never existed at all. Stewart held his breath, distantly aware of that now familiar sound, those clumsy, blundering movements fading in the distance.

His mouth opened. No sound came out.

When the night was silent once more, he rose from the chair and walked slowly over to the ravine, stooping to retrieve whatever the thing had left there for him. His hands touched it, and he felt a sharp jolt.

A photograph. An old black and white picture.

For a moment, he thought it was the same photo he'd found when he'd arrived at the cabin, somehow, impossibly, risen phoenix-like from the ashes. He quaked with equal parts sorrow and terror before realizing that it was not the same picture at all. Close. The same subject. The same year. But not the same photograph. This one was faded, crusted with dirt, parts of it torn or eaten away by time and dampness and, he thought, the touch of malformed hands that had taken it out often for study and remembrance.

"Oh God, Dale," he breathed to the silent night and dark ravine. "Dale, believe me, I'm so sorry . . . ."

But it was not enough.

***

At five minutes past sunrise, Stewart walked again to the edge of the ravine. He was freshly showered and shaved, dressed in the last change of clean clothes he had brought with him. A hundred yards behind, the cabin that had once belonged to his father and now belonged to him was engulfed in hungry, greedy flames. The sky above was choked with clouds of smoke. It would bring people from town eventually, he supposed, but by that time it would be over. The cabin would be gone, and all the memories would be dead.

He looked down and saw them waiting for him: his

escort, the small cluster of forest animals. They seemed possessed of perfect patience, complete and utter calm. He smiled at them, a pure expression of acceptance and peaceful satisfaction.

It was time, that voice had said to him. He had hidden for too long. He had stayed away. He had kept the truth inside, denying it. He had let their father die without knowing. He had let the world go on without hearing. Forty years. Four decades. Two score. Too long. He was overdue, so very long overdue, but now it was time. All secrets must be confronted. All truths must be spoken. All debts must be paid.

That's what his brother had said to him, and of course he had really said none of those things, or if he had, they had been spoken in a dead language, in words beyond Stewart's comprehension. But still, he had heard them, and he had somehow translated them in his heart. He had understood.

The memories will be dead. The debt must be paid.

He looked to his right, toward an ancient, gnarled maple that grew at the edge of the hillside. There, high up the trunk, he had spiked a certain photograph on a bent and rusty nail. It was the photograph that he remembered Dale carrying with him everywhere in the pocket of his jeans—two boys, brothers, grinning brightly at the camera, the cabin in the background, and beyond that, two upright poles crossed with a willow branch above a pile of ancient mattresses.

The photograph, beyond the reach of the flames, fluttered in the breeze. The maple leaves rustled their secret messages around it.

For one last time, Stewart saw a picture of Dale in the air—but not as he had been on that final day. Oh, no. This was a picture of Dale as he *should* be, Dale on the day they had high jumped in the side yard. Dale soaring upward, almost flying, his back arched and his smile eternal, unbeatably dazzling, a thing of the gods.

Dale.

Reaching for the sky.

They were perfect, the memory and the remembering.

All debts must be paid.

A moment later, he started down into the ravine.

BLOODYBONES

PART ONE
I

S HE WAS GOING to be caught; there were no two ways about it.

It was in situations like this that Amy Brackett wished the Horn River wasn't quite such a scenic wonder. If the river had been, say, a straight road or footpath, she could have made it home in ten minutes flat. But straight was not a word that came to mind when thinking about the Horn, especially here in this final stretch before it spilled into the big lake, a section that David often referred to as "six miles of water on a one-mile map." The bends in this section were tight and frequent, one hairpin turn and switchback after another. Even if you could paddle like a son of a bitch—which you couldn't, not in such tight quarters—your progress was painstakingly slow.

Yet the weather could not possibly care less about the topography or Amy's race for safety. As always, it was going to keep marching right along, dishing out its endless succession of sunshine or rain or heat or cold or sleet or snow. It was going to laugh at anyone it inconvenienced and spit in the face of anyone who dared to question or complain. It was going to say, in effect, *Yeah, right, we've all got problems, don't we, lady? Now how about a little thunderstorm to cheer you up?*

Amy didn't know if it was a thunderbumper sweeping down on her across the lake right now. At this time of year, it could just as easily be a freak blizzard or even just a monster blow—a three-day symphony of crashing waves and toppling trees that was fairly common at this time of year and often served as a prelude to something even worse. All she knew was that it was going to be bad. She could see that in the steel-and-slate color of the clouds whipping past, low over her head. She could feel it in the way the normally meek and placid Horn was throwing choppy waves at the prow of her canoe, waves that would soon enough be wearing jaunty little white caps. Most of all (people who didn't know would laugh at the idea, but to hell with them; those who had experienced it *knew,* they *understood*), she could smell it in the air around her.

Whatever was coming was going to be a classic example of Lake Superior's fury, the kind of storm she loved to watch from the comfort of home, holed up in front of the woodstove with a book and a beer. It was most definitely *not* the kind of storm she wanted to overtake her out here. Even in this place of relative safety, less than a mile by bird flight to her home, these Canadian bastards, these prolonged bursts of sound and fury, could be—and often were—genuine killers.

She paddled faster, all but spinning the canoe through the turns, and still, the landscape seemed to crawl past. If it hadn't been for the movement of the world all around her—those scudding clouds, the brilliant autumn leaves being ripped from the trees and swirling past in mad little cyclones of yellow and red—she would have sworn she was not moving at all, that she was, in fact, a canoeist in a painting, frozen in place for all eternity.

"Two strokes forward, two feet back," she muttered, although she knew it wasn't true. Worse, it was a bad idea to waste precious breath speaking out loud.

And speaking of breath: was that her own she was hearing now, rasping through her throat as she labored onward into the wind? Or was she already hearing the pounding of the Superior surf? She tried to decide, separating the new noise from the bellow of the wind, the splashing of her paddle, the hollow slap and boom of the waves on the hull. It would be better not to know, she decided at last. Nor would it be productive to wonder if those were really the first icy drops of rain she was feeling on her face, or if she had remembered to tell David her plan for the day and the estimated time she would be heading home, so that at least one soul on the face of the planet would know where to look for her if she was overdue.

A gust tore her battered white Tilley hat from her head. She felt it go and made a frantic, instinctive grab to save it, but she was too late. She could only turn in her seat and watch it sail away, skipping twice off the top of the waves like a stone before the wind lifted it higher, up and over the trees on the river's east bank, over the forest and out of sight.

"Damn," she muttered, then laughed harshly. She had really loved that hat.

The canoe started to rock and swing, driven

backwards by the wind and the current, sliding toward the inside of the hairpin turn she'd been negotiating. A few feet away was a half-submerged deadfall, a bleached portion of the gnarled trunk rising above the waves like the snout of an underwater beast, scenting the air and waiting to snare her. She put the lost Tilley out of her mind and started to paddle again, taking back control of the canoe just seconds before it would have been snagged.

A while later, after she had settled back into the hellish but essentially mindless task of moving forward, she spared a final thought for the hat, a hat she had truly adored, a hat that had been with her for more than seven years, that had seen her through times like this before. How many times? Dozens certainly, perhaps a hundred or more, including the late-spring snowstorm that had stranded her for two days on a tiny island in Minnesota's Boundary Waters wilderness and the thunderstorm that had come crashing down on top of her just last summer while hiking along the Yellowstone River in Montana—a storm complete with wind that had knocked her to her knees, thunder that made her ears ring for hours afterward, and crackling lightning strikes close enough that she could feel the hair on her head literally standing up and the ground shuddering beneath her feet.

But there was nothing to be done about it now. The hat was gone, gone, gone, and it was time to forget it. She had to keep moving on.

"Steady" was the word her father always used to describe her. "Pragmatic" was the label pinned on her by one of her old college English profs. And though the latter made her sound like a soulless scientist and the former like a faithful old dog, Amy thought both expressions were fairly close to the mark. She was steady and pragmatic, and she had to rely on those traits now. She could mourn the hat later. Now, it was time to get home.

The spray against her face was harder now, icier, and the wind had developed a cyclonic whirl, whipping her hair around her face and causing the canoe to rock sideways one moment, buck unsteadily up and down the next.

Around and around she went, navigating through one twist of the river, then another, and another. The work grew exponentially harder. Her breath whistled in and out of her throat, almost in time with her paddle strokes. Her heart thudded dully and her lungs began to burn. Her hands on the paddle felt cramped and sore, and the muscles in her upper arms ached.

How do you like me now, lady? the weather asked in its dry prankster's voice. *How's this working out for you?*

An ear-splitting crack ripped through the air, and Amy let out a startled curse. She thought it was the first report of thunder, but then realized that it was only the sound of an ancient tree along the river bank losing its battle with the wind and toppling over in sudden, violent death.

She was beginning to feel a bit rattled—an unfamiliar, unsettling sensation. Rattled was bad. Rattled was something you should never, must never, allow yourself to feel in circumstances like these. Rattled led to bad decisions. Rattled led to careless mistakes. Rattled was the quickest way she could think of to turn a precarious situation into a disastrous one.

At last, nearly forty-five minutes after she had first felt the rising of the storm and abandoned her downstream fishing hole to start the race northward, Amy rounded the final bend and spotted her landing on the eastern bank. There was the familiar muddy cut where she dragged her canoe in and out of the water, and there, just beyond it, was the path that would lead her home.

The comfort of home. The warmth of home. The *safety* of home. She dug the blade of the paddle deeper into the river, pulling with everything she had to cut across the waves and reach the landing.

Almost there now . . .

Almost there . . .

Almost . . .

II

And that is where I have to leave her, my sweet Amy. That is where I have to leave her, alone in the storm, because I can take her no farther.

Of course, I've probably taken her too far already. In fact, I know I have. But in doing so, I felt that I was at least standing on relatively solid ground, a foundation that was a bit shaky but in no real danger of collapse. If I were to go beyond that point, the supports would crumble and I'd immediately tumble down into whatever lay beneath—quicksand, most likely.

Before I continue, let me state as clearly as I can

that the preceding pages are a work of fiction. They are not the product of any known facts. They stemmed entirely from my own prosaic imagination. I wrote the pages a few months ago at the suggestion of a friend, who said the process could help me understand what happened to Amy Brackett, the light of my life, who vanished suddenly on a stormy Saturday afternoon last October.

It was Kyle Halprin who told me to write it, although what he meant and what I did were two completely different things. We were having a couple of beers at Ebenezer's when he suggested it. It was February. Cold but not too cold. Misty. Sleety. Amy had been gone for four months, nearly to the day.

I always tried to be careful when I talked about Amy. I didn't want to dwell on her too much, too often, or to the wrong people. I didn't want to let my obsession show. I didn't want that obsession to make people anxious or uneasy. I didn't want it to annoy them or, god forbid, *bore* them. I did my best to keep everything to myself, or at least that's what I usually did. But that night was different. Kyle was a sympathetic audience, and I was well on my way to being drunk, a dangerous combination if there ever was one.

I'm sure I had already been going on about Amy for quite some time and had probably started to repeat myself when Kyle leaned across the table and exhaled a cloud of Bud Light fumes in my face.

"You know what you ought to do, David? You ought to write about it. That's what you should do."

I didn't answer right away. Instead, I looked past him at the dimly-lit bar, a little nicer than most of the other bars in town but still nothing to write home about. It was the kind of place that *might* have earned a three-sentence mention should someone ever decide to write a travel article about our little corner of the world. It *might* have been just interesting enough to get a nod under the heading of quaint local color. Then again, it might have been just mundane enough to miss the cut entirely.

I looked at the handful of patrons at the other tables and the two TVs bolted high on the walls, one showing the Red Wings, the other the Pistons. I looked at two women I didn't know playing pool. I looked at the NASCAR and Lions and Tigers memorabilia that was hanging everywhere, covering every available inch of wall and ceiling, front to back, side to side. I looked at Katie Dunstock behind the bar, drawing beers for Henry Hartman and the girl he was with. And beyond all that, I looked at the big plate-glass window that should have shown a nice view of Early Street but was instead opaque with frost and fog and beads of moisture.

"You're right," I said at last. "You are. You're right. I should write about it."

We didn't talk about it again after that, but the seed had been planted.

I knew what Kyle meant, of course. He meant I should write about Amy's disappearance for the paper, going beyond the fairly standard and cursory *Press-Beacon* coverage we'd given the story last fall. Week one: basic police report, summary of the search, a photo of Amy, and a request to call if anyone had any information on her whereabouts. Week two: a brief recap of the situation and a follow-up on the search, which was described as "under evaluation" with the parameters "being adjusted," meaning essentially, "scaled down," or more accurately, "cut back to nothing." Week three: a police statement that the search had been called off, with reassurance that the case was still under investigation and a repeated request for information from the public. Week four: nothing.

Kyle meant that I should write a *real* story about the case, about Amy, and about what might have caused a stable, happy, well-adjusted woman to vanish into the blue—or, given the weather conditions that day, perhaps *into the black* would be a more accurate description. He thought I should press harder, go beyond the sheriff's department press release and the generic quotes from the commander of the state police post. He wanted me to get inside the story, to really dig, to investigate and report.

What I'm not clear about is Kyle's motivation. Did he really believe I would be able to find something? Or did he see his suggestion as a form of therapy, a way to turn my mind in a better direction, away from pointless fretting and toward something that was at least slightly more productive? Whatever the case, I'm sure he didn't expect his advice to take the direction it took. He never expected me to sit down and turn Amy's story into what amounted to a piece of fiction, a tale, a yarn, something that was about as far as you could possibly get from a well-researched, well-reasoned, well-grounded article.

I didn't expect it either, but that's what came out when I finally sat down at my laptop to write. I'd intended only to type out a few preliminary notes:

things I knew, things I didn't know, questions to ask and who to ask them of. But what came out instead was that odd first sentence—*She was going to be caught; there were no two ways about it*—and all those even odder sentences that followed. I wrote in a foggy white heat, scarcely aware of what I was doing. The whole thing was done in a little over an hour.

That fact alone saddened and scared me. A little more than an hour. Sixty minutes plus. That's all it had taken to imagine all of it, for me to take Amy as far as I could take her, and when I was done, I had no earthly idea what to do next.

III

Here is what I do know:

Amy came to town that morning, as she often did on a Saturday, to run some errands. The list included a trip to the post office to mail a package and buy stamps, a stop at Halvorsen's Ace Hardware for a set of door hinges, and a slightly longer stop at the Red Door IGA to pick up staples, which for Amy meant a few fresh veggies, several cans of Campbell's tomato soup, a box of Quaker oatmeal, a jar of Skippy peanut butter, and plenty of Diet Coke.

I should probably back up here and explain just what the phrase "a trip to town" meant for Amy. For starters, she lived seventeen miles outside of Madsen, at a place called Vessey Point on the shore of Lake Superior. Her home was the former Coast Guard light station at the point, a several-acre complex that included the old keeper's quarters, the abandoned lighthouse tower, and the old fog signal building, along with several smaller brick outbuildings and the remains of other structures that had mostly crumbled into ruins after decades of neglect.

There are three main ways to reach Vessey Point from Madsen. The first and easiest is to drive north on County Road 419 until it dead-ends within earshot of the big lake, then walk a hundred yards or so through the trees, down a gently-sloping footpath to Amy's house. The second, suitable for the more adventurous with time on their hands, involves driving up another county road, numbered 411, until you reach Farwell Junction. At one time, the Junction was a thriving lumber camp, but now it's just a wide spot in the road with a single building, home to the Farwell Bar, gas station, and grocery store, an establishment that caters mostly to ATV riders in the summer and snowmobilers during the winter months. From the bar, you walk a short distance to the Farwell Grade, an abandoned railroad right-of-way that is now a state-designated snowmobile trail, then hike about three-quarters of a mile east on the trail until it passes just south of Vessey Point.

Amy could, and did, use both of those routes to travel between home and town. But being Amy—by which I mean, being a contrarian as well as one of the top outdoor writers of her generation—she preferred to take the third route, because it was the longest and most difficult. That meant that for about seven months of each year, from ice-out in April to ice-in in November, she kept her Ford pickup at the Madsen State Forest Campground, about fifteen miles north of town. She would walk from her house to a wide spot along the Horn River about three hundred yards away. There, she had created a small landing—a place to pull her canoe out of the water and tether it to a fallen maple tree. The Horn actually continued on from there, rounding a final sharp bend and passing directly alongside her house before carving a widening channel in the sandy beach and emptying into the lake in a frothy mix of tannin-brown river water and the frozen-glass water of Superior, clear enough to read through at a hundred paces. Amy could have paddled all the way from the campground to her back door, but because that final stretch of river was exceedingly shallow and the current exceptionally strong, she had chosen that quieter upstream spot as her arrival and departure point. She would walk to the landing, float the canoe, climb aboard, and paddle for nearly an hour until she reached the campground. Then, she would tie up the canoe at the base of a wooden fishing pier, scramble up to shore, hike to the parking lot, get in her truck, and drive the rest of the way into town. At the end of her visit, she would reverse the process—a homeward commute that would seem ridiculously and needlessly difficult to most people but had been a simple fact of Amy's life for seven years.

On that October Saturday, she left home around eight in the morning for the trip into Madsen. A few hours later, errands done, she met me at the Pine Street Café for an early lunch. At that time of day, at that time of year, there were only a handful of people in the place. Most of them were staring raptly at their smartphones or tapping away on laptops. No one was paying the slightest attention to us as we talked about nothing in particular.

BLOODYBONES

Amy did, in fact, tell me that she was going to do some fishing on the way home. There were several spots along the river where she liked to stop and drop a line. That day, she said she would be trying for brook trout in a place she called simply "the hole," a spot where the Horn had cut deeply into the adjacent banks, creating a quiet spot about thirty feet long and more than sixty feet across, a place where you could escape the endless current, stop paddling for a while, and merely drift. Calm, deep, cool, and shaded by the overhanging branches of towering hardwoods, it was a place where you could occasionally haul in your limit of brookies in under an hour.

Based on the time Amy and I left the café, I estimate she would have reached the campground by noon or so and would have paddled her way north to the hole by one at the latest. The storm that blew in from the northwest arrived about two-thirty, but it was clear that something bad was on the way nearly an hour before that. So Amy would have fished for thirty minutes or so, then seen or felt the drastic weather change that was bearing down on her, quickly stowed her gear, and started the last leg of her journey home.

I know the trip would have been difficult, based on the winds that afternoon, which according to the National Weather Service blew a steady thirty-five miles an hour, with several gusts topping out above fifty. I know it would have been wet, just based on the amount of sleety rain and watery snow that hammered us in town. But I know she persevered through all of that and made it home because her canoe was found in its proper spot, pulled out of the river and up the bank to the old maple tree, where it was securely tied.

There was also a trail of relatively fresh boot prints leading away from the canoe and down the trail toward her house, where they eventually petered out and were lost in a bog of sand and pine needles and soggy autumn leaves.

There was no evidence that Amy ever got all the way home. The old lightkeeper's quarters was not locked, but that in itself meant nothing; Amy seldom locked the place during the off-season. Even in the height of summer, when tourists might come stumbling along at any time, she was known to leave the door open during trips into town, fishing expeditions, or afternoon hikes. Only when she went away for a day or more, which she often did when traveling for a story, would she bother to secure the premises.

Despite the unlocked door, however, there were no signs that Amy had been inside the building that afternoon. The lights were off, the woodstove cold. Her computer was shut down and the manuscript that sat next to it on the table—several drafts of a piece about the evolution of walleye lures—was just where she had left it, the corners neatly squared and a simple glass paperweight resting neatly on top. The windbreaker she had been wearing when we met that morning was not hanging from its usual hook beside the door. Her boots were nowhere to be found.

There was also no trace of the things she would have been carrying. No little bag containing hinges from Halvorsen's, no bags of groceries, no fishing rod, and no pocket-sized flip-top box containing her favorite trout flies.

That's nearly the extent of what I know about that

day. There is only one other thing. The hat. It was the only object that was ever found. A volunteer from the county search and rescue spotted it the following week, caught seven or eight feet up in the branches of a tamarack tree half a mile upstream from Vessey Point.

Even now, months later, there are still many moments during the day that I am caught completely off guard, overwhelmed with sudden grief or confusion, frustration or—most of all—a kind of gut-wrenching, teeth-grinding anger. There is no predicting, no explaining what triggers these moments. They do not arrive in any reasonable or recognizable pattern, and they never announce themselves in advance. Often, they are brought on by absolutely nothing at all.

There is one thing, however, that is guaranteed to unleash a rush of grief every time I think of it. Of all the things it could be, it's that hat, that stupid, beat-up, should-have-been-thrown-in-the-trash-years-ago Tilley hat. That's all. Just the image of the Tilley hat snagged in the branches of that tamarack, waving like a flag of surrender.

The hat that I had given her not long after we'd met. The hat that I then proceeded to make fun of, pretty much non-stop, ever afterwards. The hat that she would defend in long, impassioned, flowery speeches, like a puffed-up, hyperbolic legislator praising the virtues of an unpopular bill.

That ridiculous hat.

Damn it, but she really loved that ridiculous hat.

IV

From the parking area at the end of 419, you can just see the top of the lighthouse poking above the trees. During the minute and a half or so that it takes to hike from the road to the point, the view gradually becomes better as the seventy-five-foot tower is revealed a little bit at a time.

As I approached the structure, I was struck with a rapidly-shifting range of emotions, some predictable—that familiar anger and sorrow again—and some a complete surprise—a sense of weirdly childlike excitement, of returning home after a long absence.

It was the tail end of April, more than six months after Amy's disappearance, and it was my first visit to Vessey Point since those dreadful days last November, not long after the search had been called off.

There was snow on the ground the last time I'd been here—not enough to cover all of the grass but just enough to make things slippery and make your footfalls sound like muffled gunshots. Amy's parents had come from New Hampshire a week or so earlier, wanting to be close, to be there for whatever might happen—or not happen. Later, when it was clear that the search was a bust and that Amy was not going to miraculously walk in the door of the Pine Street Café with a grin and a cheerful, "Hey, all. Didja miss me?" her father and I spent several gray days securing her house and property.

Bob Brackett was retired after forty-seven years as a family practitioner in Concord. He'd been in the game long enough to remember when there were no family-practice docs, just guys they called GPs, those yeomen who treated everything from stubbed toes to heart disease and could still be persuaded to make a midnight house call or, if necessary, deliver a baby in somebody's living room. Over the course of his career, I imagine he'd held the hands of many grieving spouses and parents, offering comfort and counseling and the occasional prescription for something stronger. But he had no words or pills to help himself.

I had met him several times before and always found him to be an eager and cheerful conversationalist with an intriguing, slightly wicked sense of humor—not unlike his daughter. But during the two and a half days we worked side by side in Amy's house, he was something quite different, a virtual shadow of himself, a ghost, a quiet gray presence that shuffled, bent-backed, from task to task. He only laughed when absolutely required—when I tried to lighten the mood with a lame joke, for example—and the sound of it was brittle and broken, a little manic, even frightening.

It was a blessing to be alone when I returned last week. There was still a thin crust of snow underfoot—the end of the season this time rather than the beginning—but everything else about the day was different. The sky was high and blue instead of that close, cloudy, claustrophobic dome that had loomed over us in November. The sun was providing a weak blanket of warmth instead of merely cold white light, and if you looked closely enough at the grass and trees, you could imagine that the world would eventually manage to shrug off its monochrome springtime mantle and recolor itself in shades of green.

Lake Superior was calm, an unbroken sheet of

blinding blue glass dotted with the white flecks of lingering ice floes. I stopped briefly to appreciate the view then took the narrow boardwalk that led across the sand to the base of the tower and followed the short extension from there to the keeper's quarters. I dug out the ring of keys Amy's father had left with me and was about to open the side door when I felt it—the touch on the base of my neck.

I didn't move. I didn't cry out. But I did stop breathing for a moment. It felt as though something had frozen in my throat, tight enough, sharp enough, that air could not squeeze past.

The touch lasted for only a second, longer than a passing whisper of wind, though not by much. By the time I finally turned around to look, it was already long gone.

I knew immediately that it was only my imagination. Certainly it had not been Amy touching me in that small spot at the very top of my spine, that place where she would sometimes lightly rest her hand when we were watching a movie or sitting side by side at the computer. It was not her gentle, almost imperceptible touch that would sometimes make my arms break out in goosebumps or elicit a surprised giggle. I knew before I turned that there would be nothing there, and of course, I was not disappointed. The whole of Vessey Point was empty, and the only sandy boot prints on the boardwalk planks were my own.

I opened the door and went in.

Stepping into the keeper's quarters was like walking into an icebox. Shut up for months with blinds drawn, the old brick building had done an efficient job storing every bit of the winter's cold. The place felt like an unearthed tomb, abandoned for eons, an impression not helped by the sheets and drop cloths Bob Brackett had insisted on placing over all the furniture, turning every object into something vaguely threatening, ghostlike.

I walked among those looming presences in the shadowy gloom for several minutes, unsure what I was looking for or why I had even come. There was little of Amy left there: furniture, rugs, dishes in the cupboards, and silverware in the drawers. Books on the shelves in the downstairs sitting room. Clothes in the upstairs closets and dresser. Bob and I had discussed removing all of those things last fall, and while there were solid arguments for and against it, neither of us had been able to make that choice, opting instead to leave everything as it was until some undefined point in the future. In the end, all we removed were her desktop and laptop computers and her iPad, along with a few boxes of loose papers, a four-drawer file cabinet that constituted her professional life, a strongbox stuffed with important personal documents, and a few other items most likely to fall prey to marauding snowmobilers over the winter months—namely, her stash of wine and beer, her half-dozen cameras, her considerable stockpile of fishing gear, and her gun collection. Those items went into our trucks, the perishables went in the trash, but everything else stayed exactly where it was and got neatly covered with one of Bob's awful funeral shrouds.

But while all of those possessions were there, they were not Amy. They were not Amy any more than the items we had taken out of there last fall were Amy. Amy was not tightly drawn blinds. She was open windows and streaming sunshine. Amy was not careful, almost clinical preservation. She was an open bottle of Diet Coke on the dining room table, the morning's dirty dishes in the sink, muddy boots in the entryway, and a Tilley hat tossed onto the couch.

There were none of those things there now.

Feeling a sick weight in the pit of my stomach, I climbed the curving staircase to the second floor and poked my head into each of the four ancient rooms. But though the sight of her bedroom summoned a momentary pang, the overall impression was the same as downstairs. The keeper's quarters had become little more than an empty museum. It was no longer a home, certainly no longer *her* home.

I went back down and headed outside, leaving the door ajar—an excuse to come back one last time to lock up. I walked down to the beach, enjoying the feel of the sun, the scent of the pines and the lake, the sense of freedom, which felt ridiculously good even after such a short time enclosed in that tomb of a house.

As I crossed the sand, heading for the water, it seemed that I felt that brief touch on the back of my neck again. But it was even faster, lighter, more illusory than the first time, and I pretended that I hadn't felt a thing.

V

I walked along the water's edge for a while, marveling at the silence of the day—a preternaturally calm Lake

Superior, the utter absence of any sound but my own footsteps, the lack of wind rustle or wave wash or even birdsong. I wondered if the absence of birds was common for this time of year, and I felt another pang when I realized that Amy would have known and, if asked about it, would have immediately launched into a detailed explanation—lengthy but somehow coherent and entertaining—covering everything from avian migration and traffic patterns to meteorological trends, with probably a bit of regional history and local folklore thrown in to season the stew.

The lakeshore was its usual springtime mess. Within a hundred yards or so I had passed enough driftwood to construct a small fortress, stepped over mounds of weeds and pebbles and sandy muck scraped onto shore and left behind by the recently-departed ice, navigated around a dozen or more dead fish in various stages of decay and mostly pecked apart by seagulls, and even come across a deer carcass—bones, mostly, tied together with bits of waterlogged hide and sinew—that had washed in from god only knows where.

If I continued in the same direction for a few hundred yards more, I would come to the edge of Vessey Point and officially pass beyond Amy's property onto state-owned land—forest and shoreline that was exactly the same but, to me, would be significantly, fundamentally different.

It was hard to explain, bordering on ludicrous, but leaving the Point would feel entirely too much like betrayal. It would feel like walking away from Amy, and I wasn't prepared to do that, not at that moment. Rather than risk crossing that invisible boundary line,

I decided to go just a short distance more, choosing a piece of driftwood up ahead where I would stop, turn around, and head back to—

"David, look." It was her voice.

It was Amy's voice.

I heard it as an actual, corporeal thing, not imagination, not just a sound inside my head. Amy's voice, soft, almost a whisper, but real, tangible, part of the physical world around me.

I spun around so fast that I almost lost my balance, giving me a quick, disorienting image of my body sprawling clumsily on the sand and Amy standing above me, extending a hand to help me to my feet, laughing at my awkwardness. But I didn't fall, and Amy did not put out her hand for me because she was not there. Of course she wasn't. Amy was not there now, and she had not been there yesterday or the day before, and she would not be there tomorrow or next week or the month after next. Amy was gone. Amy had vanished more than half a year ago, blown suddenly out of my life and taken somewhere else in the gnashing teeth of an October gale.

But I heard her voice again all the same.

"David. Please look."

Pointlessly, I turned around again, glancing behind me at the lake, from side to side at the beach and the keeper's quarters and the light tower and the fog signal building. I thought I saw something up high, behind the glass at the top of the lighthouse, in that now empty room where a mighty Fresnel lens had once rotated endlessly, beaming its signal more than 25 miles out across the lake, providing crucial information to sailors in those days before radio navigation beacons and Loran and GPS, letting them fix their location on the chart and simultaneously warning them away from the rising lump of limestone called Vessey Reef that lay less than a half-mile offshore.

I thought for a single breath of a moment that I saw a face up there, peering down. A white face pressed against the glass, eyes wide, nose grotesquely flattened, mouth open in soundless speech.

"Please look."

I jumped, startled again. The face vanished, and I understood that what I had really seen was exactly what you might expect it to be—not a person but a reflection of the sun, a momentary illusion caused by light bouncing off the glass.

But that voice, *her* voice, still left me shaken. It was just as imaginary as the lighthouse vision, but it had been so distinct, so clear, so real in that otherwise silent place on that otherwise silent morning.

That's when the impossible happened, and I saw something that was not an optical trick or sun mirage.

That's when I saw her.

VI

She was standing just beyond the buildings, not far from where the little footpath came out of the trees, dressed in jeans and a gray hooded sweatshirt. She was not wearing the Tilley hat, of course, and her black hair hung loose around her face. There was something in her hands. From this distance, I could not quite tell what it was. It might have been a small package, a fanny pack, or even one of the cameras—the pricey Leica, maybe, or the small Nikon—that Amy carried with her on every writing assignment and most of her daily hikes.

She was looking right at me.

I don't know how to describe the feelings that swept over me in that moment. I literally do not have the vocabulary to explain the sensation, but I believe the phrase *crashing joy* might come close.

She raised her hand then and waved at me—a slow, oddly languid gesture, hesitant, uncertain, as though she did not know exactly who I was but realized I was someone to be acknowledged. For a reason I don't understand, that beautiful, euphoric, all-too-brief sensation of unfettered happiness was blown away in an instant by that wave, which sent a chill spiderwalking down my spine.

"Amy—" I said, but the word came out small and strangled. It could not have been heard ten feet away, let alone across the distance that separated us now.

She started walking toward me—and why did I react the way I did? Why did I suddenly feel as if I wanted to run not toward her, as I should have, but away? Why did the sight of Amy starting toward me down the beach make me want to sprint as fast as I could in the opposite direction?

I would have run—I'm quite sure I would have—but my legs did not seem to work. They felt weighted with lead, holding me to the spot.

The Amy-thing (and why did I suddenly think of her that way? What created *that* weird image?) kept coming, getting closer, while I simply stood there, rooted. My mouth opened again, but this time no sound at all came out.

"Excuse me," she called across the ever-narrowing gap between us. "Can you tell me—is this Vessey Point?"

Everything changed in that instant. The fear that had gripped me left as suddenly as it arrived, flooding out of my body like a wall of water released from a dam, washing the confusion away with it. With new clarity, I saw what I should have seen earlier, understood what I should have understood right away.

This person was not Amy. Of course it wasn't. It never had been Amy, not even for a moment. It was someone else, just a woman, another woman, not Amy, just a visitor to the point like me, a stranger on the shore.

I'm not sure how I could have thought, even for a half-second, that it was Amy, although I comforted myself with the knowledge that distance and location and nostalgia and longing, combined with a few vague similarities like height and hair color, had been enough to create the illusion. I would cling to that for now, I decided, and deal with the other issues later. Like that strange fear, for example—the way a simple wave had transformed joy into terror—and the troubling way I had suddenly thought of Amy as a *thing*.

"Yes," I said, finally finding my voice.

She arrived at my side a moment later, and I saw that the object in her hand was indeed a camera, not a Leica or a Nikon like Amy's but a Canon digital SLR with a fairly large zoom lens.

"Yes?" she repeated—a question, though, not a statement. "Vessey Point?"

I nodded and gestured in the direction of the tower. "That's the Vessey Point Lighthouse."

"Finally," she said, flashing a grin that hit me like a fist in the center of my chest. "It took me forever to find this damn place. I was driving up here, and I turned where I thought I was supposed to turn, but I ended up on some dirt road that went . . . well, I don't really know where it went, but it didn't come here, I'll tell you that much. I swear it went around in complete circles a few times, like about ten times, and finally ended up in a little muddy two-track trail. I had to back up what seemed like forever before I got to a place that was wide enough to turn around and drive back out."

I laughed. "Welcome to the Upper Peninsula, where decent roads go to die in the mud." I pointed at her camera. "Taking pictures of the lighthouse?"

"Among other things," she said, an evasive response that somehow didn't seem evasive accompanied by that grin. "That's all right, isn't it?"

"Sure," I said with a shrug. "I mean, technically, this is private property, but that really doesn't—"

"It's all right," she said, the smile fading slowly. "I knew the person who used to live here."

I felt my breath catch in my throat. "You kn-knew Amy?"

"In a manner of speaking. I used to know her. A long time ago. Many years." She glanced down at the ground then back at me. "Amy was my sister."

VII

"I just wasn't ready. Not today. So I did everything backwards.

But I guess fate had a different idea, didn't it?"

BLOODYBONES

We were sitting side by side on one of the dead tree trunks that had either washed onto the beach in last fall's storms or been dragged ashore by the winter ice. The sun was on our faces, the lighthouse and keeper's quarters at our backs. A good twenty minutes had elapsed since our unusual meeting, and I still hadn't entirely come to grips with what was happening.

"It's definitely strange," I said, nodding. "I didn't expect to see anyone out here. Not at this time of year. And then, out of all the people in the world, I end up running into—"

"My thoughts precisely. Don't take this the wrong way or anything, but you were the last person I expected to see. You were the last person I *wanted* to see." She laughed. "David Mahon. *Amy's* David. I mean, c'mon, really, what were the odds?"

It had taken all of five minutes to discover that I liked her. I liked her immensely. Karen Brackett— actually Karen Brackett Shumacher; she still used her ex-husband's name though they had been divorced for two years—was nothing at all like Amy yet exactly like her at the same time. Much like their physical appearances, there were just enough vague, general similarities in the sisters' personalities to tip off an astute observer that he was dealing with members of the same family, but not enough real or direct resemblance to ever cause confusion.

Karen seemed to share Amy's wry view of life and the universe along with her sardonic sense of humor, but at least on early acquaintance, I didn't detect any of the accompanying darkness I'd sometimes felt from Amy, that unconfirmed suspicion that she was laughing at the world because it disappointed her, because shrugging things off with a grin was better than crying about them. In contrast, Karen seemed to laugh because she was genuinely amused.

I'd known, of course, that Amy had a sister. If an inquisitor had put hot coals to my feet, I might have remembered that her name was Karen. I knew that they were estranged, had not really spoken much, if at all, over the past twenty years. But I never really knew why. I had approached the subject with Amy once or twice and had been led to believe that it was no big deal, just one of those things, just two siblings with different interests, following different courses, another bit of proof that blood could certainly be thicker than water but didn't necessarily have to be.

I didn't get much more than that from Karen, though I did ask how long it had been since she'd last seen her sister.

"What day is this?" she asked.

"Friday."

"Then if this is Friday, it's been . . . let's see, Monday, Tuesday, Wednesday, Thursday—I'd say about twenty-two years." She smiled, and I responded in kind. "The last time I saw her was Christmas vacation of my freshman year in college. She was a junior in high school. I kind of fell away from the family after that. You know how that goes. You decide to stay away over spring break. Then you get a job at school for the summer. Maybe you fight with your parents over a guy or an apartment or your major, or maybe a little bit of everything. The next thing you know, years have gone by. By the time I came home again, Amy was off on her own, climbing every mountain and fording every stream."

I saw no point in pushing further so merely nodded. Whatever had happened between the sisters, or between Karen and any of the other Bracketts, didn't seem to matter much now.

"How long did you know her?" Karen asked.

I didn't even have to think about that one. "Seven years," I said. "I met her when she bought the lighthouse. I work for the paper in town, and I came out to do a story about her. She was already something of a celebrity when she moved in. There were folks in town who'd read her stuff in the outdoor magazines, and the library had copies of her first two essay collections. But I'm not much of an outdoorsman, so I'd never heard of her. I did the usual Madsen *Press-Beacon* puff piece and thought that was it, but a month or so later she showed up in my office and asked me out to dinner."

"She asked *you* out. That's Amy. Ever fearless. She thought the world of you, you know." She paused, giving me an opening. I deferred, waiting for her to go on. "I never talked to her, of course, but she talked to Mom and Dad about you all the time. When I was getting ready to come up here, Dad told me to find you and get the keys to the place, in case I wanted to look inside. 'How will I find him?' I asked. He told me to check at the paper and gave me your phone number, but he also said, 'You won't have any trouble finding David. According to your sister, he's the most important person in town.'"

I laughed at that but also felt something in the center of my chest—a wound I thought had finally started to heal—open up again with a sharp, stabbing pain.

"So, David, I ask you—as the most important person in town and the most important person in Amy's life, what do you think happened to her?"

I turned away and looked at the lake, thinking, wondering, trying to see if I'd come up with any new answers to a question I had tried my best to stop asking. I could only shrug.

"I honestly don't know."

Karen nodded, as if she had expected that exact answer. Then she said, matter of factly, "I think she drowned."

It was a natural assumption. Everyone who knew Amy and every expert from every agency involved in last fall's search had entertained the idea. But, if you'll pardon the expression, it simply didn't hold water. I began to explain that to Karen, describing the sketchy facts of the case, the tethered canoe, the footprints leading away from the landing toward the house. She was nodding impatiently before I was half finished.

"I know all that, David. Mom and Dad told me, and I read their copies of the police reports. I saw the articles online, in your paper and others. But I still think she drowned."

"Okay, I'll bite. Why?"

She gave me a long, level stare. "You'll think I'm crazy." She hesitated again, then pushed on. "I keep dreaming about her. Ever since she disappeared, I keep dreaming about her. It's the reason I finally went back to Concord to see the folks. It's the reason I came here. I thought—I thought, you know, that I needed some kind of closure. I thought if I could see the place, look around, talk to people, see where she lived . . . I thought I needed to reconnect with her somehow, make up for all those lost years. I thought maybe if I did that, I'd get some closure and get rid of those dreams."

"I still don't understand. What does that have to do with drowning?"

"That's what I see in the dreams," Karen said softly. "It's crazy, I know. I barely know what Amy looked like anymore. I've seen the pictures at Mom and Dad's place and the jacket photo on her books—you know the one, where she's standing next to the canoe wearing that stupid white hat. But the picture of her in my mind is always the way she looked when I saw her last—the seventeen-year-old tomboy, the debate team captain, the midfielder on the soccer team, the kid who worked at Dairy Queen every summer and spent every afternoon fishing on the Merrimack, who spent every night in her room tapping away on Dad's old Olympia typewriter. She had shorter hair back then. And freckles. Lots of freckles. Did she still have those, David? Did she still have the freckles?"

"Right across her nose," I said, swallowing hard. "I called them Amy Major, her own personal constellation."

"Well, in the dreams, I see Amy the way I knew her back then, and she's always underwater."

"Underwater?"

"Clear, green water. Cold. I never touch it, but I know it's cold. It looks almost like ice. I see her face looking up at me, the way she looked back then but white and bloated, and she's looking up at me, always looking up at me. Her eyes are wide open. And she's reaching for me. Her hand is white too, and she's reaching up, trying to break out of the water and reach me, trying to touch me."

I realized she was crying, but I didn't know how to respond. I wanted to say something or take her hand or put my arm around her shoulder, but I didn't; I don't know why.

"I've had that dream every night since she disappeared. Every single night. Amy in that green water, reaching for me, like she wants me to rescue her."

"Karen, I'm sorry—"

"That's how I know, David. That's how I know my sister drowned. Because I see it again and again, every goddamned night."

VIII

Before we left the point, I gently tried convincing her to look inside. I know it's not what she had intended that day, and I understood why. She had already said it herself: she simply was not ready. That's the reason she hadn't called me in advance or stopped in Madsen and tried to track me down. She wanted to see the place first, walk around, get the lay of the land, maybe snap a few pictures and try to figure out what she felt, *how* she felt. It was to be a step-one visit, a tentative outreach. Later, if and when she felt up to it, she could take the next step and actually enter her sister's domain.

But I had changed that. Through a bit of coincidence so bizarre that it quite frankly unnerved me, I had decided to make my long-delayed trip back to the lighthouse on the very same day, at the very same time, that Karen had chosen for her first visit.

And since I was here, with the keys to the place jingling in my pocket, it only made sense that she adjust her plans and take a look inside today. It would be foolish to wait. Or so I thought.

After a bit of cajoling, Karen agreed. But a few minutes later, standing at the door of the keeper's quarters, she almost changed her mind.

"David, wait." She put a hand on my arm. "Maybe not today."

"It's okay," I said. "I know where you're coming from, but believe me, it will be all right. I didn't want to go in either, but once I did, I realized it was just a place. It's just a building, nothing more."

I could see her wanting to argue with me, and again, I understood. There was a world of difference between what I had felt earlier today, stepping into a place I had been a thousand times before, a place that was nearly as familiar as my own living room, and the emotions Karen would feel walking into the home of a virtual stranger. It would be the closest she had been to her sister in more than two decades.

After a moment of internal debate, she evidently decided not to argue after all. Instead, she stepped aside and let me open the door.

The arctic chill swept over us as I led her inside and seemed to dig in its claws as I showed her around the place, pointing out the window overlooking the lake where Amy had kept her desk and done most of her work, the kitchen where she'd cooked her meals, the parlor where she'd watched TV and read on winter evenings.

I also told her what I knew of the history.

Vessey Point had for a number of years been home

to two divisions of the federal government: the U.S. Lighthouse Service, which built the tower in 1895 and ran it until nearly 1940, and the U.S. Lifesaving Service, which had maintained a separate home, now long gone, with a crew that stood round-the-clock ready to race to the aid of sailors in peril out on the lake.

The lifesaving station was eventually abandoned, while the lighthouse and its keepers came under the jurisdiction of the Coast Guard. That system remained in place for many years, but it could not last forever. Like nearly every other lighthouse on the Great Lakes or ocean coasts, Vessey Point's days as a manned outpost were numbered. The light was automated, the last keeper relieved of duty, and the keeper's quarters shuttered in the early 1970s. Within fifteen years, the place was closed down completely, its duties taken over by a smaller light and radio beacon located in the shipping channel a mile offshore.

Eventually, the Vessey Point property was deeded to Madsen Township, which partnered with a volunteer group and obtained several grants to restore the tower and home. Before they could renovate the fog signal building and other structures or build the small public park they had envisioned for the site, the majority of the volunteers had drifted away, moving on to other, less labor-intensive projects with faster returns. After several failed attempts to resurrect the organization and revitalize the cause, the cash-strapped township was forced to sell the property to the highest bidder.

The first private owners were a retired couple from Ohio, who tried to run the place as a bed and breakfast for several years. When the task proved too much for them, to say nothing of too unprofitable, they put Vessey Point back on the market, where it eventually caught the interest of a young and adventurous outdoor writer named Amy Brackett.

Karen listened to this tale politely, but her interest was clearly someplace else. Even parts of the story I thought would intrigue her the most—for example, the fact that Vessey Point had at one time actually been a small town with its own store, post office, and one-room school—barely generated a brief nod.

She was lost in her own little world, or Amy's little world, or whatever hybrid of the two had formed in her mind. As I talked, she walked slowly from room to room, lifting the corners of the drop cloths and peering underneath, opening cupboards, gazing with unusual interest at the floor tiles and throw rugs.

I took her upstairs and showed her Amy's old room, where she silently studied the clothes in the closet and the handful of items—pocketknife, nail clippers, clip-on reading light, pens and bookmarks—that littered the night stand.

"You weren't kidding," she said at last, sitting on the edge of the bed with a sigh. "When you said you and dad left almost everything here, that was no exaggeration."

"We only took out the real valuables," I said. "Remember, that was last fall. It was only a month after she went missing. We were still thinking—hoping—that she might come back any day."

"And now? What do you think now, David Mahon?"

I stared at her, trying to determine what she wanted from me.

Optimism? Hope? Comfort? The truth?

"I haven't given up hope," I said at last. "But I'm realistic. I know what the odds are. I knew what the odds were even back then, the day she disappeared. I don't think I'll ever stop hoping, but I don't expect the impossible."

It seemed that I should add something else, but she had already stopped listening. As I spoke, she had gotten off the bed and moved to the window. I didn't have to join her to know what she was seeing; I knew the view well. I knew that she could see the beach to the east of the house, which continued for just a short distance before encountering a low stone wall, three sides of a square with the fourth side mostly missing, all that remained of the foundation from the old lifesaving station. A little farther along, several wooden pilings still poked up out of the water, remnants of the dock where the lifesaving crews had launched their tiny rescue boats into the angry Superior surf. Just down from there, more pilings formed the skeleton of another pier, this one the place that supply boats had once moored, bringing mail, winter rations, fuel oil, and other necessities to residents of the point.

"Karen?"

She didn't answer. She needed to be alone.

I turned away and left the bedroom, heading back for the ground floor. I was halfway down the stairs when I heard Amy's voice beside me again, just as I had earlier on the shore.

At first, there was just a single word: "David."

I froze where I was, my chest tight.

Then there was more, coming in a rush: "He's here, David. Bloodybones. You have to get out now.

Bloodybones is walking. He's here. He's walking. He's coming to the house, David. Get out, get out, *get out!"*

I barely had time to register the words when the air was filled with a tremendous shrieking noise. It drowned out the voice in my ear, which of course had never really been there to begin with, and seemed to fill every inch of the building. It felt like an incredible wave of pressure, and it increased rapidly to a crushing force, taking up every inch of space between the walls, using up the oxygen, making it difficult to breathe, threatening to blow out the windows and rip off the roof.

Heart pounding, I pivoted and raced back up the steps to the bedroom where Karen Brackett was screaming.

She was still standing at the window, and as I approached her from behind I saw that she was trembling, her entire body quivering from head to toe. Her scream went on and on, a long, uninterrupted siren shriek. This close, I thought the sound of it might cause my skull to crack open and fall in pieces to the floor.

I reached out to put a hand on Karen's shoulder, but just before I touched her, she fell silent. The abrupt cessation of noise was startling, as jarring as a punch to the midsection, and I pulled back, frightened.

She turned to face me, still trembling. Her face was as white as salt, her eyes wide, staring blindly.

I took her hand and was astonished at how cold it felt, like frozen granite.

Her mouth opened slowly, as if on rusty hinges, and a low, flat voice came forth.

"Amy's in the pool," she said.

The skin on the back of my neck tightened.

"Black water, blue water, green water," she chanted. "Deep water, dark water, dead water."

I dropped her hand and backed up a step. Her eyes stared at me, unseeing, from the middle of that dead white face.

"Black water," she intoned again. "She's in the pool now. Amy Lynn is in the pool."

"What pool?" I asked, my voice scarcely more than a strangled croak. "Where is she, Karen?"

But Karen did not answer, at least not directly. She only looked at me with those unseeing eyes, where tears had begun to brim and spill slowly over the edges, cutting glistening tracks down her marble-white cheeks.

"He put her there," she said in that strange, flat voice.

"Who?" I asked. "Who put her there, Karen?"

"He put her there," she said again. "Bloodybones put Amy Lynn into the pool."

IX

"So wait a minute—you don't know what happened to her? You just dropped her off and haven't seen her again? Haven't heard anything from her?"

Kyle gave me a level stare across the bar room table. It was nine o' clock on Monday night, and Ebenezer's was as quiet as I'd ever seen it. In fact, except for Katie at the bar, we were the only two people in the place. Only one of the TV sets was on, tuned to CNN, the sound muted.

BLOODYBONES

"Not for lack of trying on my part," I said with a shrug, refilling Kyle's glass from the beer pitcher on the table.

I honestly do not remember how long it took for Karen to snap out of it (regain her senses, wake up, come around, come to—what exactly is the correct term for something like that?) on Friday afternoon. Those few seconds after she turned around to face me were a blur in my mind. The entire interval from hearing Amy's voice on the stairs to Karen's final flat incantation—*Bloodybones put Amy Lynn into the pool*—was mostly a blur.

I could recall the highlights, however. They came as half-remembered images, like pictures glimpsed in the fog, bits and shards and slightly larger fragments: the terrible too-white color of Karen's face, the terrible feel of her too-cold hand, the strange and soulless sound of her voice, the absence of any life at all in her eyes, followed by something almost as bad—the sudden appearance of silent tears welling up and spilling down her cheeks.

I don't know how long the entire incident lasted, but it ended abruptly, and when it was over, Karen had no memory of it. She could recall looking out the window at the water and the beach. The last thing she saw, she told me, were the pilings of the two old piers running out into the lake. She said they looked like the broken teeth of an old giant, leading me to believe that some of Amy's writing talent was familial. After studying the piers, the next thing she was aware of was me leading her down the stairs and out the front door. Everything between was a blank.

We both were a bit wobbly as we hiked to our cars,

but by the time we got there, she was doing better, steadier and noticeably stronger. After talking to her a few more minutes, I judged that she was well enough to drive, but I still drove slowly as she followed me back into town. I waited while she checked into the Dreamview Motel on state highway 187—the same place her mother and father had stayed last fall—then said goodbye, handing her a sheet of paper from my pocket notebook on which I'd scribbled my work and home addresses, e-mail address, and cell number.

On Saturday I went to the office, hoping to make up for the time I'd lost by going to Vessey Point. I spent most of the day waiting for my cell to ring, but it never did. On Sunday I went to work again, intending to spend another hour or two catching up, but I was anxious and uneasy, distracted. Instead of editing press releases for next week's paper, I called the Dreamview instead.

Marie Rooney rang Karen's room for me but came back on the line when no one picked up.

"Are you sure she's still there?" I asked.

"Oh yeah, she's here," Marie said.

"You've seen her?"

"Well, not lately. Not since Friday night, when she came in the lobby to get a bucket of ice from the machine. But she hasn't checked out. I can see her car from here, parked in front of number 9."

I tried again later in the day and got pretty much the same answer, this time from Marie's husband. Ron Rooney had seen Karen drive away around noon and return maybe half an hour later, carrying a white bag that looked like the kind they used at the State Street Pharmacy. While she wasn't picking up her phone, she was definitely in her room. Ron could see her car from where he was standing, yes, parked right in front of good old number 9.

I tried a third time Monday morning with the same result and at lunch time drove over to the motel myself. Karen's car was gone, but Marie assured me she had not checked out. She had only "gone out for a bit" after inquiring on the whereabouts of certain local amenities, including the library and a laundromat.

"I told her you were trying to get in touch with her," Marie said. "If she hasn't gotten back to you, it might just be she doesn't want to talk to you."

I finished the day at the office, grabbed dinner, and drove past the Dreamview again on my way to cover the monthly township board meeting. Karen's car was still gone.

"I'll bet I've tried ten times to reach her," I told Kyle now. "I tried calling again after the board meeting, just before I drove over here, but the phone rang and rang. I guess Marie was right. She doesn't want to see me."

"Or she's just crazy," Kyle said matter-of-factly. "From what you told me, her behavior doesn't sound exactly—what would you call it? Rational? What was all that about, anyway, out there at the point?"

I shrugged, thinking how easy it would be to write off the incident in the bedroom as the antics of a madwoman. I realized the term was a dramatic one, so maybe I should temper it a bit. Not *madwoman,* but how about *seriously disturbed?*

But of course there was more to the story. There was something else. There was the part I had not told Kyle. If Karen was crazy for seeing whatever she had seen—might have seen, *thought* she had seen—outside the bedroom window, then where did that leave me? Hadn't I seen my own minor hallucination that very same day? Hadn't I imagined a face in the lighthouse tower? Hadn't I felt Amy's touch on the back of my neck, and even more, hadn't I heard her talking to me several times, the last time just moments before Karen's own disturbing episode?

I had not allowed myself to think about any of that, but it was pretty clear what the whole thing meant.

Madwoman, madman, I thought dourly, taking a double swallow of beer.

It was after ten-thirty when I left the bar, having come to no conclusions but having reached an agreement of sorts with Kyle: the next time I went to the point, with Karen Shumacher or without her, he would be tagging along.

"I don't get any of this, but I want to find out," he said. "I want to find out what this Bloodybones crap is all about. What does that mean anyway, Bloodybones? Is it a name? A person?"

Bloodybones is walking, I thought crazily. *He's here, he's walking, he's coming to the house.*

I shook my head a little to clear it and gave him a thin smile. "Your guess is as good as mine, buddy. I have no idea."

We made a tentative date for Wednesday morning, after that week's paper was on the street. It would be a relatively light day for me, and Kyle, who sold cars at Tadger's Chevrolet, said he could call in sick and not be missed.

"It's Wednesday, it's April, and the handful of tax-refund sales we had basically wrapped up a few weeks ago," he said. "If my choice is sitting in the office watching Dan Winslow play online poker all day or going with you to Vessey Point—no contest."

I drove away from Ebenezer's, going down Early Street to State, where I hesitated longer than necessary at the four-way stop. A left turn would take me the two blocks to Cherry Street, where another left turn would take me to my house. I turned right instead and headed back out to the highway.

Karen's car was in front of room number 9, where a soft light glowed through a gap in the drapes. I hesitated again, but only briefly, before pulling into an open space two doors down and shutting off the engine.

She answered the door immediately, as if she'd been waiting for my knock.

"I knew it would be you," she said, taking my hand and almost dragging me across the threshold. "Get in here. I want to ask you something."

I had never been inside the rooms at the Dreamview, but they were exactly what I expected: a simple arrangement of two twin beds with a nightstand between them, a double dresser, and a low, round table by the window. Cheap art on the walls. Cheap carpeting on the floor.

Karen must have been working at the table when I knocked. There was a laptop sitting there along with several books, a half-empty bottle of water, and a half-filled glass beside it. A partially-eaten slice of takeout pizza was sitting on a napkin beside the computer. It looked desiccated, ancient.

"I've been trying to reach you, Karen."

"They told me," she said with an impatient nod. "What is that?"

It took me a moment to understand what she was asking. Then, I noticed that she was pointing at a picture on the laptop screen. I bent down and looked at it, frowning. Frankly, it didn't look like much of anything—a long, gray blur surrounded by larger blurs of green and brown.

She noticed my confusion. "Sorry about that. Out of focus.

How about this one?"

She clicked a small white arrow on the right side of the screen. The fuzzy image slid neatly out of view, and a clearer, sharper picture took its place.

I felt a faint chill.

"Where did you get that?"

"I took it. This afternoon."

"You went out there again? Today? By yourself?"

"Yes, David," she said with more than a touch of impatience. "I went out there again today, by myself. Do you know what it is?"

I looked at the image, which showed a long stone wall—about two feet high in most places, less in areas where the top portion had crumbled away—running across a stretch of sand and beach grass.

"It's what's left of the old Vessey Point Lifesaving Station," I said. "The place was abandoned for decades. Kids used it for parties, but I don't think anyone else had been inside for at least fifty years. Most of the windows were busted out. Part of the roof had collapsed. It caved in completely sometime in the eighties, not too long after I moved here. The pile of rubble sat on the beach for years. I think it was that out-of-state couple, the ones who owned the B and B, who finally cleaned it up."

BLOODYBONES

"That's what I thought," Karen said.

She lowered herself into a chair and reached for one of the books. I noticed a sticker on the spine and a faint MADSEN AREA SCHOOL AND PUBLIC LIBRARY stamp on the page edges. When I looked closer, I recognized the volume too—*A Pictorial History of Madsen Township,* published seven or eight years ago by a group of volunteers, mostly elderly women, who called themselves the Historical Advisory Committee.

Karen opened to a page in the middle of the book. It featured a black and white photo of Vessey Point from a much earlier time, when both the lighthouse and lifesaving station had been in operation. Lake Superior was in the background, monochrome waves forever frozen in place. In the foreground, an overturned lifeboat rested on the beach, waiting for the next call of duty out on the lake. Two men stood beside the boat, holding up wooden oars that must have been at least six feet long. While everything else in the picture was startlingly clear, their faces were obscured, little more than fuzzy white blobs.

I thought of that strange moment last Friday when I thought I'd seen a pale face pressed against the glass at the top of the lighthouse tower, a face that turned out to be nothing more than a trick of the light. The faint chill returned, a little stronger this time.

Karen had been marking the page with a piece of white office paper on which another photograph had been printed. I recognized it right away. It was another picture of the foundation walls, taken from a different angle than the one on the laptop monitor—from the opposite side, in fact, looking west toward the lighthouse instead of toward the beach east of the point. I was going to ask if she had taken this photo as well, but I realized it had been snapped at a different time of year. This was not an April picture. This was midsummer from the look of it. The beach grass and weeds were lush and green. The scrubby birches and tag alders that had sprouted inside the foundation walls were in full leaf.

"Where did you get this?"

Karen hesitated for just a moment then smiled. It was the same broad, appealing grin she had flashed at me last Friday, when we'd first met.

"I stole it," she said. "From Amy's house."

"I don't understand."

"It was while we were looking around the other day. You were in the kitchen and I was in the living room. I lifted one of those bed sheets that was covering the bookshelves, and there it was."

"You found a picture and just took it?"

"No, David. I didn't find *a* picture. I found about twenty of them. Twenty pictures of this same thing. All different angles, different times of day, different times of the year. Amy must have taken them all and printed them out. They were stacked on the shelf—that middle shelf by the desk, where she kept all her maps and atlases."

"I didn't even notice," I said. "When your father and I were closing up the place, I sort of gave the bookshelves a once-over. I saw the maps and neatened up the pile a bit, but I never saw—"

"I noticed them right away. It just seemed so crazy that Amy would take so many pictures of the same thing."

"It is, a little," I said. "She loved her cameras, and she took about a million pictures a week, but I never knew her to take more than two or three of the same thing. Once she was sure she had the exposure and the focus right, she moved on to the next subject. And why would she take all those pictures of something she could see right out her window? That old foundation is a hundred yards from her door. She could walk over there and look at it any time she wanted."

"Maybe she did," Karen said cryptically.

I looked at the photo in my hand and glanced at the one on the computer screen, wondering what they meant. Outside, a truck droned by on 187. The only other sound was the laptop fan humming quietly.

"So I took the picture," Karen continued. "And today I went to the library and got this book. I was pretty sure the photo was something on the property, and that I'd seen it the other day. When I opened up to the chapter on Vessey Point and saw the photo of the old lifesaving house, station, whatever it is—that's when it sort of clicked. And I went back out to the point this afternoon to take pictures of my own."

She stood up and walked across the room, her voice dropping until it was barely above a whisper. "There's something else, David. As long as I'm confessing and all, there's something else you should know."

I waited. Nearly a minute went by. Then Karen crossed back to the table and picked up the other book. Until that moment I had barely noticed it, but I recognized it now.

Amy was as technologically savvy as any person I had ever known. She could troubleshoot computer problems, design websites for her friends, set up a wifi network in under a minute, and do about thirty other things I couldn't even begin to describe. She had once written the first draft of an article on her smartphone while waiting for a floatplane to come pick her up from a remote lake in Quebec. In other words, she was no Luddite. She was, in fact, a geek. But she was also a traditionalist, prone to habits that were charmingly old-fashioned. She still preferred sending letters to friends rather than e-mails. When the mood struck her, she liked to take notes and write the occasional draft in longhand. She collected fountain pens. And she kept a handwritten journal, making entries at least once a week, sometimes daily, writing not in cheap spiral school notebooks from the State Street Pharmacy but in hardcover blank books bound in dark red faux leather that she bought by the dozen from some retail site online.

The book Karen was handing to me was one of those journals.

"It was on the same shelf with the photographs," she said.

My hands trembled slightly as I opened the cover. Her familiar lazy scrawl filled the first page:

The Journals of
Amy Lynn Brackett
Vol. 28 27
July 17, 2016–

My eyes stung, and I had trouble drawing a breath.

Seeing her handwriting was bad enough. Seeing the mistake she had so casually corrected—a very Amy-like thing to do—was just as bad. But seeing that missing second date was the worst. It was her final journal. The last one. The one she'd never had a chance to finish.

"Flip to the page I marked," Karen said.

I was confused at first, until I noticed the torn scrap of hotel stationery poking out of the book just around the halfway point. I opened to that page.

August 9, 2016 7 p.m.
Sky: Overcast, peeks of sun p.m. Wind:
Light/Variable—SW 10 late afternoon
Morning low: 57 degrees. Afternoon high:
81 degrees.

I saw him again today.
It was mid-morning, around 9:30. I
was putting my boots on, getting ready to go
out and fill the birdfeeders and check the rain

gauge after last night's downpour. I sat down at my desk because I am, as we have so firmly established over these past several months, officially turning into an old fart, and I can no longer perform the daring, acrobatic feats of youth—such as reaching up to get the cereal down from the top shelf or bending over to tie my boots—without feeling that damn twinge in my back. I was finishing with the right boot when I happened to glance out the window and saw him.

He was walking along the beach, past the old pump house. From there, he disappeared behind the fog signal building. It was just like the last time.

Part of me wanted to race outside and

intercept him, but—and this is a big, tough admission for Beverly Brackett's little girl— I was afraid, and so I just sat there stewing.

He was dressed the same as before. Black coat with shiny buttons. Gold, I think. Black pants. Black shoes. His head was bare, and I mean that in more ways than one. He was not wearing a hat, and he had very little hair, if any. From where I sat, he looked as bald as an egg.

Why did this man make me afraid? There are always visitors to the point at this time of year. I can look out the window almost any time of day, and occasionally at night, and see hikers, birders, photographers, artists, picnickers, people launching or beaching their sea kayaks. In fact, this afternoon I counted at least seven visitors, including a family of three—mom, dad, and little girl—who opened up the door of my house and walked right in, thinking this was just another tourist trap and not a private home. As I've said before, these people range from perfectly lovely to comically entertaining to mildly annoying. I've never found any of them the least bit frightening.

But of course, this was no ordinary visitor. I had plenty of evidence to tell me that.

He emerged from behind the fog signal building. I had to stand up and lean across the desk, craning my neck to follow his progress as he moved down the beach. He was *close to the spot that I confronted him on that crazy-ass cold day last spring. Another twenty paces and he'd be there. This time I chose not to go outside and only watch.*

I looked up at Karen. "I'm not sure I understand any of this," I said.

She looked disappointed. "I was hoping you would. She keeps talking about the first time she saw this guy, but there's nothing else in the journal about it. Of course, if it happened last spring, it wouldn't have been in this volume, would it? She never mentioned anything to you?"

"Nothing," I said. "Which is strange. She always told me everything. I mean, I thought she did."

"What about that?" She jabbed a finger at a line of the text a few sentences below where I'd been reading. "Do you know where that is?"

I read: *He got to the secret garden and stopped.*

I laughed. "I know exactly where that is. And it's funny—you do too." I tapped the printout of the color photo. "It's that place. The old lifesaving station."

"*That's* a secret garden?"

"That's what Amy always called it. She said the foundation walls and the way all the weeds and scrub trees just took over in there reminded her of the book. She said it was the kind of place that Mary and Dickon and Colin and Ben would all hang out. It needed to have taller walls, of course. Garden walls. And a gate.

You can't have a secret garden without a gate. But she didn't care. That's what she called it. She said someday—someday she would clear it all out and put a real garden there. I teased her about it once. I said nothing *real* would grow in all the sand and rocks, but she was determined. She said give her enough time and she could get anything to grow there."

The words were meant to be light, but they felt heavy and dead. There were no more *somedays* for Amy. No more next week, next month, next year. Her time to turn the remnants of the lifesaving station into her own secret garden was gone. No more looking up from her computer and gazing across the beach at crumbling stone walls. No more imagining Mary Lennox helping Colin Craven learn to walk among the weeds. No more clearing. No more planting.

Karen tapped the journal again. "You might as well finish reading. It gets better."

It did.

He turned back then, facing in my direction, and instinctively, I shrank away from the window. When I dared to lean forward enough that I could see past the edge of the curtain, I realized that he wasn't looking at me or even the house. His gaze was turned upward, toward the top of the tower, and I had a crazy notion that he was checking to make sure the light was lit.

"You're a generation too late for that," I whispered under my breath.

His bald head jerked downward suddenly, and he looked right at me. He couldn't have heard me speak. Someone sitting five feet away in the same room wouldn't have heard. But something had caught his attention, and he was looking right at me. I tried to pull back again, behind the curtains, but I couldn't move. I literally was frozen to the spot, like the time with the bear in Manitoba. My brain was engaged, moving a million miles an hour, but my body was locked in place, limbs paralyzed.

It was the first time I had seen his eyes directly and not from an oblique angle. They were bright. Silver. They looked like bullet holes of light in the middle of his pale face, like coins reflecting the sun. I felt a strange heat across the distance, and I knew (without knowing how I knew) exactly what it was. I felt it as clearly as if he was in the room with me—maybe the same way he had heard me speak. I don't know. I don't even pretend to understand it. But I felt that heat, and I understood it perfectly. He was angry. The fierceness of it was crushing, overpowering, making it hard for me to breathe. It was fury and rage and boiling, thrashing, churning hatred. It sizzled across the distance between us like an electrical charge.

My mouth opened, and words came out, thick and slow and painfully heavy, like in a dream.

"What do you want?" I asked him.

I also wanted to say something else: "Who are you?" I wanted to say. "Are you him? Are you Bloodybones?"

But it was too late. He was already gone. He had vanished. Again.

I don't know how to describe what I want to say next. Maybe if I was a fiction writer, I could pull it off, but that's not me. I make my living describing what I see and do and think. I've never been good at finding ways to make someone—me or anybody else— believe the unbelievable. So I'll just do what I do and describe what I saw.

He had vanished, but for a split second I saw a trace of him still there, an afterimage in the air. Then that was gone too. But even then, the two silver nuggets of light remained, still giving off that ugly white heat.

"Leave me alone," I whispered, and the lights disappeared.

The journal entry continued for another page or so, but I had suddenly lost my taste for reading it. I put the book down and looked at Karen.

"My sister saw a ghost," she said.

The way she said it made me want to laugh, but I couldn't. My brain was awash with a dozen unrelated but crazily interconnected thoughts. First and foremost was what I had just read and the knowledge the Amy had had this experience, encounter, whatever it was—that Amy had gone through this and never said a word to me. It seemed impossible. She almost always told me about the visitors to Vessey Point, be they fans or colleagues or simply nosy tourists. But when she had one of the most unusual visitors of all—more than once, apparently—she never said a word. I wondered what that meant, and I wondered what it said about the nature of her experience and the nature of our relationship.

I was also thinking about last Friday, the way I had heard Amy's voice in my ear, and about that dreadful moment when Karen's shriek had filled the lightkeeper's quarters. The way she had looked. The way she had sounded.

Amy Lynn is in the pool.

I studied Karen closely for any sign that she was thinking the same things. But of course she had no memory of that day in the bedroom, and I had only told her a very small part of the story—namely that she had screamed and said something about her sister.

"There are other entries," Karen said, indicating the journal. "The last one was in October, just a few days before she disappeared. I haven't read them yet; some of them are pretty long. You can take it along and read them tonight if you want."

Frankly, I wasn't sure if I wanted to see the other entries or not. After a brief internal debate, I declined. Another day, perhaps. Not now.

We talked a few minutes more, but it felt awkward and uncomfortable. I wanted to ask Karen what she was trying to accomplish. Trips to the library. Trips to the point. Secretly stealing books and photos from her sister's house. Was there a reason for any of it? Was it a mission? A game?

I knew almost nothing about Karen Shumacher's life, but I had a few of the bare-bones facts: that she had been a reservations manager for an Arizona hotel before going back to school in her late twenties to become a teacher. Most recently, she had taught various elementary grades somewhere in the Midwest—Oklahoma, Kansas, Nebraska; I really couldn't remember which. She had resigned her latest position shortly after Amy's disappearance last fall and was considering another trip back to school to study— well, I wasn't quite sure. I think Bob Brackett had mentioned something about it when we spoke at Christmas, but if he'd provided the details, I could no longer remember them.

Did Karen's trip to Madsen represent yet another course correction? Did she suddenly fancy herself a detective? And more to the point, where did she think her efforts would lead? Amy was gone, and it was beyond unlikely that reading her old diaries would tell us where.

As I was leaving the motel room, Karen stopped me, putting her hand on my arm. Before she even uttered a word, I knew what she was going to say. I also knew I didn't want to hear it.

"Will you go back with me?"

I thought of my conversation with Kyle earlier that evening and the tentative trip we had planned for the morning after next. I was not surprised that Karen wanted to go. I had always expected she would. What surprised me were my own feelings—the aversion I suddenly felt to seeing Vessey Point again. I did not want to go there. I wasn't sure I even could.

But there was another truth, and it was one I wasn't quite ready to face.

BLOODYBONES

I had to go back. Not for Karen and whatever futile amends-for-the-past mission she was on, and not for Kyle, whose only mission was to escape a day of longingly watching the front door of the dealership, hoping a customer would walk in. I could say that I had to go back for myself, and there was certainly a measure of truth in that. But that wasn't the whole story either.

I had to go back for Amy.

I could not make sense of anything that had happened since Friday afternoon, not in any kind of literal or concrete way. I could not understand that unmistakable sensation of Amy's hand on the back of my neck or her voice speaking to me out of the silence. I could not make sense of Karen's shrieking or that dread-filled word, *Bloodybones,* or that terrible phrase, *Amy Lynn is in the pool.* I could not interpret the journal entry I had just read or sort out the feelings that had washed over me when I realized Amy had not shared as much of her life with me as I had always assumed.

Right then, all of those things seemed like jumbled pieces of code, broken bits of an intercepted message, and I did not have the key I needed to decipher them. I wasn't sure if the key was actually out there, hidden just out of sight, awaiting discovery, or if the key even existed. For all I knew, everything that had happened had not really happened at all. For all I knew, it was just some kind of crazy joint hallucination, some shared madness between Karen and me, a delusion brought on by mutual grief.

But I didn't believe that.

I believed that the key was out there. I believed that it was somewhere at Vessey Point.

That alone was an amazing realization, and it arrived with a jolt, a power that blew away the fear and doubt that had gripped me just moments ago, leaving me feeling strangely excited, almost giddy. Just last week, I had firmly believed the opposite. Just a few days ago, I had been convinced that Amy's disappearance was an insoluble riddle, a mystery that no one would ever unravel. Now I felt the answer was . . . not in sight, not exactly, but somewhere close.

The key was out there, and when I found it, whatever *it* was, everything would finally make sense. I would be able to decipher the code. The craziness, the irrational, and the impossible would all be explained, and all of us would finally know what happened that day Amy Brackett paddled away into the heart of a gale, never to be seen again.

A voice in the back of my head spoke up, trying to drown out the rising excitement, trying to bring back the trepidation and skepticism and misgivings. It told me that I was wrong. It told me that I was being foolish. It told me that I was grasping for hope where none existed.

I looked past Karen at Amy's red-bound journal, still lying open on the table. Even from here, I could recognize the familiar strokes of her writing, a hand as familiar to me as my own, and the sight of it caused my heart to break and sing at the same time.

Maybe the voice was right, I thought. But right or wrong, I owed it to Amy to find out.

X

I dreamed of Amy that night. It was the first time I had dreamed of her in months. The last time I could recall had been in December, a few days before Christmas, when she'd suddenly turned up in a generally nonsensical fantasia that hopscotched around various locations in Madsen and the southern Michigan towns of my youth—a surprise appearance, which in the inevitable logic of illogical dreams scarcely seemed surprising at all.

This time, there was no crazy quick-cutting of scenes. There was only one.

I was standing on the shore at Vessey Point, my tennis shoes mired in wet sand, the lake at my back and the buildings in front of me appearing and disappearing in a thickening fog. The sky was dark, and a fierce north wind was howling at my back, the sound of the breakers like thunder. There was something in my hand—Amy's journal, the fake leather cover cool and damp against my fingers and palm.

Fighting the wind, which seemed eager to steal the book from my grasp and send it cartwheeling across the beach, I opened to the middle, expecting to once again see Amy's free hand flowing across the pages. But where there should have been writing, I found only blank white space. I turned the page and found more of the same, again and the same, again, again, just emptiness, just white, nothing but white, the journal as empty as the angry lakescape roaring behind me— white space, white noise.

Something caught my attention. A flash of movement, maybe, or a glimpse of color. I found my gaze drawn to the top of the light tower, which was momentarily lost in the scudding fog. Then the veil was ripped apart by the wind, and I could plainly see that there was someone there. It was almost like the (*vision mirage hallucination apparition*) the last time I was there, when I'd briefly imagined a white face staring down at me. But this was different because it was not just an unidentified visage up there. It was Amy. There was no doubt, no mistake about that. It was Amy, down to the very last feature, the very last curve of her lips and bend of her nose, the very last freckle, the Detroit Red Wings jersey she was wearing, and the hat—her damn beloved Tilley hat—perched atop her head. It was also different because of the lamp room itself, which was completely filled from floor to peak with water. A part of me knew that was impossible. For the lamp room to be filled with water, the entire tower would have to be filled, all seventy-five feet of it. Otherwise, any water would simply drain away down the spiral staircase that led from the first floor to the top. I tried to imagine the immense tower filled like that, the millions of gallons that would take. The pressure would be enough to blow out the tower walls, sending bricks and glass and twisted iron raining down in a deadly cascade.

Amy's eyes stared sightlessly down at me, wide, bulging. Her hair floated limply about her face. Her arms lolled by her sides, the hands appearing to float aimlessly toward the glass like puffy aquarium fish then drift back and away. The fingers were moving listlessly, opening, closing, but whether of their own volition or some slowly eddying current inside the lamp room, I couldn't tell.

BLOODYBONES

The tower top disappeared again behind another curtain of fog, and a voice beside me, a man's voice, said sharply, "They went into the pool."

I spun around into the teeth of the gale, but there was no one there. I turned back to the tower, which was sporadically visible again through wispy breaks in the scudding clouds, and saw Amy's face still tilted down at me, except now her eyes were closed, giving her an oddly serene expression amidst the nightmarish quality of the scene. Her mouth opened slowly, and a string of bubbles streamed out. Then her eyes opened too, only they were no longer eyes. They were two tiny bullets of bright, shining light, silver fire glittering like beacons in their watery glass prison.

I woke up, gasping for air, as if I had been the one trapped inside the lamp room. Perspiration was beaded on my forehead and chin, and my pillow was soaked with sweat. I heard a distant pounding that I eventually realized was the sound of my own heart thudding in my chest.

A small red glow from the alarm clock was the only light in the room. It cast a thin, cold half-circle of illumination that didn't even extend to the edges of the nightstand. Everything outside that radius was perfect blackness.

Yet . . .

I saw something just past the end of the bed, or maybe sensed something, a rough shape rearing up beyond the footboard, not really a shape at all but just a blacker patch of blackness. It seemed, perhaps, to be moving, swaying slowly from side to side.

I reached for the bedside lamp, closing my fingers around the knob. It felt hot to the touch. When I turned it, there was a loud sizzle and pop, and I was momentarily blinded by a brilliant flash of light, blue-white and magnesium bright, as the filament in the bulb incinerated, instantly returning the room to darkness.

The brief explosive glare left yellow-orange circles dancing before my eyes, but out of that crazy quilt of shifting color, several brighter spots gradually emerged—seven or eight at first, then five, then four, resolving themselves at last into two points of fine silver light, hanging there in midair, suspended in the darkness.

I instinctively understood that they were not really spots at all but eyes. They stared at me, unblinking. As my own eyes gradually adjusted to the room, I saw what was behind them, that vague dark shape still hovering at the end of the bed, moving almost imperceptibly from side to side. It was a body, lumpy and ill-shapen, but with enough familiar form to discern arms and legs, shoulders and neck and head. A face without features but with a rough texture, as if it was covered with crude cloth. And, of course, those tiny silver-bullet eyes peering out through punctures in the fabric, looking back at me, watching me.

I tried to speak—*Who are you?*—but the air had trouble escaping through the narrow channel of my suddenly constricted throat. All that emerged was a smothered, unintelligible sound, a soft groan of agony.

I tried to speak again—*What do you want?*—but it came out as a mournful moan, as if I had become a ghost, wanting to, needing to, but helpless to communicate with the living souls around me.

I thought of Amy's journal and her own unspoken

words—*Who are you? Are you him? Are you Bloodybones?*—and felt my chest being crushed by a mixture of unutterable sorrow, bewilderment, and dread.

The shape shifted, leaning forward, leaning toward me. Its left arm hung downward, but the right began to move, rising slowly, stretching out, reaching. Without thinking, I shrank away from it, fearing its touch. I thought I saw a shadow appear on that empty face, a change of light or a flicker of movement, something different in the area where the mouth should be, a dimpling, a rippling, as if something was moving underneath the heavy, course fabric that covered the head.

A sudden rushing roar filled the room, and in the same moment, all the lights came on at once: the bedside lamp that had burned out just seconds before; the smaller lamp on the dresser across from the bed; the overhead light that I distinctly remembered turning off from the switch by the door hours earlier, before heading to bed.

I threw up my hands, shielding my eyes against the glare, but I could already see that there was nothing else in the room. Certainly not a person standing at the foot of my bed. Certainly not a man without a face, reaching for me.

But that wasn't completely right. There was no person standing there, but there was *something*. There was a puddle on the hardwood floor, just beyond the footboard, exactly where the figure had been standing, swaying in the darkness. I could plainly see the overhead light reflected in the water, which had begun to trickle slowly toward the closet, following the uneven path of the floorboards that sloped ever so slightly in that direction. It was that tiny detail, silly and seemingly insignificant, that convinced me what I was seeing was real, not my imagination, not a lingering fragment of my earlier dream, not some crazy, confused hallucination.

I threw back the covers and climbed out of bed. I walked over to the puddle and knelt down. I reached out, hesitating for just a second before allowing my fingers to brush against the water.

It was cold, near freezing; the feel of it sent a sharp, shuddering jolt up my arm. I jerked my hand away, as if burned.

I stood up shakily and backed away from the puddle, keeping a wary eye on it the entire time. I don't know what I expected to happen. It was only a puddle, after all. It wasn't as if the water would suddenly change direction, stop trickling toward the closet and reverse itself, running uphill, coming for me instead. It wasn't as if the puddle would suddenly deepen, becoming a bottomless pool into which I might stumble and fall. It wasn't as if the water would begin to move, churning, swirling, coalescing into a solid shape, a body that would rear up from the floor and reach for me with grasping fingers. It wasn't as if the puddle was going to do anything at all—anything, that is, other than what it was doing now, sitting there on my bedroom floor, utterly inexplicable and utterly real, reflecting the overhead light like a beacon.

I brushed my hand against my sweatpants, drying it off, but I could still feel the impossible ice-chill of the water on my fingertips for a long time afterwards.

PART TWO
XI

"I know I'm not the sharpest fork in the drawer, but I'm still not sure what we're looking for."

Kyle and I were standing a few feet from the northern wall of the old foundation. The sun was almost directly overhead, but it was just light—flat, glaring, springtime light—with precious little heat. We had left Karen in the keeper's quarters to look through Amy's library while the two of us had come out here to look for—well, like Kyle, I really had no idea what we were looking for.

The tangle of growth inside the old foundation walls provided no clue why Amy had been so fascinated with the place. To me, it looked exactly as it always had, like a small, unruly jungle. The only thing I could imagine was that she had been planning for the future, taking pictures by day and perhaps pondering them at night, as she brainstormed ways to turn her imaginary secret garden into a real one. That had to be it. There was nothing else that could have drawn her focus—not even an extraordinarily large shrub with branches poking this way and that or a tree trunk twisted into some amusing or unlikely shape. That, I could have understood. Amy was, after all, the woman who was endlessly intrigued by unusual cloud formations, the patterns traced upon the water by a rising wind right before it begins to churn the surface into whitecapped waves, or the suggestions of faces or symbols or almost-legible words that she would inevitably see in the gnarled driftwood littering the lakeshore.

"We're trying to figure out why Amy was so hung up on this place," I told Kyle. "You saw those pictures. We want to know why she took them."

I wondered, not for the first time, if it had been a mistake to bring Kyle along. Not that we'd really had a choice. I had already promised he could join us on our next trip to the point, and that was before he'd learned about my Monday night visit with Karen, before he'd seen Amy's journal, before he'd looked at the photographs. Once that happened, there was no hope of changing his mind. Not after he'd read Amy's account of the silver-eyed visitor.

Kyle flashed a lopsided grin. "I understand that, David. I'm actually pretty bright when I've had my three hots and a cot. What I mean is, *what* are we looking for? A ghost? The bones of Jimmy Hoffa? The hidden entrance to Cibola?"

That should have annoyed me, but his breezy manner took the sting away.

"I suspect Jimmy Hoffa's buried over there," I said, jerking a thumb toward an empty stretch of beach. "I'm betting on Cibola. Or maybe just an old stump that Amy thought was pretty. Let's find out."

I led the way forward, stepping over the wall into the old lifesaving station. Kyle followed, and we made our way cautiously around the site, slogging through long grass and thick weeds that would have reached nearly to our waists if they hadn't been crushed into matted mounds by the weight of winter snow that had only recently departed. Growing among the mounds were swarms of tag alders and shrubs along with the scattered saplings of larger trees. Beneath the mounds lurked hidden hazards—old stumps and frost-heaved ground and fragments of what had once been walls or doorframes. There was also a surprising amount of debris—rotted pieces of wood, broken chunks of brick, shards of shattered glass that crunched beneath our boots, the moldy remnants of newspapers and magazines, and many jagged fragments of steel and iron. It was impossible to know how much of the rubble had come from the old station and how much was just the flotsam and jetsam that inevitably accumulates in places like this. The majority of it was barely visible, buried so deep in the weeds that it was impossible to see until you stepped on it—or tripped over it.

"It's a fool's errand," Kyle said after a few minutes. "A fool's errand, and we're fools for being here. There's nothing to see in here. And—please don't take this the wrong way, David; you know how much I liked Amy— but if she was so nuts about this place, maybe she was a fool too."

I bristled reflexively but bit my tongue, wondering if he might be right.

We shambled about for a very long time, following our own aimless paths, occasionally wandering away from each other and occasionally circling back, passing in close proximity or crisscrossing the same areas like planets with eccentric orbits, but it was becoming increasingly clear that Kyle had summed up the situation perfectly: we were wasting our time.

I lost that conviction abruptly a few moments later. I was nearing the eastern wall of the foundation and was about to surrender, but first, I stopped to examine an object at my feet. My eye had been caught by a glint in the weeds, but it turned out to be nothing, just a fragment of an old bottle, a bit of shattered brown glass with the words DOCTOR WURTZ'S on one line and the abbreviated phrase WONDERFUL ELIX immediately below.

That was when Kyle barked out, "Who the hell is that?"

I straightened up and looked toward the shoreline, where Kyle was pointing. It took my eyes a second to adjust to the change in focus, and in that heartbeat, I thought I saw someone standing there—a large hulk turned into a dark, almost shapeless silhouette by the bright gray glare of the lake behind it.

"Hey!" Kyle said, but it was already too late. He was talking to an empty stretch of beach. Whoever had been there—or more properly, whoever I had *imagined* was there—was gone.

Except that couldn't be right, could it? I couldn't have imagined it, because Kyle had seen it too. We had both seen it, seen *him,* seen whatever it was. Yet there was nothing but sand and rocks and driftwood there now, nothing but the beach, behind which sprawled the vast expanse of the lake and, somewhere in the invisible distance, the endless shadowy forests of Canada.

Kyle took a step in that direction, hesitated, looked at me, took another step, stopped again, and shook his head.

"David, did you—"

"Yeah, I saw it."

"Well, what the hell, man? There was a guy standing there, wasn't there? I mean, I just looked up and saw him there. There was a guy, no joke, standing there staring at us—big as life and twice as ugly."

"I know," I said, nodding slowly, although all I had really seen was that amorphous silhouette.

I didn't want to do what I did next, but I couldn't help myself. I turned and looked up at the light tower, close to certain that I would see Amy up there staring down at us, her mouth yawning wide in a silent scream. But I was wrong. The sunstruck windows revealed an utterly empty lamp room.

"This place is seriously weird," Kyle said behind me. "I mean seriously, David, it's deranged."

Something in his voice made my blood cold, and I pivoted slowly back to face him. It wasn't the words that I noticed; it was the tone. It was so unlike the usual Kyle Halprin, the guy who occasionally said serious things but seldom said them seriously. It was a different tone altogether, one I'd never heard from him before, flat and featureless, as if the words were falling from his mouth like dry sand. I was reminded chillingly of Karen staring out the bedroom window in the keeper's quarters, chanting in that low, expressionless voice—*black water, blue water, green water, deep water, dark water, dead water*—except that Kyle was not speaking from the same kind of trance. He was standing there, clearly awake, looking at me with eyes that were comically wide.

"Bloodybones," he said then in that same cold tone.

"*What?*"

"I think we better go check on Karen."

"I—"

"I think Bloodybones is in the house."

His face had gone as white as winter bone, and his eyes were no longer wide but had narrowed down to fine, dark points, like shutters closing against the light.

303

Looking into them, I felt a strange, floating disconnection and a bleak certainty that something—the moment, the situation, maybe the entire world—was slipping away from me. In no time at all, in the two seconds or less it had taken Kyle to bark out his baffled *who the hell is that,* our trip to Vessey Point had spun off like a cyclone into a kind of alternate reality. Everything looked the same. But everything was different.

I barely had time to process that sensation before Kyle turned his back to me and stumbled away, heading through the underbrush toward the nearest wall of the old foundation. He reached it and stepped over clumsily. It looked as if he was about to lose his balance and topple face forward into the sand, but he caught himself and took off for the keeper's quarters at a fast walk, almost a trot.

Suddenly, everything seemed to happen at once.

I opened my mouth to call out for Kyle but stopped when I heard another voice instead—a distant shout coming from the direction of the keeper's quarters. The words were indistinguishable, but the origin was unmistakable; it was Karen.

I looked toward the house and spotted her immediately at the side door, standing on the little concrete stoop, leaning out over the wooden railing and looking in our direction, beckoning to us. I heard her call out again but still couldn't make out a thing that she was saying.

I wasn't sure if Kyle had seen or heard her too, but it scarcely mattered. He was plunging ahead in her direction all the same, moving with that same awkward speed, like a mechanical soldier whose key was wound just a turn or two too tight.

BLOODYBONES

I started to follow him, but my foot came down on something hidden in the scrub growth. My ankle bent sharply to the inside, and a hot bolt of pain shot up my leg, exploding all the way from ankle to hip. I barked out a curse as I felt myself start to go down, falling awkwardly to my right. My arms pinwheeled crazily, and the world spun past in flashes of sand and grass and water. I think I might have cursed again—I growled something at any rate—sure that any second I would be face down in the weeds. Somehow, though, I caught myself before passing the point of no return and stood there gasping, wincing against the pain that burned deep inside my leg and had already become a faint, twisting nausea in my belly.

From the house, Karen was calling again, but I didn't pay any attention. I was looking down instead, staring at the thing I had stepped on, which I had assumed was just another piece of debris, another chunk of busted bottle or broken brick.

Except that it wasn't.

A dull pressure filled my chest, and a small groan escaped my lips as I stared at the object hidden in the weeds. It was a hand, a human hand, lying there in the brush, palm up, flesh bleached white, bloated, puffy, malformed fingers spread wide, as though grasping for something.

I stumbled a half-step back, triggering a fresh bullet of pain in my ankle, and a gust of air exploded from my lungs, making me aware for the first time that I had been holding my breath. I looked up and saw Kyle still hurrying toward the house, Karen still beckoning from the stoop.

When I looked back down, the hand was gone.

There was nothing important there at all. Just an old piece of wood, bleached almost white. It was laying almost perfectly flat, half buried in the sand, hardly enough to create a hazard. It was difficult to even imagine how stepping on it could have twisted my ankle so sharply and thrown me off balance so suddenly.

It occurred to me that I was losing my mind. It wasn't a disturbing thought; more of a clinical observation. It came in a brief flash, a broken mental shorthand, and it seemed utterly, inescapably natural. I was losing my mind. Of course I was. In some ways, I had been losing my mind since that Sunday morning last October when I had tried repeatedly to contact Amy—by phone, by text message, by e-mail—and gotten no response, or perhaps the moment that afternoon when I'd driven out to the point to look for her and found the house cold, dark, and empty, or the following day when I'd stood on the side of County Road 419, talking to a small knot of police officers and search-and-rescue volunteers while red and blue roof lights strobed around us, each flash driving home the point that something was seriously, maybe deadly wrong.

Oddly, the thought that I had been losing my mind for the last six months didn't trouble me at all. On the contrary, it seemed mildly comforting, as if it explained something I had sensed but not understood.

I looked up and saw that the picture around me had changed. It must have been nearly a minute, maybe longer, since I had looked down and seen the bloated hand that turned out to be nothing at all. In that time, Kyle had reached the house and was now standing on the bottom step, talking to Karen with animated gestures. But something else farther away claimed my attention first.

The man Kyle and I had seen was back again, but this time, he was three or four hundred yards from where I stood, beyond the house, beyond the light tower, near the edge of the woods. I could not make out his face or features, but I was sure it was the same man; the size and shape was identical to the hulking black silhouette that had startled Kyle a few minutes ago, that I had seen for a split second before it vanished.

He was coming toward me, head down, moving quickly, dragging something along behind him through the sand. It took me a few moments to realize what it was, and in that time, my mind interpreted and rejected several things: an old piece of furniture, a heavy sack, a tree trunk with broken limbs jutting off in several directions.

But it wasn't any of those things.

It was a body, being dragged by the feet.

The pressure tightened in my chest again, and it felt as if my throat had closed down to a channel no wider than a pin. I struggled to draw a breath, and when I did manage to pull one in, it made a sad, sick buzzing sound, like a slowly dying insect. My hands felt numb, the fingers tingling; I didn't even realize right away that I had closed my palms into crushing, bloodless fists.

The man and his cargo were approaching the light tower now, still moving quickly. Soon they would be at the back corner of the house. Although he was still too far away to see much, I could almost make out his face now, and I could see—I saw—

I'd initially thought the body he was dragging was limp and lifeless, but I could see now that was not the case. The body was moving, thrashing, legs trying to kick, arms flailing wildly as it was dragged along through the sand.

I looked toward the steps, where Karen and Kyle were still engaged in conversation, oblivious to me and to the nightmare duo that was approaching them around the back side of the house. I opened my mouth to cry out—a simple notice, a warning, god only knows what—but stopped myself before making a sound. It was absolutely crazy, I knew, but I didn't want to attract the attention of the man who was coming my way, who was still heading steadily, inexorably toward me but did not yet seem to have noticed me.

Instead of calling out, I tried silently signaling, waving my arm back and forth in a wide arc, but Karen was looking down at Kyle from the stoop, and he was looking up at her from the bottom step, and neither of them were paying me the slightest attention.

I could now make out the man in perfect detail, and I recognized him immediately as the man in Amy's journal. He was dressed the same way she had described him, wearing a dark coat with bright gold buttons. His perfectly bald head glistened in the sun. Even from here, I thought I could see beads of sweat standing out on the crown, from the exertion of dragging the struggling body along the beach.

It's Bloodybones, I thought without the least understanding of what that meant. I'm honestly not even sure the thought was my own; it was like someone else's voice screaming inside my head: *It's Bloodybones, and he's coming your way! He's coming for you!*

BLOODYBONES

I tried again to catch Kyle and Karen's attention, and this time, it worked. They had finished their conversation and turned toward the lifesaving station. When they spotted me, they both broke into wide grins and waved.

"Hey! David!" Kyle called out, but I made a frantic *no, no* shushing gesture with my hands and pointed to the south of the house, where the man and his load were getting closer and closer.

With terrible clarity, I could now see that the person he was dragging was a child, a boy, maybe ten or twelve—no more than that and quite possibly less—wearing dark overalls and a red and white checked shirt. The boy had fine, blond hair that hung down across his face in wet, matted strands. There was something dark on the boy's forehead and cheeks. Mud or blood. He was still thrashing wildly. His eyes were wide, and his mouth was open wide in a soundless scream.

Karen and Kyle tried to see what I was pointing at, but the man and boy were still blocked by the south wall of the house. He would have to drag the poor child another forty feet or so before he would reach a point where they could see him.

The man looked up at me then, and I was not at all surprised to see that his eyes were shining like bright silver coins. His gaze locked with mine, and I was instantly reminded again of Amy's journal, her description of the boiling hatred she had felt coming from the man, burning into her even from a distance— a distance that, coincidentally or not, was about the same as the gap between us now, from the house to Amy's secret garden. My heart skipped a beat or two then raced erratically in compensation, like an injured runner staggering toward the finish line.

That was when my cell phone rang.

The combination of my annoyingly bright electronic ringtone and the simultaneous vibration in my right front pocket made me jump, and I almost cried out, but the sight of those rage-filled silver eyes still coming closer kept me silent. I dug the phone out and only then turned my gaze away from the man's face to glance quickly at the screen.

This time I did cry out, timed perfectly with the second ring. I jerked reflexively, and the phone flew from my grasp as if knocked loose by an unseen hand. It thudded into the weeds a foot or two away, face up. Of course it did. Of course it landed face up. In this crazy losing-my-mind or *lost*-my-mind universe where I was trapped, landing face up was the only thing that made sense. How else could I have seen the screen with that little thumbnail picture in the center? It was a picture I had uploaded to my contacts directory late last summer, the same day I took it. I remembered it all perfectly, as if it had happened eight minutes ago instead of eight months. I remembered snapping the picture of her outside the office of the *Press-Beacon,* both of us in silly moods, giddy because it was a Friday afternoon and we were both done working for the week and we would have several days to spend together without demands or interruptions from the outside world. We were going to go camping; she wanted to show me a new fishing spot she'd discovered an hour or so to the west in the Pictured Rocks National Lakeshore. I had just made some silly joke about her new Salewa hiking boots and immediately taken her picture—a woman captured forever in a bright, silent laugh, a spray of freckles across her nose and a worn-out white Tilley hat perched atop her head.

It was impossible for that picture to be on my phone screen now, just as it was impossible for those words to appear below it in white block letters: AMY'S CELL.

I bent and picked up the phone, which was already on its fourth ring. My hands were trembling violently. The impossible picture and impossible legend gleamed up at me, pixel-perfect and preposterous.

I tapped the green button that said ANSWER and put the phone to my ear.

The sound I heard there was dreadful. It was a low, howling whistle, like a midnight wind blowing through an empty canyon. It was the sound of nothingness and despair, of absence and loss and longing, the sound of deep space or beyond, the void far past the edge of the universe, the place where the monsters dwell.

Was there another noise in there too? A voice, soft and fantastically distant, virtually inaudible, lost beneath that howl from the eternal darkness? I'll never know because the connection went dead, turning the cell phone into a lifeless brick in my hand.

I looked up, then, and saw the man with silver eyes had stopped. He was just beyond the corner of the keeper's quarters, still out of sight for Karen and Kyle, who were looking at me with questioning gazes. The man was staring at me too, but I barely noticed. I was too busy looking at what was behind him, the body he had dragged all that way along the beach. A minute ago, it had been a small boy with tangled, blond hair, thrashing and crying out in silent terror.

Now, it was Amy.

She was lying in a crumpled heap beside the man, her body utterly limp and still, her neck twisted at an odd angle so that I could see most of her face. Her eyes were open. She was staring at me. But I don't think she was seeing. I don't think she had seen anything in quite some time.

My phone rang again. The sound started out as loud as ever but then dropped off abruptly, fading or falling away as the world spun around me, color and movement gradually absorbed by a great darkness that rushed up to swallow me whole.

XII

Darkness turned slowly back to light.

I don't know how long I was unconscious in the weeds, but when awareness came swimming back to me, I was already on my feet, Karen supporting me on one side, Kyle holding me up on the other. They were moving me toward the house, both of them talking at once. I heard only scattered words and phrases—*journal* and *what were you* and *pointing* and *did you see* and *newspapers* and *Amy found* and *Bloodybones* and other words that sounded something like it; they might have been *Robert Dough*. I couldn't make sense of any of it then. I was struggling too hard to get the fog and the fuzziness out of my head. I was also looking westward, toward the keeper's quarters and just beyond it, to the place I had last seen the man standing with Amy's body crumpled at his feet.

They were not there now. That stretch of beach was

empty but for the sand and the beach grass and the lengthening afternoon shadows cast by the house and the light tower and some banks of high clouds that were starting to scud in from the north.

I stopped walking and pulled abruptly away from them, looking down at the phone that I somehow still held in my hand. I unlocked the screen, but it was blank. I switched to the directory of recent calls, but there nothing unusual there: a call from Kyle this morning, a call I'd placed to Karen at the Dreamview last night, predominantly work-related calls before that.

"David?" Karen said.

"Nothing, it's nothing," I said, shoving the phone in my pocket and allowing myself to be led the rest of the way to the house. It was still catacomb-cold inside despite the fact that Karen had been running a pair of space heaters for the last several hours; the chill almost took my breath away when I entered.

They took me into the living room, where I stopped, gaping at the scene in front of me. My impression was that Karen had spent her time here ransacking the place like a burglar. Either that or a bomb had exploded. What I saw were loose papers, newspapers, and books strewn everywhere across the desk, the couch, and much of the floor. It took longer to see the sense in that seeming chaos, in part because of the very different kind of chaos that was still rattling inside my head, where a flurry of confusing images swirled madly and that deadwind still whistled its cold, barren song.

We sat in that frigid living room and talked, hesitantly at first, then with increasing confidence and speed. I could not explain most of what happened to me during that wild stretch of two or three minutes on the beach. I could remember the sequence of events well enough, beginning just as Kyle scrambled out of the secret garden and started hurrying toward the keeper's quarters, worried about Karen's safety, and ending with the two of them holding me up and propelling me toward the house. But I could not find the words to describe much of it and was hesitant to discuss the rest. How do you, after all, talk about the hallucination of a severed hand lying in the weeds? How do you admit the vision of a silver-eyed man dragging an injured, terrified young boy along the shoreline? How do you explain getting a phone call from a woman who has been gone—dead—for over six months?

I was not the only one who had trouble talking about his experience. Kyle vaguely remembered seeing the man standing near the waterline and vanishing as suddenly as he had appeared. He did not remember anything that happened after that, certainly not his desperate certainty that "Bloodybones is in the house" or his urgent need to go check on Karen. When I described those moments to him, I got only a blank look in return. When I pressed the point, he snapped at me angrily. He only recalled what happened after he arrived at the house, when Karen met him on the steps and excitedly started telling him what she had discovered.

Karen.

She had the most to talk about, and as she did, I felt a wrenching sensation deep inside my gut, as if I was being pulled in two directions at once. In a very real sense, I think I was. For the first time since I had returned to Vessey Point last week and heard Amy speak to me—*David, look*—I was beginning to grasp some answers, or at least the faint, distant shape of answers, the *suggestion* of answers. But at the same time, I felt as if I were being roughly dragged somewhere else altogether, away from answers and deeper into confusion, into mystery. Or to be brutally honest about it, deeper away from the precarious edge of sanity and closer to the madness I had sensed earlier after stumbling on the severed hand that did not exist.

Little by little, Karen told us and showed us what she had discovered during her exploration of Amy's shelves and drawers. The afternoon waned, and the light through the windows grew dim. The space heaters finally began to have an effect, but at best, it was a weak, paltry warmth, just enough to make the living room bearable, not nearly enough to approach true comfort. I could have fought the chill by bringing in an armload of firewood for the woodstove, the fireplace, or both. But I didn't. The cold that lingered in the room felt weirdly appropriate for the conversation that was unfurling between us. But there was another reason too. I did not want to go outside, even for just the few minutes it would take to get to the woodpile on the other side of the house, gather up a load of stove lengths, and return. I did not want to go outside with the light beginning to fade and the shadows beginning to lengthen across the sand.

I was frankly impressed with what Karen had accomplished in such a short time. She had uncovered a vast wealth of information—so much, in fact, that I was shocked and chastened all over again at the amount of things Amy had never told me. I could not understand why she had kept so much a secret, and I vaguely understood with a wave of heartbreaking sorrow that I probably would never know.

The story Karen uncovered was revealed in two long streams of information. There were the entries in Amy's journals, both the final volume that I had looked at in Karen's motel room the other night and the volume that immediately preceded it, which she had located on Amy's shelf that afternoon. She had carefully marked each applicable entry with a sticky note from a pad she found in the drawer and occasionally highlighted portions of those entries with additional notes, some of which had cryptic symbols— a lone question mark or exclamation point, and in one case the statement *WTF?*—written on them.

Then there were the other materials strewn about the room. They included several newspapers that had to be a hundred years old or close to it—I recognized the bold *Press-Beacon* masthead that had been used from the paper's founding in 1887 into the 1920s or so—along with dozens of photocopies. There were faded duplicates of articles from the *Press-Beacon* and other papers, pages from *A Pictorial History of Madsen Township* and a few additional books, and what appeared to be copies of original source material that might have been journal entries or old letters or maybe just the notes of an earlier researcher.

Finally, there were Amy's photos of the secret garden. Karen had told me there were many of them, but I was still astounded by what I saw. There were twenty or more images printed out on regular white paper and scattered among the other documents. Each one showed the crumbled foundation and its overgrown interior from a different angle—from the beach looking inland, from the opposite side gazing toward the lake, from the keeper's quarters looking east, and from the east looking back toward the house and light tower. Some of the images were untouched. Others were marked with a red circle or a black X pointing out a particular spot inside the walls. It appeared to be the same spot each time, a location roughly near the southern side of the foundation, though the different angles and focal lengths made it difficult to tell for sure.

"So this man you saw is the same man Amy saw," Karen said at last. She took a sip from the bottle of water she was carrying in her knapsack then looked back up at us triumphantly. She had already been talking for more than an hour and was nearing the end, presenting her conclusions with a flourish, like a whodunnit detective addressing his room full of assembled suspects. "She saw him, and you two both saw him, and somehow—it makes no rational sense, but there doesn't seem to be any way of escaping it—somehow that man is—"

"Albert Robideaux," I said, holding up a copy of an old photograph. "Apparently, known around these parts as Bloodybones."

The photo had taken my breath away the first time I saw it. There was no doubting or disputing that it was the man on the beach, the man who had been dragging the struggling young boy from the woods toward the house, the man who had stopped and looked at me with that terrible gaze, those eyes shining with silver hate. The eyes in the photograph were not silver. They

317

were tiny, black, expressionless specks in the middle of his wide, pale face, almost as if they weren't eyes at all but pinholes that had been punched through the paper. But everything else was identical. The nose. The thin-lipped scowl. The bald pate. It was the same man.

The photo was stapled to another photocopy, this one a newspaper clipping on which Amy had scribbled *Press Beacon October ? 1914.* The story, set in the typical miserly eight- or nine-point type of the day and made blurry by the poor quality of the copy, was headlined *Butcher of Vessey Point Revealed* and beneath it, *Madman Succumbs to Self-Inflicted Wound.*

The article apparently marked the conclusion of a story that had played out here for close to a decade, from the spring of 1905, when a thirty-one-year-old former shoe salesman from Indianapolis named Albert Eugene Robideaux had joined the U.S. Lifesaving Service and been assigned to the lonely, windswept stretch of Lake Superior shoreline known as Vessey Point.

Except in those days, the point had not exactly been lonely. In addition to the lighthouse with its keeper, assistant keeper, their families, and the lifesaving station with its crew of half a dozen or more men, there was a thriving lumber camp a mile away and what amounted to an entire fishing village within a quarter-mile of where we now sat—thirty-odd families, a schoolhouse that doubled as a church on Sundays, a general store, a post office, a blacksmith and livery stable, a net works, and a saloon that seemed to come and go as business demanded, usually opening up in the winter when the lumberjacks were working in the frozen cedar swamps nearby, shutting down during the quieter summer months.

According to Amy's research, as reconstructed by Karen, the first reports of trouble had begun in the early fall of 1905, when several children at the school announced that they would no longer go outside to play during the noon-hour recess break. They complained that someone was watching them from the woods across the road from the schoolyard. Within a few days or weeks, other pupils were tearfully reporting the same thing, claiming to see a man glowering at them from the edge of the trees. Their descriptions were sketchy at best. Several of the children began calling him "the shiny man," a phrase that was not fully explained but may have stemmed from something the man carried with him—a metal implement, perhaps a lantern—or maybe some physical characteristic.

The schoolmistress, a seventeen-year-old Madsen girl named Abigail Arnette, could not assuage the children's fears. She was likewise unable to find any trace of the shiny man herself although she tried several enterprising surveillance tricks, including spying from inside the schoolhouse and, on one occasion, lying flat on her belly beneath a clump of shrubs next to the outhouse while the children played nearby. Eventually, several area men began staking out the schoolyard as well, but they had no more luck than the teacher. Sightings of the shiny man were still reported, even at times when other adults were nearby, but he seemed to be invisible to anyone over the age of ten.

"People made the obvious assumption that the

whole thing was just a hoax, a prank," Karen said. "Nowadays, it would all be different, especially because the children were so damn vehement—anxious, crying, terrified. Parents would pressure law enforcement to keep up a constant presence around the school. The media would be relentless. If they still couldn't find anything, they'd start to look at other explanations. The school district would call in an army of shrinks, and you'd probably hear people batting around terms like 'shared hallucination' or 'mass hysteria.' But obviously, that kind of thing didn't happen back then, at least out here in the middle of nowhere. Back then, the adults just told the kids to act their age and stop fooling around, and then they went back to the business of catching fish or cutting trees or whatever it was they did around here."

One morning in October, a seven-year-old boy by the name of Noah Redding burst into the classroom in a panic, tears streaming down his face, and told of being accosted by the shiny man during his walk to school. The man had stepped out suddenly from behind the blacksmith shop and blocked Noah's path, telling him there was something *very interesting* to see behind the stable. Terrified, Noah shook his head and stammered no. But it would not take long, the shiny man said. It would take only a moment. Noah could look and still make it to school before Miss Arnette rang the final bell. And think of the story he would be able to tell his friends! Noah protested and tried to dart around the shiny man, who was also, as it turned out, a *tall* man and a *broad* man. The man sidestepped nimbly and blocked Noah's path again, and when Noah tried to reverse direction and run the other way, the man reached out and grabbed his right arm, jerking it so hard that Noah's shoulder still ached two days later.

There is no telling what might have happened next had not a low, thick bank of fog been creeping slowly across the lake that morning. Watching it develop over the last hour or so, the ever-dutiful keeper had fired up the steam-powered fog signal on the grounds of the lighthouse, which suddenly went off with its first deep-throated bellow. The sound, a more-than-common one around Vessey Point, barely distracted the shiny man, but it did distract him just enough, causing him to turn his head toward the lighthouse and loosen his grip on Noah's arm. The boy was able to wrench free, and he ran the last quarter-mile to school, screaming at the top of his lungs.

"Nothing much happened for a long time after that," Karen said. "It was at least two years before the next major incident. There were periodic sightings of the guy. Usually, it was around the schoolyard, but once in a while, he'd be seen at other places in town. Always looking from the shadows, at least according to the stories. The kids still talked about the shiny man, but not with the same fear they had before. At least until August of 1907, when he tried another—I don't know—abduction, I guess." She stopped and rubbed the bridge of her nose as if she had a headache. Kyle and I never took our eyes off her, waiting for her to go on. "This time, it was a little girl who was approached, not on her way to school but while she was walking home from the store with a bag of flour for her mother and some penny candy she'd bought for herself. Sarah Haapalien. Nine years old. The man surprised her by popping out from behind a dray wagon. She was quick and got away before he could grab her, but she was also a pretty observant kid, and she was able to give the constable from Madsen details that none of the other children had ever been able to provide."

"Details?" Kyle said. "You mean like a description?"

"Partially," Karen nodded. "She couldn't describe the man's face any better than the other children had, but for the first time, she was able to tell the grown-ups why. The guy was apparently wearing a mask—whitish, maybe, or light gray, maybe even a little silvery. Some sort of thin cloth. Sarah said it was like sparkly linen. She said it caught the sunlight and made his face look 'bright.'"

"Shiny," I said.

"Shiny," Karen agreed. "There was a slit cut for a mouth and two holes punched where the nose should be. There were also two holes for the eyes, and when she looked in them, she could see his *real* eyes. She said his eyes also caught the light. They were pale, and she thought they reflected the sun. They looked . . . well, you guys know how they looked. They looked like silver. Personally, I have no idea what that means."

"I know what it means because I saw it. But I don't understand it," I said. "The man in that photo certainly doesn't have silver eyes. But I'm as sure as can be that it's the same man."

"It's the same man all right," Karen said. "I know it's the same man because he told Sarah his name."

"He told—"

"He told her his name, but she didn't understand it. He must have been trying to calm her down, you know, win her trust and convince her not to run. He was trying to sound like her friend, and what do new friends do? They introduce themselves. But in her fear or her hurry to run away or whatever was going through her mind, she barely heard what he said. She heard only a vague sound. He told her his name was Robideaux, but that's not what she heard."

"For goddsakes, Karen, what did she hear?" Kyle said, leaning so far forward that I thought he might topple out of his chair.

Karen sighed. "He said his name was Robideaux. But what Sarah heard was much worse. She heard the word Bloodybones."

XIII

I was totally unsurprised when Karen explained what happened next. With that single logical misunderstanding—a somewhat unusual name misheard by a little girl in the grip of utter terror—the child-stalker was instantly elevated to the level of folklore or myth. Bloodybones, the man with the silver eyes. Bloodybones, the creature that watched from the edge of the forest, that lurked behind buildings, that jumped out from behind wagons. Bloodybones, the legend. Bloodybones, a monster more than a man.

Over the next several years, the legend only grew. Most of the area children and more than a few of the adults claimed to have seen Bloodybones lurking in the shadows, most often in the early morning or during the evening hours, just around twilight. A few described encounters with the demon, hair-raising stories of extremely close calls, although there was no way of knowing how many of those tales were true. The name became a schoolyard chant—*Bloodybones, Bloodybones, coming in the night; Bloodybones, Bloodybones, carrying a knife; Bloodybones, Bloodybones, has a silver eye; Bloodybones, Bloodybones, see it and you die*—and a threat used by parents—*If you're not good (eat your vegetables, go to bed, finish your schoolwork, do your chores), Bloodybones will come and take you away*. One day in 1910, two brothers named Isaac and Christopher Lovesey failed to show up for school, and the story spread like wildfire through the town: Bloodybones had snatched the boys away. The fact that it later turned out the brothers had gone with their parents to visit a sick aunt in Sault Ste. Marie scarcely dampened the glee with which Vessey Point residents imagined their demise.

Interestingly, despite the fears, despite the stories, despite the chants and the rants, despite the swooning fascination people held for their very own local ogre, to the best of anyone's knowledge, no one had yet died at Albert Robideaux's hands. But that was soon to change.

Not long after the incident with the Lovesey boys, on a blustery and rainy afternoon in late October of 1910, a stuffed blue gingham doll that belonged to six-year-old Esther Toyra was found at the edge of the woods behind her house.

"It was covered with blood—the doll and everything around it," Karen said.

In fact, the ground for ten feet around was soaked with blood, and several wide arcs made by spattering droplets had sprayed as much as fifteen feet in various directions. There were signs that the little girl had been ruthlessly carried away by someone heading east. A bloody trail of bootprints and unmistakable drag marks were carved through the dirt in that direction but grew fainter and fainter over the distance, eventually vanishing completely near the lakeshore, where there was no protection from the rain, which had been falling for hours in wind-driven sheets. The only other trace of the girl was found at that spot, lying there in the sand. It was her left shoe. The laces were still tied, but the leather was scuffed and ragged and torn, as if someone had brutally ripped it right off of her foot.

That was just the first of the killings.

Although it had taken years for them to begin, once they started, it seemed they could not stop, could not *be* stopped. Between October of 1910 and October 1914, no fewer than nine local children—five boys and four girls—fell prey to Bloodybones. Not one of the bodies was found, but there was always evidence left behind. In several of the cases, the amount of blood and devastation at the scene made the site of Esther Toyra's abduction look like the aftermath of a church picnic. In other cases, there was hardly a sign of struggle or injury, perhaps as little as a broken branch, a bit of disturbed earth, or in one case, a single torn scrap of a red checked flannel work shirt.

"That was Joseph Adderly. Twelve years old and probably retarded. The accounts of the time described him as a simpleton—ah, what an enlightened age that was. He was the son of Willard Adderly, the lighthouse keeper. He lived in this house," Karen said.

Kyle and I exchanged a glance and then, weirdly, both looked toward the staircase at the same time, as if we expected to see the ghost of Joseph Adderly standing on the top step, watching us.

The disappearances—murders—began to drive people from Vessey Point. Little by little, families packed up and moved away: to Madsen, to Paradise, to Sault Ste. Marie, to Newberry, or to places in Lower Michigan and even more distant. While history would record that the little community on the point died for the same reasons as countless other towns, fading away as the timber and fishing industries slowly failed, it was pretty clear that the terror of Bloodybones played a significant role as well.

It was not until the fall of 1914 that the nightmare came to an end, and it happened the way such things so often do: with a careless mistake on the part of a perpetrator grown bold and fat with visions of infallibility or immortality or both. In this case, Robideaux made two crucial errors. He attempted to take someone much older than his usual victims—a nineteen-year-old girl named Florence Kinnunen—and he attempted to do it in what passed for the center of town, a wide stretch of dirt path between the store and the post office and the building where fishing nets were made.

Florence, a savvy, work-hardened, big-boned northwoods gal, instantly recognized the danger she was in. She screamed at the top of her lungs the moment she saw Bloodybones and lashed out with both hands, pummeling the man's body and clawing at his face with a strength his previous victims had not prepared him for. Her cries were loud enough to summon a crowd of people from the store. They scrambled out into the road and raced to her aid, but by that time, the killer was already fifty yards away, sprinting toward the woods at the edge of town and the lakeshore beyond. Several men took up the pursuit, while the women gathered around Florence, who was standing in the middle of the road, sobbing and looking down with an uncomprehending gaze at the object in her hands: Bloodybones' silver-painted linen mask.

Seen in full view and broad daylight, with his distinctive bald head uncovered, Robideaux was instantly identified by the men giving chase. There was some element of confusion, however, because Robideaux, like everyone else who lived at and around Vessey Point, had been questioned at length several times over the years as various local and state authorities had investigated the string of child abductions. In the heat of the moment, his pursuers could not understand how someone could have gone through those rounds of interrogation and not been discovered. Nor could they grasp the fact that the person who had terrorized them for so long could be someone they saw every day, a good neighbor, a respected member of their community, and a savior to boot, a selfless individual who risked his own life to rescue those in peril on the lake. The fact that Bloodybones had worn an actual mask was easy to comprehend. The fact that he had worn a very different kind of mask, that he could be an accomplished liar as well as a psychotic killer, seemed unthinkable.

"They chased him all the way to the lifesaving

station," Karen said, waving a hand toward the room's eastern window, in the direction of the secret garden. "When they got there, he was nowhere to be found. They tore the place apart, and after about an hour, they found him. He was at the bottom of a ladder that led from the pantry down to some sort of root cellar. Not dead. Almost. He was bleeding out. He'd slit his own throat with the butcher knife he was carrying and was maybe a minute or two away from death. After that, the stories vary a bit. Okay, a lot. The official version is that they wrapped towels around his wound and got a truck from the lumber camp—one of the only motor vehicles that was out here in those days. They started taking him to the doctor's office in Madsen, going as fast as they could on whatever passed for roads back then, but he died a few miles outside of town."

"That's the official version?"

Karen nodded. "What actually happened, or so it seems, is that they found him lying at the bottom of that ladder in a pool of his own blood and proceeded to beat, kick, and stomp him until he was dead. Then, probably hours and hours later, they put him in the truck and took a nice, leisurely drive into town."

I shuddered. It was all too easy to imagine.

Despite an intense effort lasting several weeks, the bodies of Albert Robideaux's victims were never found. The presumption was that he had dumped them somewhere far back in the woods, probably miles away from Vessey Point, where they likely would never be discovered. Nevertheless, there was plenty of evidence to clearly tie Robideaux to the victims. In his quarters at the lifesaving station, shoved far back underneath the bed, were two wooden crates full of children's belongings, some of them still covered in blood. A ring. A locket. A small photograph of Esther Toyra's mother. Two shooting marbles. An empty shotgun shell. Joseph Adderly's pocketknife, engraved with the legend *To Joey from Mama and Papa.*

They also found a journal Robideaux had kept in fits and starts, sometimes writing long, rambling entries day after day, sometimes not writing a word for weeks or even months on end. The journals described each abduction and murder in intricate detail, the unspeakable things Robideaux had done with and to each victim, the way they had struggled, the way they had pleaded with him, the expressions on their faces as he entered them, the tears, the shrieks, the way the blood spattered as he began to dismember them, the sound of flesh tearing and bone grinding, and the way the light had faded from their eyes when death had finally, mercifully rescued them from the horror.

While every entry was vastly different, they all concluded the same way. At the end of each terrible account was a single line, identical each time, just five short words: *They went into the pool.*

I felt a fierce, hot pressure in the center of my chest.

"Amy Lynn is in the pool," I murmured.

I glanced at Karen, and our gazes locked.

She was crying.

XIV

The windowpanes rattled, and all three of us jumped like frightened children.

I would be lying if I didn't say my first thought was, *He's out there. Bloodybones is out there.*

But I realized immediately that it was only the wind.

The sky was darker than it should have been even at that late-afternoon hour. Clouds were beginning to pile up above the lake, towering cliffs of cumulonimbus that had formed in the northwest and were now moving swiftly toward shore like an attacking armada. The few trees I could see from this angle were beginning to bend inland, away from the stiffening breeze, and the lake, which had been calmly reflecting sunlight like bright glass just a few hours ago, was dappled and shadowy, broken by long, marching rows of angry whitecaps.

But while the weather explained the change in light and the noise at the window, the knowledge did nothing to calm me. It might not have been Bloodybones out there rattling the glass, but I was under no illusion. He was out there someplace, and not far away. My experience earlier that afternoon convinced me of that.

A stray thought pushed its way into my head: Which victim had I seen that afternoon? Which young boy had Bloodybones been dragging down the beach? At the end, the vision had changed and I had seen Amy lying at the phantom killer's feet, dead. But before that, who had it been? What boy was it I'd seen fighting for his life, crying out for all eternity in soundless terror?

Almost as soon as the question occurred to me, I knew the answer. I'm not sure how I knew, but I had no doubt that I was right. If I could see a picture of him right now, it would be the same child, the same lanky limbs, the same overalls, the same red checked shirt, the same limp hair, so blond it was almost white.

The boy who had lived here, who had played in this room, who had perhaps sat in the very spot I was sitting now, drawing pictures or whittling with the pocketknife his parents had given him, occasionally looking out the window as spring thunderheads rolled in across the lake.

Joseph Adderly.

The lightkeeper's son.

XV

The rest of Karen's story was quickly told.

She described how Amy had first seen Bloodybones in the spring of last year while returning from a hike along the beach. According to her journal, she took a shortcut through the remains of the old lifesaving station, stumbled over something buried in the grass, and fell face first. It knocked the wind out of her, and it took her a minute or two to catch her breath, get back to her feet, and dust herself off. That was when she saw a man standing a short distance away, staring at her.

I felt the skin on the back of my neck tighten when I realized how similar Amy's encounter was to my incident that afternoon.

The man vanished almost immediately, leaving Amy to doubt her powers of observation. Quite naturally, she assumed that she'd been fooled by a trick of the light, a stray shadow, or who knew what? She had spent enough days and nights in lonely, wild places to know that your mind sometimes showed you things that weren't there, especially when turning quickly, looking up suddenly, or perhaps after recovering from a stumble and fall.

But over the next month, she saw the man seven or eight more times, usually while she was safely inside the house, looking out. He would be walking along the beach or staring off into the distance. Several times, he was looking toward the house or the light tower, scanning, as if searching for something. Once, she thought she saw him dragging something heavy through the sand past the fog signal building. There was no pattern to the appearances except . . . except that there was. More times than not, he seemed to come and go from the lifesaving station, appearing and disappearing either from inside the crumbled foundation walls or from the area just outside, which naturally triggered her sudden fascination with the place. She began to study her secret garden with a newfound intensity, strolling around the perimeter, walking through the interior, and of course, taking several dozen photographs from every conceivable angle.

"She was intrigued by how intrigued she was," Karen said with a humorless laugh. "She was positively entranced with the place and didn't really understand why. This strange man she was seeing seemed to linger there, or show up there, or vanish there. But he wasn't *always* there. So what was it? Why was she so fascinated? She wrote at one point that she wanted to *stop* being fascinated. She tried to drop the whole thing a couple of times, but the place kept calling her back, like the bottle calling to an alcoholic."

Amy clearly understood that the situation was abnormal. Not just her interest in the lifesaving station but everything. She never got to the point of admitting, at least in print, that the man she was seeing wasn't real. She never used the word *ghost*. But she knew that something was "otherwordly," Karen said, quoting one particular journal entry verbatim. She knew exactly what was happening whether she put it down in black and white or kept it inside.

One day in May, a bitter cold day with a harsh north wind surging off the lake and late-season snow flurries whirling through the air, she looked up from her laptop and saw the man standing stock still on the beach, midway between the house and the walls of the secret garden. With no thought or plan, she jumped up from her desk and raced outside, sprinting across the beach in nothing but a T-shirt, sweatpants, and bare feet. The icy wind cut like a saber, but she ignored it.

She called out, "Hello! You! Hey, hello!"

The man had his back to her and did not acknowledge her cries. The distance between them was now just a few yards.

"She shouted to him again, and he started to move," Karen said. "He was turning around to face her, and Amy was able to see what he had in his hand. Or she thought she did. She thought she saw a knife, but as he kept turning, she realized it wasn't a knife but some kind of grappling hook—the kind a lifesaving crew might use during a rescue. And then she saw again that he wasn't holding anything at all. His hands were empty. And then he was gone."

"Gone?" Kyle said.

Karen nodded. "He vanished. Instantly. One

second he was there, turning toward her, maybe with something in his hands, maybe not. The next—well, he just wasn't there anymore. That's when she used that word, *otherworldly,* when she wrote about it that night. It was also the first time she mentioned feeling afraid."

Amy did what her writer's instincts told her to do, what she had always done when confronted with something new or different or difficult to understand. She threw herself into research. In between a professional visit to a Montana resort and a trip to compete in a northeast Wisconsin walleye tournament, she began visiting the Madsen School and Public Library to scour their small collection of area history books and scroll through the morgue of old *Press-Beacon* issues they maintained on microfilm. It wasn't a complete collection of papers—quite a few rolls of film had been purloined by unsupervised researchers over the years—but since the newspaper office itself had been severely damaged twice in its history, by fire in 1937 and flood in 1968, it was the closest thing to a complete run anywhere around.

She also paid several visits to the "research library" maintained by the Historical Advisory Committee, which was really nothing more than a half-dozen shelves of old books and a battered filing cabinet housed in a pole building behind the log cabin Madsen Museum on Shelton Street. Among their small collection were quite a few family histories compiled as an aid to genealogists. Several of those histories focused on families who had once lived near Vessey Point.

Although she had to peruse some twenty-five to

thirty separate sources to do it and extrapolate to fill in a number of gaps, Amy eventually pieced together the full story of Albert Robideaux. She also felt a growing certainty that Robideaux was the man she was seeing—at least once or twice a week by that time in early July—and that his presence on the point was connected to her unshakable obsession with the old lifesaving station. She continued to resist the use of words like *ghost* or *phantom* but seemed to accept the general concept easily enough. At one point, she wrote a detailed journal entry recalling the many times her work had brought her into contact with what she termed "spiritually-aligned people." It was a diverse crew covering a broad spectrum from backwoods fundamentalists to mountain-dwelling Wiccans, fishing guides who cast the runes before an expedition, hunters who used a "third eye" to unfailingly sight their targets, Christian proponents of sustainability through adherence to the "green gospel," Druids who sang beneath the moon, and Native American healers who quietly went about their work in little towns from Michigan to Alaska and everywhere between.

Karen showed us that entry, which concluded, *I have heard so much. I have seen so much. I have felt so much. I have been within touching distant of the infinite so many times in so many places. I am no longer the skeptic I once was. You can't stand beneath the northern lights and listen to an old woman speak with wolves and still be a hardheaded rationalist. I find it impossible to doubt things I don't understand. Sometimes, I think the things I don't understand are the only things I'm sure of.*

She also confessed to a sense of mounting dread.

335

"Yet she never said a word to me," I muttered, unable to get past that single, unavoidable fact.

"She wanted to," Karen replied. "She wrote about it. She wanted to talk to you and to our father. But she was afraid what you would think. She didn't say it, but I'm guessing she was worried a little about her sanity. Or maybe she was just worried that *you* would question her sanity. A couple of times, she sat down to write you an e-mail. One time, she picked up the phone and started dialing your number. But she always chickened out. She thought she would do it later. That was her plan. Always later."

Tears stung my eyes as I thought of Amy out here by herself, watching Albert Robideaux stalk around the grounds, understanding what but not why, afraid of being alone but afraid to reach out.

When I looked up, I saw Karen watching me closely. She gave me a small, sad nod of understanding, and I remembered her telling me about her dreams, dreams of Amy, recurring nightmares of a seventeen-year-old girl who no longer existed, a sister she had never really known. We were too much alike, Karen and I. We both ached to help someone we were too late to help.

"I don't understand any of this," Kyle said as another burst of wind rattled the windows. The gusts were rising steadily and had begun to whine around the eaves. The sound was faint, fearful, like a child crying in the distance, lost and unreachable. "What's the connection for all of this? If that's really the vengeful ghost of some old child murderer walking around out there—if that's who it is—why? Why now? It's been over a hundred years. Why is he back? Amy lived out here for years. Why didn't she see him before? What changed last spring? Trances, visions, dreams—it doesn't make any sense, any of it. I'm sorry, guys, but I just don't get it."

"I do," I said, surprising myself.

Kyle and Karen looked at me expectantly, and I thought, *The things I don't understand are the only things I'm sure of.*

"I don't get it either," I told them, "but I think I know what started it."

A splatter of rain struck the window, and beyond it, I could see breakers beginning to crash onto the shore.

"Get your coats," I said. "Come on."

XVI

Wind and water were roaring as we made our way across the beach. We kept our heads down, turned away from the mix of stinging rain and flying sand. It seemed brighter here, outside the confines of the keeper's quarters, but not by much. It was hard to believe that it wasn't yet five o' clock. The light looked like the end of day. The sky felt low enough to touch.

Karen must have figured out what I was doing (*excellent,* I thought, *at least somebody's figured it out*) because she stopped me just before we reached the old foundation, grabbing my arm and turning me to face her.

"David, are you sure you want to do this?"

The things I don't understand are the only things I'm sure of.

"I'm not sure of anything," I said with a shrug. "Let's go."

"David, wait—"

"What is it?"

"I didn't tell you about Amy's last journal entry."

She led us a short distance away from the angry water, behind the dubious shelter of twin leafless birch trees.

"If you're going where I think you're going, you and Amy are an awful lot alike," Karen said. "She figured it out too. The thing that started it all. A simple little thing. A stupid accident. When we were just kids, my mother used to call us Careless and Clueless. I must have been about seven, so Amy would have been five. We'd look at Mom with these goofy angelic expressions and say in perfect unison, 'Which one am I?' Then all three of us would laugh like mad. She must have remembered that when she was writing about what happened that day because she called it, 'a careless and clueless kind of accident.'"

"What the hell are you talking about?" Kyle said.

I answered for Karen. "It all started the day Amy was cutting through the old lifesaving station. She tripped on something and fell, just like I tripped out there today. I'm thinking—I'm almost certain—that we both stumbled over the same thing."

"I don't . . . " Kyle began then trailed away with a puzzled expression. The light dawned a moment later. "Oh, my god," he murmured.

Karen nodded. "Amy realized she must have stumbled over the entrance to the pantry staircase, the ladder, whatever it was that led down into the root cellar where Robideaux slit his throat. She didn't know how, exactly, but she knew hitting that spot had—I don't know, pick your term. Awakened the spirit? She theorized that these images of Robideaux walking around the point were like a movie of the past, and somehow, tripping over the cellar entrance had turned on the projector."

She came to that realization on a Tuesday morning, four days before she disappeared, and didn't waste any time putting her theory to the test. By lunch time she had gathered up her camera and her little snub-nose Taurus .38—*I knew there was nothing I could shoot at out there. Whatever I might find could not be wounded by bullets. But I felt better carrying it anyway,* she wrote—and started for the lifesaving station. She wished she also had a blueprint of the old building, but she would have to make do without one.

As it turned out, the lack of a floor plan scarcely mattered. With that first day still fresh in her mind, she was able to find the place almost immediately. She knelt in nearly the exact spot she had tripped and parted the weeds with her hands, feeling a rush of excitement that quickly vanished in disappointment. She had been wrong. There was nothing there but the same mix of loose soil and dirty sand that covered the whole interior of the secret garden.

Then she saw it.

It was just barely protruding from the ground. She might not have seen it at all if it hadn't been for a pair of long, jagged scuff marks in the dirt, left behind by her own boots the day she fell. At the beginning of those twin tracks was a curved piece of rusty iron, no more than an inch or two long, rising out of the sand.

She dug it out and discovered a heavy ring perhaps four inches in diameter.

Amy pulled. Nothing. She cleared away more of the sand but still could not get the ring to budge. It ended up taking a good fifteen minutes to dig out the entire area, revealing a wooden trapdoor, four feet long by perhaps three wide, on heavy black-iron hinges.

"She opened it and realized right away that she'd forgotten a critical piece of equipment: a flashlight," Karen said. "It was pitch dark down inside the opening, of course. So she pulled out her cellphone and used the screen as a light."

When she knelt and thrust the phone into the hole, the sunlight from above and the digital glow from her hand were just enough to show her the first five feet or so of a built-in wooden ladder with thick, heavy rungs descending into the black at about a fifty-degree angle. She didn't hesitate. She started down. While she'd gotten the impression that she had only seen a small portion of the ladder, that turned out not to be the case. In fact, what she had seen was almost the entire length. After descending just eight or ten feet, her boots thumped down on a hard-packed earthen floor.

She found herself in a room perhaps ten feet square, lined on three sides with wooden shelves. The shelves were mostly bare but for a scattering of Mason jars full of withered, unrecognizable contents. In the far corner stood some kind of large container, a wooden crate, perhaps, or an oversized steamer trunk. Strands of cobweb hung from the ceiling like cheap Halloween decorations. The air was cool, smelling of damp and mildew.

She pointed her phone at the foot of the ladder,

wondering if this was the exact spot they had found Robideaux sprawled in the dirt, bleeding to death. The thought gave her a weird, uncomfortable thrill. But if she had expected to see anything—a man-shaped depression in the dirt or a dark, dried blood stain—she was disappointed. The floor was flat and undisturbed and as clean as it ever had been or ever would be.

She started to walk toward the far wall, intent on checking out the room more closely, when there was a loud bang from above and the shaft of sunlight that had been shining through the trapdoor vanished, plunging her into near total darkness, broken only by the small, faint half-circle of light emanating from her phone.

Amy let out a startled cry and hurried back to the ladder, confirming what she had thought. The trapdoor had slammed shut. It was impossible, of course. There was no wind that day, and even a fifty mile per hour gale would not have been enough to lift that heavy wooden door from the ground, swinging it up and over to the point that it would fall closed on its own. But impossible or not, the door was closed now.

She didn't waste time trying to puzzle it out. She shoved the phone in her pocket and scaled the ladder, taking two rungs at a time. She was afraid that she would get there and find the door impossible to open, locked, but she didn't spend time worrying about that either. Instead, when she reached the top, she raised her shoulder and threw all her weight against the wooden planks. The door immediately lifted, letting in a blessed wall of light. She steadied herself on the ladder and grasped the door with both hands, pushing it open the rest of the way.

As she was scrambling out of the hole, she felt something grasp the sleeve of her windbreaker. It was the kind of feeling you might have snagging your coat on a tree branch or door handle. Or if another person had grasped the fabric and tugged. Blinking rapidly, trying to get her eyes to adjust to the flood of daylight, she struggled to figure out what might have caught her. But she could see nothing. She pulled her arm away and felt that invisible force pull back. This time, it was actually strong enough to drag her arm up and away. She felt a sharp pain in her shoulder, and her feet were lifted several inches off the top rung of the ladder.

She barked out a curse and yanked back with all her might.

Her arm came free, her momentum almost carrying her backwards off the ladder. It was a near thing, but she caught herself, steadied herself, then sagged forward, collapsing against the edge of the trapdoor opening, her hands clutching sand and weeds, heart pounding, breathing hard.

"By the time she wrote about it that night, she had convinced herself it never happened. She was very firm that it was all her imagination," Karen said. "But that didn't stop her from putting the whole thing down in detail. She described it all explicitly—how it felt like someone was trying to pull her up, jerking her, actually dragging her out of the hole. It was almost like she was using the journal to debate herself, spelling out very clearly what happened and arguing very insistently that there was no way it *could* have happened."

"She didn't go back down in the root cellar?" Kyle asked.

Karen shook her head. "She went back to the house

and had a drink. Then she did what she knew best. She sat down to work on her latest article. It wasn't until hours later, almost midnight, that she wrote about it in her journal. Her last entry. There was nothing more after that."

I felt a fresh wave of sadness wash over me, but this time, there was a small white flame of anger too. I thought of what I'd seen earlier that day, the image of Bloodybones dragging Joseph Adderly along the beach and how that had changed into a picture of Amy crumpled in a lifeless heap. The anger grew.

Part of me was mad at Amy for her secrecy, for what she had kept from me, what she was afraid to tell me.

But a bigger part was mad at something else.

I saw another image: Amy being pulled out of the hole not by an invisible force but by Albert Robideaux—huge and horrible, wearing a mask that sparkled in the light, pinpoints of silver shining through the eyeholes.

"This is going to end," I said. The words seemed right although I didn't exactly know what they meant. "This has *got* to end."

Kyle and Karen looked at me expectantly. I tried to look back but could not quite meet their eyes.

Nobody spoke. The wind howled around us.

I turned and stalked away, heading back toward the foundation.

A moment later, they followed.

XVII

My wild guess turned out to be right, a fact that did not surprise me in the least. The place I had tripped that afternoon was the same place Amy had fallen last spring. It was easy to spot now that I knew what I was looking for. What I had mistaken for a broken piece of wood was in fact part of the trap door, and it wasn't bleached white, it was painted white, or at least it had been almost a century ago.

Despite the fact that Amy had used this door just six months earlier, only about a third of it was still visible. The rest, including the iron ring, had already been reburied by the blowing, constantly shifting sands. It took less than a minute to clean it off.

"David?" Kyle said, putting a hand on my shoulder. "To be honest with you, I'm not exactly thrilled about the prospect of going down there."

"Don't go," I said, not even looking at him. "You can stay up here if you want. You can both stay up here."

"Don't be a prick, David. I want to go with you. But—but I don't understand what you're looking for."

"I don't either," I said, thinking again, *the things I don't understand are the only things I'm sure of.*

"There's nothing down there," Kyle said. "It's just a root cellar, right, Karen? It's just a dirty old room with some cobwebs and old jars. Grandma Josephine's pickled beets, expiration date 1922."

I wiped rainwater out of my eyes and grasped the iron ring. "You're probably right," I said. "But I'm going down anyway. I don't get it. It doesn't make any sense. But it started here. Maybe it can end here too."

I pulled, and the trapdoor came up, sand-clogged hinges squealing. At the same moment, a bright flash filled the sky, and the first clap of thunder exploded somewhere far out over the lake. All three of us jumped, and Karen let out a startled cry.

"Sorry about that," she said with a sheepish laugh. "I must say, that was pretty good timing though. Think someone's trying to tell us something?"

"Just another bit of Vessey Point weirdness," I said. "You guys have your phones?"

We took them out and turned them on. Another burst of thunder sounded. This time, none of us jumped.

"Okay," I said, swallowing hard. "Okay."

I started down the ladder, Karen following and Kyle bringing up the rear.

The last thing I saw as I climbed down was the lighthouse tower reaching skyward behind blowing curtains of rain. There might have been an indistinct white face peering back at me from the lamp room, or it might have been a trick of imagination and weather. I could not say for sure.

I reached bottom, stepped off the last rung, and moved slightly to the right to make room for the others. As I did, my foot connected with something hard. I heard it thump and saw a shadowy glimpse of a small object rolling a short distance away. I aimed my phone screen downward to see what it was.

"What?" I whispered, so softly I couldn't hear my own voice.

I blinked stupidly, uncomprehending, unable to grasp why I should be staring at a jar of Skippy peanut butter here in this underground room, here of all places.

My brain felt dense and sluggish, unable to process the information. It was such a dull, prosaic object, yet it did not belong here. Commonplace, out of place.

And then I remembered.

Slowly, agonizingly, I turned to the right and saw the rest of it. Two plastic bags with the legend THANKS FOR SHOPPING AT right above the familiar Red Door IGA logo. One of the bags was still intact. The other had torn down the seam, spilling its contents onto the hard-packed floor: the jar of peanut butter, a box of oatmeal, two potatoes, and a bunch of celery that had withered and turned black. The oatmeal container had broken open. Dry white oats had sprayed across the dirt in a wavering arc, like a messy elementary school art project.

"David?" Karen said beside me, and I almost screamed. "Do you know what this is?"

I nodded. "They're Amy's. They're the things she bought in town that morning, the day she disappeared."

"Christ," Kyle said softly. "You're sure?"

"Oh yeah, I'm sure. I saw all of this sitting on the bench seat of her truck when she drove away from the café. There should also be . . . yep, there it is. The bag from the hardware store. She bought hinges that morning. She was going to fix the door to her upstairs bathroom."

An odd thing happened then. As if we all had the same thought at the same time, we turned in virtual unison and shined our phones around the root cellar. None of us said what we were looking for, but it was obvious. If Amy's belongings were here, it was possible Amy was too.

I held my breath, tensing myself, preparing for the

346

dim light of my screen to sweep across a familiar face and form sprawled on the floor. I could see every terrible, grisly detail in my mind. I could see what her eyes would look like, her skin, her mouth. I could see her twisted form, arms and legs at crazy angles. I could imagine the pain tearing my heart open from the inside out. I could hear the sobs that would break from my throat. It was almost as though I were remembering something that had already happened.

But Amy was not there.

At least her body wasn't.

Karen noticed something else right away. At first, it appeared to be some kind of spot or stain on the floor, but when we moved closer, we could see it was a torn piece of navy blue nylon, no bigger than the palm of my hand, sitting there in the middle of the room, just beyond the second grocery bag.

Karen bent down and picked it up. "Was this—"

"Her windbreaker," I said dully.

Kyle said something that might have been another muttered curse or perhaps just made a low noise in the back of his throat.

I felt another fierce wave of anger. It washed over me like fire.

"She was here that day. There's no doubt about it," Karen said. "But where is she now?"

I opened my mouth to answer but realized I had nothing to say. I turned back and looked at the ladder, which was being pelted by icy raindrops. Above it, the wind roared past the trapdoor, sounding a little like that low whistle I had heard through my phone earlier in the day. It was a dumb, dead sound that offered no guidance, no hope.

Suddenly, Kyle grasped my arm.

"Do you feel that?" he said.

"I don't—"

"You don't feel it?" He looked at me closely, turned to Karen, turned back to me. "Don't either of you? Really? Don't you—you've got to—my god, don't you *feel* that?"

He looked exactly as he had on the beach earlier, when he had suddenly started babbling about Bloodybones being in the house. His face was china white, his eyes small and dark. His mouth quivered, and his breath made a strange rasping noise in the back of his throat.

"What is it, Kyle?" "He's here."

"Who?" I asked, but of course, I knew the answer already. "Is it him? Robideaux? Kyle, is Robideaux here right now?"

Kyle turned and stumbled away from us, simultaneously letting out a ghastly sound, part scream, part strangled sob. "There!" he cried, pointing toward the darkness at the back of the root cellar. "There! He's there! He's there he's there he's there he's there he's there *he'stherehe'stherehe'sthere!*"

I ran after him and saw what he was looking at. There was a wooden crate in the corner, tipped up on its side. The lid was off, and a drift of excelsior packing material had spilled out onto the floor. But Kyle wasn't paying any attention to the crate. He was looking at what was underneath the crate, or what had been underneath it until it had been overturned and shoved aside.

A second trapdoor, standing open.

"Kyle, don't—" I shouted, but it was too late. He had plunged into the open trap and vanished.

There was a startled cry, a muffled thump, a splash.

Then a louder crash as the trapdoor above us slammed shut.

XVIII

In the darkness, my cell phone rang.

I turned it over and looked at it, utterly unsurprised to see the words AMY'S CELL staring up at me again. I touched the ANSWER button and put the unit to my ear. This time there was absolutely nothing, no noise at all, no wind howling from the void, no sound of any kind. It was as if the phone was turned off.

I stabbed the red button to end the call, and as soon as I did, the ring tone sounded again.

AMY'S CELL.

I shoved the phone in my pocket, still ringing.

I was aware that Karen was sobbing beside me. I think I might have reached out to squeeze her hand, but all I was really aware of was pulling away from her and starting to walk toward the place that Kyle had disappeared.

"Get up that ladder and see if you can get the trapdoor open," I told her.

"David, no—"

"Get the trapdoor open!" I barked. "We're going to have to get out of here. But be careful. Remember what happened to your sister."

I didn't know if she listened to me or not. I didn't care. I was already at the other trap, kneeling, looking down.

My phone was still ringing when I pulled it out of my pocket. I briefly caught the word AMY'S before turning it over and shining it down into the hole.

The faint light revealed a drop of four or five feet down to some kind of platform made of wooden planks, almost like a pier. But it was the other thing— what was beyond the pier—that shocked me, sending a sharp, stabbing pain through the center of my chest.

My phone stopped ringing as abruptly as it started.

"Oh," I murmured. "Oh, my god."

I was looking at an opening that might have been twelve or fifteen feet across that was entirely filled with water. Part of me accepted that as perfectly natural. Down here, after all, we were no doubt well below the water level of the lake. But that still didn't explain what this room was doing here in the first place. Why would they have made a sub-basement below the root cellar when they must have known what the result would be? Why dig down here at all, and more to the point, why dig until their pit had flooded? Why this hidden lake? Why the wooden platform? What was this place?

The water looked cold and deep. The surface caught the light of my phone and sent a dull reflection back.

Black water, blue water, green water, I thought. *Deep water, dark water, dead water.*

I leaned farther into the hole. "Kyle?"

There was no answer.

I turned around and lowered myself into the opening. There was no ladder here, so I simply dropped with a thud to the wooden pier below.

"Kyle? Where are you?" Nothing.

BLOODYBONES

Once again I thrust my phone forward, and that was when I saw them.

Bobbing in the water in the middle of the pool, arms out, face down, as if in perfect parody of a dead man's float, was Kyle. His jacket had ballooned up behind him like a red parachute.

Beyond that, in the southeast corner of this underground lake, was Amy. The only part of her that was visible was her head, canted at an impossible angle, wedged into the corner formed by two earthen walls. Her hair floated limply around her face, which was bone white and bloated. Her mouth gaped, her sightless eyes stared toward me.

"Oh, Amy," I said softly. I felt hot tears, like acid on my cheeks. "Oh, my dear, sweet girl."

There was a splash, and the image of Amy's face vanished as I was cast into total darkness. I was so distraught that it took me a moment to realize I had dropped my phone. I looked down and saw it sinking to the bottom of the pool. It landed face up, the screen still illuminated.

The first thing I saw was that the pool was not nearly as deep as I had thought. Resting on the bottom, my phone was only five or six feet away. It looked close enough to reach out and grab.

The second thing I saw was where the phone had come to rest. The faint light showed me several feet of the sandy bottom, enough to see that the area was littered with bones. They were scattered in all directions, dozens of them. I saw a long, straight bone that might have been a femur. A platelike scapula and a portion of ribcage. Something small and crooked that might have been a finger. A jawbone with several teeth still intact. Another straight one, smaller, perhaps an arm. And more. So many more. Little bones. *Tiny* bones. The bones of children.

Then the light on my phone went dead, and I could see no more.

"They went into the pool," I said aloud in the darkness.

Above me, Karen screamed.

XIX

"David, look out!" I heard, and with that cry, above it, below it, everywhere around it, was something else—a loud, bellowing roar.

I looked up toward the trapdoor but could see nothing in the pitch dark.

"David, it's Bloodybones! He—"

Her cry was cut off abruptly, but that monstrous roaring went on and on.

Then I saw it, his face filling the opening above me. Although that's not exactly right. I could not see his face. It was much too dark for that. I saw his eyes. Those small, silver bullets of light glaring at me. I could feel his savage, soulless anger pour down on me from above, and I could hear his crazed, unnatural bellow going on and on and on—whether in the air or only in my head, I did not know.

For the first and only time, I wondered exactly what I was facing. Earlier in the afternoon, listening to Karen so thoroughly recount her sister's extensive research, I didn't think of it at all. I heard nothing that made me wonder if Albert Robideaux was more than he seemed. His story was terrible, bizarre, but sadly common for all of that. It was a tale told again and again throughout history—the child snatcher, the baby killer, the deviant, the psychopath.

But now . . . now . . . seeing those unearthly silver eyes inches away, feeling that unimaginable hatred boiling down over me like a tangible, physical force . . . I wondered if I wasn't facing something other than a man. Something bigger than a man. Something inhuman. Something from beyond.

I lashed out toward the eyes, both hands clutching, grasping. I didn't actually expect to feel anything, but again I was wrong. My fingers sunk into soft, cold flesh, and Bloodybones' horrible roar grew louder.

I brought my right hand back and curled the fingers into a fist. I struck out again, driving my arm forward with all the force I could muster, and felt my knuckles crash into the face, mashing against something that might have been the nose or lips.

Then he—it—whatever it was—leaped and fell upon me. I was knocked to the wooden deck and the air was blown out of my lungs in one painful gust. My head struck the planks and a burst of bright light went off behind my eyes. I struggled to roll out from underneath the body, but it was too heavy. And cold. So cold. Frozen. It felt as if Robideaux had just swum up from the depths of Lake Superior, emerging from beneath the churning waves to attack me, to keep the intruder away from his private, personal death chamber.

The monster was clawing at me now, huge, unseen hands ripping at my face. I tried to move, to fight back, but I could not free my arms enough to get loose or get a grip. Invisible fists pummeled me, and that raging voice went on, growing louder and louder. I was aware of another sound too—the sound of my own panicked cries rising in the dark.

The silver eyes were inches from my own, and as I looked into them I imagined I could see it all reflected back to me, every second of the terrible truth, all the children, everything he had done to them, all the ways he had made them suffer, the ways he had tortured them and used them and finished them and then brought them here, tearing them to pieces, carving them up and dumping them into the hidden pool. The children. And Amy. I saw my poor, dear Amy in those eyes too, her final moments, the dark, cold water rising up to swallow her forever.

Then Karen was beside me. I could sense her as much as see her in the dark.

"You son of a bitch!" she cried, and I felt the weight on top of me lessen just a bit. "This is for Amy, you son of a bitch!"

I felt a searing pain in my right cheek as Robideaux's fingers gouged me, tearing away a scrap of flesh, but then the weight was gone completely and I was free. I rolled over and scrambled to my knees.

"Here, David, here, help me!" Karen panted, and I realized that she was striking the monster repeatedly, slapping, punching, kicking. I saw the silver eyes flashing up at her—at us—with overpowering anger.

I managed to stand up and immediately raised my right leg, bringing my foot down with every ounce of strength I could summon directly on top of the creature's eyes.

BLOODYBONES

The bellowing sound rose higher and higher, becoming a deafening shriek.

I brought my foot down again and heard a strange, eerie sort of crunching noise, not breaking bone but something else altogether. Again I raised my foot and drove it downward, and again, each blow harder than the one before. I was aware that Karen was still next to me and that she was doing the same.

Again. Again. Again.

I thought of Karen telling the story of Bloodybones' demise: *They proceeded to beat, kick, and stomp him until he was dead.* That statement and the image it conjured sent an incredible, terrible sense of hateful joy surging through me.

I don't know how long we continued. Surely it was no more than a few seconds, but it felt much longer. Longer, but not long enough. Crazily, it occurred to me that I could go on kicking this monster for hours, maybe days, maybe forever.

I did not get the chance.

As quickly as it had all started, I suddenly realized that my foot was no longer hitting Robideaux's face. It was coming down instead on the wooden planks of the pier. The thing was trying to escape. It had managed to roll away from us and was getting to its feet.

For a single moment, I could feel its raw, furious power gathering again, the same force I had felt when the silver eyes first appeared in the opening above me.

"David—"

"No!" I cried. *"No more!"*

I leaped forward and threw myself against the body, head down, shoulder first. I struck the thing in its huge, hard midsection, knocking it backwards and sending it over the edge of the platform. There was a tremendous splash, and dark water rained down on us, so cold it felt like fire.

For a half-second I thought I had used too much force, that my momentum would carry me forward and into the pool. I felt myself literally hanging on the edge of the pier, teetering, arms pinwheeling, and I saw an image of myself landing in the water beside Bloodybones. I saw him rising up beside me like a sea-dragon, silver eyes flashing, pushing me beneath the black surface, dragging me under and down forever.

Deep water, dark water, dead water

Then Karen grasped my arm and pulled me backwards, hauling me to safety, away from the edge, away from the pool.

I turned and clung to her, aware of how quiet it had gotten. The only sounds in the chamber were the sounds of our own gasping breaths.

"Where—w-w-where are we?" she said. "Give me your phone."

She handed it to me and I turned it on, shining it down into the water.

Robideaux was lying on the bottom of the pool, directly in the middle of the field of bones. He was on his back, arms spread wide. His eyes were open, but they were no longer silver. They were tiny black BBs, barely visible in the weak light. His mouth was closed, but a thin stream of bubbles was emerging through his lips, rising toward the surface.

I will never be quite sure of this next thing. I will never know if I actually saw it, if it actually happened, or if I only imagined it. It could be that I hallucinated the whole thing. It could be that my mind simply showed me a picture of something that was nonsensical and impossible but also quite wonderful. I asked Karen about it later, asked if she had seen it too. She said no, of course. That's probably what I would have said in her position. But she also gave me an odd, indecipherable look, and I chose to believe that look was her real answer.

Real or not, as I looked down, it seemed to me that the bones began to move. Several of them skittered or vibrated on the bottom of the pool. Several others rose up from the sand as if floating, lifting an inch or two and then settling back down. As I watched, those movements intensified. Several of the bones now shifted position by a few inches or even more, and it seemed—it *almost* seemed—as if there was purpose in their movements, as if they were trying to go somewhere, as if they were trying to move toward Robideaux.

I thought I saw the monster turn its head then, as if it realized what was happening. Its eyes widened. Its mouth opened. The stream of bubbles increased to a momentary jet flow.

Then it was over. If what I had seen was real, if the bones had moved, that brief bit of magic was finished, and they were moving no more. Robideaux lay perfectly still, once again staring blindly up at us. There were no more bubbles rising toward the top.

A second later, there was no more Robideaux either.

The thing on the bottom of the pool started to fade then abruptly vanished altogether, leaving nothing behind, nothing but what had been there before, nothing but what had lain in the sand for so many long, long years: a field of bones, silent and undisturbed.

Karen was sobbing.

"What did we do, David? What just happened? Do you know? What in the name of God did we do?"

The things I don't understand are the only things I'm sure of, I thought.

But that's not what I said.

What I said was: "I don't know, Karen. I wish I could tell you, but I can't. I don't know what we did. But I do know who we did it for."

XX

I can almost take her the rest of the way now.

I still don't know everything, of course. But I know so much more than I did that day in February, when Kyle looked at me across the table at Ebenezer's and encouraged me to work out my agony on paper. I know so much more than I did when I sat down and wrote what amounted to a tall tale about a young woman racing a storm to safety. I no longer have to leave her where I did back then, stranded in the middle of the Horn River. I can now take her farther along the journey. I can almost take her all the way home.

It is so easy now to see what must have happened that day—not all the bits and pieces, not the nuances, but the broad, terrible strokes. I can see her as clearly as if I were there beside her, coming up the path from the landing, head down into the wind, eyes narrowed against the rain, still cursing her lost Tilley hat. I can see the grocery bags in one hand, her fishing rod case in the other. The fate of that case is one of the mysteries I still haven't solved, but I don't think it's especially important. At first, I thought it might be at the bottom of the pool with her, but when the authorities pumped the area dry and recovered the bodies and bones, there was no case to be found. Now I'm thinking it's still out on the beach somewhere, buried in the sand. Perhaps shifting winds will reveal it someday, a nice little find for an accidental treasure hunter.

I can imagine her breaking out of the trees and seeing the house, the light tower, the safety of home. I can imagine her grinning, thinking of a warm fire and a cold beer. Knowing Amy, she had already picked out the movie she would pop into her DVD player, and perhaps she was already beginning to compose in her head, laying out the e-mail she would send to tell me about her close call with the weather. She always told me things like that. Of course, I once thought she told me everything, and look how very wrong that was.

She is halfway across the open stretch of beach when she sees him there, Bloodybones, rearing up in her path and blocking the way home. She tries to detour around him, but he comes for her. She tries to run, maybe heading back toward the river or racing to go around the house and reach the safety of the fog signal building, but he is faster. Maybe he confronts her. Maybe there is a scuffle. Maybe there is a fight. Maybe she swings at him with the rod case, which flies from her hands and lands a short distance away, where it is soon covered by blowing sand. Maybe he catches her and drags her away across the beach the way I saw him dragging poor Joseph Adderly, struggling, screaming. Or perhaps she runs away again, seeking to escape to the only place she can, the only place she can think of: the underground root cellar she had only discovered a few days before, that room beneath the trapdoor where he eventually cornered her.

It might not have happened like that, but I think it probably did.

Karen thinks so too. She thinks that's the story, or very close to it. She thinks that's what she sensed all of those nights that she would wake up, sobbing, from dreadful dreams of her sister floating in cold, green water. She thinks that's the story Amy wanted her to come here and find.

It may be asking too much for us to understand more than that.

In all honesty, we're not even sure of everything that happened to us on that final afternoon. I do remember what I saw when I jumped down into the pit. Karen remembers going in the other direction, climbing the upper ladder and forcing the trapdoor open. She remembers feeling something blow past her then, almost knocking her off the ladder, a powerful but invisible presence. She remembers feeling cold all over and turning to look back down then suddenly seeing a shadowy form, the suggestion of a person, stalking across the cellar, heading for that other trapdoor where Kyle and I had disappeared moments before. I remember the eyes. I remember the nightmarish, bellowing roar of the creature as it attacked. We remember fighting together, side by side.

We remember those things, but we're not sure we understand any of them. And that's all right. It's the way it has to be.

BLOODYBONES

It is summer now, and the story is finished. Amy's house is empty. Her possessions have been carted away, sold off. The property is on the market, and it gets quite a few visitors, though I think it might be a while before it is sold. The local agent listing the site said he gets calls almost every day but few serious inquiries. One Madsen entrepreneur approached me a few weeks ago, wanting to get in touch with Amy's family. He didn't want to buy the site but rent it. Just for the fall, he said. Just for the month of October, actually. He wanted to open a haunted lighthouse. Now that the police have stopped questioning Karen and me, now that their investigation is closed, now that the media attention has faded, that seems to be the direction everything is going. Hucksters. Promoters. Even the little old ladies of the Historical Advisory Committee have been busy. They have begun work on a new book: *Bloodybones: The Terrible True Story of Albert Robideaux.* I try to get angry, but I can't.

What I feel these days is much different than that. What I feel is something very much like gratitude.

I think of where this all began for me, with the hellish fury of that storm last fall, and how everything that happened after that eventually led us to the underground chamber and the hidden pool, to Amy and, more importantly, to the remains of nine children who are now at rest. They were down there in the dark, those little ones, down there in the pool, lost and alone, for more than a century. Now they lie in a mass grave at the Madsen Township cemetery, beneath a marker with their names and a plaque telling their story. It's not justice, but it's as close as any of us will ever get, and to me it feels like a small sort of miracle.

It is summer, and the story is finished, and I feel good. But there are still days—days and especially nights—when I am not quite sure.

Last night, for instance.

I had been asleep for several hours when my phone rang. I awoke, gasping. The alarm on the nightstand said 2:18. I reached for my phone, but as soon as I touched it, the ringing stopped, and the screen went dark. Just before it did, I thought I saw two words there, two words that could not be there, two words that caused my chest to tighten and my stomach to clench and my eyes to sting.

I opened the directory of recent calls, but it was empty.

I didn't put the phone down right away. I just lay there in the dark, holding it tight in my hand, waiting to see if it might ring again. Wanting it to ring. Willing it to ring.

I may take a drive today. I may climb in the truck and head north on 419. I may park at the end of the road, and maybe I'll get out there and take a little walk. I haven't been there in a while. It might be good to go back.

So often I find myself remembering how close we were, how unceasingly we shared the minutiae of our lives—an almost overwhelming intimacy that started like a spark during our first meeting and quickly grew into something that felt, at least to me, like a sacred, unbreakable bond. But then I think of a phone call with nothing on the other end, nothing but a distant echo, a faraway, hollow emptiness, and I'm struck by the things I never told her, the things she wanted to tell me but couldn't.

Someday, I think, my phone will ring again, and this time when I answer it, she will be there on the other end, ready at last to tell me everything.

"Come out to the point," she will say. "Come see me."

And I will go.

I've almost gotten her home now.

Someday, I know she will help me take her the rest of the way.

THE END?

Not quite . . .

Dive into more Tales from the Darkest Depths:

The Third Twin—A Dark Psychological Thriller by Darren Speegle—Some things should never be bred . . . Amid tribulation, death, madness, and institutionalization, a father fights against a scientist's bloody bid to breed a theoretical third twin.

Embers: A Collection of Dark Fiction by Kenneth W. Cain—These short speculative stories are the smoldering remains of a fire, the fiery bits meant to ignite the mind with slow-burning imagery and haunting details. These are the slow burning embers of Cain's soul.

Aletheia: A Supernatural Thriller by J.S. Breukelaar—A tale of that most human of monsters—memory—Aletheia is part ghost story, part love story, a novel about the damage done, and the damage yet to come. About terror itself. Not only for what lies ahead, but also for what we think we have left behind.

Beatrice Beecham's Cryptic Crypt by Dave Jeffery—The fate of the world rests in the hands of four dysfunctional teenagers and a bunch of oddball adults. What could possibly go wrong?

Visions of the Mutant Rain Forest—the solo and collaborative stories and poems of Robert Frazier and Bruce Boston's exploration of the Mutant Rain Forest.

The Final Reconciliation by Todd Keisling—Thirty years ago, a progressive rock band called The Yellow Kings began recording what would become their first and final album. Titled "The Final Reconciliation," the album was expected to usher in a new renaissance of heavy metal, but it was shelved following a tragic concert that left all but one dead. It's the survivor shares the shocking truth.

Where the Dead Go to Die by Mark Allan Gunnells and Aaron Dries—Post-infection Chicago. Christmas. There are monsters in this world. And they used to be us. Now it's time to euthanize to survive in a hospice where Emily, a woman haunted by her past, only wants to do her job and be the best mother possible. But it won't be long before that snow-speckled ground will be salted by blood.

Tales from The Lake Vol.3—Dive into the deep end of the lake with 19 tales of terror, selected by Monique Snyman. Including short stories by Mark Allan Gunnells, Kate Jonez, Kenneth W. Cain, and many more.

Sarah Killian: Serial Killer (For Hire!) by Mark Sheldon—Follow foul-mouthed and mean-spirited Sarah Killian on an assignment from T.H.E.M. (Trusted Hierarchy of Everyday Murderers), a secret organization using serial killers to do the dirty work for their clients. Sarah's twisted sense of humor alone makes this Crime Fiction/Horror/Thriller a worthy read.

Gutted: Beautiful Horror Stories—an anthology of dark fiction that explores the beauty at the very heart of darkness. Featuring horror's most celebrated voices: Clive Barker, Neil Gaiman, Ramsey Campbell, Paul Tremblay, John F.D. Taff, Lisa Mannetti, Damien Angelica Walters, Josh Malerman, Christopher Coake, Mercedes M. Yardley, Brian Kirk, Stephanie M. Wytovich, Amanda Gowin, Richard Thomas, Maria Alexander, and Kevin Lucia.

Blackwater Val by William Gorman—a Supernatural Suspense Thriller/Horror/Coming of age novel: A widower, traveling with his dead wife's ashes and his six-year-old psychic daughter Katie in tow, returns to his haunted birthplace to execute his dead wife's final wish. But something isn't quite right in the Val.

Tribulations by Richard Thomas—In the third short story collection by Richard Thomas, *Tribulations*, these stories cover a wide range of dark fiction—from fantasy, science fiction and horror, to magical realism, neo-noir, and transgressive fiction. The common thread that weaves these tragic tales together is suffering and sorrow, and the ways we emerge from such heartbreak stronger, more appreciative of what we have left—a spark of hope enough to guide us though the valley of death.

Devourer of Souls by Kevin Lucia—In Kevin Lucia's latest installment of his growing Clifton Heights mythos, Sheriff Chris Baker and Father Ward meet for a Saturday morning breakfast at The Skylark Dinner to once again commiserate over the weird and terrifying secrets surrounding their town.

If you ever thought of becoming an author, I'd also like to recommend these non-fiction titles:

Horror 101: The Way Forward—a comprehensive overview of the Horror fiction genre and career opportunities available to established and aspiring authors, including Jack Ketchum, Graham Masterton, Edward Lee, Lisa Morton, Ellen Datlow, Ramsey Campbell, and many more.

Horror 201: The Silver Scream Vol.1 and *Vol.2*—A must read for anyone interested in the horror film industry. Includes interviews and essays by Wes Craven, John Carpenter, George A. Romero, Mick Garris, and dozens more. Now available in a special paperback edition.

Modern Mythmakers: 35 interviews with Horror and Science Fiction Writers and Filmmakers by Michael McCarty—Ever wanted to hang out with legends like Ray Bradbury, Richard Matheson, and Dean Koontz? *Modern Mythmakers* is your chance to hear fun anecdotes and career advice from authors and filmmakers like Forrest J. Ackerman, Ray Bradbury, Ramsey Campbell, John Carpenter, Dan Curtis, Elvira, Neil Gaiman, Mick Garris, Laurell K. Hamilton, Jack Ketchum, Dean Koontz, Graham Masterton, Richard Matheson, John Russo, William F. Nolan, John Saul, Peter Straub, and many more.

Writers On Writing: An Author's Guide—Your favorite authors share their secrets in the ultimate guide to becoming and being and author. *Writers On Writing* is an eBook series with original 'On Writing' essays by writing professionals.

Or check out other Crystal Lake Publishing books for more Tales from the Darkest Depths.

ABOUT THE AUTHOR

Paul F. Olson has been a professional writer and editor for over 30 years. His first novel, *Night Prophets,* was published in 1989. He is also the author of the dark suspense novel *Alexander's Song,* plus many short stories, essays, reviews, interviews, and other works. In the late 1980s, he published and edited "Horrorstruck: The World of Dark Fantasy," a trade magazine for horror fans and professionals. With the late David B. Silva, he co-edited the anthologies *Post Mortem: New Tales of Ghostly Horror* and *Dead End: City Limits,* and created the award-winning newsletter "Hellnotes," which he and Silva edited together for five years. His recent work includes the Cemetery Dance anthology *Better Weird,* co-edited with Richard Chizmar and Brian James Freeman, and the short story collection *Whispered Echoes.* After spending nearly two decades as a small-town newspaper editor, he has returned to a full-time focus on fiction. He currently lives in Brimley, Michigan, not far from the shores of Lake Superior.

CONNECT WITH THE AUTHOR

Website: http://paulfolson.com

Facebook: https://www.facebook.com/pfolson

Twitter: https://twitter.com/pfolson

Instagram: https://www.instagram.com/pf_olson/

Hi, readers. It makes our day to know you reached the end of our book. Thank you so much. This is why we do what we do every single day.

Whether you found the book good or great, we'd love to hear what you thought. Please take a moment to leave a review on Amazon, Goodreads, or anywhere else readers visit. Reviews go a long way to helping a book sell, and will help us to continue publishing quality books.

Thank you again for taking the time to journey with Crystal Lake Publishing.

We are also on . . .

Website
http://www.crystallakepub.com/

Books
http://www.crystallakepub.com/book-table/

Blog
http://www.crystallakepub.com/blog-2/

Newsletter
http://eepurl.com/xfuKP

Instagram
https://www.instagram.com/crystal_lake_publishing/

Patreon
https://www.patreon.com/CLP

YouTube
https://www.youtube.com/c/CrystalLakePublishing

Twitter
https://twitter.com/crystallakepub

Facebook page
https://www.facebook.com/Crystallakepublishing/

Google+
https://plus.google.com/u/1/107478350897139952572

Pinterest
https://za.pinterest.com/crystallakepub/

Tumblr
https://www.tumblr.com/blog/crystal-lake-publishing

We'd love to hear from you.

With unmatched success since 2012, Crystal Lake Publishing has quickly become one of the world's leading indie publishers of Mystery,We do not just publish books, we present you worlds within your world, doors within your mind from talented authors who sacrifice so much for a moment of your time.

This is what we believe in. What we stand for. This will be our legacy.

Welcome to Crystal Lake Publishing.

We hope you enjoyed this title. If so, we'd be grateful if you could leave a review on your blog or any of the other websites and outlets open to book reviews. Reviews are like gold to writers and publishers, since word-of-mouth is and will always be the best way to market a great book. And remember to keep an eye out for more of our books.

THANK YOU FOR PURCHASING THIS BOOK